Return to Elysium

Lucina is a Greek girl who grows up in an utopian enclave, Elysium. As she matures, her natural psychic talents unfold—putting her at odds with the skeptical, scientific philosophy of Elysium. So she and two friends sail to Rome, which is just emerging as an empire. There she becomes a priestess in a Delphic temple, dispensing wisdom and healing to any who come. Her reputation grows quickly, but at the height of her success, she abandons it all to run away with her lover Nigellus, a Roman senator.

Return to Elysium is a delightful book to read, filled with insights into the human being. It is also a profound commentary on the power of self-deception to prevent us from understanding ourself and our destiny.

"During the last twenty years, seven books of mine have been published as historical novels which to me are biographies of previous lives I have known."

Joan Grant

BOOKS BY JOAN GRANT

Far Memory Books:
Winged Pharaoh
Eyes of Horus
Lord of the Horizon
So Moses Was Born
Life as Carola
Return to Elysium
Scarlet Feather

———

Far Memory

———

The Scarlet Fish and Other Stories
Redskin Morning

———

The Laird and the Lady
Vague Vacation
A Lot To Remember
Many Lifetimes *(with Denys Kelsey)*

RETURN TO ELYSIUM

by Joan Grant

ARIEL PRESS
Columbus, Ohio

First published in Great Britain
by Methuen & Co. in 1947
First Ariel Press edition 1987
Third Printing

This book is made possible
by a gift from Richard Wythe
to the Publications Fund of Light

ISBN 0-89804-145-7

table of contents

PART III

IN PERMANENT FRIENDSHIP FOR
alec kerr-clarkson

JOan GRant

Joan Grant was born in England in 1907. Her father was a man of such intellectual brilliance in the fields of mathematics and engineering that he was appointed a fellow of Kings College while still in his twenties. Joan's formal education was limited to what she absorbed from a series of governesses, although she feels she learned far more from the after-dinner conversations between her father and his fellow scientists.

When Joan was twenty, she married Leslie Grant, with whom she had a daughter. This marriage ended soon after *Winged Pharaoh* was published in 1937—a book which became an instant best-seller. Until 1957 she was married to the philosopher and visionary Charles Beatty, who is the author of several books, including *The Garden of the Golden Flower*, a treatise on psychiatrist Carl Jung. In 1960, Joan married psychiatrist Denys Kelsey.

Throughout her life, Joan has been preoccupied with the subject of ethics. To her, the word ''ethics'' represents the fundamental and timeless code of attitudes and behavior toward one another on which the health of the individual and society depends. Each of her books and stories explores a facet of this code. As Denys Kelsey has written, ''The First Dynasty of Egypt once knew the code well, but lost it and foundered. Eleven dynasties were to pass before it was recovered, but those were more leisurely times when the most lethal weapon was an arrow, a javelin and a club. We feel that in the present troubled days of this planet, these books must be presented.''

RETURN TO ELYSIUM

author's note

There are both Greek and Roman characters in *Return to Elysium*, so to avoid confusion I have used throughout the more familiar Latinized spelling of proper names.

PART ONE

CHAPTER ONE

the Quay

Three days before my thirteenth birthday Elissa told me I was going to a place called Elysium. I was very excited, for I had always lived on the island and even in clear weather the Greek mainland was only a blur on the horizon. She did not tell me how many days I was to stay, but I knew it could not be long for I heard her tell Dictys, her husband, that she would leave food for him while we were away. I spent the last afternoon explaining to the goats that I would soon be home again, and that while I was gone they must obey Dictys and not wander if he took them to the high pasture.

I knew Elissa was my foster-mother, but she had never told me before that I had a guardian called Aesculapius who was one of the most famous men in Athens. She kept on reminding me that I must always be polite to him. 'He is a good man and very clever, Lucina, but he expects people to be obedient. So you must not argue as you do.'

We went down the mountain at night; Dictys striding ahead and Elissa holding me tightly by the hand, as though she were afraid I was going to get lost in the dark. If she had known I had often been out alone at night, when I was supposed to be asleep, she would not have been so anxious about me. There were lights in the houses of the village street. Through an open door I saw people crowding round a narrow table, and wine-skins hanging from the rafters. They were singing and looked friendly, so I said I was thirsty; but Dictys only grunted, and hurried me past the house.

When we reached the harbour, a man carrying a flaring torch came up to Dictys, spoke to him in a low voice, and handed him a small leather sack. I saw Dictys counting coins which shone yellow in the light. The resinous smoke from the torch got into my throat and made me cough: Elissa thought I was cold and told me to put on the woolen cloak which she had woven for me during the winter.

Our boat was larger than those which were drawn up on the beach. We were not going to start until dawn, but Elissa and I got into it, and Dictys said good-bye to us, rather gruffly. In the stern there were cushions under an awning, and Elissa made me lie beside her, saying we had better sleep while we had the chance. The waves made a soft sound like butter slapping against the sides of a churn. I thought I was too excited to sleep, but woke to see the chief sailor, whose name was Phocion, hauling up the sail. It was red-brown patched with blue, and flapped like the wings of an angry bird.

The sun was still low in the sky and the waves were caved with shadow under their crests. When we got outside the harbour, Phocion let me help him steer. Elissa lay huddled under her cloak and moaned when Phocion asked her if she would like something to eat. He gave me a basket of green figs and small purple grapes, and taught me not to spit the pips to windward.

All that day there was only sea and sky to look at, except for two small islands which were too far away to be more than shapes, with coloured dots for houses; but next morning we were in sight of Athens. We were close enough to see people, small as ants in the distance, walking in the steep streets. Then we turned westwards along the coast, which was hilly, with mountains showing through the haze beyond. The wind had changed and was blowing strongly from the land, so we had to go sideways, drawing very slowly nearer to white beaches which curved among the rocks. There were large houses among groves of trees, and many boats, their sails curved like tulip petals.

'We shall soon reach Elysium,' said Phocion. Elissa got

up from the cushions and staggered towards me. 'Don't be frightened,' she said. 'Everyone in Elysium is kind. You mustn't be frightened of them, Lucina.'

Until then I had not been at all frightened, and felt shy because I was not used to Elissa being so affectionate.

'Do you know Elysium? Were you happy there?'

'Yes,' she said slowly. 'I was happy in Elysium. Promise me you will be happy.'

'Of course I shall,' I said firmly. And for the first time wondered if I should enjoy being away from the island, even for a few days.

'Now you can see the landing-steps,' said Phocion, pointing to a wide bay protected by jutting headlands.

He turned the boat across the wind. It lurched so suddenly that I fell against the mast and grazed my arm; but I was too interested to bother about the sharp hurt of the salt.

There was a man on the landing-stage. As we came closer I saw he was young and had curly hair. The sail came down with a clatter. Phocion pinioned it as though it were a hen being taken to market.

The young man helped me out of the boat. 'My name is Clion,' he said. 'I am very glad that you have come to Elysium.'

I was relieved to see he was so friendly, for now Elissa would stop being worried about meeting strangers.

'Elissa,' I said without turning round, 'Elissa, this is Clion. He is glad we have come to see him.'

Elissa was standing beside the mast. Tears were running down her face. Phocion was hauling up the sail.

It was only then that I realized she was not coming with me. 'Elissa, don't leave me here...Elissa!'

Already there was a narrow strip of water between the boat and the hard white stone of the quay. I ran, but the water was too wide to jump.

'Don't leave me here! Please don't leave me!'

The boat bent to the wind. Elissa had to cling to the mast

5

to prevent herself from falling. 'I can't help it...everyone has to do as *he* says.'

'Don't leave me!' To make her hear I had to shout until my throat ached.

'Don't be unhappy. You promised not to be unhappy.'

Her voice was brittle against the sound of the sea. I could not see her properly: everything was blurred, but I knew she was crying too. Elissa had gone away, without even telling me why.

In sudden terrible loneliness I clung to Clion; he wasn't Elissa but he was better than nothing. He must have known I was crying, yet he said, as though nothing terrible had happened, 'There is a rock-pool further along the beach, with red sea-anemones. Shall we go and see them?'

I nodded, for I knew my voice would be unsteady; and followed him along a path between high rocks until we came to a stretch of sand. The anemones were interesting, and curled up when I touched them. There were shrimps in the pool too; and a small crab which Clion showed me how to catch, by dangling my hair-ribbon in front of its claws until it hung on and I could pull it out. Further on we came to more rocks, covered in brown seaweed which popped when I squeezed the pods.

'Shall we have a swim?' he said. 'I forgot to bring a towel but we can dry in the sun.'

I hesitated. He might think me silly if I told him I couldn't swim, but it would be worse if he thought I was afraid. I decided it was necessary to be honest. 'I can't swim. I was never allowed to leave the mountain.'

'Then I will soon teach you,' he said kindly. 'Leave your things on that rock and then they won't be sandy when you want them again.'

Elissa had always been fussy when I went outdoors with no clothes on, but apparently they were more sensible in Elysium.

Clion stood on a rock, waiting to dive. His body looked

like gold against the blue sky: his hair was gold too, but darker than mine. He swam out a little way and then turned back to where I waited for him in the shallow water.

It was fun learning to swim: at first he kept his hand under my chin, but later I could take three or four strokes without even a toe on the bottom. We lay on the hot sand until we were dry; my skin felt sticky with salt but very clean.

'Hungry?' he said.

'Very: though I hadn't noticed until now.'

'I thought we would eat by ourselves on your first morning, so I asked Epicurus to send one of the servants down to the pavilion.'

'Who is Epicurus, and what is a servant?'

'Epicurus is one of the men who live here—he looks after the household and chooses the meals. Servants are people who work—cooking and gardening and making clothes.'

'Then what does Aesculapius do?'

'He is a philosopher.'

'What is a philosopher?'

'Someone who knows the answers to the changeless questions, and who remembers that there are always more answers to discover.'

'Are you a philosopher?'

He laughed. 'Sometimes I think so, but usually not.'

'Can I learn to be one?'

'That is what he wants to discover, Lucina: that is one reason why he brought you here.'

'What are the other reasons?'

'He is your guardian, which means that as you have no parents he looks after you instead.' I thought it an odd way of looking after some one, not to see her until she was thirteen, but decided it might be wiser not to say so. 'He is my guardian, too,' Clion continued. 'He adopted me as a son twelve years ago, when he left Athens and came to live in Elysium.'

We had reached the pavilion, which was only a roof supported by six slender pillars. Several dishes, covered with white napkins, were on a stone table, and there was a stone bench, with a ram's head carved on the back, for us to sit on. It was an absorbing meal: fat prawns to dip in a green sauce, slices of chicken with cold asparagus, and small, sticky cakes to eat with the cream cheese.

'Full?' said Clion. 'Shall we sleep, or would you rather explore?'

Sleep seemed a waste of time. 'Explore—if you don't mind.'

There were always new things to discover in this garden: statues gleaming against dark trees; a pool fringed with iris, cool with the sound of water dripping from the mouth of a stone dolphin; secret paths winding through thickets of bay and myrtle. We came to a narrow stretch of turf, so smooth that I had to run across it.

'Who taught you to crouch and clench your hands before a sprint?' said Clion.

'I can't remember. I woke up too quickly. It may have been something the young man knew.'

'What young man?'

I hoped he would not laugh at me. 'The one I made up because I wasn't allowed to talk to the shepherd boy. When I became him I could run much faster than the ordinary me. It was disappointing that when I was awake my legs didn't remember how to do it.'

'You run very well. If you hadn't already a better name we might call you Atalanta.'

'Who was she?'

'A woman who lost a race because of golden apples.'

We had come through an olive grove into a glade where there was another statue. I was just going to ask why Atalanta wanted golden apples when I realized that the statue was a man standing on a stone plinth: he wore a bronze helmet and held a short sword in his upraised hand.

'It's only Agamemnon,' said Clion. 'But he won't like

it if he knows we saw him.'

He pulled me back into the shelter of a laurel bush. Agamemnon began to shout orders as though he was surrounded by a crowd of people. Then he thrust at the air with his sword, so violently that I thought he was going to fall. He looked very funny and I began to laugh.'

'Not so loud, or he'll hear you,' Clion whispered urgently. 'Creep away, and *do* be careful not to let him see you.'

When we could no longer hear the shouting, we sat on a fallen tree while I picked twigs and dead leaves out of my hair—we had crawled through low bushes to avoid being seen.

Clion seemed embarrassed. 'Some of us may appear a little odd until you get used to Elysium. For instance, Agamemnon isn't the *real* Agamemnon.'

'But you just said he was.'

'I mean he is no relation to the hero of the Trojan war. Most of us are given new names when we come here, to remind us of the direction in which our talents should develop: that is why our sculptor is called Praxiteles, our poet Euripides, our steward Epicurus.'

'I never heard of any of them. Ought I to have done? Were they all heroes? Who was Aesculapius, or is that his own name?'

'Aesculapius was the greatest of all physicians, endowed by his followers with magical powers and eventually worshipped as the god of medicine. *Our* Aesculapius took the name to remind himself never to be influenced by the awe which all wise men receive from the ignorant; who cannot understand that miracles are only the question of natural laws.'

I had no idea what he meant, so I said, 'What *is* a god?'

'They don't exist—but most people think they do. Did nobody on the island have a statue to which he gave offerings on special days; or even a sacred tree?'

'Dictys had no statue, and though there was a very old olive tree beside the house I don't think it was particularly important. I am afraid I don't know much about people. Until I left the island I never spoke to any one except Dictys and Elissa.'

'Didn't they let you play with other children?' He sounded sorry for me, so I wondered if I ought to feel sorry for myself.

'No one else lived on the mountain, and Dictys never took me to the village. I tried to make him, but he only got annoyed so I had to give it up. That is why I had never been in the sea until to-day.'

'How lucky for me,' he said cheerfully. 'I shall be able to teach you to dive, and to catch fish with a trident. You will be very happy here, Lucina.'

For the first time it was safe to think of the island. The high pasture was not so exciting as Elysium, and instead of the ordinary anemones and asphodel and tulips there were much more interesting flowers. And the food! Meals would be an adventure instead of only a way to stop being hungry. It was sad that I could not bring the goats with me, but perhaps there were goats here too.

'Would Aesculapius let me have a goat?'

'I am sure he would; if he thinks it is good for you.'

I was disappointed; for whenever Elissa made me do something disagreeable she said it was good for me.

We were getting close to the house; it was coloured a soft pink and gleamed like coral among the flowering vines that wreathed the windows and hung from the pillars of the central loggia. Aesculapius must be very important; probably even more difficult to understand than Clion.

'Need I see any one else to-day?'

'Of course not. I didn't realize it was so late. I will take you straight to your room and explain to the others that they must wait until to-morrow to welcome you.'

As we passed the kitchen quarters I saw a man peeling

onions, and another plucking a goose. They both looked up and smiled, but we did not stop to talk with them.

'In Elysium you will find only friends,' said Clion.

It was a comfortable thought to take to bed with me, and I told myself very firmly that I was going to be happy: it would be terrible if I started to miss Elissa again before I went to sleep.

the GaRÐeneR

Next morning I woke reluctantly, unwilling to break the thread which might lead me back into a curious and exciting dream. An unfamiliar sound made me open my eyes, to see a young man, holding a cup in one hand and a plate of fruit in the other, standing beside my bed.

He smiled and asked me how I had slept. I sat up, and stared at him for a moment before I recognized Narcissus, who had come to see me after Clion had gone.

'I slept very well. I am sorry I forgot to thank you for being so kind. I must have been very sleepy.'

'Why should I be thanked? I was only carrying out instructions.'

'Because no one has looked after me before, except Elissa. How did you learn to look after children? Have you a daughter?'

'I have no children...the gods be praised!' He paused to glance at the open door, then crossed the room to close it. 'Please forget I said that...the gods are not mentioned in this house.'

He began to peel figs for me; 'You had better drink your milk: I thought you would prefer it cold, in case you hate

11

skin as much as I did at your age.'

'I do,' I said fervently, sipping the milk and watching him over the crescent of the rim. 'Narcissus, what *are* the gods? I heard about them yesterday for the first time.' I hesitated, perhaps it would be unwise to mention Clion. 'Some one said they were a kind of statue, or else a tree; but I saw several statues here, and hundreds of trees, and none of them seemed at all secret. One of the statues was really a man called Agamemnon: but he wasn't frightening, only funny.'

'Agamemnon!' he said scornfully. 'There is nothing to fear in Agamemnon; but treat him with respect or he will think you are mocking him. He is difficult when he's angry, and he *enjoys* fighting.'

'Why does he shout orders to people who aren't really there?''

''How should I know? My role is to be obedient, not to ask questions.'

'So you are not a philosopher?'

'No, I am only the servant of a philosopher; because I find it easier to obey than to accept responsibility.'

I sighed. 'The conversation here is very puzzling. Perhaps it is only because I am so unused to people. Shall I like being here, do you think?'

'We are all happy...in our own way.'

'Are you happy?'

'Me? Why shouldn't I be?' He sounded defiant, too decisive to be convincing; as I was when telling myself not to be afraid after waking suddenly in a dark room.

'Then you like him...the man to whom Elysium belongs?'

'Why do you think I stay here?'

I felt embarrassed at having asked a question which so obviously disturbed him. 'I don't know...you see I only arrived here yesterday. I've not spoken to any one except you and Clion. I haven't even seen *him* in the distance.'

'If you want to run away, go *now*, before you see him. If

you stay you will love him...and then you will never be able to go. He is so much stronger than any of us, so much wiser...so very much too wise.'

Opposite the door there was an archway covered with a blue curtain. Narcissus nodded us towards it and said casually, 'Your bath is ready in there, and you will find clothes in the chest, the painted one under the window. Call me when you want me to do your hair.'

Beyond the curtain there was a small room with a marble pool set in the floor. It was half-full of warm, scented water, and three steps led down into it. There was a brush to scrub myself with, and oil to use after I had dried on the embroidered towels that were spread over a stool. My hair was sticky with salt from the sea, so I let it float in the bath: it tickled like the mouths of small fishes I had met in one of the rock-pools. Sun was pouring through a round window high in the wall, and I lay in the hot patch it made on the floor until my hair was dry. I had felt oil on my skin before, but only plain olive oil which Elissa had given me when the weather was very cold. The one I used smelt of roses, and the second flask was warm with violets.

Most of the clothes in the chest were tunics, leaving one shoulder bare and showing my knees, but there were also two pleated dresses, which went down to my feet and were bound under the breasts with coloured ribbons. As I hadn't grown proper breasts yet they looked rather silly, and I thought I might trip over the hem; so I chose a white tunic with a blue border.

I began combing my hair before I remembered Narcissus, so I called him to finish it in case he might be offended. He did it very well, holding it close to the scalp when he came to a knot so that it should not pull.

'You have admirable hair and good bones,' he said. 'If you take trouble you should be a beautiful woman. You will have to let your nails grow, they are far too square and the cuticles are distressingly ragged.'

13

'I never noticed them,' I said. 'I'm afraid they are usually rather dirty.'

He opened a box and showed me various curious instruments I was expected to use. There was a spike for cleaning my nails, tweezers to pluck my eyebrows, and a thing he said was for removing blackheads.

'Fortunately you have excellent skin,' he said magnanimously, 'so this is redundant. In due course I shall teach you a judicious use of paint and suitable unguents, but to-day we can leave your hair braided until I think of some amusing conceits.'

'It is very kind of you,' I said hesitantly, 'but won't it be enough if I am clean and fairly tidy?'

'As the only female in Elysium you have a certain obligation,' he said severely. 'Even the slaves who make our clothes are men, a tiresome fad of Aesculapius'. By the way, ''slave'' is another word which is not used in this house. Until I came here there was an appalling lack of the more delicate civilities—the flower arrangements were an offence against decency, and Praxiteles frequently forgot to shave.'

He sounded so outraged that I giggled. 'Is Aesculapius very fussy about unimportant things?' I said anxiously.

'That depends on what you consider important. He expects to be obeyed, and yet is scornful if one shows too little initiative.'

'Is Narcissus your real name?'

'Of course not! But it is considered more appropriate than my own. It is intended to remind me that I was nearly destroyed by self-pity, that I am incapable of loving anything except myself. Aesculapius thinks I was in love with my mother, and saw her as a projection of my hideous conceit. He may be right—I tried to kill myself when she died, which is why I was sent here.'

'Poor Narcissus—won't they let you go away?'

'Why should I try to escape from the only security I have ever known?'

14

While I was wondering how to reply he walked towards the door. 'We eat at noon on the terrace. You can amuse yourself in the garden until Aesculapius sends for you.'

The door slammed behind him. Had I said something tactless or was he always so complicated?

Hoping to find Clion I spent most of the morning exploring more of Elysium, but though I saw several people in the distance he was not among them. Beyond an orchard I came to a large field in which vegetables were growing in orderly rows, each kind divided from the rest by paths of white pebbles. A man was digging there, pausing between every few spadefuls to wipe the sweat off his forehead with his strong, brown forearm. He was naked except for a loincloth, and his body looked so young that I was surprised his hair was white, nearly as white as his short, curly beard. He must have heard me for he turned round and smiled, a friendly smile that made his blue eyes crinkle at the corners. He was a very restful person; for he talked about vegetables and did not expect me to think hard for the next remark. He reminded me of Dictys, so I told him about the island and how I had helped to grow things in our fields.

'I am quite useful at weeding,' I said, 'if you would like me to help you at any time. I am good at remembering the shapes of plants so I shouldn't pull up the wrong ones.'

'I also like weeding, so we shall enjoy each other's company.'

'Planting is even better,' I said, hoping that he would not agree with Dictys, who considered it too important to leave to me.

'Weed first,' he said. 'Get the ground clean and then the right plants take care of themselves. A little judicious pruning in the proper season, of course, but weeding is the main task of the good gardener.'

'I am glad there are some ordinary people here, like you and me,' I said, and then thought he might be offended at being called 'ordinary,' so added hastily, 'Perhaps that

15

sounds rude, but I only meant it is rather bewildering to meet people who talk in riddles and expect you to understand. Narcissus explained that there were no slaves here, only servants, but it wasn't very helpful as I don't know what a slave is.'

'A slave is a man or woman who belongs to some one else, having been bought for a sum of money.'

'Sold like a goat or a cheese? But people can't belong to other people, can they?'

'Unfortunately your natural grasp of ethical principles is not yet widely shared.'

Suddenly I remembered the bag of coins which had been given to Dictys. I had been sold, so I was a slave!

'Is it wrong to own slaves?' I said.

'It is, in my opinion.'

'Then you must help me to escape from here. Please help me! Aesculapius bought me, so you must tell him that I am very stupid and so hideous that the goats will go dry if I milk them—tell him *anything* so that he won't try to bring me back.'

'Aesculapius did not buy you: he sent for you because he believes you will be happy here.'

'Is he kind or are philosophers horrible people?'

'My dear, what a difficult question to answer with modesty and yet without false humility. You see, I am not only a gardener, I am also Aesculapius.'

I ought to have felt embarrassed, but somehow could not help joining in his laughter. We laughed until I got hiccoughs, but luckily they stopped in time for me to enjoy the melon we shared.

When we had to go back for the noon meal, he showed me a shorter way from the kitchen garden than the one I had taken. A winding path led through a vineyard, and then followed the bank of a stream that presently widened into a formal lake. A flight of shallow steps led up between ranks of cypresses to a wide terrace in front of the house.

16

Servants in white tunics were setting dishes on a table under a yellow awning. Several men were leaning over the balustrade, waiting for us to join them. I recognized Clion, Narcissus, and Agamemnon, and wondered if the others would be alarming. As though I had spoken aloud, Aesculapius said, 'Euripides is the one with red hair; you will enjoy his company, he can make you laugh or weep according to the role he decides to play. Fortunately he prefers comedy to tragic drama. The man beside him is Epicurus; he looks after the household, and we had better conceal that I have been feeding you with melons or he will accuse me of having blunted the fine edge of your appetite.'

'Not nearly enough to stop my being greedy!'

The third stranger came running down the steps towards us. He was very tall with remarkably broad shoulders.

'Our sculptor,' said Aesculapius. 'Praxiteles, here is new inspiration for you: I insist that you give us a change from your unrestful athletes.'

Praxiteles laughed down at me. 'Would you prefer to dance in a frieze or to be a fountain?'

'A fountain would be horrid in winter.'

'Agreed,' said Agamemnon, smiling at me as though we had known each other for days. 'I refuse to allow Lucina to be left in some chilly grove instead of filling a warm and comfortable niche in the house. You must sit beside me, so that this great barbarian cannot persuade you against our better judgement. It is necessary to be firm with him. I get cramp whenever I see myself trying to throw a discus which never leaves my marble hand!'

'It is a good statue,' said Euripides. 'Much better than the one of me as the squatting scribe.'

'No doubt he was encouraged by a superior model!' Agamemnon laughed, and I found it surprising that he was the same man I had seen yesterday.

'Now that Lucina has arrived we may be spared the discomfort of holding some unlikely pose far longer than conceit allows,' said Epicurus. 'Do you mind sitting still, Lucina?'

'She will be lucky if Praxiteles allows her to *sit*,' said Clion with feeling. 'She will probably have to pretend to be running; a most difficult pose, as I know from experience. I kept on getting cramp in the calf muscles. Praxiteles complained that I had no proper appreciation of art, and sulked for the rest of the day.'

'Sulked!' exclaimed Praxiteles in feigned anger. 'With the word you prove you have no understanding of the frenzy of genius. Genius described in terms of the nursery!'

'Do we ever entirely outgrow the nursery?' Aesculapius smiled as he said this; every one laughed politely, as though he had made a familiar joke which they did not think very funny.

We ate small fish fried in butter and a pastry stuffed with raisins: I enjoyed them but they were not so interesting as yesterday's prawns. I hoped that when the meal was over Clion would suggest giving me another swimming lesson; but instead Aesculapius asked me to go back to the kitchen garden with him. He wanted to finish the row he had been digging and told me I could sleep in the shade until he was ready. It was hot, and flies settled on my face unless I fanned myself. I wondered if any one would mind if I went down to the beach, but decided it might be tactless.

When I woke, Aesculapius was lying flat on his back with an artichoke leaf on his head to keep off the sun. His mouth was open, and he snored, a comfortable sound like a cauldron simmering over charcoal. I wondered what happened to people when they slept; it made even Aesculapius look young and defenceless. Who was he now? He brushed a horsefly off his chest and was suddenly completely awake; so suddenly that he caught me staring at him.

'What are you thinking, Lucina?'

The question was too unexpected for me to have time to consider the answer. 'I was wondering who you were...

18

while you were asleep, I mean.'

'Why not Aesculapius?'

'Are people ever only their ordinary selves in a dream? I'm not, but that may be because I'm not old enough to have grown used to being me.'

'Who are you, when you are not Lucina?'

For the first time I felt shy in his company: the truth sounded silly, yet he was not a person with whom it seemed practical to lie. 'Sometimes I am a young man who wins races against a lot of other runners—there is a crowd watching and I am given a wreath of green leaves to wear, which seems very important.'

'The father image,' he said, and then added hastily. 'I am sorry; I was talking to myself, a most discourteous habit. Do you imagine yourself fighting against enemies—enemies which you expect to meet in your dreams?'

'Yes,' I admitted reluctantly. 'When Elissa wouldn't let me go out after sunset—it was after I heard the piping and Dictys was so stupid he wouldn't believe it was only a goatherd—I thought I had better be quite sure whether disobeying would be frightening...really frightening I mean, not just the anticipation of being scolded. So I decided to imagine the kind of thing I might meet. The thing was a large goat with the head of a man. It had horns that shone red in the dark...I don't know why I invented the horns but they seemed to make it more convincing. I imagined him so well that I could almost hear him pattering round the house when I was supposed to be asleep...his hooves made a sharp, dry sound on the gravel path.'

Aesculapius leant on his elbow, and I noticed again the brilliant blueness of his eyes. 'What happened then?' He sounded interested, but not inquisitive.

'I imagined myself as a woman who wore a white robe and carried a silver sickle in her right hand—the sickle was the shape of the young moon. When the goat-man tried to attack her she held up the sickle and a brilliant light shone from it. His horns faded, first to a dull red glow and then they sizzled like a piece of charcoal dropped into water. He put his hands up to his head and the horns came out...like loose teeth; there was no blood, only two small holes in his head above the ears. Then he was quite ordinary; a little black man lost on the mountain. So I told him to follow me, and he did; very quiet and obedient. There was a path I knew very well, and when we reached the place where I had to turn home I showed him where his path went...it was towards the village, I think, but I am not sure.'

'Then what did you do?'

'Just to be certain I had imagined right I went up the mountain in the middle of the night. I heard the piping again and tried to find the goat-herd. He must have gone to sleep and not heard my calling, for nothing interesting happened. I went a long way...everything was quiet and friendly, and ordinary.'

'Does the word ''Pan'' mean anything to you?'

'No,' I said. 'Ought I to know it?'

'I am glad that you don't—forget that I mentioned it. I should have brought you here sooner.' He smiled. 'When you have plenty with which to occupy your mind the dreams will cease, so I assure you there is no need for anxiety.'

I wanted to tell him that I enjoyed dreaming, but thought it might be rude to interrupt.

'You will begin your education to-morrow,' he said, 'and we will establish a healthy, cheerful routine. Euripides can instruct you in the languages and the arts, Praxiteles has already insisted that he will teach you to write, for he thinks no one else is sufficiently concerned with the shape of letters. Agamemnon can teach you history, Epicurus mathematics. I shall reserve the interesting subjects to myself, the others can provide the raw material from which I create the structure of your personality.'

I was appalled at the weight of this potential knowledge. 'Do I have to learn all day?' I said.

'There will be plenty of time for relaxation and amusement; you will of course join in our athletics—running, throwing the discus, various games to increase your speed of co-ordination. You will never have time to be bored,' he said cheerfully. 'You will be able to be perfectly natural, with every opportunity to become a balanced individual, unaffected by preconceived ideas, unbiassed by ignorant instruction.'

I wished I had the courage to point out that I seemed unlikely to be given time to have any ideas of my own, but he embarked on what I realized was a favourite theme. 'When you go outside Elysium, you will see carved on the lintels of great buildings, ''Know Thyself.'' Thousands, and tens of thousands, go through those doorways and never understand the conditions for their right of entry. Know Thyself: the strength and the weakness, the youth and the age, the ignorance and the wisdom. Only then can you be free to accept responsibility according to your capacity, without trying to escape either from life or from death. Know Thyself: and become one of the Realists, the vanguard of a race who will rule the world because they know themselves.'

CHAPTER THREE

the hero

While the weather was still warm I did lessons in one of the garden pavilions, and often found it difficult to learn because my thoughts followed the thread spun by the curve of a sail, or a cloud, or soaring gulls against the sky. It was easier when the autumn chill drove us indoors: the frescoes made a pattern of stillness like letters on a page; the steady glow of the charcoal brazier was no more exciting than the knowledge found in books.

Praxiteles taught me to write. A blot or a misshapen letter really hurt him, so I often had to ask Epicurus to give me more papyrus. I used to tear up the spoiled sheets until I realized Epicurus disliked waste and expected me to keep them so that I could do lessons with him on the backs.

I learned to read with Euripides, both in Greek and Latin. He considered Latin a vastly inferior language, but said it was necessary to be able to converse freely with people who were as yet too uncultured to appreciate our more subtle tongue. I wished the Romans had been more intelligent so that they could have had the trouble of learning Greek.

If I felt bored I asked him to read me one of his favourite plays; some I considered rather dull until he let me act them. He used to make me say the same lines over and over again until I caught the right inflection and made the gestures look spontaneous. It was much more difficult than I expected, to laugh or cry on purpose, to discover how to *feel* like the character I was supposed to represent: but it was well worth the trouble for it proved very useful in getting my own way. Even Praxiteles ceased being tiresome about blots if I looked convincingly pathetic—fortunately he never guessed that I was only being Hecuba mourning the griefs of Ilium!

Euripides let me wear the right clothes when I could remember my lines perfectly. Narcissus used to help me to dress up—I think he enjoyed it even more than I did. It was rather tiresome having to sit still for so long while he arranged my hair, for if I wriggled he stuck one of the pins into my scalp and then apologized without sincerity, and when he demanded formal curls I had to sleep with my hair screwed up in wet rags. Both of them enjoyed acting female roles. Narcissus preferred being a goddess, but Euripides was usually a miserable old woman, who wailed so effectively that the kohl ran off his eyelashes and made black streaks among the painted wrinkles. Sometimes they both looked very funny, but I never laughed unless they had been annoying.

History with Agamemnon was the only lesson I really disliked. He wasted a lot of time telling me about strategy, which he illustrated with plans of battles, but only those our side had won. I felt there must have been other battles, or the foreigners would all have been killed long ago. I was supposed to remember dull lists of wars, which seemed to be caused by quarrels over something too trivial to be mentioned. I always pretended to understand the plans, for Agamemnon took so long to draw them that I could sit watching him and think about something else. He sometimes used to get really angry, and I had to spend hours making up for the time I had deliberately wasted: but this was before I knew about the spiders.

I went to his room one day, to tell him I was sorry I had missed our lesson, but that I had been talking to Aesculapius so it was not my fault. He was lying on the bed, huddled down under the covers. I thought he was ill, until I saw he was staring at a spider which was lowering itself from the ceiling above his head. So Agamemnon didn't like spiders: he probably liked them even less than I liked history!

'Some people don't like spiders: and some are not very good at remembering names of unimportant battles,' I said briskly. 'I shall not mention spiders, unless you tell Aesculapius that I am being deliberately lazy.'

Then I climbed on a stool, caught the spider and put it out of the window. For the next two months Agamemnon even let me sleep during lessons if I felt inclined. When at last he lost his temper with me again, I pretended I had to go out of the room. When I came back, a spider, a large one with very hairy legs, fell out of a fold in my tunic. I had found it in the wood-stack outside the kitchen. While I was looking for it Epicurus saw me, so I had to pretend I was hungry and wanted a piece of bread. He gave me a thick slice with honey, and I had to eat it, hoping that the spider would not run down my leg and escape. It was very fortunate that Agamemnon was afraid of spiders instead of scorpions, for I did not like scorpions or snakes.

If I thought at all about Agamemnon brandishing a sword on the stone plinth in the olive grove I suppose I imagined he was only rehearsing the lines from a play—I had no idea that he was fighting a real enemy. He always seemed so excessively brave that I found it amusing to have found a secret chink in his armour. Whenever he was diving I had to go off a higher rock than I enjoyed, even when he climbed trees with me I had to go further than was at all pleasant. He wrestled with such ferocity that I was glad Clion had decided it was the only sport which I could not share, for even Praxiteles, who was taller and heavier than any of the others, had to exert himself to throw him.

Aesculapius must have noticed that I often quarrelled with Agamemnon, for he gave me several hints to stop, and after I had been stupid enough to ignore them, he summoned me to his room.

'I had hoped Lucina, that you might have been helpful to Agamemnon, but I perceive that your personal experience of the reality of phantasy has not increased your understanding. Therefore I must reluctantly inform you of certain facts which I should have preferred him to tell you himself, for if the harmony of our community is to be preserved, it is no longer possible to wait for you to outgrow this childish desire to dominate your companions by playing on their fears. It is for you to decide whether knowledge of the circumstances will be sufficient to change your attitude, or whether I must find more stringent means.'

I had never seen Aesculapius look so stern: did he mean that I was to be sent away from Elysium? I opened my mouth to plead with him, but he said coldly, 'You will hear the story; we will discuss the implications afterwards.'

I listened, at first in bitter resentment and then with increasing shame.

24

'I thought you would tell Agamemnon how you were able to destroy the panic fear of the goat-man by creating the opposite image of the daughter of the virgin moon—that you would have described it in your own words would have increased rather than diminished the force of the example. Remember, Lucina, that your object in Elysium is to learn to overcome fear both in yourself and in others. When you deliberately increase a fear you betray your integrity.'

He must have seen I was finding it difficult not to cry, for he continued in a milder voice, 'Agamemnon, like yourself, has an unfortunate ability for creating subjective images and then seeing them objectively. You see yourself as the conqueror, but he is open to every suggestion of defeat. You are of a naturally combative temperament, who will always attack rather than retreat—even when the most effective plan would be non-action. He has to be outwardly aggressive to conceal that his real tendency is to escape by abject flight from every challenge which he thinks will find him vulnerable.

'He is an only child: the son of a military hero, killed in the last phase of the war against the Persians, and a woman of dominant and destructive character who saw every one in her environment as a source of personal aggrandisement. First she saw herself as the daughter of a famous man—he was an orator but irrelevant to this narrative—then as the wife of a hero. She found the role of widow inadequate so she determined that her son would be the third means of making her influential—he must become a hero so that she could be the mother of a hero.

'She nurtured the child on vastly exaggerated tales of his father's prowess, and made him practise the arts of war at an age when he should have been playing with other children. When he complained of pain she upbraided him as a coward; when he failed to win in the Games she said he had dishonoured his ancestors; when he fainted at the sight of his favourite dog killed by a chariot she had all his animals slaughtered in front of him, to harden him against showing his feelings.

'The boy tried to become the hero she demanded: he made phantasies of himself leading an army to victory, of himself watching his friends killed while he remained invulnerable and disinterested. At seventeen he experienced his first real battle, a frontier skirmish in which he sustained a minor wound, little more than a deep scratch in the arm. But she had forgotten that the theme of all her stories, the core of all his imagery, was the *death* of the hero: death had been made the purpose of his living. The wound became infected, by his terror of failure. When they brought him home he was very close to the death he coveted.

'I was asked to attend him, and though I seldom accept patients the fee was too considerable to ignore. He was in delirium and by listening to his ravings the source of his imminent dissolution became clear. I took considerable pleasure in telling the mother she had tried to kill her son as certainly as though she had exposed him at birth. I called her a murderess and an incestuous harlot. I am afraid I was not without resonance to her anger.' He smiled. 'I think she might have been able to defend herself with the remnants of her pride had I not pulled aside a curtain and discovered the bier, wreathed in the bays of the hero, already prepared for the dying boy: the bier beside which she expected to play the role of stoic mother who again had made the great sacrifice on the altar of Greece. She made no protest when I ordered my servants to carry the boy from the house and bring him here.... That was nearly two years ago, but she has not asked for news of her living son, who betrayed her only because he did not die too young.'

'What did you do to stop him dying?'

'He saw standing beside his bed a man wearing the bay-crowned helmet of the traditional hero. The man said his name was Agamemnon, and that the boy was to recover his health and bear the same name in honour. He said that battle was only one of the many ways of dying and that the hero was the man who learned to live. The boy no longer wanted to die, so his fever abated and the clotted, yellow poison of fear drained out of the wound until the flesh was clean and could heal.'

'Who was the man in the helmet? Was he real or only a dream?'

'He was real enough: a friend of Clion's, wearing a gold helmet which I borrowed from a friend who has a collection of antiquities in Athens.'

'Does Agamemnon know he was tricked into getting well?'

'Yes...perhaps he was told too soon. I hoped that the knowledge would complete his cure.'

'But it didn't, or he would not still have to fight his enemies?'

'Very few people, Lucina, have the courage to be themselves, without being led by an ideal or driven by fear. If Agamemnon had been content to see himself as an ordinary soldier he could have replaced that image by something equally valid which was within the scope of his natural powers, for his mind is not of the quality from which outstanding personalities are developed. But Agamemnon cannot, as yet, accept a small role, though he knows it to be inevitable. Most of the time he is content to adjust himself to the niche which nature intended for him, and which will be suitable when he leaves here: the owner of a small, well-ordered property, content to identify himself with other men's triumphs as a spectator at the Games or the theatre.

'But whenever he considers he has been vanquished by something trivial, such as a spider, especially a spider which a girl can use as her ally, he seeks strength in terms of the original phantasy. He is inevitably defeated, being identified with one-half of the personality against the other, instead of arbitrating in the conflict from the viewpoint of the integral self. Each defeat makes him more sensitive to ridicule and therefore more determined to mock other people; more afraid, and so more boastful; more terrified, and so more desperate to act the bully in an attempt to prove his courage by a display of physical dominance.'

'I ought to have recognized how he felt,' I said humbly. 'How could any one know better than I do what it feels like to boast because one is ashamed of being so terribly inadequate?'

He was suddenly the kind, gentle Aesculapius again, so it was impossible not to be anguished because I had disappointed him. 'We grow through our failures into our success,' he said. 'Remind me of that, Lucina, when I despair because I cannot help Agamemnon—remember it yourself, for you also will never be satisfied by bays already won.' He patted me consolingly on the shoulder. 'But you will have bays, Lucina—and may they be earned with honour.'

I had to find some way of letting Agamemnon know I was sorry, but what could I do? I realized, only too well, that to tell him I knew he was afraid would make it more difficult; it would only make him hate me even more—how could he do anything else if he thought I pitied him? The plan I decided on was silly, but curiously enough it worked much better than I hoped.

I found a scorpion in my room and waited until I knew Agamemnon was outside the window. Then I began to scream, and when he came running to find what had happened I clung round his neck and wept and said how terrified I was of scorpions. He was so kind to me that after he left I cried real tears, for the Lucina who was often so unpleasant to discover in myself.

CHAPTER FOUR

merchant's Scales

Even at meals, when the conversation was never profound, for Aesculapius said that mental effort interfered with
digestion, Epicurus seldom laughed unless some one made a
deliberate joke. Then he would pause, to make quite sure
that humour was intended, throw back his head and make a
honking noise which reminded me of wild geese flying over-
head in winter. His eyes were grey, with short, thick lashes;
and his body had a solidity which made him a little clumsy
with the discus though he could wrestle better than any one
except Praxiteles.

I had never liked him particularly until the day he took me
to the storeroom, which was not until I had been in Elysium
about six months. Here, in his private world, he seemed a
different person; interested, alert, eager to share his
enthusiasm.

He opened jars of honey for me; from Mount Hymettus,
from Delos, from Rhodes; honey dark as bees or pale as sunlight. He told me to use a different finger for each kind so
that I could compare the flavour, and listened to my opinion
as though I were Aesculapius deciding the merits of wines.

Then he loosed the cords that bound the bales of stuffs
from which our clothes were made. The wool for winter
cloaks came from the fleece of wild sheep and there were
more ordinary kinds which the servants wore. The thinnest
wool came from Cos, which also sent us cotton for summer
tunics. While he showed me linen, some so fine that it was
transparent, he told me how he had been to Alexandria and
travelled by barge up the Nile to Heliopolis.

He let me rub ointments on my hand so that the warmth of
my skin brought out the scent, and crumble dried herbs until
they sifted between my fingers in odorous powders. How

could I have thought Epicurus dull, when everything he showed me was the clue to an exciting story? Why had I been so slow in discovering that tallies could be more interesting than books?

'So you share my love of *things*, Lucina?' he said. 'You are not bored with the steward?'

'Please can I come here often? I will even learn to add properly if you will let me help with the tallies, and try to remember the different ways in which things are measured and weighed and sold.'

'For one so resistant to lessons in the art of numbers that is a great concession and I am deeply honoured!'

'I am not really stupid when I want to learn,' I said frankly. 'But numbers which don't belong to anything real are such a waste of memory.'

'We are all supposed to be seeking in Elysium, but I seem to be the only one who realizes that *things* are real. The others pretend to despise what I value, but don't let yourself be decoyed into following them. People are too unreliable as objects of devotion, being subject to constant change which cannot be accurately predicted—even by Aesculapius.'

'Wouldn't people be very dull if they didn't change?'

He looked surprised. 'Does an ingot of silver lose its quality because it cannot turn into a lump of cheese, or find itself transmuted into gold?'

'But you are a man, not a metal. You can't help *thinking* so you have to grow, and growth must mean change. Don't you want to grow, Epicurus?'

'I want to know, about real tangible things. I want to know why figs from Attica are better than any others, and why Attica also produces the finest olive oil—it is nonsense, of course, that this is due to the groves being under the special protection of Athene. I want to discover the precise value of each commodity in relation to all other commodities: the *real* value, not the false which is made by men who cannot decide what they want or why they want it. Within every lifetime there is war and famine; men die in thousands because merchants cannot agree. And why can't they agree, why do they lie and haggle and cheat? Because they try to falsify the basic values to enrich themselves.'

'Or is it because people find it too difficult to be honest?'

'People!' His voice was near to tears. 'People spoil everything, silly, cruel, squalid little people. Their horrid tastes which have to be satisfied on other men's blood. They are idiot children, to be pacified into temporary good humour; and they call this "freedom"! They go to war because it makes them feel important, and die for futility which they have not the courage to recognize. They are born because their parents lacked discrimination: why should children be born unless a surplus of goods justifies an increase in population? Why? Because people are too lazy and cruel to realize it is wicked to invite more people than the house can feed.'

'Don't women sometimes have babies because they want them; want to love, I mean, not because they might be useful?'

'Of course they do! I said the world was full of irresponsible adolescents, who refuse to grow up even when they are senile!'

'I don't know about the world: I have only lived in the island and here.'

'Well, stay here, if you wish to go on believing that it is safe to love people: if you intend to leave Elysium, learn to love things; old, beautiful, solid things, which days and months and centuries cannot spoil. You had better hear what can happen in the world, and then you won't let it break you if Aesculapius dies and we have to leave here. It is not a pretty story, do you want to listen?'

I nodded, and he began, 'My father collected imperishable beauty: vases from Attica and Rhodes; figurines from Crete; bronzes from Andros and Sparta. He was happy until he tried to collect the living beauty of a woman. He built a

31

house for her near Athens which was considered one of the jewels of the city—the marble alone cost him ten thousand staters. In the gardens were statues by Phidias and the real Praxiteles. She wanted fountains and ornamental pools, so he built an aqueduct which could have supplied a town.

'He wanted a large family, but I was their only child, the limit of her generosity. He gave me everything: she could not be bothered even to choose my clothes, saying that she had nothing to contribute to a son already so lavishly endowed. Her lack of appreciation was incredible. I remember him giving her a vase from Mycenae, over a thousand years old, and she complained that as it was cracked it was useless for flowers. She kept embroidery threads in a casket which had come from a royal tomb of Egypt and wore a pectoral that had belonged to the same queen as though it were a string of coral beads.

'Instead of realizing that she was too stupid to value his gifts, he thought her taste so fastidious that he must find still more beautiful things to satisfy her. She must have known he was ruining himself, but she made no attempt to stop him. I overheard their final quarrel. He confessed in abject abasement that he had spent his last sack of coins and owed vast sums to merchants. She laughed at him, and said he deserved poverty for having tried to buy her clemency because he was too cowardly to entrust her with his heart.

'That night she poisoned herself. I found her body. She was lying on a gold and ivory couch that had belonged to a Ptolomaic princess. Beside it were coffers, their lids open to display the treasures he had given her. She had even made her own funerary wreaths and set lamps at her head and feet. There was a scroll beside her, and on it was written in her fine, delicate hand, ''I cannot wait any longer to use your only gift which has not disappointed me: the memorable sarcophagus made for the woman you forgot to love.''

'I fled from the house to a wine shop...and woke two days later to find it was not a hideous dream. I went back to the house. It was empty, save for beauty destroyed by a man driven insane. The floors were covered with shards of pottery, splinters of ivory, jewels wrenched from their settings, precious ointments trampled into charred carpets which had taken five years to grow on the loom. The curtains had been slashed, the furniture hacked to pieces, fire had blackened the walls and cracked the frescoes.

'I found my father in the treasure room, the *empty* treasure room. He was sitting on the floor, playing with a little gold statue of Ptah, an Egyptian god, as though he were a child with a toy. He looked up at me, and said in a small pitiful voice, ''He is too strong, too beautiful to destroy. Do you think she will let me keep him? I gave her everything else, but it was not enough.''

'I was only sixteen; ignorant, except in learning, for I had always been indulged and protected. At least I had the decency to hide my father from other men's pity. I took him to a small farm which belonged to a freed slave who had reason to wish to repay my father's generosity. From the ruined house I saved a few things which had escaped destruction...gold is still gold even when only its value as metal remains. When I no longer had these fragments to sell I worked for a foreign merchant, who found useful my knowledge of where he might find buyers. I, who had often been a guest in those houses, was not recognized when I went to the servants' courts to beg for my wares to be considered by the master!

'My father lived another three years. He thought that he was a child and I the slave who had looked after him. He could not wash himself and had to be fed with a spoon. His only pleasure were toys; small, brightly coloured toys which the slaves buy for their children. He had a doll, and a wooden horse with a red saddle...he never played with the gold statue but kept it hidden under his pillow. He said it was a present he was going to give to a beautiful woman when he grew up. I buried it with him.'

Suddenly he began to cry. I put my arms round him as he knelt beside me, his body shaking convulsively, his tears dripping on my bare knee.

'I loved him, Lucina,' he said desperately. 'I loved him, and that is why I am never going to love any person again. Please help me find things to love, don't let me believe in people again.'

'Your father loved things, and they didn't make *him* happy.'

He raised his head and looked at me. 'But I don't want rare, irreplaceable things. I only want to know about figs and wine and spices, things which belong to every one, things of which there will always be enough for every one who isn't greedy.'

'Aren't there enough people for everybody?'

'No. There is too little love in the world, only enough to make you hungry for more. And there is never love without fear: people *die*, Lucina. They take your heart into the ground with them, or you take theirs. You cannot dare to love unless you are very brave, and if you are brave you don't need any one to help you. Aesculapius is strong; if we all died he would still be the same person. He believes in himself...but I don't; I don't believe in *anything*.'

'Dictys and Elissa are very ordinary people and not very brave; but I think they love each other, even if not very much. They know that it will be lonely for the one who is the last to die, but they will have memories to help them, like a lamp in a dark room. Can't you forget the hurt of your father's sorrow and remember the strength your loving gave you? It did bring you strength, dear Epicurus...it made you able to look after him and give him the things he wanted when he really needed them.'

'A toy from the market...a wooden horse given to me out of charity by a pedlar!'

'But they were the things he *wanted*: he felt like a child because life had been too difficult in the way he lived it. Perhaps your mother felt like an ordinary woman, who wanted to work for her husband, to be loved in small commonplace ways. She may have been a real person, and neither of them knew it.'

'So real that she killed herself to enjoy the full taste of hatred!'

'Or because they were both so very lonely?'

'Lonely!' He stood up and rubbed the back of his hand across his eyes. 'Lonely! What do you know about loneliness? Spend ten years cringing to foreigners, ten years cut off by poverty from your own kind of people...and spend another three living in Elysium, among people who think you are cold and remote, content to live by tallies, to weigh your heart in a merchant's scales. Do that, at your peril. Then talk to me of loneliness and I will weep for pity!'

'I don't need to wait so long: thank you for not seeing that I have been crying too. I am young, and very unimportant, but I can understand much better than a statue... even a very beautiful statue. We can help each other, if you don't mind my being so young. Both of us need to learn how to be brave enough to love.'

'Love,' he said slowly. 'Is love not the enemy...is love perhaps the only freedom?'

'I think so,' I said. 'But I am not very clever.'

He smiled, the first time I had ever seen him smile like that, 'Aren't you, Lucina?' He kissed me on the forehead. 'You have seen me cry, and I am not ashamed. Isn't that very clever?'

lamplight

The western headland of the bay was joined to the rest of
Elysium by a narrow neck of land, and the cliffs were steep
enough to make it almost as secluded as an island. On it was
a deserted house, a small white house protected from the
north by ancient pines. It looked an interesting place to
explore, but one of the servants told me it was haunted. I
asked Aesculapius about the ghost, but instead of being helpful he said impatiently that ghosts had no existence save in
the inferior minds of the credulous. I could not question the
servant for he was sent away from Elysium that same
evening.

I wondered why Aesculapius had been so annoyed, especially when he maintained that curiosity was the primary
virtue. He used to say, 'Answering questions is the privilege
of philosophers; and they remain philosphers just so long as
they remember there are always more answers to discover.'

If ghosts did not exist why was the house abandoned?
Why was the path leading to it from the mainland overgrown
by brambles? After careful thought I decided that it might be
wiser to avoid the place until I knew more about ghosts and
what to do if I met one.

In calm weather it was easy to go beyond the headland,
for there was a ledge of rock, between the cliff and the deep
water, which led to a long sandy beach. I sometimes went
there for a solitary walk, usually after I had been defeated in
an argument and wanted to enjoy a comfortable quarrel inside
my head, in which I always made witty remarks instead of
thinking of them too late.

It was on one of these occasions, a cold afternoon in early
spring, that I was too busy being clever to notice black clouds
driving up against the wind. Thunder suddenly roared; I

knew it was only a natural phenomenon, but it would have been easy to believe that the sound was made by gods bellowing at each other, angry gods, probably angry with *me*.

I could not help remembering the tree I had seen struck by lightning. If Zeus decided to aim his fire at me I should soon look like a carcase left too long in the oven! I tried to laugh at myself, but the joke seemed too probable to be funny.

I wanted to get home very quickly, not only because it had begun to rain. Waves were dashing against the cliff, and the ledge was under water. If I tried to cross it I should be sucked into the sea by the undertow. Could I swim round? The sea was too rough: I should be driven on the rocks before I could get beyond the headland.

If I went back along the beach there was another way home—but it was much further, and it would soon be dark. I should have to pass close to the deserted house. Did the ghost inhabit the garden too?

I began to run, which is never sensible when you are frightened. The steps were slippery with spray. I fell and grazed my knee. At the top there was a solitary pine, its branches dark and tormented against the livid sky. The wind was so strong that I had to cling to the tree to stop myself being blown over the cliff. The rough bark was strangely reassuring, the only protection in a world of hostile water.

I should have to shelter in the empty house until the storm lessened, until I could fight my way through the brambles which barred the way home.

The shutters of the west window were swinging in the lash of the gale. As I pulled myself up to the sill, the broken plaster of the outer wall stripped the skin from my other knee. Lightning showed me a long narrow room, the walls frescoed with faded lilies.

The shutters creaked disconsolately, like the knee-joints of some one very old. I tried to close them, but the bolt was too stiff with rust. I crouched against the wall for protection. In the glare of another flash the painted lilies watched me, scornful of the girl who huddled beside their placid stalks.

Why had I thought the room was empty? There was a bed, and a painted chest under the east window.

A woman was lying in the bed, a woman with honey-coloured hair tangled on the pillow. She was asleep, breathing very slowly...I could see the green coverlet move with the shallow rise and fall of her breast.

I could hear water dripping in the sudden silence...water dripping from my hair, small precise drops marking the passing time. The woman opened her eyes, sea-green under the weary lids. I tried to speak to her, to tell her she was no longer alone. I felt my lips move, but the sea was too loud for her to hear me.

A child came into the room, a child with curly hair bound with a fillet of pale flowers. She carried a lamp, shielding the small flame carefully with her hand. The wind must have died down, for I could hear the soft fall of the child's bare feet on the tiled floor. The child stumbled—she had caught her foot in the fold of a small carpet near the bed: the carpet was brown with a pattern of white deer. She began to cry, and the oil from her lamp spilled on the floor, spreading into a narrow pool of light.

The woman got up from the bed, slowly as though she were afraid of falling. I saw her straighten herself and move towards the child. She took the lamp and the flame was steady...a much brighter flame, for they were no longer in shadow. The child looked up at her, the tears glittering on its lashes. They smiled at each other, and hand in hand went to the far window. I heard the shutters open, and saw the sunrise; then the light was too bright for me to see them.

Some one was shouting outside the house. 'Lucina! Lucina, where are you?'

'Here!' my voice sounded very loud in the quiet room. Where was 'here'? Why was I lying on the floor...why was I wet and shuddering with cold?

Against the green, storm-clean sky I saw Euripides

climbing through the window.

'I saw you on the headland. I came back to look for you when I realized you couldn't have reached the path before I did. Were you frightened by the thunder?'

'Only when I dropped the lamp...before she held it for us.'

I could only see his face as a shape against the sky, but I knew he was staring at me. 'Something has happened, Lucina. What is it? You're still frightened.'

He bent down and lifted me from the floor. He smelt of wet wool and warm, human skin. I clung to him, hiding my face against his shoulder.

'I'm going to make a fire, ' he said. 'I left dry wood in the next room when I was here last month...there is even a towel and an old cloak that I use after bathing.'

I watched him coax the pine-knots into strong flame. I sat close to the hearth, hugging my knees to try to keep myself from shivering. He took off my wet clothes, and rubbed me with the rough towel until I began to feel warmth creeping back to my body. Then he wrapped me in his cloak, which smelt of seaweed, and sat with his arm round me in the warm fire-light.

'What happened to you, Lucina? You needn't be afraid to tell me. I shan't laugh, for I know there is something here.'

'How do you know?' I wanted to tell him: but it would be terrible if he could not believe in what I had seen.

'Shall I tell you why I come here, then you needn't say anything if you feel I wouldn't understand?'

'Yes,' I said, 'but please don't be angry if I don't tell you anything.'

'Why should I be angry? We can both pretend nothing happened except a thunderstorm.'

He threw another log on the fire and I leant against his shoulder.

'I came here for the first time three months ago; for the

very ordinary reason that I thought it would be a good place to work in, where no one would interrupt. I meant to go on with a play about the Trojan war...but I started to write something entirely different. I felt the characters belonged to this house, and instead of having to create the background it flowed quite naturally into the pattern. I knew even such small details as clothes and furniture. The only curious thing was that time went backwards instead of forwards....It began with a woman dying: she died in the other room.'

'On a bed facing the south window?'

'Yes: and I think there was a child's bed in the room, but I am not sure of this. I'm uncertain about the age of the child, sometimes I think she was a baby, and then I cross that out and make her about three years old. She had pale yellow hair, like the mother.'

'Go on...*please* go on.'

'The woman had a rare stillness, as though she listened for a sound on the edge of silence. She was content to drift on the current of the seasons, as though her world held nothing more complex than the sound of the sea, or the tranquil pattern of trees against the sky. But she had to guard her quietness, holding it like a fragile shell cupped in her hands. She had suffered some great sorrow, and only by a deliberate forgetting could she protect her unborn child.'

'She knew that if she let herself remember it would be so very easy to die,' I said softly. 'And when the child was born?'

'Then she dared to relive the past—to remember the love that was stronger than any other reality.'

'She wanted to find my father, but she couldn't go to him until she was sure I was strong enough to carry my own lamp. Euripides, why didn't you tell me that my mother died here?'

'Because I didn't know, until you told me.'

We walked home under a sky of many stars. Euripides wanted me to go straight to bed and not see Aesculapius until the morning. But how could I sleep with so many questions unanswered?

I went to his room, though it was understood that he was not to be disturbed after the evening meal unless by his express invitation.

'Is anything wrong, Lucina? You appear agitated. I hope you found adequate shelter from the storm?'

'Most adequate,' I said. 'In the room where my mother died—in the house on the headland where I was born. Why did you lie to me?'

He paused, as though considering whether evasion was still practicable. 'I considered it wiser to conceal the circumstances of your birth until you were older.'

'Then you admit I was born in Elysium?'

'Have I ever denied it?'

'You said my mother was a patient of yours in Athens; that you promised to look after me because it was her dying wish and I had no relations.'

'That is perfectly correct; if you will allow me to explain my reasons for not telling you the full story until now, I think you will find nothing discreditable in my motives.'

Then his face softened, he took my hand and drew me towards him. 'Don't stand there accusing me before I have had a chance to tell my story—sit here beside me. How can we quarrel, when I loved your mother as you would have loved her if she had lived.'

'I am sorry I was rude. It was a shock, finding out so suddenly.'

'Who told you?'

'No one—I discovered it for myself.'

It was obvious that he thought I was defending somebody. I thought he was going to try to find out who it was, but instead he said gently, 'Your mother was beautiful in mind and body, and she would have been proud of you, Lucina. She was a priestess, in the temple of Hera at Mycenae. She was dedicated to lifelong virginity, but she

41

fell in love with a young Athenian. She loved him more than her sterile vows; you were conceived and he persuaded her to flee with him to Athens. They hid in a poor quarter of the town with his foster-mother, waiting for a boat to take them to Alexandria. It was the Olympiad of the Games and he yielded to the temptation of renewing his laurels. I think it must have been very difficult for him to relinquish the acclaim of the crowds who had made him the most famous athlete in Greece.

'Your mother eagerly awaited his return, there had been a messenger to say that their ship would sail at dawn. She heard the lamentation of the crowd, and in sudden terror ran out of the house. It was your father's name which echoed through the weeping throng; he had been killed in the last bout of the wrestling. She watched his body carried through the streets on a bier garlanded with the laurels of his companions. She said he looked as though he smiled in his sleep: no one could have told that his neck was broken.

'When she collapsed, a passer-by carried her to my house. I heard her story and offered her the sanctuary of Elysium. In those days there was only the cottage on the headland: it was not until I decided to live here permanently that I built this house.' He smiled, 'It was because of your mother that I became a philosopher instead of a celebrated physician.'

'Why did she change you?'

'I tried by every means at my command to save her life, but I did not know enough to win against the false gods which destroyed her. My skill was useless; it was only sufficient to convince me that she suffered from no bodily disease.'

'Then why did she die?'

'She believed herself guilty of your father's death, that in him the gods she worshipped had revenged themselves for her disloyalty. I tried to give her a sense of reality, but she refused to listen: saying that if I took away her fear of the gods she would no longer be able to believe she would in time rejoin your father. I thought that when you were born her love for a child would increase her will to live. But she had only been waiting to give you life before she felt free to stretch out her arms to death.

'Are you surprised, Lucina, that I try to make you strong enough to resist the hideous infection of superstition? You resemble her so closely that often I fear for you. But I *will* protect you! I will teach you to accept reality even if the process must estrange you from me. I beg of you to believe that only truth, unclouded intellect, can give you security.'

'You want me to believe that she has no existence save in our memory?'

'I know it, Lucina. Here and now are the place and the time of our living, not in some amorphous afterworld which cowards conceive to hide their fear of death.'

'You are wrong, Aesculapius. I saw her this afternoon— if you don't believe me ask Euripides, he was there too.'

'How dare he contaminate your mind with his phantasies!'

'I *saw* her—and I saw myself, as a child of three years old for whom she lit a lamp.'

He leant back as though relieved. 'A child of three? This proves beyond all doubt that your vision was purely subjective—you left Elysium at the age of two months.'

'You promised her to look after me, so why did you send me to the island?'

'I was determined that you should not share her needless suffering. The influence of heredity is strong, but not more so than the childhood environment. I wished you to be free from all contacts which might cause you to develop the mystical strain which had been dominant in the maternal parent. Elissa was loyal, obedient and healthy, but incapable of abstract thought. Her husband was of the same type, and after due consideration, was willing to swear that you should be kept in strict seclusion so that you should hear nothing appertaining to the supernatural. As a token of his acceptance of my wishes I made him destroy his household god in my presence: I knew this would remove any temptation to break his word, for he would not be likely to invoke gods he thought he had insulted. He made a sound bargain: a clay image in exchange for a home and sufficient land to secure his future.'

'Only the immediate future: in exchange for immortality.'

'You think it dishonest to barter a shadow for a substance?'

'No, but I think it is cruel.'

'Unfortunately a physician who has the courage of his convictions must be prepared for the patient to see only the temporary pain instead of the final health which will result from the removal of a malign growth.'

'You still haven't been able to explain how a baby could remember the pattern on a carpet, the position of a chest, the colour of her mother's eyes!'

'Do you?' He smiled indulgently, but his mood had altered, he was no longer sympathetic to affection. I described the room, but though he agreed that every detail was accurate he remained unconvinced.

'A most brilliant demonstration that the perception of infants is far more acute than is generally accepted. It is also illuminating that the baby had already developed a concept of itself at a more advanced stage. You were in the room when your mother died—I had no idea that the end was so close or of course I should have had you taken away. Already you were conscious of the difference between light and darkness, and found the lamp reassuring. Your mother was afraid of the dark; you must have contracted this fear during the pre-natal period. You see how *interesting* it all is when the process is explained?'

I made no reply and he took my silence for assent.

'The influence of the symbolic name is most gratifying. You were her daughter, the projection of herself which might well have proved strong enough to combat her fears. What did she call you? Lucina—the lamp, or, in a wider aspect, the light bringer. She tried to protect herself from a fear of death as darkness, by a pitiful belief that the light of affection could endure beyond mortality: the symbol of that light was the child with the lamp.'

He crossed the room to take a small terracotta lamp from the table on which he wrote all his theses. 'This was beside her when she died—it is unchanged, but she will never use it again.' He held it between his hands, looking down at the small, clear flame; for a moment he seemed young and curiously defenceless.

Then he said gently, 'I am very grateful, Lucina, that you have told me she did not die in fear—she was so afraid of the dark.'

What could I say to comfort him, or myself? Perhaps he was right—perhaps I had only seen her symbolic vision which somehow had lingered in the room where she died. He had told me that ghosts were only a subjective image created by one person and perceived objectively by another. But if he were wrong, how could I be so cruel as to tell him that after the physician had watched her body die the philosopher had left her soul alone in the dark, because he was too blind to see beyond the horizon of mortality?

CHAPTER SIX

Sea Urchin

A fly settled on the nose of the nymph opposite me. Instead of brushing it off she continued to stare at the pomegranate in her hand with her foolish smile unchanged. It was easy enough for her; she was marble. Blocks of stone, a half-finished frieze, a broken torso: all of them kept their interminable pose without effort, but Praxiteles seemed to have forgotten that his model is alive. He turned to select a broader spatula and I gave a quick rub to my right thigh which was protesting against this laborious inactivity.

'Tired, Lucina?' He sounded resigned, the parent trying to be patient with the difficult child.

'Why should I be? I've only been standing here for three hours!'

He ignored my sarcasm, glanced at the high window and said cheerfully, 'Good. I thought it was much later. I shall be able to finish your left buttock before we leave off.

'I will tell my buttock that it may feel duly honoured.'

''Buttock! Cease complaining! You are being immortalized: consider how smug you will feel when you are safe in the best quality Pentelic marble while the rest of me is only a handful of ashes.'' '

'Don't talk...unless it helps you to keep still.'

'Don't answer, Buttock! He is not interested in our opinions; only in the shape to which we have contorted ourselves for his convenience.'

Pellets of clay continued to fall on the floor. Praxiteles began to whistle through his teeth; usually a sign that he was impatient. If he got sufficiently impatient he would pause only long enough to cover the clay with a wet cloth and then rush out of the studio. He stopped whistling; there was no immediate escape which I could accept without loss of pride. At least I could move my eyes without displaying weakness. They showed me five Lucinas, though three of these were only in clay. Lucina the child who had come to Elysium three years ago, looking pensively into a rock-pool...this had been intended for a fountain but was never finished. Lucina aged fourteen carrying a wine-jug on her shoulder. Lucina asleep, her hands folded, her feet resting against a young ram: this had been one of the early models for the sarcophagus of the daughter of an Athenian merchant, an acquaintance of Epicurus. There was also Lucina throwing a discus, and Lucina

46

as Artemis with a young hind.

No one found it odd that I could stand here and see five people who were separate entities and yet an integral part of myself; but if I claimed to have been people who belonged to other centuries instead of only to other years, I was considered a fool. Perhaps I *was* a fool; otherwise I should not have held this pose so long, much longer than Euripides or any of the others would have done.

'Enough for to-day!' Praxiteles sounded pleased with himself, at least I should be spared further effort for the sake of my right buttock—or was it the left one? I was too tired to bother.

'Are you coming to watch me wrestle with Agamemnon? We want to practice a new throw, it might be interesting.'

Watching them wrestle always made me afraid, which of course, I could not admit; so I quickly thought of an excuse. 'I promised Epicurus to get some sea urchins—he wants to find out if they go well with the new sauce he invented for crab last week.'

'It was a good sauce,' said Praxiteles with kindly patronage. 'A considerable improvement on garlic and mussels— even if the mussels had been free of sand it would still have been an error of taste.'

Criticism of Epicurus always annoyed me. 'Luckily some of us have grown beyond the primitive desire for mutton in prodigious quantity—to quote Aesculapius, ''A subtle palate is an indication of the mature intellect.'' '

He grinned, 'Preoccupation with the belly is apt to make it bulge—not that your figure shows any such tendency as yet, my dear Lucina.'

Why had I said I was going to collect urchins? Now I should have to do it or else let Praxiteles think he had scored. But the alternative would be throwing the discus with Clion and Euripides, or else running against them. I should have enjoyed the two hours we had to spend each day on some kind of athletics if only I had not had to exert myself to the utmost to maintain a measure of equality. At least I no longer had the humiliation of being given a start in each race, but it had not been easy to train in secret so that no one should know how terribly hard I had to try at everything.

I fetched a basket from the kitchen, and was on my way down to the beach when I met Narcissus and Aesculapius. Narcissus was carrying a cushion and obviously intended to spend a lazy afternoon.

'I am going to get urchins', I said briskly. 'The least you can do is to hold the basket.'

Narcissus smiled. 'Nothing would please me more, Lucina. Especially as you are far too fragile to be trusted on the beach alone.'

The presence of Aesculapius made it impossible to retort adequately so I pretended not to notice the insult.

About three hours later Narcissus stood just out of reach of the ripples, still holding the basket.

'Surely you've got enough now?' he said plaintively. 'There were twenty-three when I last counted.'

'I want at least twelve more. It's your fault we've taken so long; if you had helped instead of grumbling we would have been home by now.'

After making sure it was dry, he sat on a rock, staring disconsolately at a long green smear on the front of his tunic: he had fallen down while I was urging him to hurry across a wrack of slimy weed.

I found another urchin lurking in the sand at the water's edge. I was feeling impatient with Narcissus, so instead of taking it to the basket I threw it to him. Instinctively he caught it, and then yelped with pain.

I ought to have remembered he had taken off his gloves, thick leather ones we always used when handling urchins. I knew how painful the spines could be, for I had got one in my foot a month earlier and could not run properly for several days. Perhaps it would have been easier to show sympathy if I had not an uncomfortable feeling that I had known his hands were bare and thought it would be funny to punish him for being too lazy to help me.

'Does it hurt much?' I said, fighting a sudden urge to giggle. 'I'll pull out the spines and then you can suck it to stop the bleeding.'

'The taste of blood revolts me, and I might swallow a spine and choke.'

I took one of the silver pins which I used to keep my hair out of the way when I was too busy to do it properly. 'I shan't hurt you if you keep still.'

There were three spines: two came out easily but I had to dig deep to get out the last without breaking it. A little blood oozed out of the hole and trickled down his arm. 'I'll lick it as you mind the taste,' I said kindly.

To my shame, he seemed genuinely grateful. 'Thank you, Lucina. I must apologize for thinking you threw it on purpose—of course I know you mistook it for a pebble. It's extraordinary how pain can make one temporarily lose all sense of justice.'

He sounded sincere: but could he really be so guileless? Did we all underrate him? Perhaps we did: I looked at him with new respect.

The basket had fallen over. I picked up an urchin, forgetting that I had taken off my gloves.

'Poor Lucina, how very distressing, you got far more spines than I did! Can I help?'

I could have cried with pain and humiliation, but I said, 'No, thank you: I can manage quite well.'

Several of the spines had broken off. I knew that if I did not get them out they would probably fester. I had to use the pin with my left hand, which made the operation more complicated. Narcissus watched me, his lip grave, his eyes alert as a child who sees a new toy being unwrapped.

'Does it hurt much?'

I sucked my palm, which tasted of wet leather and fish scales. 'It doesn't hurt at all,' I said firmly. 'I like blood;

it is a more dramatic scarlet than anemones.'

I saw this disturbed him a little, so I held my hand over a rock-pool and watched the slow drops spread through the water, fanning out until they looked like a new kind of sea-weed.

'You are rather like a sea-urchin yourself, Lucina,' he said reflectively, 'soft-hearted and delicious, but not without menace if handled carelessly.'

I thought it wiser to take this as a joke. 'And no trouble to any one so long as he doesn't tread on me!'

'But who does? Certainly not I; is Clion, perhaps, a little apt to be obtuse?'

'Clion? What has Clion got to do with it?'

'A trivial remark, quite unworthy of serious consideration. It only seemed that there were occasions when he over-emphasized that we had all been told to ignore the obvious fact that you might be our complement instead of our rival.'

'You mean that instead of throwing a discus I should be content to sit making a wreath with which humbly to reward the victor? And I suppose I ought to keep silent in discussions; eager to enrich my inferior mind with such morsels of wisdom as may be thrown to me!'

'Nothing so crude, Lucina. It is only that I find it distressing to see you consistently trying to exchange your natural talents for those of the less complex male. For instance, you had to *tell* me, in the presence of Aesculapius, that I was to carry this basket for you: I obeyed, you must admit, with no trace of resentment. Had you been a less exacting personality I should have asked, even perhaps implored, you to let me do this trivial service. I should have admired the charming composition made by your yellow hair against the varied blues and greens which the sea so thoughtfully provides for a background. I should have helped you to collect this unnecessary trophy, instead of taking pleasure in the fact that you are getting tired, but too proud to admit it; are wet and dirty, but too lazy to notice it; have been doing a man's work, but are too stupid to be ashamed of it.'

I was more surprised than if a strand of seaweed had suddenly coiled to hiss at me. Then I realized it was worse than this: he wasn't being unkind, he was *sorry* for me!

'So you think I'm a fool? You may be right: I had never really thought about it before.'

He deliberately tore a strip off the hem of his tunic, took my hand out of the water and bandaged it. Narcissus, not caring if his tunic, and it was a new one, was spoiled; not trying to escape from the sight of blood—and there was quite a lot of blood!

'Hadn't you better learn to let people do things for you?' he said gently. 'You're fighting nearly as hard as Agamemnon; and you don't need to fight us unless you insist.'

'What else can I do? I'm younger than any of you, and not so clever about the knowledge which comes from books. Aesculapius has told me not to believe the things which none of you understand: he says I have got to be strong, that I must never let myself be dependent on other people. I have to run faster, think quicker, be more sure of myself than any of you; and all the time I know you are just being *kind*.'

'Well, even if we are, is kindness an insult?'

'It is when one doesn't deserve it.'

'Has it ever occurred to you, dear and rather silly Lucina, that we like you for all the things you despise in yourself? If I want to admire an athlete I can turn to Praxiteles; if I want to be impressed by learning, there is always Aesculapius; if I want to be burnished by some one else's superior wit I can seek the company of Euripides.'

'I know that perfectly well,' I said bitterly. 'That's why I have to try harder and harder at everything all the time.'

'Why not accept yourself as you are?'

'And be sent away, because I have shown that a woman can never be a competent philosopher?'

'She might be; if she was first a competent woman, or even a competent girl.'

'Why should I want to be a woman? All of you despise females; in Elysium they are not even good enough to wash clothes! Look what happened to my mother: she died because she gave up being a priest and wanted to be loved as an ordinary, safe, silly woman. She died: and I am not nearly ready to die yet!'

'So why not try living for a change?'

'I am *not* a coward,' I said passionately. 'I don't try to escape from being hurt. My hand hurts more than yours, but I didn't make nearly so much fuss.'

'I only pretended it hurt me because I wanted to make you feel guilty...make the other person feel ashamed and you are half-way to victory. If there were more of the true female in you, Lucina, you would have learned so obvious a strategy.'

'I thought strategy was only used by soldiers.'

'Did you? How curious, for you are not lacking in subtlety...though at times you are a little crude in your methods. The urchin, for instance; surely you don't think I really believe you mistook it for a pebble?'

'I wasn't sure,' I said frankly. 'At first I thought you couldn't be such a fool, and then...well, now I know you couldn't.'

He laughed, 'The first real compliment you have ever paid me!'

'And it won't be the last...if you don't hate me for being so disgusting and so blind.'

'I am the only person here who has not been asked to share in your education, but if you feel inclined to accept my devoted service I think I might prove not entirely useless.'

'I should be very grateful if you would teach me, Narcissus. What do you want me to learn?'

'You needn't sound so depressed: the lessons will not be without interest. I want to show you how to use the natural weapons with which you have been most generously endowed.'

'What weapons?'

'The power of the female over the male; invincible if properly used, for we are defenceless against an opponent who does not deign to accept a challenge in our own terms.'

'Go on,' I said. 'It doesn't matter if we don't get back until late. If the others have finished I can get us something to eat from the kitchen.'

'No, Lucina: if you listen to the first lesson with attention you will *not* go to the kitchen. You will look a little tired, having taken care that you hair is becomingly disarranged instead of leaving it screwed up on your head, skewered by pins which would be more suitable for a trussed fowl! You will take these revolting fragments of marine complexity to Epicurus; show him your hand with a brave smile—but make it clear that you lost a lot of blood. He will be filled with remorse that you have suffered on his behalf. So it will be Epicurus who hurries to the kitchens, or even to the store-room, in search of delectable morsels to tempt your appetite. And you must insist on being tempted; no mere bread and honey for you, no cold meat or hunk of cheese. If he should have the temerity to bring such an inadequate token of apology you will say you are too tired to eat: I shall assist you to bed, and return, obviously distressed, to say that you will undoubtedly have fever unless I can persuade you to take some nourishment. If that doesn't produce any pronounced effect I shall fetch suitable food; and make him feel thoroughly miserable that he hadn't the wit to think of it himself.'

'Perhaps you know a lot more about women than I do,' I said thoughtfully. 'It seems a pity you were born a man.'

'It is much more than a pity, it is a tragedy,' he said. 'But in you I hope to find a vicarious satisfaction for the talents of which circumstances have denied me the full use. You will notice I said the *full* use, for the more intelligent male is not without female subtleties.'

'Narcissus; why do you pretend to be weak when you are really stronger than any of us?'

'Because, with the lower animals, I share the instinct of self-preservation. By being outwardly compliant I get a lot of things done for me which otherwise I would have to contend with myself. It amuses me to wait on you, for, certainly until now, the process has daily increased my feeling of superiority. When you feel in the mood to let me choose your clothes, and achieve the desired effect with your hair, I have the satisfaction which Praxiteles no doubt feels for a statue...but with the advantage that I am working with living structure instead of laboriously hewing at unresponsive stone. It is not *you* they admire, Lucina: it is me, Narcissus, the creator of living beauty. Most satisfactory, I assure you.

'But it can't be fun for you to be ordered about by Agamemnon.'

'No? Then you have never suffered from the boasting of the followers of Mars. I have, and it is most soothing to old wounds to play the indulgent parent to a small boy who still wants to strut his silly little pace. I am not so foolish as to create a phantasy of the enslaved woman: I am not the wife watching her beloved husband go off to battle while she weeps: I am the woman who is delighted to see him go, knowing she can pursue some more interesting pastime during his absence: an absence which leaves her free, and yet with the added glory of being envied for her stoic calm!'

'Don't you mind when Aesculapius deliberately makes remarks which he thinks will drive you into independence? I have often thought it horrid of him to do it in front of us, especially at meals.'

'I know. It has usually made you kind to me for the rest of the day; and even the less sensitive make a determined effort to show they desire my company. I am most grateful to Aesculapius, I assure you. When you first arrived at Elysium I had only been here three months. I still believed I wished to learn to stand without support, having not yet learned the simple truth that when ivy climbs a tree it is the tree which dies. I am now much wiser. I am docile, for then others protect me; I am incompetent, so no one gives me disagreeable tasks. Epicurus ceased asking me to help him with the tallies after I had deliberately added them wrong three times in succession. Aesculapius thought it would be good for me to take an interest in husbandry.' He shuddered. 'Earth under the nails, sweat running down my face, the soft pulp of slugs... and so easily avoided by using the minimal intelligence!'

'How did you manage it?' I asked with fervour: remembering the hours I had spent digging thistles from the kitchen garden, content to work through long, hot afternoons for a word of praise.

'It was very easy. I displayed a remarkable ignorance of the most elementary botanical principles. It was obvious that I was trying pathetically hard; yet no precious seedling was safe from me, time after time it wilted on the rubbish heap, because poor, stupid Narcissus had mistaken it for a noxious weed. I always asked to be given another chance: I think it was some rare bulbs from Macedonia, which I sent to the kitchen instead of onions, that at last convinced Aesculapius that I could no longer be usefully employed in the garden. I was careful to conceal my elation: you may remember I sulked in my room for two days after he refused to let me help him any more.'

'Wasn't it very dull, sulking alone, I mean?'

'Nothing is dull, Lucina, if it is part of a careful design which is emerging on the loom provided by your less knowledgeable companions.'

'Don't you respect Aesculapius at all?'

'But of course!' he sounded genuinely shocked. 'If I did not hold him in real and sincere admiration, surely I should not let him do all my important thinking for me? I may say that I *revere* Aesculapius; he has given me the greatest of all boons; I am spared the painful necessity of making any decisions for myself.'

As I had not brought a hair-ribbon with me, Narcissus

made me a wreath of sea-pinks before he went back to the house.

'There is no point in us both missing a meal,' he said frankly. 'But you must stay out until sunset, or later still if you are not too bored. If you let them think you lost your way in the dark it will make your entrance more effective—I shall prepare the stage for you by feigned anxiety.'

'I shall look such a fool! I *can't* pretend to be lost in Elysium.'

'You will never learn to be clever until you are willing to appear foolish. I do not expect you to believe in me until I have proved that I know what I am talking about, so I will make a bargain: if you do not get your own way, and a better supper than the rest of us, I will collect a hundred urchins without wearing gloves and you can sit and laugh at me!'

'Very well,' I said grudgingly. 'But if Epicurus only grumbles because I didn't bring the first course in time *you* will have to find something for me to eat.'

'Good! Already I observe a distinct improvement. Before our little talk you would have been perfectly content to gnaw a chicken leg in the kitchen.'

I watched him climb the steep path from the east beach and disappear among the pines. Had he really taught me something very important, or was it only an elaborate joke? It was true that I regarded them as rivals—only when I felt no need to challenge their strength could I afford to love them. When I discovered that Agamemnon was afraid, so afraid that he was much more vulnerable than myself, I no longer had to torment him with spiders. I had never dared to love Epicurus until I saw him cry. I had despised Narcissus until to-day, when I discovered he would have been so much happier as a woman—and could never forget it.

They said too often that women were the inferior sex, that I enjoyed a special privilege in being accepted as an equal. If this were true why did they have to shout it so loud? Suddenly I realized that every one in Elysium was afraid of women—the women on whom they had once been utterly dependent; the mother, the nurse, perhaps even the wife who might have loved them enough to give them real security.

Surely it was obvious? Why were there no female servants in Elysium? Because they would not have been sufficiently impressed by their master's importance. Why was Agamemnon here: because his mother had nearly destroyed her son as well as her husband. Why did the father of Epicurus return to childhood: because the woman who had been the main source of his life had deserted him, and so he had tried to return to the security of the infant. Euripides saw himself not as the hero, but as the heroine of his dramas. Why? Because he knew that only a goddess could tolerate the amorous antics of Zeus. And Aesculapius? My mother died because she loved my father more than the philosopher or her child. Aesculapius said she had been destroyed by faith in false gods, that she had no more substance than ashes caught by the wind. But was she not still more powerful than the philosopher, who had created Elysium as a sanctuary in which to hide from the love of women? Perhaps he really wanted me to be a philosopher, thinking it would protect me from the harsh light of emotion, thinking it would save him from being hurt through me.

Or was I to disillusion his pupils so that they would be invulnerable to women when they went back to the world? Was I to be used as a demonstration that female intuition can be explained in material terms? Were they to be told I was unique among my kind, knowing I should still be an object of affectionate contempt, who might with impunity be indulged and patronized, but never allowed to become the sun in a lover's sky?

Had I been warned in time by Narcissus that I should throw away my weapons, destroy my heritage, if I still tried to be a better man instead of a more subtle woman?

Soliloquy becomes unsatisfactory when a cold wind is

blowing from the sea, when your hand is aching and your belly insists that it is time you had something to eat. I watched the sun, a scarlet seal on the grey parchment of the sky, slowly erased by the horizon.

I picked up the basket, and found my right leg had gone to sleep—it felt as though it was being attacked by the ghosts of sea urchins. Even a hunk of cheese would be welcome, and I could get warm in bed even if there were no hot water for a bath.

But I found that Narcissus had not overrated his skill in strategy. Epicurus brought me my supper in bed: red mullet cooked with wine and olives, a salad brisk with radishes, a sweet dish he had composed for me—shards of almonds in smooth cream under a coverlet of crystallized violets.

CHAPTER SEVEN

Amphora

A few days later, Narcissus woke me soon after dawn. I was sleepy, and muttered 'It is much to early to get up.'

'You had better hurry,' he said abruptly. 'Aesculapius wants us—we're to wait for him in the loggia.'

'Why?'

'He didn't tell me. He said he wanted to speak to all of us except Praxiteles...anyway, Praxiteles couldn't come for he went to Athens yesterday—he heard that a shipload of marble had arrived from Pharos.'

'Is anything wrong?' I scrambled out of bed and looked for my tunic, which had fallen behind one of the chests.

'I've told you I don't know. I can't stay here making futile guesses. I haven't woken Euripides yet.' He went out, slamming the door.

He was in such a bad temper that I thought it unwise to annoy him, so I combed my hair and made sure my nails were clean before joining the others. Aesculapius must have been watching through the window, for before I had time to ask any questions he came out of his room.

'You will remember,' he said gravely, 'that I recently gave to each of you a cloak of Tyrian purple: there were only six so I could not get one for Praxiteles. You wore them for the first time, five days ago, at Lucina's birthday feast. I have disquieting news: the merchant who sold them to me has died of plague; a scourge prevalent in Syria but very rare in Greece. So far as my medical knowledge goes, and it is not inconsiderable, there is no effective remedy. However, as I have told you many times, unless you allow fear to enter your mind, your body will almost certainly remain invulnerable.'

I hoped none of the others saw the blood drain from my face, or knew my hands were cold with sweat. I tried to make my voice sound as though I were asking an ordinary question. 'How shall we know if we've got it?'

'The early stages are sometimes confused with insect bites. Then a rash develops, small red blisters, usually first observed on the hands and chest: this is associated with pain in the joints and a mild degree of fever. I shall not alarm you with details of the last extremity of this terrible disease, which is mercifully brief, death being probable on the seventh day. If you remember that life is far stronger than death you will have no cause for anxiety.'

'What shows that life is winning?' I said.

'If you sleep soundly, if you eat without vomiting, if you are free from sudden cold sweats.'

'And if we get the rash?' Clion's voice sounded much more convincingly calm than mine and I instinctively moved closer to him.

'You will have two or three days during which your mind should remain clear; in which to digest your experience, a process few men learn even in extreme age. You will find nothing alarming in death if you have eaten the essential core of the fruit of living, the seed of the tree of serenity.'

'If any of us follow the merchant, can anything be done to prevent its spreading through the household?' said Epicurus, his first consideration still for his stewardship instead of only himself.

'You will be segregated, in the house on the headland, until the danger of infection is past. Food, and such other necessities as you may require, have already been sent there. Should one of you die the body must be burned and the ashes thrown into the sea. Remember, all of you: death, to the realist, is no more than the seal on the record of a life. Could I stand here, unswayed by emotion, unless I had learned the acceptance I have tried to teach? I commend you into the keeping of your integrity: there are no other gods.'

Then he turned and went to his room; slowly and without looking back, as though he tried to believe he was sure of seeing us all to-morrow...and to-morrow. For the first time I felt pity for Aesculapius: I saw him as a man hiding behind a mask, a man who also gained his strength in unreality, who desperately needed the concept of the dispassionate philosopher to protect him from human emotion.

In silence we took the familiar path to the forsaken house. Aesculapius had often spoken of the circle of life; was my circle to be so meticulously joined that it ended where it began, in the same small room whose faded shutters swayed to the wind of timeless seas? But I had no child for whom to light a lamp, no vision of the future to warm a tenuous mortality. Seven days...could I live enough in seven days to learn to accept impermanence?

'We must forget yesterday and to-morrow,' said Clion. 'We shall bring fear with us if we allow ourselves to think how profoundly a few words have changed this morning from all other mornings. The sky is the same, the sea is the same, *we* must be the same. Remember he said none of us would die if we had sufficient courage.'

'What did the merchant fear?' said Agamemnon.

'Poverty, or the superior cunning of a rival, or a loss in exchange of goods...merchants are never free from fear. At least we need not echo *his* fears.' Epicurus sounded scornful, and the others, who had never seen him as I had, stared at him in surprise.

'I thought you considered merchants a superior race,' said Narcissus. 'You have often told us that everything would be all right if people accepted a standard of real values instead of being swayed by transient and illogical preferences.'

'Perhaps your idea of my standard of values is not complete. You had better ask Lucina about them; she knows more of my thoughts, for what little they are worth, than any one else.'

'Isn't he a merchant at heart, Lucina?' said Euripides. 'It has always been my opinion that he is closer to the poet than to the trader.'

'Poets don't have the practical intelligence to keep accurate tallies, or to tempt stomachs which are already filled with the wind of discourse,' said Agamemnon rudely. At which remark Euripides smiled, in the manner we knew from long experience was intended to provoke an argument. He enjoyed arguments, especially if they grew beyond the limits of debate, for he claimed they provided him with raw material for his plays.

'Have poets any practical use?' Agamemnon seldom let himself be drawn so openly into conflict, for he knew his quick temper usually prevented him winning a battle of words.

'Have they, Euripides?' I was surprised that Clion seemed to be encouraging the quarrel, until I realized he knew a heated exchange of remarks would help to warm the cold fear lurking inside us.

'I believe that the lower orders of life are content with a fulfilment of their basic needs; even the more elaborate plants discern in the bee no more than a vehicle of pollination; a bull when approaching a cow does so without tormenting himself in a search for appropriate phrases to describe the sweep of her horns or the opulance of her udder. A bull, in fact, behaves according to his nature, dependent for initiative only on the seasons.'

'Poets therefore have neither the common sense of plants nor the robust realism of animals?' Agamemnon looked round to see whether we were aware that at last he seemed to be defeating Euripides on a field which had appeared unfavorable.

Euripides remained unruffled. 'Poets are the only completely practical members of any community...if you accept that the continuance of life is at all desirable.' He realized this remark had been tactless, so sat down on a fallen tree to show he was in no hurry. 'Were there no poets there would soon be no people. The act by which children are primarily created, is, as we have all agreed, one which the philosopher does not find seemly. It is undignified, it disturbs the mind which might otherwise be occupied with matters of importance; it necessitates the company of females, who, with the shining exception of Lucina, are unworthy companions even for the less intelligent male. What are women? Our inferiors as animals...for what woman could hope to win in the Games? Our inferiors as realists: for what man would see his body distorted, and his night made hideous by the sound of infant pulings, merely because the desire for flattery was greater than the most elementary common sense? Our inferiors as objects pleasing to the eye: for even Praxiteles has had to admit that his statue of Lucina as a nymph might have been carved in lard instead of marble, the female curves being too soft to endure any permanent medium.'

'I am enjoying this,' I said, 'and greatly honoured that you should allow me to listen to this discourse between superiors.'

'But we don't think of you as female,' said Agamemnon

kindly; 'we accept you as one of ourselves.'

At which I smiled, to conceal that I should have preferred to slap him.

'To continue,' said Euripides. 'If it were not for poets the human race would disappear, or else be bred from those primitives who most closely share the single-mindedness of rams. Poets, however, allow people to see each other in heroic roles. It is shameful to be decoyed into complacency by a woman, but not to assume the same position for the benefit of a goddess. So we allow women to escape beyond the narrow confines which nature had provided; she is no longer bound even by the limitations of her appearance, she can paint her face to resemble some improbable ideal, arrange her hair as a net to ensnare the unwary hunter. She is no longer a female, she is Selene, hot to the scent of an Endymion...while he, poor, foolish shepherd, is content to dream, until he wakes to find her satisfied!'

'So poets are not only the fathers of the race, but the rulers of Olympus,' said Clion. 'No poets, no children: no poets, no gods.'

'But of course poets created Olympus', said Euripides complacently. 'Who else could have supported such a divine and illogical conception? Zeus and the shower of gold...how delicious and unlikely! Had Epicurus conceived it, the unfortunate girl would have been badly bruised by ingots or else taken before the magistrates for trying to pass illicit coins! And Leda...he would have sent her to the poultry yard, and hurried away to think how to use a swan's egg of phenomenal size. He might, perhaps, have marked the occasion by seasoning the dish with asphodel, which is inferior to the common onion, and no doubt highly indigestible.'

'Asphodel is often planted on graves,' remarked Narcissus sombrely.

'Some people use it to kill mice,' I said hastily.

Clion followed my lead, 'It is also said to be beneficial to pigs. I forget whether they are supposed to eat it or hang it in their sties to conceal from themselves their less agreeable qualities. Or do pigs enjoy their own smell? I have often wondered.'

'A farmer!' said Euripides. 'Clion nourishing secret thoughts about swine. How charmingly bucolic! Do you see Lucina as a ripe Hebe, carrying a cornucopia which you have bountifully filled with the fruits of your toil? I must put you in a play; it shall be performed in late summer, so that the chorus can wear wreaths of corn and carry pumpkins.' He struck an attitude. 'I can see it quite clearly: plump young women with lavish breasts to echo the fertile curves of gourds and melons. And a quantity of pomegranates, or do you consider them too virginal? There is something very unawakened about a pomegranate.'

'There would probably be something very unawakened about the audience,' said Agamemnon, still hoping to wrest victory.

'Surely you would not fill *all* the seats with your friends? We know that the warrior must occupy his leisure by deep draughts of lethe, to conceal from himself that he cannot bring home laurels which do not rapidly wilt in the rarefied air of cultured intercourse, but surely it is his duty to replace the population that he and his kind so frequently deplete, instead of straining his little intellect by listening to his superiors?'

'I doubt whether you would have found it so easy to compose if the Persians had taken Athens, or even the Romans.'

'You misunderstand me, Agamemnon. I was not trying to decry Greek warriors, who have fought well in defence of our culture, but warriors as a creed.' He pretended to shudder. 'So barbaric, this glorification of destruction; such crude colours, old blood and tarnished metal, and the distressing yellow of decaying wounds!'

'Stop it, Euripides!' said Clion sharply. 'You know we are trying to keep off unpleasant subjects...can't you and Agamemnon have a quarrel about something else?'

64

'A quarrel? Was I having a quarrel?' He turned to Agamemnon. 'I thought it was only a friendly discussion on the relative merits of poets and other species of the human animal.'

Agamemnon blushed. 'I was only joking...Clion shouldn't have taken us seriously.'

'As the only female present,' I said, still somewhat annoyed that I was considered to be of an inferior sex, 'I hesitate to suggest that as Aesculapius has not provided us with servants we had better go to the house and do something towards making it comfortable and seeing if we can cook...or will Epicurus attend to the meals?'

'I am better in theory than in the sordid effort of actual preparations,' he said genially, 'but no doubt I shall think of some new and delicious conceit under the inspiration of so delightful an assistant. You will assist me, Lucina, if I do the more unattractive tasks such as cutting up raw meat and peeling onions?'

'Of course I will: Narcissus can make the beds while the others scrub the floors and light a fire. The house will probably be damp, for it smelt very musty last time I was there.'

'When was that?' said Epicurus. 'I didn't know any one went there.'

Euripides saved me from the need of answering. 'She comes with me sometimes...when we wish to read lines without being interrupted by an illiterate audience.'

'Oh...' said Agamemnon, 'I thought the house...never mind, it's not important.'

'You thought what?' I didn't want to hear his answer but I could not resist asking.

'It was only a silly story I overheard from the servants. Something about the place being left empty because it was haunted. Nothing in it, of course. How could there be when we don't believe in ghosts?'

'Don't we?' said Euripides. 'Shades are always popular

in the drama; some one has got to inhabit Hades or the place would be redundant. How difficult it would be to point the moral if there were no retribution for the wicked or rewards for the hero who dies in the last act!'

'Plays,' said Agamemnon scornfully. 'Food for cowards who try to escape from reality.'

Euripides began to whistle under his breath: I knew the tune was familiar, but did not recognize it as the marching song, a favourite of Agamemnon's when he was caught up in his phantasy, until I saw him swing away from the path and scramble down the steep rocks to the beach.

'That was horrid of you, really horrid!' I said angrily. 'Now he will go into a mood and make it much more difficult for everybody. He'll probably start one of his battles, and as we have got to keep to the headland there is nowhere really private for him, so we shall have to stay in the house and pretend not to hear.'

'How terrible is the wrath of a virtuous woman! I am abashed to have been the unwitting cause of disturbance in our harmonious company.' He went down on one knee and poured a handful of sand over his head. 'No ashes are available, so will this serve to prove my abject abasement?'

I tried not to laugh, but it was always impossible to resist Euripides. 'You may be forgiven if you accept a penance: you can fill the water-jugs, and the spring is sufficiently far from the house for you to hope that none of us are very thirsty!'

'Water! Surely Aesculapius has not lost all regard for the common decencies! He sends us into exile, but promised to supply us with necessities...and what is a necessity if wine is denied that honourable title? I must go ahead to discover the full horror of our plight: should I not return you will find me prostrated with grief. I beg of you not to attempt to revive me with water: it would be cruel as well as useless, and only add to the burden I shall have to support to-morrow.'

He ran between the trees and I saw him pass the corner of

the house. Then he reappeared, waving his arms and shouting, 'We are saved! Ten jars of admirable wine!'

I watched him go up the path towards the spring carrying a water-jar on his shoulder. Clion went to look for Agamemnon. Narcissus and Epicurus climbed down to the beach to collect drift-wood. I hesitated, and then decided not to go with them.

The house slept in the sun: the rosemary under the windows drowsed with bees, balm and verbena joined their quietness to the still air. The door opened smoothly, as though too idle to protest against intruders.

In the main room a huddle of soiled feathers lay in the ashes of the hearth. It had been a seagull, driven here by fear of a storm, too bewildered to find its way back to the sky. I carried it outside and dug a grave for it; the earth was hard and I had to use a shard of broken pottery before I could make the hole sufficiently deep.

Had Aesculapius deliberately sent the original furniture to the house, even the chests in which my mother's clothes had been stored away? The hinges were stiff; pungent herbs, brittle with age, fell from the pleats of fine linen; brown dust had gathered in the folds of woollen cloaks.

My mother had been a little taller than me, but our feet were the same size. The leather of the first pair of sandals was so dry that the toe-thong snapped when I tried to fasten it.

In a box, carved with doves, that held the things she had used for her toilet, I found a silver mirror. It was tarnished, so I polished it with sand that had drifted through the shutters: the sand must have been too harsh, for the bright surface was marred by scratches. Did I look like her? Would she recognize her daughter? The unguents in the alabaster jars were dry or rancid, but the perfume in a narrow phial held the ghost of violets. So that was why I loved violets. Aesculapius would be gratified to find another proof of ancestral memory. Or had the baby remembered the scent as a symbol of lost security?

It was dangerous to think of my mother; here in the room where she had died, where I was under the threat of death. She had protected a child from fear; love for a child had been strong enough to break the spell in which she lingered. If I wore her clothes, her perfume, the wreath of gold and silver flowers, so supple that it still held the shape of her head, I might gain a measure of the courage which had made her strong in love.

I remembered seeing a lennet valiant on her nestlings as she tried to drive off a hawk. If I could make myself believe that the men with me were children who needed protection I might forget to be frightened. Are men always children: who have to fight and boast and create philosophies to conceal from themselves that they can never outgrow an incurable adolescence? Do they try to keep women prisoners of the household to revenge themselves on the nursery from which they never completely escape? Had Narcissus and Praxiteles been trying to find in each other the solace of a foster-mother? Perhaps that was why they had been so embarrassed when I surprised them in the cave. And Agamemnon, was he only a small boy, shouting to keep up his courage?

I went to look for Agamemnon and to my relief found him in the kitchen, helping Clion to pluck three ducks which Epicurus was going to cook when he had finished peeling mushrooms.

'Aesculapius must be optimistic about our chances,' said Clion cheerfully. 'There is enough in the storeroom to feed us for a month.'

Narcissus came through the further door: 'I've made the beds,' he said. 'We get straw pallets but Lucina is having the front room—rugs on the floor, furniture—*most* civilized.'

I wished the rugs were not so familiar: I wished the furniture did not remind me that it could watch me die just as easily as it had watched me being born.

We managed to keep up the pretence that it was an ordinary day: six people having a holiday from familiar routine, laughing rather too easily, keeping together as though solitude had suddenly become another source of infection, preparing much more food than was eaten, and burying the remains furtively to conceal our lack of hunger.

At sunset we carried one of the wine-jars down to the beach and lit a fire of driftwood among the rocks. A fire gives more light than a lamp against the darkness. There was no wind and even the waves whispered; so we sang, loudly and without much consideration for the tune so long as it was stronger than the silence.

CHAPTER EIGHT

tyrian purple

I dressed with unusual care, in a robe of pleated linen bound between the breasts with violet ribbons, and selected a pair of scarlet sandals studded with turquoise. Perhaps the gold and silver wreath was a little elaborate for the morning, but it was so becoming I decided to wear it instead of looking for suitable flowers. I painted my eyelids green, reddened my lips and put perfume behind my ears. Narcissus would be glad to see that at last I was being an obedient pupil!

I found Euripides lying on a mattress in front of the house. A wreath of ivy partially obscured his right eye, and a bunch of it was folded between his hands.

'Why the ivy?' I said amiably.

'To remind Dionysus that after I have poured such copious libations in his honour he cannot in decency allow this torment to continue.'

'What's wrong with you?'

'Rather should you ask what is *right*! While I indulged in innocent, defenceless sleep, some ill-intentioned fiend has sawn off the top of my skull and filled it with scorpions and boiling lead. You perceive a soul who will find no unfamiliar pang among the Underworld's most robust conceits. Would you like some ivy? Dionysus appears too preoccupied to heed my pleas, no doubt he has troubles of his own, but it might be worth trying. Clion will probably have the charity to collect some for you...he found mine on a dead tree.' He closed his eyes. 'Some ill-omened sculptor is hammering my skull, having foolishly mistaken it for a block of granite, no doubt to erect a memorial to a dead poet. Could you persuade him to desist?'

I was annoyed that he was too preoccupied to notice my appearance. His skin had a greenish pallor under the tan which I should have found disturbing if I had not seen him like this before...and for the same reason.

'Ivy, why should I wear ivy?' I said maliciously.

He sat up, clutching his head as though afraid it might topple from his shoulders. 'To placate Dionysus, of course! Come, lie here beside me, my poor deluded child, and we will take solemn vows (which I have no real intention of following, for my wits have not entirely forsaken me) to drink water instead of regarding it as a fluid suitable only for filling baths.'

'What has Dionysus done to offend you? He gave us good wine, and sleep. What makes you think him angry?'

He groaned. 'Lucina, the only thing which has sustained me through this dolorous morning is the thought that you must be feeling worse even than I, and so would need my help and comfort in affliction. I distinctly remember seeing Clion carry you to bed; after you had fallen flat on your face, grunted with the charm of a sucking-pig, and gone irrevocably to sleep. Very pretty you looked, too, and I should have been delighted to carry you if my legs had not suddenly emulated strands of seaweed.'

'How did Clion manage?'

'Either his mother was a maenad or else his sweat turns wine to water. He drank more than any of us, and was the only one to remain entirely sober. He was disgustingly cheerful this morning: he whistled, Lucina! *Whistled*, though he must have known that in so doing he drove hot copper wires through both my ear-drums.'

'Perhaps wine suits me, for I feel very well this morning.'

'And they say women are weak!' He groaned and buried his face in his arms.

'*I* didn't say that!'

'How true, how terribly and disquietingly true.' His voice was blurred, but it carried heartfelt conviction.

So Clion had been sober: Clion had carried me to bed. He was the only person in Elysium who used his own name, a name which was neither the symbol of a fear to be conquered nor an ideal to be attained. I had never seen him angry or in tears...he had always seemed a little dull compared to the others. Or were people who had the courage to be themselves, instead of only *talking* about reality, the reverse of dull?

Narcissus came down the path from the stream, carrying a water-jar. He nodded towards Euripides. 'I thought I had better do this to-day, for he seems to be undergoing sufficient penance: if we waited for him, the dishes would have to stay dirty...and there are no more clean ones.' Then he noticed my headdress. 'You are looking very beautiful this morning, Lucina. Why didn't you wear those clothes before?'

'I found them in the chest in the south room.'

'Oh...I see.' He looked embarrassed. 'Well I had better ask Agamemnon, if he is awake, to help me, you would be certain to spill something on your dress.'

I felt rather unkind not to insist on helping, but it was *his* idea that I was unsuitably dressed. He could get Agamemnon to do my share of the work; or do it himself. It was good for men to realize that women had better things to do than wait on them!

Epicurus, with a dripping towel tied round his head, was sitting on a bench outside the kitchen disconsolately peeling onions. I avoided him, for when he had a headache he was apt to be disagreeable. I could not find Clion, so I went to the top of the steps to see if he was on the beach. I saw him standing on a rock beyond the breaking waves, the sun glittering on the trident in his hand. This was annoying; if he did not get enough fish soon, he might spend the morning there, perhaps not even come back for the noon meal. I had planned to be discovered standing pensively beside a tree, or sitting, gazing out to sea, so that I could look up, as though startled, when he was close enough to appreciate the full effect. Now I should either have to wait until later in the day or else go back to change into an ordinary tunic: I disliked watching people do things, which Clion knew; so even if he came closer to the shore there would be no point in pretending that I had only come to see how many fish he had caught. It did not take me long to run back to the house. I climbed through the window in case some one was in the outer room.

From the steps I shouted to Clion, but the waves must have been too loud for him to hear; so I left my tunic on a dry ledge and swam out to the rock.

'A mermaid,' he said, stretching down a hand to help me out of the water. 'I must capture alive this rare addition to our aquarium.' Then, pretending to be surprised, 'Why, it is only Lucina! However, I have been unlucky this morning so you can try to get fish for us...perhaps they will be more willing to approach if they too mistake you for a mermaid.'

The 'only Lucina' rankled, but I took the trident and managed to get two red mullet in less than half an hour. Perhaps fishing was more interesting than thinking about the impression I had hoped to produce, for the morning passed so quickly that we were both surprised to hear Epicurus shouting that food was ready.

On the way back I noticed a stack of driftwood in one of the shallow caves. 'Are we going to have a fire so far from the house to-night?' I said.

'I put it there in case of... well, in case of an unlikely emergency.'

He did not have to explain any further: it was to be used as a pyre. Which of us would burn, alone on the beach until our ashes dissolved in the immeasurable sea?

It was rather a dreadful meal; a stew of meat and onions too strongly flavoured with sage. No one ate very much, but at least the wine of the previous evening provided an excuse which allowed every one to be unhungry without anxiety. Agamemnon announced that he was going for a long walk, and the tone of his voice made it clear that he did not wish for company. Clion and Epicurus decided to bathe, so I could find nothing better to do than pick flowers—there were still a few among the encroaching weeds—and arrange them in the two stone urns I had found abandoned in a tangle of brambles beyond the terrace. Later I went to sleep and did not wake until sunset.

They had again lit a fire and carried down a jar of wine; but no one talked much and we sat listening to the waves, too subdued even to sing. Clion, rather pointedly I thought, gave me only one cup of wine and did not offer to refill it. Perhaps I had looked as silly as Euripides; perhaps Clion had only carried a helpless child because he was sorry for her. It was an uncomfortable thought, and I was glad I had decided not to try to look beautiful.

'I think I shall go to bed,' I said, and stood up, yawning to show that I was genuinely sleepy.

'Agamemnon went back to the house some time ago, so he will be there if you want anything. We shall all be coming up soon.' Clion sounded kind but disinterested.

The door leading into the room where the men slept was half open. The house was very quiet and I stood listening to the silence, wishing I had waited until we all came back together.

Then I heard a small, furtive noise, too loud for a rat. What was it? My heart began to thud and my legs wanted to run: but in which direction? Towards the beach? Or was the thing outside, waiting to grab me if I left the house? Into my room? But there was no way of barring the door, and it might follow me before I had time to escape through the window.

I heard the noise again: it was human, and relief left my knees limp as asparagus. It was a man crying, the sobs muffled as though he was trying to hide his head under the pillow. Agamemnon, having one of his lonely defeats. I was enormously grateful to him for making me feel strong and competent. *Dear* Agamemnon!

I pushed the door wider and he shouted 'Keep out...don't come near me! Leave me alone!'

'It's only me, Lucina. The others are still down on the beach.'

'Go back to them...tell them to stay out of the house!'

'Don't be silly; you know it doesn't matter if you cry when it's only me.'

'Won't you ever learn to be obedient?' There was desperation in his voice. 'You silly little fool: do you want to die? I've got the plague...won't you even give me the credit for wishing to die alone?'

The men were still sitting round the fire talking in low voices and they had not heard me running across the soft sand.

'We can all stop pretending,' I said. 'Agamemnon's got it.'

They stared at me in silence, then Clion said calmly, 'Is he very afraid?'

'Yes. He wanted me to warn you to leave him to die alone. I thought it better not to argue until we were all there. We have *got* to make him believe that none of us are afraid;

74

Aesculapius said courage was the only remedy.'

'You mustn't go near him, Lucina.' I knew Epicurus meant to be kind, but I turned on him as if he had flung a stone at me. 'If you want to let fear kill you it's your own business, but you're not going to kill *me*. I'm the only woman here, and women are better than men at dealing with real things, like sickness and death.'

'But you're so *young*.'

'Not too young to have more sense than any of you! I am going to look after Agamemnon and you can all do what I tell you...the sooner you all understand that, the sooner we can do something useful to help: instead of my having to argue with you as though you were idiot children.'

'She is right,' said Clion. 'If we made her keep away from the house it would be worse for her than sharing the danger.'

'It's not a case of what you *allow* me to do, it's what I have *decided*.'

I turned and walked resolutely back to the steps and heard them following me, talking in whispers which I was too angry to try to overhear.

While they were persuading Agamemnon to be moved into my room, I went to put clean covers on the bed and drag the chest of clothes through the doorway. At least I could put on a fresh tunic every day, for Aesculapius had said it was important to be very clean when looking after sick people. I called Narcissus and told him to bring something for me to sleep on. When he protested I lost my temper. 'Do what I *tell* you. A sick man is like a child; he mustn't be left alone in the dark.'

'But I'll stay with him, Lucina.'

'A man is no use. Can't you drive that simple idea through your thick skull?'

He shrugged his shoulders and came back carrying one of the pallets which he put in the corner under the window.

Without thanking him I said briskly, 'Now go and get a

lamp...two lamps, and cut the wicks carefully so they don't flicker.'

While he did this I rolled up the rugs and threw them out the window. I am not sure why, but I think it was because they reminded me too much of the child Lucina whom I was trying to forget.

Agamemnon did not look very ill, but there was a rash on one shoulder and his forehead was thick with sweat. Clion offered to carry him, but he said coldly, 'I am not dead yet; you can reserve that courtesy for my corpse.'

When the others had gone out of the room he let me tuck in the covers and even thanked me for bringing him a cup of wine and water. I sat on the floor holding his hand until he fell into a fitful sleep.

Was he going to die? Aesculapius had said we should know in seven days. Did he mean seven days from the time we came here, or seven days from the first rash? I wished I had been sensible enough to ask this important question before it was too late.

Next day the rash was no worse...and no better. I smeared oil on his shoulders, but that only increased the irritation so I washed it off with warm water. He asked me about the rash so often that at last I gave him the silver mirror so that he could see it for himself. He said he would vomit if he ate anything, but I managed to persuade him to drink a little milk, and later, two eggs beaten up in wine, and though he retched he kept them down.

To keep myself awake, I spent the first two nights crouching on the floor beside his bed. I agreed to sleep in the afternoons, so long as Clion stayed in my place. Epicurus brought me bowls of strong broth and always seemed to have something ready when I was hungry. Narcissus scrubbed the floors several times a day as though sand and water could kill the enemy who held us in siege. Euripides spent most of his time sitting on the bench by the door, covering sheets of papyrus with his small, untidy writing. It was not until later that I knew he was composing a funeral ode, in which he had carefully left alternative lines so that it would fit any, or all, of us. I do not know whom he thought would read it over the ashes of the last to die.

The only times when I was really afraid were while Agamemnon slept and I had no stimulus to make me forget my own fear. I knew now why mother had seen the child spill oil from the lamp; she had thought of the flame licking up to its hair, the flesh charring in the cruel heat. It was easy to be brave when I had to demand strength to help some one weaker than myself. But at night I could not help looking at my shoulders in the mirror. Was that an insect bite on my neck, or the start of the rash? I was sweating...but the room was hot, wasn't it? I didn't feel hungry; of *course* I didn't feel hungry, how could I when I was so tired?

Sometimes Agamemnon was gripped with cold, and shivered so violently that I thought he was going to fall out of bed. I sent Clion to get hot stones, which we kept ready in the ashes in the kitchen fire, wrapped them in a piece of blanket and put them against his feet. After the shivering stopped he was drenched with sweat: I washed him in wine and then rubbed him dry with hot towels. I knew this was the thing to do, for Aesculapius had told me it was correct for any kind of fever.

When Agamemnon was awake he watched me all the time; his eyes too bright and very wide. He seldom spoke, except to tell me when he was thirsty or to thank me whenever I did anything for him. In his sleep he muttered about a sword. He seemed to think the sword was going to fall on him. Then his eyes would jerk open and he would lie staring at the ceiling until I stroked his forehead. I thought he was watching for spiders; but there were no spiders in the room. Or did he see imaginary spiders: would he have seen them if only I had not been so cruel as to play on his secret fear? Would it help if I confessed that I had brought spiders hidden in my dress...or would it spoil the little confidence that I was able to give him? The indecision was worse than the lack of sleep, but I reluctantly decided that I could not afford the luxury of sharing my guilt with a sick man. When he was better I could tell him...*when* he was better. I must believe it was only 'when'.

'The sword...why won't they let the sword fall? I can't wait any longer...please let the sword fall.' The words fell slow as blood from his parched lips. I woke him and gave him a sip of wine, but his eyes did not recognize me. 'The sword...why doesn't it fall?'

Aesculapius had told me that the vision of my mother had been only a resonance to her idea, so strong that it was almost material. Perhaps I could make myself see the sword which was torturing Agamemnon. If I could see it I might be able to change the pattern, as the child had broken the thread which had bound my mother to this same bed.

I stared at the ceiling, but I saw only the cracks in the plaster and the dark patch where rain had seeped through the roof. Perhaps it would be easier with my eyes shut....

I was in a great banqueting hall; men and women in foreign clothes...they were all foreigners, and very cruel. A man was sitting in a high, carved chair on a dais at the head of the table. Above him was a sword...suspended on nothing...or was there a thread supporting it over his head?

The man was Agamemnon...and yet not Agamemnon as I knew him. He was trying to pretend the sword was not going to fall; it meant more than life to him for the people to believe he was unafraid.

Now I could see the stranger and the familiar man on the bed at the same time. Both were staring up at the sword. The other people had faded into the background, insubstantial as shadows. If I could take the weight of the sword neither of them would be in danger any longer.

I felt myself get up from the floor and walk towards the bed, though I was not conscious of having told my body to move.

I had to grow tall to reach the sword...I could feel it in my hand: cold metal against my palm. The blade was dark, crusted with old blood. I tried to rub it clean, but the stains were too deep.

Agamemnon always used a sword to challenge his enemy; would this sword help him, even though it was brittle with age?

I put the sword in his hand, and saw his fingers close round the hilt. The hilt was red-gold studded with turquoise.

Then I was only Lucina; standing beside a man who smiled in his sleep.

I dared to rest that night for I knew Agamemnon was going to get well. He woke before I did and when he saw my eyes open he said gently, 'I am not going to die, Lucina: because of you I am not going to die.'

Then he began to cry, as a child cries when it has found something it thought forever lost.

Epicurus stared at me when I said that Agamemnon was hungry and wanted a bowl of broth and at least two eggs. 'And you had better send Clion to get some fish,' I added, 'for he will be hungry again before long.'

'*Hungry?*' said Euripides. 'We thought he was certain to die before evening. Are you *sure* he's hungry?'

'Would I look so cheerful if I weren't sure? So cheerful that I am not even cross that you are all so unbelieving?' Then fear suddenly coiled like a snake. 'Where is Clion? Is he all right?'

'Clion?' said Euripides vaguely. 'He was here a moment ago. There is nothing wrong with him: there is nothing wrong with any of us. I had a pain in my stomach yesterday, but it was only because I ate some mussels which were a little stale. I feel quite well this morning.'

'*How* silly of you! I hope you had the sense to drink salt water until you were thoroughly sick.'

'I did, as you wish to know the nauseating details. I assure you I did not eat them from greed; only to keep myself from starvation, due to Epicurus being too occupied with thinking of food for you and the invalid to have any consideration for the rest of us.'

'I suppose you were too lazy to cook anything for yourself.'

'Not too lazy, too busy,' he sounded really offended. 'Too preoccupied with the melancholy task of writing your funeral ode. It would have been my masterpiece; chanted at sunset while the pyre flamed as a torch to light you to the company of the immortals. I should have used scented oils to annoint your body—luckily I found some in the chest you left in the main room.'

'And what part was Agamemnon to play, or did you let him live because you needed him as one of the mourners?'

'I think you are showing supreme ingratitude: we have tortured ourselves with the thought of your untimely death. Already we had endowed you with some of the attributes of a goddess and in a few years we would have been convinced that you dwelt serenely on Olympus. And now you are proving yourself only the clay from which the sculptor makes a promise in which fools believe.' He sighed. 'The world is the place of disillusion; it was unnecessary to create Hades.'

He was trying to break the tension and bring me back to normal, but I still saw myself as a heroine who had rescued Agamemnon from death, or perhaps I was too tired to appreciate any attempt at humour. To my shame I started to cry; not the kindly tears which slide slowly down the cheeks and darken the lashes, but noisily with my mouth open.

Suddenly Clion was there, saying, 'Sometimes, Euripides, I should like to hit your silly face so hard it would hurt you too much to open your mouth for months! Go and tell Epicurus to take Agamemnon something to eat. He is quite all right and Lucina needs looking after now. Hurry, you fool, or I'll help you to run!'

I clung round Clion's neck as he carried me down to the beach, away from the people who did not understand, away from the house where I had waited for death to come through the door. I cried until my nose would not let me breathe properly, until my face was swollen and ugly: and yet it did not matter. Clion was the one person with whom it was safe to be only me.

I told him about the sword and how I knew Agamemnon would get well as soon as I had broken the spell. 'Aesculapius will try to explain it all away with long, clever words. But I *know* it was real...much more real than ordinary things. Don't let Aesculapius pretend it wasn't important. It was the real reason why Agamamnon was always fighting; he thought it was his father's sword he had betrayed, that it was modern soldiers to whom he had to prove his courage. But it was much further back in time...I don't know how long, I think two or three centuries. He was always afraid... not only when he had one of his moods. The sword was waiting to fall on him, much more dangerous than spiders, much stronger then clever explanations by philosophers!'

Clion tried to comfort me, 'Aesculapius will understand... he *must* understand when we all tell him that Agamemnon was dying until this happened. You can't destroy something which has saved a man from death.'

'He will say I only found a way to stop Agamemnon being afraid: he will be so terribly *reasonable*, as he was when I felt happy because I thought mother was safe with my father. I didn't mind *where* she was, I only wanted to be sure they were *somewhere* together, that all her loving had not been wasted.'

'Love is never wasted. Isn't it life, Lucina? Isn't it the only thing which is stronger than death?'

'You won't let Aesculapius take that certainty away from me? Please, Clion, don't let him take that away.'

'No one can take it away: and if you ever forget I shall try to remind you.'

81

the ScaBBaRÒ

It was the morning of the seventh day: to-morrow we could go back to Aesculapius, tell him that our courage was stronger than Tyrian purple, that affection was more powerful than philosophy. I had intended to collect mushrooms with Agamemnon, but instead we idled in sound of the waterfall and basked in the autumn heat.

'It is wonderful to lie here,' he said. 'Doing nothing, thinking nothing except the kind, trivial thoughts which come from watching water slide gently over rocks. I have never had time to notice the shape of small, unimportant flowers or to listen to the murmur of bees. I was blind except to the harsh challenge of banners, deafened by battles which were never joined. It is terrible, Lucina, to have been a coward so long.'

'You were never a coward: it was only that the man in the past had an ordeal too hard for him. You took his guilt on your shoulders, and looked forwards instead of backwards in search of a shield against his sword.'

'You found the sword; you had the courage to take it by the hilt and draw it out of my heart.'

'Because I loved you, because you gave me the strength to forget my own fear. I told you about the linnet; she must have loved the hawk for making her brave, even though she thought it was only her nestlings that she loved. Love is the only thing which is stronger than fear: love can make all women strong in defence of their young, all men brave in protection of women, all soldiers heroes in defence of their country...if only they love enough.'

'Why didn't Aesculapius tell me that?'

'Because he will not accept it. He never told any of us that we have to love ourselves before we can love any one else.

He let you go on hating yourself; he tried to give you courage by reminding you of weakness. It was not clever of Aesculapius.'

'You are *sure* it was a real sword, a real man in that banqueting hall?'

'Yes: I am sure that the past is as real as the future. It is nonsense to say that both are only a reflection of the present. I didn't *imagine* I used to be an athlete: he was a part of the whole, of whom Lucina is another part. I am Lucina, and the athlete, and the woman who challenged the goat-man...and probably lots of other people I cannot remember. They were real, and Lucina is real. When Lucina dies I shall still be real; not only a memory, or an idea, or a shade in Hades or an immortal on Olympus. I shall still be a *person*, quite solid and ordinary, as you and I are ordinary, here and now.'

'Perhaps the past and the future are always here and now...nothing to fear, nothing which needs elaborate words to describe.'

'We must both cling to that truth, Agamemnon. We have proved it for ourselves, no one can take it away from us. You had a disease which Aesculapius admitted was incurable. You were dying, and then you accepted the past and were no longer prisoned in it, and so you got well. Only six days ago you were too weak to hold a cup, and now you can carry two water-jars, two *full* water-jars!'

'You gave me that truth,' he said, and kissed me on the shoulder. 'I suppose Aesculapius would say you freed me from guilt.'

'And you freed me—when I told you about the spiders and you didn't hate me.'

He smiled. 'That wasn't difficult. I always knew you produced spiders to frighten me: but I never had the courage to tell you, or to laugh, or even to hate you. You know very little history, because I never forced you to learn in case you brought back more spiders. Will you forgive me for your lack of education?'

I leant on my elbow so that I could see him better. 'I am not very interested in knowledge,' I said contentedly. 'It never seems to give you the important things and it is such a trouble to acquire!'

I heard Clion whistle, the tune he used when he wanted me to answer. 'We are by the waterfall,' I shouted.

'Come back. We want you.' His voice, muffled by the trees, sounded excited.

Aesculapius was with the others outside the house. I had expected him to be glad to see us healthy, to praise us for having withstood the plague; but he looked just as he always did when embarking on a sea of words, and the others seemed curiously subdued.

'So I hear that my little experiment was not without incident,' he said, his eyebrows raised to show he was amused, 'Lucina, my dear, I must congratulate you on showing remarkable courage and initiative.'

'I am glad you find it *interesting* that none of us died: or has that spoiled the full value of your discovery? Would it have been more satisfactory if one had died and the others lived; you will never be *quite* sure that the cloaks held death?'

'But I shall, I *am*, Lucina. I knew that the cloaks could produce no more than a harmless rash, due to some quality of the dye, annoying, but, I assure you, not in the least inimical to health.'

'Then why did you lie to us? Or have lies become the coinage of philosophy?' I knew I was being rude but was far too angry to care.

'Have I not impressed on you that it is necessary to fight an enemy in his own terms? To teach you to conquer a real fear I thought it advisable to provide an imaginary one.'

'Agamemnon was dying,' said Clion hotly. 'You weren't here, so you can't judge. None of us are fools, so you can't make us believe he wasn't very dangerously ill.'

'You misjudge me, Clion. I am fully aware that I exposed

84

you all to danger, great danger which might have been fatal. However, I consider it my duty to train you to take your place in the world: and the world is not the nursery, you are not children who can still demand entire security.'

I was cold with anger. 'You treat us as children so that you can play the role of the wise father. Do you enjoy it, are you *sure* you enjoy telling lies to make your deluded children shiver in the dark?'

'It seems, Lucina, that you have not outgrown the phase of childish temper.' He was not even angry, he was only tolerant and amused.

'At least I am not buried in the pomposity of age, which has made you forget what it feels like to be human!'

Even this did not ruffle him, though Clion whispered, 'Don't say too much, Lucina.'

'You are all displaying a natural emotion, due to the belated recognition that you have suffered an unpleasant experience created by your personal fears. If I had not a deep and lasting affection for you all I should not have undertaken an experiment which, though beneficial to yourselves, may possibly undermine your faith in me. I wanted to give you confidence, the real confidence which comes only through experience. I admit I was conceited enough to feel sure that my faith in the reality of my philosophy was built on solid rock.'

'And if we had died to prove your philosophy, that would have been our own fault?' Epicurus spoke quietly but I knew he was nearly as angry as I.

'Precisely; but I should have left Elysium, to return to the practice of the ordinary physician...or I might have decided that I was better employed in some way which is not directly concerned with the lives and happiness of my fellows. Before we enter into a dispute about what *might* have occurred, let us calmly consider what has in fact taken place. We will start with Lucina, who seems to feel more violently than the rest of you, and who therefore is in more urgent need of a balanced view of the situation. However, as we are likely to take some time, I think it would be better if we were to assume postures congenial to conversation.'

He took his place on the bench by the door and the others sat on the ground. I made them wait while I fetched a cushion: the tiles were hard and I wanted to show I was not impatient to hear what he had to say.

'Now that Lucina is comfortable, she will, no doubt, be willing to listen to pompous age.'

I smiled politely, delighted that at least one thrust had found a chink in the sculptured folds of his robe.

'Though Lucina, on many occasions, has displayed a remarkable degree of intelligence, I have frequently been disturbed by her tendency to ascribe to natural phenomena some supernatural source. Instead of accepting that her unusual perception allows her a degree of awareness into the thought projections of people closely connected with her, she prefers to believe that these subjective mirages have an objective reality. I have explained to her that the mind has depths of which only the surface is visible to the casual beholder: I used the analogy of a turbid fluid in a jar, the fluid is deliberately stirred, or the jar shaken by some outside disturbance, and the surface pattern is immediately altered. In her mind, as in all our minds, there are thousands of constituents which, though out of focus, are constantly present. For instance, Lucina as a child was deliberately given an extremely restricted environment. The two people in whose care I placed her had an almost bovine intelligence. Yet Lucina must have heard them describe the training of a runner: she may have overheard them talking in the next room when she was half asleep and therefore retained no conscious memory of their conversation. It was from this drop added to her jar that the dreams of herself as an athlete were projected. She accepted my explanation, until under the stress of violent emotion (to children, and all primitives, thunder and other manifestations of natural laws are an active stimulus to hereditary fears) she imagined she could not only see her mother, and herself as a child of two or three years old, but that she had some power by which the child was able to appeal to the mother for help. She extended this phantasy until she 'saw' the mother walk across the room, and in so doing become free to go to some unspecified realm where she could enjoy the companionship of the man from whom circumstances had irrevocably separated her.

'I consider this factor in Lucina's character to be a dangerous weakness; indicating, as it does, that she finds life too difficult and longs to escape into some nebulous after-world. As she has a highly developed faculty for creating mental images, I think it probable that this after-world has all the advantages of the normal environment. On her Olympus the ambrosia resembles raspberries and cream—or even prawns; both retaining, you will notice, the rosy hue of mountain clouds at dawn: her nectar may still be closer to fruit juice and honey than to the great vintages, but no doubt she will in due course make such minor adjustments as the maturity of her palate demands.'

I hoped no one realized how close this came to the meals I had planned for my parents in Olympus. Why should they not eat prawns if they liked them? Could not Immortals enjoy the pomegranates they have invented for the pleasure of other people?

'As Lucina does not feel inclined to make any comment, I will presume that I am not entirely irrelevant in my remarks.' He was warming to his theme, nothing would stop him now and we were expected to listen in attentive silence. 'However, when Lucina found herself in a situation which demanded immediate practical action she discarded the phantasy for the reality. She remembered that fever responds to sponging with wine, that the sick need nourishment in small but frequent quantities; and, by far the most important, she knew that the cause of the disease, as of all diseases of mind or body, was *fear*. Agamemnon imagined he saw a sword suspended over his head, but instead of trying to argue with him she let him believe the sword was real and therefore that she could remove it. A most excellent demonstration of the power of the stronger mind to heal the weaker.'

He smiled benignly at me, 'I hope you will all pay due attention when I say that I am delighted with Lucina. In her you see what I sincerely believe will be the first female philosopher, the first female realist, which our civilization has produced!'

A few days ago I should have been flattered. Now I only felt insulted because he had not the wit to recognize that he could no longer coax me into accepting his ideas.

'As you are so wise why didn't you see the sword yourself; why didn't you take it away from him?'

'Because the sword appeared only under the stimulus of the false illness: if it had been relevant before, he would have told me about it during the course of our many conversations.'

'It was a real sword.'

'Then no doubt you will bring it here to show me. If you can produce a sword, such as Clion said you described, I will admit myself justly rebuked.'

'You know it wasn't an ordinary sword...not the kind you can *feel*.'

'So your claim that the hilt was cold against your skin was a pardonable exaggeration?'

'I *did* feel it!'

'But you said it could not be felt.'

'You are only trying to confuse me with words. I *hate* words, they never describe what I mean; they are nets to catch birds, which until they were trapped could see further than blind, stupid ants of humans.'

'Birds, ants, nets...and a moment ago it was a sword! Surely there is confusion in your mind, which must be resolved before we continue the pursuit of truth?'

Clion tried to rescue me from the morass into which I was being lured. 'I believe in the sword, so does Agamemnon. Ask him.'

'How comfortable for Agamemnon! No doubt a much more desirable state than the imaginery fever which preceded this new belief.'

A red flood of embarrassment spread upwards from Agamemnon's neck to his forhead. I thought he was going to cry; perhaps Aesculapius regretted the cruelty of his last remark for he gave him no opportunity to speak.

'The sword has always, or at least during several millennia, been the symbol of conflict. Agamemnon has an adequate share of courage for any normal situation he is likely to meet. That he has always tried to drive himself beyond these limitations is, as you know, the product of an unfortunate background and the absorption, during the formative childhood period, of a false standard of behaviour. Agamemnon is a historian; it is therefore certain that he has learned many fragments of the past which he does not clearly remember under ordinary conditions. The sword, suspended by a hair over a man who presumed to exceed his authority, is an historical fact; it took place in Syracuse, a whim of Damocles the Elder, who was a tyrant. Even the banquet has been recorded by one of our more famous writers.'

He turned to me, 'So you see, Lucina, that I was not unfair to state that the sword was real only in so far as any story is real which can impinge on the imagination.'

'I have never heard of Damocles,' I said flatly, 'and I don't suppose Agamamenon has either.'

'Have you, Agamemnon?'

There was a long silence. 'Yes: I have just remembered... though the name was unfamiliar. My father told me the story, when I was a child...before he went to the last battle.'

'I said the sword and the man were real,' I said passionately. 'It doesn't make them less real because somebody bothered to write them down. Why shouldn't the man have been another part of Agamemnon; why shouldn't he have remembered his *own* sword?'

'Why are the trees green instead of blue: why is blood red

instead of yellow? Those questions are not yet within the scope of our consideration; we are only able to assess those factors of which we may hope to discover the cause.'

I had promised myself that Aesculapius would not be able to destroy my new confidence; and yet I could not think of any way to make the others believe me...or even to be sure that I believed myself.

'What about me,' said Euripides. 'Did I behave according to your pattern?'

'Entirely. I hoped that you would continue to see your emotions as separate entities of which you could maintain control even in extreme stress. You have proved that you possess the finest quality of the dramatist, who projects his ideas on a wider stage than that of his trivial identity. Your ode is excellent; the lines superbly balanced, no overstatement, no self-pity; unless I mistake my judgment it will equal the best work of your illustrous prototype.'

'And Epicurus?'

'He again was entirely creditable: instead of trying to play some unsuitable role, he continued to remain calm, to see that food was provided...the faithful steward.'

'At least I had the intelligence to accept my mediocrity,' said Epicurus bitterly.

Did none of the others hear the disillusion in his voice? Were they all such fools that they paid no tribute to his deep humanity?

'Narcissus scrubbed the floors, so I am told: he remained content to leave the directive to others.'

'Some one had to scrub,' I said. 'He was only doing what you told him...keeping the place clean so that there was less chance of the plague spreading.'

'Exactly. And do not mistake me; obedience is an estimable virtue, if it does not become the ruler of initiative.'

'I shall remember that, and continue to allow myself the privilege of making my own decision.'

He smiled, 'Have I ever denied you that privilege, Lucina?'

I could find no adequate answer: Aesculapius never prevented us from doing exactly as we wished...he pruned our wishes until we could grow only in the shape he selected.

Aesculapius, calm and urbane as usual, went back to the house of Elysium, taking Epicurus with him: no doubt we were to be provided with a special meal, as though we were children being rewarded with sweetmeats for a lesson learned. I stayed to put my mother's things away: if Aesculapius bothered to look in the chests he would see the clothes had been unfolded and some of them worn; it would amuse him to tell me that I had tried to escape into her image. To me she had been a light in a dark room: now he was trying to make me believe it was only a false light, a flicker over the marshes of materialism, without warmth or promise of sanctuary.

'Don't hate him, Lucina.'

I swung round at the sound of Clion's voice. 'Why not?'

'Because we promised to remind each other that love is life. It is true, Lucina; so hatred must be the blood of death. Don't hate him, don't hate any one.'

'Not when they hurt people I love? Not when they try to take away courage?'

'Is that quite fair? He has seen far more of the world than we have. He knows how easily people are destroyed through seeking blind faith instead of accepting personal responsibility for their lives. He has told us about the hideous sacrifices made to blind gods; gods who are not even immortals, but only invented by men to excuse their petty hatreds and desires. I think it is true what he says; that we create our own future. If you accept gods, Lucina, you discard your freedom of choice, betray your integrity as the pilot of your destiny. You showed a magnificient courage with Agamemnon: why not recognize it as part of your essential character, not something which came to you through the action of some outside force you don't really understand?'

I sat down on the closed chest; no longer angry, almost indifferent. 'So has he convinced you so easily? Yesterday you believed it was a real sword; you opened a window which showed a new horizon to us both, a window through which we could glimpse a country whose boundaries are wider than the empires of mortality. You were happy, Clion: I know you were happy. Now you want the security of your little room: safe from the past, shuttered against the future...and it doesn't matter to you that the room is dark, and cold.'

'No room is dark to me when I share it with you.'

How much I had longed to hear this warmth in his voice: but now he was only Clion, neither lover nor enemy. 'Words won't bring us any closer to the truth: you have got to find your own experience, and so have I. When we are old, old as Aesculapius, we may be able to explain what now we can only feel in our hearts...if we still have the courage to believe in the heart.'

'You mustn't forget you saved Agamemnon: you mustn't let any one take that away from you.'

'Agamemnon? Yes, he was happy this morning: really happy for the first time in his life. But the happiness I can give is not armoured against the wisdom of philosophers.'

'Nor is my happiness proof against the vision of mystics!'

The door slammed behind him and I heard him running across the terrace. Philosophy and mysticism: were they only two ways of making people lonely, because they could not find a link of understanding?

I spent the rest of the afternoon in the woods beyond the headland: and when the long shadows told me it was time to go back I knew I had very little of which to be proud. I had tried to prove myself stronger than the men; stronger even than Aesculapius who could not make Agamemnon happy. But the strength had come from them, because they had made me fond of them all: I had been strong in love and now I was deliberately trying to make myself weak in hatred...for are not all things weak which have to attack because they know themselves defenceless? I had nearly allowed myself to hate Clion: because I had wanted him to love me more than he did. I had tried to think him a fool...for no woman admits that she loves a fool. Was I really so great a coward that I dare not love for fear of being hurt?

I washed my face in a stream: the water was cold, clean and direct as reason. Reason is good as bread when you are hungry: reason could even make Lucina laugh at herself. Was it true laughter: or was I terribly afraid of something which lurked beyond the careful circle of my thoughts? The dark trees were suddenly instinct with menace: I ran between their crowding trunks towards the lighted windows of the house.

Narcissus had filled my bath and put fresh clothes ready for me. I closed the shutters, for I did not want to look out to the dark garden. I could hear the servants singing in the kitchen: the sudden crash of a dish breaking on tiles was kind as a friendly voice to a lost child. I dressed slowly; re-arranged my hair-ribbons in neat rolls, each in an exact gradation of colour; gave fresh water to a spray of late roses which some one had put in a terracotta vase.

It was still too early to join the others on the terrace: if I got there first I should be alone with the whispering trees; an audience expectant beyond the balustrade. I found the manuscript of a part written for me by Euripides: it was suddenly vital to memorize the lines which had no relation to actuality, whose life was dependent only on the rhythm of words which had no urgent meaning. Perhaps Aesculapius was right: men and women could not afford to abandon the narrow frame through which they could see themselves in exact proportion to their small capacities.

My place was set at the right hand of Aesculapius, and I was relieved at this sign that he had no quarrel with me. The conversation deliberately ignored the last sorry days: Praxiteles described in detail a new statue he had seen in Athens, and we listened as though it was of supreme importance. Epicurus and Euripides exchanged a trivial witticism, and we laughed immoderately, betraying the tension which each tried to conceal. We waited for Agamemnon, and at last Clion went to find him. Clion came back to say he had gone down to the beach to spear fish, taking a servant to hold the torch. I tried to assure myself this was a proof he had not taken the judgement of Aesculapius too seriously.

The dishes were cleared from the table, but no one made any move to leave. Praxiteles was now engaged in a half-hearted discussion about the value of the frieze in lending emphasis to the background of the formal grouping of a chorus. Aesculapius leant back in his chair while he complimented Epicurus on the selection of certain Alexandrian wines which had arrived during our absence.

'A finer vintage than I have known since I visited the Delta ten years ago,' he said sententiously. 'It has not the profundity of a Maronean, the hospitable adaptability of the wines of Sciathos, nor the noble austerity of the Pramnian: but to the discerning palate it contains a honeyed echo of the Egyptian sun.'

Clion listened, but only with a surface interest, as I knew by the way he kept looking at me. Narcissus cracked almonds, with a meticulous care which I should have found exasperating if I had not known he tried to conceal a deep unease. An owl hooted three times: the conversation trickled back to fill the sudden silence.

The room seemed unbearably close. I got up from the table, drew aside the heavy curtains (they were harsh, red wool, embroidered with an acanthus pattern) and walked out to the terrace. Some one had left a cloak on one of the benches: I wrapped it round my shoulders and went to sit on the balustrade, listening to the garden flow down towards the sea.

I felt, rather than heard, some one in the deep shadow below me. 'Agamemnon?' I said in a low voice. He did not answer, but I knew he was there: he could see me against the lighted house but he was only a blur against the darkness.

'Agamemnon...don't hide from me. The others are inside, they can't hear us.'

Words came; spoken so quietly, so fast, that they ran together like drops of water: water, formless yet very clear in its essential substance.

'I can't go away until I know you forgive me, Lucina. I don't want to see any one else...no one else believed me. I had to be sure it was a real sword; to prove to myself that although I never had the courage to live by the sword I was not afraid to die by the sword.... Never let them make you betray life, Lucina. Never believe that you can escape life by dying...you can't escape anything by death...life is so much stronger than we are...so much longer...so lonely without love. Please love me, Lucina...Lucina.'

I heard myself say, 'There is nothing to forgive, and so much to remember. I love you, Agamemnon.'

'I love you.' These words were loud and distinct. Were they only an echo of my voice? The silence was like an empty jar waiting to be filled. 'Lucina...light in the dark. I love...I am no longer alone.'

'Agamemnon! Agamemnon, remember me....'

The small sounds of night rushed in to drown the living silence. Again the owl hooted, and fear touched me on the forehead with a cold finger. Beyond the curtain I heard some one laugh; a strident laugh, mirthless, cold. I had only to walk across the terrace to be among ordinary humanity. Why did I stay here: lost in the shadows between two worlds? A nightingale began to sing among the cypresses: I got slowly to my feet and went towards the sword of light which thrust between the heavy curtains.

I stood looking in at the lighted room. Clion was the first to see me: his half-finished sentence snapped like a thread of

rotten linen. Flat and static as a wall-painting they stared at
me.

'Agamemnon has killed himself,' I said.

No one spoke, and in the same expressionless voice I
heard myself repeat, 'Agamemnon has killed himself. He
just told me.'

Clion came forward, moving slowly and carefully as a man
walking in sleep. His hand was warm against my shoulder,
but I could give no response. 'Agamemnon is dead. Have
none of you the charity to treat his body with respect?'

'You are dreaming, Lucina!' Aesculapius spoke with
authority; trying to bring the room back to its secure
normality.

'No; it is not a dream. You will find I have spoken the
truth; a truth which you will never be able to explain away. I
know Agamemnon is dead; but he didn't tell me where he
had left his body. He died by the sword: the sword I put into
his hand, and which you turned against his heart.'

'You are exhausted by a long ordeal, my child.' Aesculapius came towards me, his hands outstretched, his face showing concern and real affection. 'I will give you a sleeping-
draught. I blame myself for forgetting how greatly you
needed sleep.'

'Lethe, Aesculapius? Or the little lethe of poppies? I
promised to remember: I said I would not escape into forget-
fullness.'

'The mind plays strange tricks on us when we have
worked too hard. Let Clion take you to your room: sleep,
and let the rest of us look for Agamemnon. If you wish, we
will bring him to see you when he comes back, so that you
are reassured.'

'Agamemnon will not come back...yet. I shall help you
to search for his body.' I looked at Euripides. 'I am glad it
was a great ode you wrote for his death...you always knew
he was going to die, didn't you, Euripides?'

They tried to persuade me to go to bed, to leave to them

the mournful search of the dark groves where the night wind whispered a lament to the sleeping trees. When they knew I could not be deceived they sent for torches, and walked, silent, beside me.

I went first to the house on the headland and then to the waterfall, where only this morning Agamemnon had been happy. I should have known he would not choose either place.

There was a pale streak of dawn in the sky before we came to the olive grove, and our torches were guttering in the rising wind.

The stone plinth was empty: the statue had fallen, to lie forsaken in the rank grass. His eyes were open: blank as empty lids of marble. The sword was still fast in his hands: the blade hidden in the scabbard of his ribs. The blood which had seeped from the wound was dark on the hilt of the sword.

I knelt to kiss his forehead. 'I tried to clean the sword, dear Agamemnon. The stain was too deep...but will you believe that I tried to clean the sword before I gave it back to you?'

Clion stood beside the body of the man who had been our friend, staring down as though it had suddenly become horrible and dark with terror. It was Epicurus who caught me when my knees crumpled under the weight of my body which I was too tired to carry: Epicurus who sat beside my bed until the kindly little sister of lethe bore me into sleep.

the Dramatist

Euripides sat on one of the chests in which we kept the clothes we used for acting, watching me rub oil on my face before taking off the paint which had turned me into the passable likeness of an ancient crone. I had used a blend of kohl and lard to draw the wrinkles; they were difficult to remove and my hair was stiff with flour.

'Next time I shall wear a wig,' I said firmly. 'I know horse-hair isn't very convincing but it's far less trouble.'

'Nothing is too much trouble if it is really effective,' he said. 'I have got a splendid idea for Medusa's headdress... real snakes, stuffed of course. I've told one of the gardeners to catch some for me...seven should be enough.'

'They would be seven too many! I am *not* going to wear snakes on my head even to please you.'

He sighed. 'Sometimes you show a distressing lack of artistic appreciation. As you take the trouble to *believe* in your roles you might at least *act* mine properly.'

'You mean I believe in what Aesculapius calls ''the objective projection of character traits''? I didn't realize you thought they were no more than that.'

He looked embarrassed. 'You're not offended, are you? I know we haven't discussed it frankly, but I thought it was understood that we share the same capacity for seeing the different facets of ourselves as separate entities....I suppose it is the fundamental quality of all genius. You are a genius, Lucina, in your own way.'

'Thank you,' I said coldly, 'I suppose you intend that as a compliment.'

'The greatest compliment any one can be offered...and I mean that, Lucina. Beauty diminishes, physical strength lessens, with increasing years: only genius continues to produce brighter flowers each season...if you use it properly instead of letting it use you.'

Euripides so seldom entered into serious discussions that I was too interested to feel annoyed. 'What exactly do you mean?'

'If you really want to know, and will try to understand instead of treating me as an entertaining buffoon, I will explain—but not in here, for some one will interrupt us. We can go to the headland. If I am going to commit the ultimate nudity of being myself, instead of remaining decently clothed in any of a hundred roles I act with tolerable conviction, I can at least assure us a certain privacy.'

Euripides, so moved with real emotion that he was shy! An experience not to be missed, and which required to be treated with tact. I knew that unguarded honesty was apt to leave one feeling limp but hungry; so I went to the kitchen to collect a basket of food so that we need not come back until we felt inclined...there is always a certain humiliation in being driven by the demands of the body.

We exchanged trivialities until we reached the bench under the pine tree. Even then he seemed reluctant to start serious conversation; first making the excuse that it would be a pity not to swim on such a radiant morning, and then climbing up to the house to fetch a cloak for me to sit on.

'Lucina,' he said earnestly, 'you mustn't think I am unaware of your difficulties: I know what they are, and I honour you for the way you have coped with them in spite of so many conflicting influences. It is all very well for Aesculapius to give wordy explanations; but you and I know that he doesn't share the same kind of experience. He plays many roles, but only because his mind considers them advisable; you and I play them because we have to...which is the great difference. When I came to Elysium my roles were stronger than me, so strong that often there was no conscious link between one and another. One morning I would wake up as a woman: I thought as a woman, felt as a woman, and even my face in the mirror seemed like a stranger who was peering over my shoulder. Then I would wake in a heroic role, a famous dramatist or a maker of laws: I could almost hear the crowds applauding in the amphitheatre, or see the people who had gathered to listen to my judgements. None of this became destructive until I began to *live* in their way: when I started to wear women's clothes one day and the next demanded the deference due to a famous orator, I thought I was going mad...and so did my father who persuaded Aesculapius to take me to Elysium. Aesculapius was clever with me; instead of arguing against my ideas he provided me with every property to play them to the full. Which is why, though I have never told you this before, there are clothes here which could dress the actors of any company in Athens. He never laughed at me, Lucina: and I hope you will never learn how great a charity the lack of mockery can be.'

'Aren't you being unnecessarily grateful? Surely the least one can do is not to mock one's friends?'

'Did you find it easy not to laugh at Agamemnon when you first came here? Remember that I looked far more funny than he ever did.'

'At first I laughed,' I admitted reluctantly, 'but only until I realized he was fighting a real enemy.'

'Aesculapius knew my enemy was real the first day I came here. It was like being given water, unlimited water, when you have been slowly dying of thirst: to be accepted without comment, without any suggestion that your mind was diseased, was like being taken from the press of a doomed battle. He taught me to accept the fact that I was a pattern made up of many threads: that the threads had become tangled until I could only see one colour at a time instead of recognizing their mutual dependence. He said I should never be sane until I could follow each thread, seeing it as separate from the weaver, who was myself.'

'So you think I am mad too?'

'No, Lucina, you are very sane, sometimes almost cruelly

sane: but you are sixteen, and I did not try to live my roles until I was twenty-three.'

'You are trying to warn me of what the future may hold unless I follow your road of escape?'

'It isn't an escape,' he said passionately: 'It is a return into freedom, a home-coming into a real, factual world. I was weak and terribly afraid: now I can watch the characters I create and learn from them. I am no longer driven by daemons. I have conceived many children who are kindly and obedient: before I discovered how to rule them they tried to destroy me because I knew I was barren.'

'You told me you had never taken a woman.'

'Does a genius have to go to bed to conceive a child? My plays are my children; the rhythm of lines is their laughter, words are their bones, the chorus the flesh which will not decay unless they are too feeble to endure the long years of immortals.'

'So you think I should become a dramatist?'

'Why not, Lucina? Why should a woman not be a poet instead of a philosopher? You torture yourself because you did not save Agamemnon's life: why not give him permanence in the theatre? You despise books: but why not use them to widen the conception you already hold of the hall of Damocles? It would make a great play: there should be an epilogue written as it happened, the girl by the bedside of a man who thought he was still dying by the sword...it would be very effective. I should let him die, just as he did: the dead man lying beneath the empty plinth with the elders staring in horror at the girl who had prophesied his death... magnificent!'

'So you have decided it was a prophecy? You don't think I really heard Agamemnon ask me to forgive him?'

'The method is not important; only the facts should be presented to the audience.'

I went back to the night when Agamemnon died, and saw the faces of the people who stood looking down at his body.

Aesculapius showed grief...and was there fear with the grief? Clion was in sorrow for the death of a friend. Narcissus looked away, to save himself the discomfort of seeing something which might disturb him. Epicurus had watched me...that was why it was Epicurus who had caught me when I fell, taken me to bed, comforted me until I slept. But Euripides had been alert; Euripides had only been interested. Had he then a secret I dare not ignore?

'Are you no longer tortured by emotion, Euripides? Have you found a shield more sure than any warrior holds?'

'Yes: and I had to find it...or die. Lucina, you must believe me! You and I share so much; let me share with you the strength, not only the weakness. We feel more intensely than ordinary people: our thoughts take on a life of their own, but we must watch them on the stage, and never forget that we produce the play in which they act. We must live our life, not their's. At Agamemnon's burial I was concerned only with the sound of the words I had written as his funeral ode: if I had allowed myself to see how closely I had come to the same death I should have wept...and more than wept. If we can set the fire of our emotions to a torch we light in praise of genius we shall never be alone in the dark: if we are ruled by that fire it will consume us...and the taste of ashes is bitter in the mouth.

'Genius is the noble metal: it is for us to choose whether we make of it a crown or the shackles of despair. At last I am *happy*, Lucina...because I have learned to feel only at second hand. When I recognize the onslaught of emotion, I set it safe in words until it is harmless as a fly in amber: the form is real, and changeless, but it cannot hurt me. Even beauty has lost her power of flight, and so she cannot escape to leave me desolate.'

'Do you never weep with Icarus? Your tears should be more bitter; the sun melted his wings, he did not throw them away because he feared to see too far.'

'So it is true that you are in love with Clion?' He said it

as one might say 'It is true that you are dying.' A statement of an iron truth which could no longer be denied.

'Why do you think so?'

'Aesculapius told me—I was a fool not to see it for myself.'

So Aesculapius had seen Clion kiss me in the pavilion. Was it more than a coincidence that Clion had been sent to Delos the following day?

'You haven't answered me, Lucina. Do you want to marry Clion?'

'Perhaps...how can I be sure?'

'Would you rather be an ordinary woman? Would you throw away genius, power, wisdom; and take instead the petty occupations of a wife who is content to be the mirror in which a man admires himself, when he has nothing better to do?'

'I might have both: he might be *my* mirror, and love me for my wisdom.'

'For a month, even for a year, you could deceive yourself. But then he could no longer believe in you, for Clion is a realist. He would know that he had stolen from you the immortal fire, and that you were chilled by the little warmth of the hearthstone. You would no longer have vision..except the visions of the anxious mother when her child's forehead portends a bout of fever; you would no longer have power over people, except the small authority of the woman who commands the trivial matters of her household; you would no longer have immortality, except for the brief span when the arms of a lover seemed to promise that you share the blood of goddesses...a promise he could not fulfil when illusion had shed it magic. You would have lost your fine detachment, which is the frame by which the artist gives less fortunate humanity their glimpse of beauty. You would have become part of nature; no more than a blade of grass, a tree, a cloud-wrack dark against the wind. You could no longer be creative, except by the animal process of the belly, and if you still retained that moiety of honesty you would know you deserved no more credit than a vegetable marrow obedient to a bee! '

'I thought Aesculapius maintains that virginity confers no special virtue?'

'Of course it doesn't. But what you are trying to do is to escape from your real talents into a stagnant little pond of domesticity. '

'Why do you dislike Clion so much?'

'I don't—and you know perfectly well he is a friend of mine. But as a husband for you he would be disastrous. You would be so bored in a few months that you'd either run away or die. And you are too stubborn to admit your mistakes so you'd choose death, or a half-life of trying to live a role you knew was entirely false to your character. '

'Why shouldn't I marry and have children? Surely it's my own business what I do with my life?'

'Burying talents alive is one of the few sins that destroy. Your talent, which is curious, and I don't pretend to understand it properly, doesn't belong only to you—it is for you to use. It is much greater than you are, it belongs to the *audience*. '

'What's the point of working to get an audience when a lover can provide a better one? Clion makes me feel clever and beautiful and important. Being in love with him makes me feel kind, and it's much easier than fighting against everything. '

'Clion has more power than any of us suspected—he's turned you into a coward in a few days. Lucina sighing to be the sheltered flower instead of being proud as a tree! What a pitiable transformation—forgive me if I find it nauseating! '

I slapped his face, so hard that my fingers ached. Instead of hitting me back as I expected, he said gently, 'Do you want to be Clion's wife or a *persona*, Lucina? You cannot be both. Please believe me before you have to find it out for yourself. '

CHAPTER ELEVEN

the Seer

In many ways they all showed me a new consideration
which I found it difficult to accept. No one said openly that
they thought I was in love, but it was obvious from the way
they spoke of Clion in my presence. The evening I heard he
would be delayed in Delos another month, perhaps longer, I
was deliberately gay. I made Epicurus laugh immoderately,
defeated Euripides in a duel of wits, and when the long meal
was over I danced for Praxiteles in the moonlight until he said
he must keep me safe for eternity in a frieze.

Yet Aesculapius was not deceived; he was only sorry for
me, and because of this I cried myself to sleep. The next
morning he called me to his room. There was a half-empty
goblet on the table though he seldom drank wine before the
noon meal.

'Lucina,' he said gently. 'I know that you feel I have not
shown a proper sympathy for your perception, which is more
subtle than my own. I thought there was a chance you might
accept my explanation of certain experiences I was unable to
share. I failed to convince you, and now I suggest that together we should explore this unfamiliar territory.'

For the first time since Clion left I found it easy to think of
something else: at last I was again to be treated as a person
instead of a patient!

Aesculapius smiled. 'So Lucina has not entirely forgotten
that Truth eludes those who do not seek her?'

'I shall never forget it, unless you are able to convince me
she doesn't exist!'

The words were sharp, but he knew they were spoken in
affection. He laughed like a boy, 'I have always boasted that
there was no risk I was unwilling to accept if it brought me
closer to reality. I now freely admit that when I found some-

thing which would not yield to explanation I tried to pretend it was only an illusion. If I had been correct in my analysis of the phenomena which you experienced, you would have believed me. Now it is our duty to determine whether you employ some faculty which as yet I cannot fully understand.'

'But have I ever claimed more than that?'

'No, and yes, the question is complex. Unfortunately you have a special genius for such questions! Do you agree to undertake an experiment which is not without risk, and to abide by the result which I believe will satisfy us both?'

'Am I such an unwilling pupil that you need to ask?'

'You must believe, Lucina, that I am not setting a trap for you: this is not another cloak of Tyrian purple, of that I give you my most solemn word.' He smiled. 'If it were not against our tradition I would offer to swear an oath by all the gods to prove my sincerity.'

'Does gold demand silver-leaf to make it noble? Why, then, should an oath be added to the word of Aesculapius?'

The philosopher blushed, and we laughed together. 'I have arranged,' he said, 'for a physician of Athens, a man who has long been interested in my findings as to the effect of the mind on the body, to send me four of his patients with whom he has failed to produce any improvement. I do not wish the others to know what we are doing, for if we learn nothing we can share our ignorance in decent privacy. I shall announce my intention of taking you to Athens for a few days: in fact we shall go to a cottage which came into my possession last year when the owner died. I had done him a small kindness he wished to repay.'

'A cottage, instead of a cock to Aesculapius?'

'And not, I hope, an empty tribute!'

'What shall I have to do?'

'I want us both to discover to what extent you can discern the latent fears of a stranger with whom you have had no previous contact. I have, after most serious consideration, decided that you can no more cease from influencing people than you can cease to breathe. When I brought you here I hoped to educate a female philosopher, but the blood of your mother is strong in you, and it is creating a priest-physician. Remember that of every hundred people you will ever meet, even if you travel to the furthest countries of the known world, ninety will be haunted by fear. You can help to free them: and it is too great a destiny to be denied, too great an honour to betray. Before you die, Lucina, demand of history this accolade: ''Because I have lived there is less fear among men; because I kept faith the lamp I lit can never be put out.'' '

Aesculapius opened the door of the cottage: the theatre where I must see my dream, the stadium in which to contest the right of bays. It was a small room, containing nothing more significant than a straw pallet, two wooden stools and a bench under the window. A fire smouldered on the hearth.

He drew aside a faded curtain which covered a niche in the wall. 'You will find bread, salt, and wine on the shelves,' he said. 'The rest of the food is in the shed where the previous owner kept his hay. Conditions here are primitive but adequate, though no doubt they would embarrass Epicurus and appall Narcissus!'

There were two other doors. One led into the room where I was to sleep, for I saw the chest of clothes which Narcissus had considered suitable for Athens. The other door was shut.

'Is that the storeroom?'

Aesculapius smiled. 'It may prove to contain rare treasure. Why not look for yourself?'

It was empty except for a narrow bed with a pillow and three covers neatly folded. There was an outer door and a high window closed by a shutter. I realized what he meant by 'treasure'; the patients were to be brought here.

I had been so elated when Aesculapius decided to treat me as an equal that I had not troubled about what I was expected to do. I realized with appalling clarity that I had no idea how to prove anything, nor did I know what manner of ordeal I was to undergo.

'What is going to happen?' I said, hoping my dismay was not too obvious.

'The patients will sleep in here, assisted by a draught of poppy, while you remain with me in the other room.'

This was even worse than I expected. 'What do you want me to do?'

'That is for you to decide: I do not wish to influence your judgment even by suggesting the possibilities.'

'You are not going to tell me anything about them, the four people I mean?'

'I could not do so even if I wished, for I am being kept in ignorance of their age, their affliction, even of their nationality—they will each be dressed in a white tunic so that we can have no clue as to their rank. Each evening, soon after sunset, one will be brought here in a curtained litter. They will have taken the drug before they arrive, to make sure that we cannot influence them by logic, reassurance, or any other ordinary means. The bearers will wait until I tell them that the patient is ready to leave: which will be after you have finished and when I have prepared a brief report to send to the physician. Until I return to Elysium, he will not send me news as to whether they show improvement, nor tell me from what disease of mind or body they suffered. I agreed willingly to this condition, for I think it best that we should not have any information which might make us unduly elated or depressed.'

'You think that if I fail with the first one I may not have the courage to try again?'

'You will never lack courage, Lucina, or so I profoundly believe. But in justice to both of us, for I too am pledging my knowledge on this trial, it is vital that we should not be biased by previous success...or failure.' He smiled a little ruefully, 'You see, Lucina, in my time I have not been immune from the pleasures of rivalry; so he is very eager to prove that since I left Athens my wits have mouldered in seclusion! It would be a satisfactory story for him to tell, if we give him cause, that the man who now calls himself Aesculapius has become credulous. We can be sure that the four patients he selects will be those whom he believes incurable. I insisted that he send four, for even one effect will prove that there is more to understand than physicians have yet acknowledged. But perhaps he will not be able to set us an impossible task: we will remember Perseus and gain confidence that the hero has resources denied to his tormentors. '

'Does it matter whom he sends? We shall either succeed, or admit I have been a fool. '

'Not a fool, Lucina; only some one who so profoundly wished to believe that she deceived herself. Even apparent failure need not be decisive, for if he sends only those people who prefer their madness, their bodily affliction, their retreat from the press of ordinary living, to the free seal of integrity, then you can do nothing for them. You could do nothing even if you were endowed with all the powers which men claim for their gods. If a man, or a woman, prefers illness to the claims of health, no one can cure his body; if he chooses emotional instability instead of the demands of clear thinking, no one can cure his mind; if he prefers the temptation of evil, the comfortable cloak of guilt, to the light of ethical maturity, no one can cure his soul. The gods do not dwell remote on Olympus, they are instinct in the centre of our being, both the core of the fruit and the host of the seed. If we accept that godliness we are immortal. If we deny it, then Zeus, Juno, or Apollo are no greater than their statues, masks of stone by which men seek to hide their slow decay. '

I was sitting with Aesculapius beside the hearth, watching the olive logs gently smoulder into white ash, when we heard the slow pace of men who carry a burden coming up the path that led to the door of the other room. Then came the creak of hinges, followed by a series of small sounds which told us that some one was being laid on the bed and covered with the three blankets. Again the door creaked, and closed with a soft thud.

'Do you want to see whether it is a man or a woman?'

'No,' I said slowly, 'not until I have tried to find out for myself.'

'It will not disturb you if I light the lamp?'

I thought he offered this because I might be afraid of the dark; but the room was not really dark and he was with me. 'I don't need a lamp when I have you.'

'If it makes no difference I should prefer one, for I want to keep an exact record of anything you may say.' He set a flaring twig to the wick and then put the lamp on the floor beside him so that his body shielded me from the direct light.

For a long time, I don't know how long by the ordinary measure of hours, nothing happened. What was I supposed to do? I had seen my mother without making any effort: I had seen the sword above Agamemnon because I had been looking for an imaginary spider. Perhaps if I pretended to be some one much wiser than Lucina it would help. She might be able to get through the wall and look down on the person lying there. If I became one of my dream selves I could enter the stranger's dream...but I must remember that I was also Lucina or I should forget everything when I woke. Or worse than that, I should remember and yet Aesculapius would think it was *only* a dream.

I tried to remain between sleeping and waking, sitting cross-legged, my hands relaxed palm upwards on my knees. Cramp stabbed my thigh; I tried to ignore it but had to change my position. Small irrelevant thoughts bubbled up in my mind, making it difficult to keep it as a clear pool in which to see the wiser Lucina's vision.

'Would it be easier to relax if you lay flat?' There was no anxiety in his voice and I was assured. I nodded, and he spread a blanket beside the fire and brought another with which to cover me. I curled up on my left side: it was not sleep which had to be fought against, but a persistent wakefulness. A steady beat sounded in the quiet room: I thought I was listening to my pulse until I realized it was rain; falling steadily, increasingly insistent.

The rain was heavy, yet there was no wind, no mutter of distant thunder. It was not the season for rain...the fields would be a sea of mud if it went on much longer...the water would slide like snakes through the groves. Animals would flee from the rising water...and not only animals. People would try to reach the mountains. But it would be difficult to run through the clinging mud; ankle deep, knee deep.

If I fall the child will be drowned in the mud...don't let me fall into the mud. The mud is more cruel than the rain; it is a hungry mouth trying to suck me into the last darkness.

The child is screaming; its hands are clutching my hair because it knows I am getting so tired, so cold, that I can't hold it securely on my shoulders. I try to tell it to keep still...but it can't hear me because of its screaming, because of the sound of the rain.

The mud is getting deeper; it presses against my thighs. If I stand still I shall sink too far to be able to move forward again. If I can keep moving, even so very slowly, we may reach higher ground. The child is struggling...it won't listen to me....I can't hold it on my shoulders for my hands are slippery with mud. Everything is mud...there is no solid rock, no cleanness anywhere.

I can't get the mud out of its nostrils...my hands are covered with mud. A dead child cannot breathe...a dead child...a dead child.

I can hear some one speaking...the rain must have stopped for I can hear the words. No voice could speak against the rain. 'Take the child to the clear pool.'

There can be no clear water in this sea of mud. How can I carry a dead child through the mud which is slowly sucking me down?

'There is rock under the mud. Remember the rock which is clean under the rain.'

My feet are bruised by the rock; but it is not cruel, not greedy as the mud was greedy. The rock is stronger than the mud, older than the mud. The rock is not afraid of the rain: because it is old as courage the rain has ceased. That is why I can hear the voice: the rain has ceased...the rain has made a clear pool on the rock.

My hands are clean because the mud is washed away. I can take the mud from the nostrils of the child, from its mouth, from its closed eyes.

I thought the child was dead...the child of a slave whom I found crying in an abandoned house beside the causeway. But it opens its eyes...it is not dead. I am not dead! I am part of the living rock which the rain came to rescue from the mud...I am free of the mud...I am free...

'Drink this, Lucina!' The wine ran out of the corner of my mouth though I tried to swallow. 'Lucina!' I was sitting half upright, leaning against Aesculapius' shoulder. He held the cup and my teeth chattered against the rim.

'You will be better in a moment. Don't be frightened...I am here, with you. There is nothing to fear.'

'I fell asleep,' I said. 'I think I had a dream, but I can't remember much about it. I fell asleep soon after it began to rain.'

I stood up and then ran to unfasten the shutters. The bolt was stiff, or my hands were too cold to pull it back.

'What are you doing?' His voice was brisk, authoritative.

I turned round. 'I only wanted to see if the fields were flooded...the path will be covered in deep mud. We must shout to warn the men not to try the path...they might be drowned in the mud.'

He threw back the shutter. It was difficult to make myself look out of the window: I was afraid of seeing a terrible desolation.

'Open your eyes, Lucina. You must never be afraid to see.'

The moon shone down on a quiet garden; a garden where paths were silver with the gleam of gentle moisture on smooth stone. The trees were secure in kindly earth which smelt clean with the memory of a summer shower.

'But I heard the rain,' I said. 'It couldn't have been only a dream. I heard the rain. I felt the terrible hunger of the mud.'

'It was not only a dream, Lucina. You have never talked in your sleep. You described to me an experience which I believe you shared with the woman who is now sleeping quietly in the next room.'

'Did she wake?' I said, trying to make myself calm enough to talk without emotion of an experiment, instead of being afraid to relive it again.

'I will tell you what happened when we both have had time to recover. But first we need something to eat, and to drink. We need a proper fire to get warm. Feel!' he gave me his hand, 'I am nearly as cold as you are.'

He fetched logs and made the fire blaze. He heated broth and we sat with hot bowls of it between our hands until the warmth made us feel secure and I no longer had to keep tense to prevent myself shivering.

'Now I want to hear what happened,' I said. 'I really want to, I'm not asking to pretend I wasn't frightened!'

'Do you want me to read what you said while it was happening?'

'Not yet,' I admitted frankly. 'I can remember enough for to-night. To-morrow it will only be words, but now it might be more; too uncomfortable!

'Good! Already you are learning a new kind of courage, which is secure because it dare admit fear instead of having to pretend it doesn't exist! I am learning it too, for I have never found anything more difficult than letting you go on when I so profoundly wanted to stop you. What you experienced was horrific, even at second hand, and I could only watch and recognize my helplessness. You would have known my feelings when you saw my writing. It looks like the prowlings of a drunken beetle, instead of the precise marks of cold reason. I shall have to make a fair copy to send to our friend in Athens!'

We laughed together and filled our wine-cups before he went on speaking. 'When the rain began—it was only very ordinary rain but audible because the night was still, the woman in the next room began to moan. I thought she would disturb you, though you seemed to have fallen asleep. The moans grew louder, and though I knew she would not wake I went in to see if she were ill. The symptoms from which she suffered were immediately obvious: she was fighting for breath, her face suffused, the mouth gaping open as she struggled for air. If I had not seen several patients of my own with the same affliction I should have thought her in grave danger, or, if I had believed in daemons, I might have considered that she was being strangled. It is an affliction which occurs in both men and women, less frequently in children. So far as I know there is no cure, though sleep-drinks help to alleviate the condition. That was one of the curious factors: she had this sudden attack while deeply asleep, and there is no physical damage to the nose or lungs, for when the attack passed she breathed without any difficulty.

'I was sufficiently anxious about her to leave the door open: as the tempo of your experience heightened so did her struggles become more desperate. When you heard the voice which spoke of the pool of clear water, there was a sudden silence. I ran to her: I thought her heart had stopped, that I should find a dead woman on the bed. She was breathing slowly, deep breaths as a runner takes when he has reached his goal. I had not heard this reassuring noise because the contrast was so great between this ordinary rhythm and the previous agony.' He smiled, 'And I think my hearing was less than normally acute because of the sound of my heart. It was thudding in a manner most disquieting to one who prides himself on being free of undignified emotions.'

'She was being drowned in the mud. Her body, this body I mean, remembered what had happened.'

'Have you any idea whether her fear came from an accident in early childhood; for instance, was she the child, and the woman a nurse—you said the woman knew it was not her own child? There may have been a storm of unusual severity, you said the mud was very deep. The child fell into the mud and thought it was being smothered. An experience of that severity would be enough to cause permanent damage to the mind; the fear remaining latent except when brought to the surface by a catalyst, such as the rain to-night provided.'

'I don't know, Aesculapius. This was different to the sword. I felt that Agamemnon was the man in the banqueting hall.... I could even guess at the time it happened, two or three centuries ago. It was I, Lucina, who took the sword and gave it to him. But this time, though I was so close to the woman that I experienced her fear and could *feel* the mud, I know it didn't happen to me. I was in two places at once, inside her mind and still thinking with my own. It was like dreaming another person's dream; real and yet in a sense impersonal. I knew I could stop knowing about her...and you can never stop knowing about yourself. I was she and not she: myself and more than myself. I'm too sleepy to be intelligent about it, but at least we know that *something* happened.'

'Yes,' said Aesculapius. 'We know that something happened: and for the first time I hope to live to a great age so that we shall be able to discover the country to which this is one of the roads.'

We deliberately spent the next day being very ordinary. There was an old spade and a sickle with a broken handle in the shed, and we worked in the garden, cutting dead wood from the bushes, digging up nettles that were choking the few remaining flowers, as though we were desperate to get the ground clean for a sowing on which our security depended. Neither of us felt hungry, but in the late afternoon we lit a fire to boil some eggs and ate them with bread and goat's cheese. We sat outside, watching the colours of the setting sun fade from the sky, until we heard some one approaching along the main road.

Aesculapius walked to the end of the rough terrace which still supported a few neglected vines. 'It is only a man driving a pack-donkey,' he said, 'but I can see a litter coming over the crest of the hill. We had better go indoors. How are you feeling, Lucina? I can tell them to turn back if you are too tired to try again to-night.'

'I am feeling very well, and not at all worried,' I said, and wished it were true.

I lay down beside the cold hearth, we had lit the cooking fire in the garden for both of us had felt inclined to stay in the open, and waited to hear departing footsteps and the thud of a door closing. To-night the hinges did not creak for we had oiled them.

Again a procession of trivial thoughts passed across the surface of my mind, clear, precise pictures which were easy to recognize but seemed without significance: Euripides tying his manuscripts with coloured ribbons, and putting them away in the box made for him by Praxiteles in the form of a child's sarcophagus; myself packing my mother's clothes in the painted chest, being so careful to replace each pleat as I had found it; Epicurus counting the tallies in the storeroom.

'I can't see anything important,' I said. 'A lot of irrelevant ideas keep coming into my head. I try to keep them out for they don't mean anything.'

'Describe them to me: don't worry if you can't see any significance. Pretend it is the memory of a dream. We have often discovered that a small, seemingly unimportant, detail is the clue to the labyrinth.'

I did as he told me, expecting that he would share my disappointment. 'There is no clue,' I said. 'All these images are ordinary memories of things which I know have happened.'

'You recognize no similarity?'

I paused, and then admitted that I could not see any connecting thread.

'Each of them has one factor in common. They are symbols of personal treasure, the treasure which represents security.'

'Of course! How stupid of me not to see it.'

'Follow the clue, Lucina. Let the pictures form without any conscious effort, and describe them to me as they occur. Ask yourself if the patient has a treasure he jealously guards.'

'Don't talk any more,' I said quickly. 'I have just realized there was another picture which kept on forming behind the others...but it was difficult to see clearly. It was like a faded fresco on which another has been painted...in much brighter pigments.'

'Look at the faded picture: look at it, Lucina!'

'There is a man, an old man, very thin...he is shut in a room without windows. There are sacks all round him: leather sacks, I think...their mouths are closed with thongs, tied very tightly and sealed with purple wax. He is very hungry: there must be food in the sacks, for he is trying to break the thongs. The wax is hard, hard as metal, for his fingers bleed when he tries to break the seal. Some one has come into the room. I cannot see whether it is a man or a woman...I can only see a right hand holding a knife. The knife would slit the sacks, but the old man won't look at it. He pretends it isn't there...I can't hear anything, but I know some one is telling him to take the knife and slit open the sacks.'

'Why won't he take the knife? *Why*, Lucina?'

'Because he thinks that if he lets any one help him he will have to share the food. There is a lot of food, but he believes

117

there is only just enough to save him from starvation. He thinks there is only one sack...but there are many, so very many. He has only just enough space to move between them. I said there was no window in the room; but there is a window, it is hidden by the sacks.'

'Can't you tell him to escape through the window?'

'He won't listen. I have tried to tell him: but he won't listen. He thinks I am a thief who has come to steal...he thinks every one is a thief.'

Then the picture faded: there was only the white ash on the hearth, Aesculapius writing down the last words I had used, the lamp making us great with shadows on the wall. I felt ordinary and rather silly, as though I had been inventing a story to amuse Euripides...and it wasn't even an interesting story, no proper ending, no drama. I wasn't cold, or tired; there was nothing to show, even to myself, that anything even a little odd had happened.

'I am sorry,' I said. 'I tried, but that was all I could see, and it is very unimportant.' Then I remembered how hungry the old man had looked; the way the ribs showed through the torn tunic, the broken nails which had tried to force the wax seals.

'It may not be unimportant to him,' I said. 'He may be a beggar who is too old even to beg. At least we can give him food and somewhere to sleep. I think it was cruel to send a starving man here, when all he needed was work or a little charity. If he is a slave will you buy him? Even if he is useless we could let him work in the garden: there must be something he could do to earn enough to stop himself being so terribly afraid of hunger.'

'Has any one been turned away from Elysium? Of course I will buy him and give him his freedom. I have never found it more easy to be the skilful physician, for no disease is more readily cured than hunger, if you have food to give away!'

I laughed. 'A few moments ago I thought that I hadn't found out anything...we don't even know if it is a man or a woman. Yet we are already certain that he is a man, and old, and hungry. We have almost decided exactly how much his freedom will cost and what kind of work will suit him!'

'It is easy enough to prove,' he said, and taking the lamp we walked towards the door.

The man, at least it was a man and not a woman or a child, slept quietly, his hands folded on his chest. But they were not the hands of a slave: they were sleek with ungents, the nails carefully tended. The beard was curled, and perfumed with ambergris; the grey hair glossy, parted above a broad forehead; the body had cause to remember many years of rich food.

I said, 'If he is a slave, then his master must be a paragon. If he is old and close to starvation, then I am a foreign wrestler with a broken nose!'

I never had greater cause to be grateful to Aesculapius than during the following day. He understood how foolish I was feeling, but he gave no sign that we had any reason to be disturbed.

We took food with us and went far up the mountain, talking of things which had no bearing on my failure. We collected several uncommon flowers to bring back to plant in the garden; we chose wild herbs for the stew I made for the evening meal with the care which Epicurus would have given to a banquet.

At least I was prepared for another disappointment, and so was able to conceal something of what it meant to me. For hours I tried to produce some effect; even a fleeting idea which could be translated into a symbolic meaning would have been as a healing ointment. But nothing happened: I was only Lucina who could think of nothing except that she was betraying Aesculapius, and herself.

When I had to admit that it was no use trying any longer, we went to look at the third patient. He was a young man, lying peacefully on his side with his right hand under his cheek. I was too dispirited, and too tired, even to wonder why a diseased mind should be contained in so healthy a body.

I had gone to bed before the bearers came to take him away. I was so miserable that I should have been glad if they had come to carry me to my funeral, for a corpse is spared the humiliation of failure!

I knew the fourth ordeal was a woman, for she cried out when she was carried into the house; there was fear in the sound, which blurred into a mutter of unintelligible words before the silence crept back.

I lay down as I had done before and tried to hold a state between sleeping and waking. I was no longer bowed with the sense of inevitable failure; almost I hoped that nothing would happen.

Aesculapius knew I was afraid. 'It is not unusual to talk under the influence of lethe; do not let yourself be disturbed, Lucina. You would not be afraid to hear some one mutter if he were deep in wine: this is no more important.'

His voice was calm, yet I think he shared my unease. It was suddenly intolerable to lie on the floor, to try to become a placid mirror in which the mind of some one else could be reflected. It was urgent that I remained Lucina; only as my inviolate self could I find strength. The strength I needed was not to be found in a concept of a different personality; I must search for it from the centre, from a hidden source of life which as yet I had only dimly recognized. I must act according to the dictates of that spring of clear water; let it flow freely, the course not misdirected by logic or preconceived ideas. Yet logic was needed too, the precise judgement, the complete mastery of fear by which alone this current could find the free waters of the sea beyond the sea.

I stood up and walked slowly across the room to unbar the shutters. The moon was full.

'Let me see myself in the moon.' I could hear my voice as though it belonged to some one I had once known and loved. 'By the light of the moon let me challenge the darkness!'

I was no longer uncertain: what I must do was clear and precise as the pattern of a ritual dance; each step, each movement was defined, to be followed with meticulous exactness. Yet I knew only the next step, the immediate gesture: I could not tell where the pattern was leading me.

I went to the cupboard in the wall: I did so with the assurance of instinct, and yet I could feel the texture of the woollen curtain and the smooth surface of pottery as I took down the flask of wine. The bread broke easily, and in my right hand I took a small portion. The salt was in a stone jar: I sprinkled some on the bread. The bread and the salt; the sword and the shield. I was no longer without armour.

The latch of the door was familiar as the hilt of a sword. The screams which I could hear were only the turmoil of battle, familiar to the soldier. The room was dark, but in the light which came through the door I had opened I could see the dark shape of a body contorted on the bed. I placed the bread and salt at her head, the flask of wine at her feet. The soldier puts those for whom he joins battle in a safe fortress before he gives challenge to the enemy.

The herald must know the name of the enemy. I knew the name. 'BAST!' In the challenge there was the sound of trumpets by which chariots are unleashed as hounds on a dark quarry.

'Bast! Is the Cat of Sekmet a whipped cur who is afraid to show her face to me, the Daughter of the Moon?'

The enemy came forth from the shadow. A woman with the head of a cat, the claws of a cat. A woman strong with youth, imperishably old.

'Accept my challenge, or let your slave go free!'

I knew for whom I fought: a girl younger than Lucina, who in fear had dedicated her spirit to the service of Evil.

The clawed hands of Bast stretched out towards me, curving for my throat. I could feel the thick, dark fur; soft and impenetrable under my hands.

'The life of the cat or the life of the moon!'

And the voice of Bast answered, 'I accept no freedom at your hands: there can be nothing except death between us.'

'Choose freedom! Choose in the Name of Ptah!'

'Bast does not give up her slaves!'

'By the power of Ptah I conquer!'

The claws tore at my throat. I felt blood pouring down my face, drenching my body until it was wet as the sweat of death.

'Ptah, protect me!'

There was strength in my hands, memory in my fingers. The goat of Pan had fled from the child on the mountain. I would conquer by the light of older victories.

My hands were drawing closer together; closer on that throat which tried to utter names of immemorial evil.

I was alone in the room; save for a woman who was no longer a prisoner of the dark.

I took the bread and moistened it with wine. The woman was lying as though death had brought her the only peace. I opened her mouth and put the sop of salted bread and wine on her tongue.

She opened her eyes: 'I will not again betray the salt,' she said, 'I will not again betray the salt.'

Aesculapius stood at the foot of the bed, holding the lamp high so that its light filled the room. The woman was very old; sparse white hair fell in disorder round a face which time had treated without kindliness.

She lifted her hand; the hand of a woman who had never been spared the lowest forms of toil. She stared at it and a tear crawled down a wrinkled course. 'I had forgotten that I am old,' she said. 'I had forgotten the slave market, the quays of Alexandria, the stews of foreign cities. I could only remember the girl who was born in the island beyond Delos...the girl who had never seen a cat.'

Then she looked up at me. 'But I am no longer afraid to be old, for I know that my grave will not be defiled by the cats; the cats who have come in their hundreds to remind me that their patience was infinite.'

She lay back on the pillow, and, smiling, fell asleep.

It was only then that I saw the look on the face of Aesculapius. There was horror and compassion in his eyes. I saw
that my tunic was splashed with blood. So the cat had torn
my face....I had felt its claws driving into my throat.

'No,' he said. 'Your throat is not wounded...your nose
bled. It is not unusual for the nose to bleed under the stress
of powerful emotion.'

'Then why are you frightened for me?'

'Because I don't understand...I don't understand. You
were in danger, Lucina. Terrible danger...I thought I had
driven you insane.'

'Aesculapius, for the first time in my life I am secure in my
sanity. I no longer have to fight for my certainty that there
are more things under the sun than have yet been recognized
by philosophers: I *know*.'

CHAPTER TWELVE

Escapist

It was noon when I woke next day. For a moment I was
surprised to be in my own room: then I remembered that
Aesculapius had brought me home to Elysium last night. It
had been a long and silent walk along the familiar paths. He
must have guessed that I had suggested we leave the cottage
because I wanted us to get back to the security of ordinary
surroundings.

We had always been separated by the relationship of
master to pupil; now, for the first time, we should be able to
talk as equals. Now I could teach as well as learn; we should
recognize each other's knowledge as two facets of the same

crystal; for I also could speak with authority.

I went to the room where he usually worked and found him sitting at a table under one of the windows. He was reading a letter and did not look up or give me any greeting when I came in. I was used to his preoccupation, and so waited without anxiety for him to speak.

It was a long letter, and he read it over again before he rolled it into a closed cylinder, tied it with one of the linen threads which he took from a pottery dish, and put it away in the box where he kept his private documents.

Then he turned to me, making a trivial remark that the weather was unusually hot for autumn. His words were flat as stale water, and he looked old and very tired.

Fear crept into the room. Had the cat been stronger than I realized? Had it come back to attack him, while I slept in the false security of the soldier who is too vain to know that the enemy has only paused to summon fresh legions?

I went to kneel beside him. 'Aesculapius, did the cat come back?'

He drew his hand slowly across his forehead as though he were trying to clear his mind of a miasma. 'Cat...what cat?'

He spoke as a man may speak of something trivial when his thoughts are deeply preoccupied.

'The Cat of Bast...you watched me fight against her last night.'

'Forgive me,' he said wearily. 'I shall never forget the conflict. I had only forgotten the form in which you explained it to yourself.'

'So you don't believe me?' I had to ask the question, though it seemed already to have been answered with such terrible sincerity. I knew he meant to be kind; it was not his fault that to me his words were cold as iron nails driven into my hands.

'I have to believe you,' he said: and he sounded like a man accepting the sentence of slow death from a physician.

'Then how can you be unhappy? Please don't be unhappy...don't try to put a barrier between us; being set apart from you is the only thing which could break me.'

'If I lie to you there will always be a barrier. You are right: I am not strong enough to lie.'

He opened the box and took out the letter. Very slowly he untied the thread and smoothed out the scroll before he gave it to me. 'Read it, Lucina. And understand why I am afraid for us both.'

I recognized the writing; I had often seen it before, when the physician of Athens wrote for a fresh supply of the medicines we made for him.

'How did this reach us so soon?' I said.

'The horseman who brought it must have ridden like a centaur...I thought you would have heard his arrival. He left Athens soon after dawn, an hour after the woman's return: the first part of the letter was written yesterday.'

After the formal greeting, I read:

'It appears conclusive that this new evidence, so profoundly disturbing, cannot be ignored, even though it may destroy the value of the work we have so painfully accomplished. If we, the Realists, are forced to acknowledge the existence of malign forces beyond our normal control, then we have little hope of curing mankind, or ourselves, of the diseases of fear and superstition. I will enumerate the facts as they are known to me, hoping you may be able to provide some explanation which will not invalidate our established premise that the individual is the master of his destiny. I need not stress the urgency of the task, nor the horror of failure. I sent these cases to you in the confidence that they would serve to help you cure the girl Lucina of a persistent, but not unusual, series of phantasies. You and I cannot escape the results of this experiment: Truth cannot be denied, even if she appears to us in the role of the destroyer.

'The first woman was sent to me by a fellow physician of Cos. He had failed to cure her of asthma, with which she was so seriously afflicted that she was unable to carry out even the most trivial duties of her household. These attacks occurred whenever she heard rain. During a storm she became almost demented with terror and has on occasion seemed on the point of death by strangulation. She married at seventeen, but would never let her husband approach her, as she said that if she had a child it would die of suffocation. When questioned she could not explain this fear, but repeated that the child would die because ''she could not clear the mud from its nostrils.'' Careful research into her family background has failed to bring to light any incident of her early childhood which might have been at least a contributary cause. Rain fell heavily yesterday evening: she showed no distress and at her own suggestion went into the garden and walked with bare feet through the mud. When I asked her why she had lost her fear, she only said, ''I don't know: I have realized it was silly...I forgot that the mud cannot destroy the rock.'' She wishes to return to her husband, and says she is now eager to have a child. Her family overwhelm me with gratitude: and make me feel a charlatan. Shall I send you the gifts which I cannot in honesty accept, or give them to the poor?

'The second patient is one of the richest men of the State. He suffers from delusions of poverty, and in spite of every argument of logic is convinced he will die of starvation. I had told him that he might find release from his fears if he would give away half his possessions, considering that they were too heavy a responsibility for him to maintain. This suggestion he received with symptoms of extreme anger, and became so insulting that I refused to continue in my efforts to help him until he offered to treble his original fee. He left my house this morning; his attitude unchanged. He was in extreme anxiety to get home, as he believes that some one has tried to break into his treasure room. The most significant statement he made was that the treasure is in coin or gold dust; that it is kept in leather sacks, which each bear his seal in purple wax. Did Lucina see his gold as grain? Was the starving slave the mental image of the rich man's conception of his inevitable destiny? Can we in honesty accept any other explanation?

'The third man was my favourite pupil. So far as I can discover he is entirely free from any disease of mind or body. I sent him as a check, to discover whether Lucina would use any suitable catalyst to project her own interior conflicts into the objective field. She was not deceived.'

Here the writing changed: it slanted across the page, and there were several blots.

'The last case was an old beggar woman whom I took because my servants were afraid of her: she had the reputation of being possessed. The symbol of her terror is the cat; even a kitten would send her into a paroxysm akin to epilepsy. When she woke from the lethe she went to the kitchen and brought a cat to the room behind the stables where I allow her to shelter. I found her crooning to the animal as though it were a child. Already my household looks at me with a new respect. I am now endowed with the capacity to cast out daemons. I have not yet had the courage to inform them that their master is both ignorant, and a fraud who accepts honours to which he has no rightful claim. But what would have happened to Lucina if the cat had won? Would she have become possessed? I humbly charge you to use every means in your power to prevent her coming into contact with any one whose full sanity you have any reason to doubt. To do less would be deliberately to expose her to the most extreme peril for which we know no cure.'

The sense of failure and inferiority fell away from me. No longer could any one laugh at *my* reality: at last I belonged in my own right to Elysium.

'So we have won...oh, Aesculapius, we have won!'

'The victory is to the enemy.'

'But I don't understand. The physician tried to trick us, and he couldn't. How can you say the *enemy* had the victory?'

'Is it so easy for you to forget the great issues in a personal triumph, Lucina? You have shown that the marble is flawed in which I tried to carve an image by which men could honour their own integrity. Why should we rejoice that we have failed to free humanity from its slavery? Unless we can discount this evidence we must admit that instead of ruling our own lives we are no more than the fevered dreams of those who sleep bemused with nectar, or gorged with bloody sacrifice in Hades.'

'How can you say that, how can you feel that, when we have found a new *cure* for people in torment? Would you discard a beneficent drug because it could become a poison if unwisely used? We must not become cowards, Aesculapius, when we have to enter a new country which is still unknown.'

'There will never be a free world, Lucina, until it is composed of people who are free in themselves: a real democracy cannot be made from slaves. Every one is a slave unless he will recognize immediate personal responsibility for his character and his destiny.'

'Have I ever denied personal responsibility?'

'You no longer find it sufficient to feed your pride. You see yourself Olympian, playing god to mortals...and you are glad!'

'Yes, I am glad! Are you surprised? You have told me to accept ''I am; what I am.'' Why should I be ashamed because I have the courage to say also, ''I have seen; what I have seen''?'

'You will also find it comfortable to say, ''I have seen; I know!'' instead of listening to reason.'

'Did reason save the woman of Cos? Why should she fight for breath because philosophers and physicians find it convenient to deny everything which does not fit into their theories? Why should a woman live in terror of cats because none of you had the vision to challenge Bast?'

'Such a small taste of power, Lucina, has made you cruel. Have I done anything to justify your accusing me of being an escapist?'

'You are doing it now! The gods may not be mentioned in Elysium...but do you think they consider this rebuke? We are not allowed to use the word 'slave'; but are there fewer slaves in Greece, in Rome, in Macedonia? We have got to recognize the power of dark gods, malign powers; and learn to fight them. Fight, do you understand...not run away, not pretend that evil has no existence except in the imagination of the credulous!'

'So you want to be a new Pandora? Is there not enough misery in the world without your trying to add to it?'

'At least Pandora had the courage to open the box: if she had had more she might have discovered how to kill the evil which escaped from it.'

'Would courage have been enough? You are young and strong: the enemy, if it was an enemy and not the personification of some factor in your own nature, was defeated... but there are many enemies of sanity.'

'So you think I am going mad?'

'I think you are deliberately choosing a road which will lead you to destruction, of mind and body.'

'You have always said that each man chooses the road of his destiny! We shall find the end of my road for I shall follow where it leads. You won't be able to stop me: how can you, when you so often claim we are free to make our own decisions?'

'I shall keep you away from every one whom I consider may be a malign influence. I promised your mother to protect you: I shall fulfil that promise by every means in my power, even if it means I must estrange you.'

'You are not going to let me help you any more? You won't let me use this power which we both know exists?

Aesculapius, don't turn us both into escapists! If only you will accept me I will gladly give my life in your service....I will give everything.'

'I know, Lucina: you would give your peace of mind, even your sanity. At least I have the courage to accept neither sacrifice.'

'What do you expect me to do?'

'It is not difficult; and I plead with you to obey me.' He took my hand, holding it between his own, and his eyes were sorrowful. 'I am a proud man, Lucina: perhaps that is why I am so aware of the dangers of pride. But now I do not command obedience, I only implore you to listen.'

Was he really unhappy, or only being clever? He knew he could never make me change my mind by bullying, so was he deliberately using the unfair weapon of an appeal for sympathy?

'Even though you are only seventeen you are already a woman, Lucina; but you are still sufficiently immature to believe that you will always be content to merge your humanity into the service of some unknown power. But I knew your mother, loved your mother, failed your mother. I watched her caught between the two extremes of the pendulum, the virgin priestess and the pregnant woman. The conflict was too great: she died. And I, the philosopher who could not share her dreams of immortality, watched her die...and knew myself powerless to bring her comfort.'

Perhaps he was right: it might be a much greater happiness to marry Clion, to have children, to be content to be as other women. I had been afraid before the battle with Bast: with Clion to think for me I should never have to be afraid.

'Then I can marry Clion? You only said I wasn't ready to make a man happy because you were remembering that love had hurt you.'

'In a few years you can marry him, if you still want to marry. But only when I am sure you no longer want to escape from yourself into the role of the mystic or the mother.'

130

So I was still to be treated like an irresponsible child! I said bitterly, 'You haven't told me what I am to do during the next few years. And you seem to have forgotten that when one is young the years are never few.'

'Nothing will be changed. You will enter into discussions, help me compound remedies, arrange the flowers; all the things which occupy your normal routine. It will be easy to forget the last few days.' He took the letter which I had left on the table beside him. 'See how easy it is to destroy a memory.' He went to the brazier and I watched the closely written lines curl in the heat. He crumbled the ash between his fingers. 'The words have gone; the incident is forgotten.'

'Nothing is forgotten, Aesculapius. You cannot escape from memory: it is too strong, strong as life, stronger than love.'

'Nonsense, Lucina! We train ourselves to remember; we can make ourselves forget. You must ignore this unfortunate experience. You must forget your feeling for Clion, until such time as we may consider it appropriate.'

He looked confident and cheerful. He thought he had been clever enough to find a reasonable solution to the problem of Lucina. He smiled as I went out of the room. He found it easy to smile, because it was convenient to believe that I had ceased to love Clion since I had been told it was inexpedient. He thought I could be persuaded to forget that already two women were happier because I had not run away from reality.

I felt no pity for Aesculapius: for this he could blame his own teaching, which had trained me to be intolerant of those who are afraid to accept the truth. Now I would work with Clion, or alone: I would fight for Lucina's vision against the world.

CHAPTER THIRTEEN

Buried Roses

I had gone to the storeroom, with a message for Epicurus about a new consignment of hemp seed which had been ordered from Syria. He gave me a letter which Clion had sent to him: it said that he was returning by boat direct to Elysium instead of through Athens as he had intended. The letter had been delayed: I no longer had to count the days, he would be back to-night.

My thoughts were clear and decisive: listening to them was almost like being given detailed orders. I must see him alone; before Aesculapius can influence him. I must make him recognize that he loves me more than anything else. But I shan't have a chance against Aesculapius unless I can see him alone...before he talks to the others, before he returns to the habit of Elysium.

Without realizing what I was doing I tore the letter to shreds and threw them behind one of the bales. 'I won't tell any of them that Clion is due home to-day,' said Epicurus. 'You and Aesculapius are fighting over him, aren't you, Lucina?'

I had never been so fond of Epicurus as I was at that moment. He patted me on the shoulder, as he might have patted a favourite horse. 'Always remember that in any fight I am on your side,' he said. 'The others are troubled about the rights and the wrongs, but I am concerned with different values: to me a friend will always be right.'

'Thank you, so very much. You do believe in me, don't you?'

'I believe we share the same values, even though we see them in different terms. You want Clion: so I will help you to get him. And I will also help you to get rid of him when you ask me to.'

I stared at him, bewildered. 'Don't you think he will be happy with me? I am not a tyrant...really I'm not.'

'You don't need to tell *me* that...I'm not blind.'

'Then why did you say you would help me to get rid of him?'

'Lucina, your destiny is not my responsibility, except in so far as you ask me to share it. I am of little account in Elysium, but you would not find me entirely ignorant of the world. If you can make yourself small enough to be a contented wife...well, stay here, and forget the rest. But if things ever get too difficult, remember that I will try to help you. I have always hated to see a caged bird. Once, when I was still afraid of poverty, I opened a cage in which a rich man kept a nightingale that he hated because it would not sing for him. I hope I shall always have the courage to free the singing bird which must forget its voice in captivity.'

So Epicurus thought me a prisoner of Elysium. Poor Epicurus: I must always remember that he had been kind to me; Clion and I must find a way of sharing our happiness with him.

He seemed to know what I was thinking, for he said gently, 'May Apollo attend you...but if he is unkind, remember that we should not be escaping from reality if we left here.'

The words were kind, but fear was cold in my belly. I had never been into the world: I knew only the island, which now seemed so remote that I had almost forgotten Dictys and Elissa; and Elysium, where every one was obedient to Aesculapius. But Clion belonged here: Clion would never let me go into exile.

Narcissus must have guessed Clion was coming home, for he had put a new dress on the bed, a beautiful dress of fine linen with a violet hem. There were sandals of gilded leather, and a wreath of white roses beside the gold hairpins which were headed with carved amethysts. For the first time I understood how to Narcissus it seemed of supreme importance to blend two perfumes into a new subtlety, and why a ribbon must be tied again and again until it is knotted into the exact way which completes the rhythm for which it was created.

Dear Narcissus! If he had not taken so much trouble with me I should have been already on the quay watching the horizon for the sail that would bring Clion home to me. I should have let the wind tangle my hair, and though I would have had the sense to put on a fresh tunic, it would probably have got torn before the moment for which it had been intended.

Without the counsel of Narcissus I should still be the girl who was content to be only a rival. Clion would never have noticed me unless we shared the magic of a summer dusk; he would never have listened unless the nightingales had sounded sweeter than the sere autumn of philosophy. Narcissus should design a dress for my marriage, and at last I would reward him by looking as he had always hoped I might. They had all tried to educate me; but only to Narcissus would I prove a distinguished pupil!

I recognized the sail even when the boat was only a shard of silver against the grey sea. The evening wind plucked at the folds of my dress; the thin stuff streamed away from my body like a pennant. A strand of hair fell across my forehead; I tucked it under the wreath, and discovered that my hands were unsteady. I knew it would be sensible to wait in the pavilion until the boat was closer: but I could not make myself lose sight of it. Clion was in the boat, coming home to me by the power of the wind which could blow the cobwebs of expediency and fear away from my corner of Elysium.

Suddenly I wished I had arranged this meeting in a different way. Clion would know that I expected him: it would be difficult to appear casual, to wait until he was ready to tell me how long the days had been for him. Why was I not walking pensively up from the eastern beach; even Narcissus allowed that my hair flying free in the wind was not unbecoming. Or

I might have worn the robes of Artemis, and pretended that I had been rehearsing a play for Euripides. This dress would have been suitable for Athens, but here, by a deserted quay on a chill evening, it looked silly! Why had I not taken Narcissus into my confidence? He had put the dress ready for me, but thought I would wear it when we gathered in the loggia before the evening meal. Because I had again been too proud to ask for advice I had spoilt the effect I was so anxious to achieve. I could almost hear Narcissus saying, 'Will you never learn to let people help you?'

'Yes,' I answered aloud. 'If only I can have Clion I will let every one help me!'

Was there time to run back to the house to change? If I ran very hard would there be time? No, the boat was coming fast across the wind. I could see the brown patch on the sail, the patch which I had helped Clion to sew when we came back after a storm three months ago. It was after the storm, after we knew we were safe from the angry sea in the shelter of the headland, that he had kissed me. He had only kissed me twice; that night of the storm, and five days later, in the pavilion before he went to Delos.

I could see him now: he was steering the boat and the waves were white crescents against the hull. I wanted to run away; it would be too difficult to conceal how much his return meant to me. If I ran back to the house I could meet him with the others; I could ask casual questions about Delos, about his work there. It was indecent not to be able to conceal my feelings: much more naked and unarmed than any lack of clothes could ever make me. 'Being in love makes me very vulnerable: why do I wait here, proud of being in love instead of resenting anything which makes me admit I am weak?'

At least I had the courage to give an honest answer to myself. 'You welcome this weakness, because through it you will never be alone any more. You won't always have to fight for yourself. Clion will protect you: that is what being in love means, being protected, and yet not being ashamed to need it.'

I heard Clion shout my name above the sound of the waves. The gulf of sea was getting narrower. I saw him give the tiller to one of the sailors and crouch on the deck beside the mast. Then he leapt, slipped on the wet stone, recovered his balance.

His hands were warm on my shoulders. I thought he was going to kiss me. He said, 'Lucina; it is so very good to see you...Lucina.'

I talked very fast; silly, trivial questions about his journey, about the sea being rough for a small boat. He smiled down at me, and forgot to answer. Why should he use words without meaning when there was so much which must remain unsaid until we were alone?

He told the men to take the chests and bales up to the house. 'We need not wait for them,' he said. Then he looked down at his tunic which was stained with salt and torn at the shoulder. 'I must hurry to change into more suitable clothes. You look so beautiful, Lucina, that I feel like a barbarian!'

'It is early yet,' I said. 'The others are not expecting you: they will be disappointed if you arrive before they are ready to greet you.'

'Formality in Elysium? What have you all been doing since I went away?'

'Nothing important...nothing,' I said. 'I want you to be a surprise for them. Only Epicurus knows you are coming home to-night. He has arranged a feast, and you know how particular he is that everything should be exactly timed.'

'How is he? Still so absorbed in his tallies that he forgets to be human? How is Aesculapius; I have so much to tell him. Has Praxiteles made more statues; new Lucinas? Is there another play from Euripides? Will you act it for me?'

Need I be jealous that he was eager for news of the others, or was he asking only because he was nervous?

'I thought you might be thirsty; in such rough weather your mouth must be salt with spray, so I took some wine to the pavilion.' I wanted to say 'our pavilion' but found that I also was too shy to put my heart into words.

'Wine is even better than prawns,' he said. 'Do you remember the prawns, Lucina?'

'Of course I remember: and the sea-anemones in the rock pool, and you teaching me to swim, and hearing Agamemnon...'

'Yes, Agamemnon,' he said slowly. And I could have pulled out a hank of my hair to punish myself for reminding him of sorrow.

I thought he would kiss me when we reached the pavilion: but instead he poured wine with a steady hand.

'The wine of Elysium is better than the greatest vintage drunk anywhere else,' he said. 'It is very good to be home again.'

Of course it was better wine than he had drunk in Delos! I had asked Epicurus to open one of the small amphorae which had been sent as a thank-offering from an Egyptian noble whom Aesculapius had cured many years ago.

'So nothing important has happened since I have been away,' he said. 'Are you sure, Lucina? I have had letters from Aesculapius and he seems troubled—about you.'

It was useless to try to hide anything from Clion: when he discovered the facts he might reproach me for not preparing him. There must be no concealment, no evasions between us. If I lied, even such a small lie as is made by not revealing the whole truth, it would be turned against me. He loved me because I was honest: should I throw away my honesty because I was trying to be clever in the manner of Narcissus?

'Clion,' I said, 'I thought I could pretend that nothing had changed since you went to Delos...but nothing is the same. What happened with Agamemnon could be hidden away and forgotten: but this can't be forgotten.'

And then I told him everything concerning the physician of

Athens. I had been carefully trained to record the details of a story, so I gave him the letter almost as though I held it in my hand and was reading it aloud...I could almost see the blots on the last side where the writing slanted across the page. I was right; memory cannot be wiped out by a smear of black ash crushed between the fingers of an old man who is trying to cling to his belief.

He listened with a terrible intensity: making me repeat any phrase whose import was in doubt, insisting on exact detail...even the fact that my nose had bled during the fight with Bast, which I had not intended to mention. But he did not ask what Aesculapius had said after he had received the letter: and I did not tell him.

'Lucina,' he said. 'Lucina: I could never have believed that I should ever be in conflict with Aesculapius, who is to me much more than any father could be to his son. But I will take you away from Elysium rather than let you be exposed to such danger. If he will not swear to protect you from any further contact with this corroding evil I will have to tell him that I am no longer his son. How can he refuse to see the danger; how can he betray everything he represents to us? He stands as the image of reason; and now he is prepared to destroy it all because of his lust for knowledge!'

'But the two women...they are happier because of me! They were so terribly afraid and now they are free! You wouldn't want us to betray them because we were cowards who could not dare an enemy who until now has ravaged people because he goes disguised?'

'There are thousand, perhaps ten thousand, who cringe before the altars of the gods, for every one who suffers from asthma, or is obsessed by cats! If Aesculapius has forgotten the many in a futile defence of the few he has betrayed his own teaching.'

'Aesculapius is growing old,' I said desperately. 'He has forgotten what it is to be young. He discounts the power of being in love; he thinks it an emotion that can be sterilized with dry, irrelevant words. He is trying to escape from life, from everything for which we honour him.'

'Lucina,' and his voice was stern, 'in spite of loyalty to Aesculapius you must tell me the truth. Is he trying to make you enter more ordeals in which your sanity is at stake? Has he become fanatical, or is there still a chance that I can make him listen to reason? If not...'

The silence was so long that I had to break it. 'If not?'

'Then I shall take you away from here; to-night. I welcomed you to Elysium because I believed it was the home of free people, where you would be safe, and happy. If you are in danger from which I cannot defend you, the least I can do in honour is to help you escape.'

I longed to lie: now that I knew he agreed with Aesculapius I had so little chance of being stronger than them both. But if I ran away with him to-night I should be free; I could be an ordinary woman, a happy woman, the woman who belonged to Clion. But he might take me to a place of safety and then come back to try to save Aesculapius from a danger which existed only in my mind. He would discover that I had lied; and Clion would hate me if I had lied to him, even though the lie was the last defence of our security.

'Aesculapius has forbidden me to use this faculty. He wants to pretend that the experiment never took place. He burned the letter; he believes that I have forgotten the proof it gave to me.'

At once the frown smoothed from his forehead; 'I am a fool, and a traitor,' he said, but the tone of his voice showed relief, not shame. 'I thought that Aesculapius had betrayed us all. Never tell him, Lucina, that I was so unworthy.'

There was only one throw of the dice left to me: I took it.

'He says that being in love is a weakness. He says that it is only another form of escape; an attempt to see oneself through the eyes of a lover because one lacks the courage to look into one's own heart. He says that lovers are cowards. He says I am only seventeen...'

'I don't think that the lover need be the coward. But that is not a problem for you yet, Lucina. Perhaps it will never be a problem...you have a full life in Elysium; we have work to do. You are going to be the first woman philosopher. Surely that is more important than being a woman in love?'

'Is it?' I said. And I hoped my voice sounded as though I were asking an ordinary question.

'Yes: to you it will always be more important. I have never been in love, but I have seen the malaise afflict others. In love: in hate; two sides of the same coin. Both of them are a snare which makes the afflicted feel that they are wiser, stronger than they have ever been before. They give up their own power because they think it can be given to them by the lover, without effort. They demand strength instead of seeking it from the core of their being. When they find that strength cannot be demanded from outside, they fall out of love into hate. That is why the priest is always a virgin, Lucina: not because virginity confers any special faculty of the spirit, but it is the symbol of energy conserved to a higher purpose. If you took a lover without love, you would betray yourself; if you took him in love you would deny your destiny. Philosophy endures though lovers have turned to dust.'

'So you don't expect to marry? You believe you will never fall in love?'

'Do you expect to marry?'

'No,' I said, 'I expect to be only Lucina.'

I was very gay at the feast which welcomed Clion home to Elysium, but I think Narcissus knew why I wore the gold headdress which had belonged to my mother. The wreath of white roses was buried in the olive garden beyond the pavilion.

When the sky showed grey through the wind I gave up trying to sleep. Euripides had taught me to act, now I should have to act all the time, the role of the Lucina who was not in love with Clion, who need not be pitied because she had been weak. If they saw me look at him they would know what I really felt; if I were afraid to look at him this might be even more revealing. How could I act all the time; day after day, month after month? It was my own fault, or so Aesculapius believed. If I could have blamed Apollo it might have helped; but if Apollo really existed he would have listened to me yesterday. I should have to work with Clion, eat with Clion, laugh with Clion...and lie every time I spoke because I could never say 'I love you,' which was the only truth I could give to him.

I put on an old tunic and took a woollen cloak from the chest. If I got out of this room which I had peopled with thoughts of Clion I might find it easier to prepare to meet him again. Rain had fallen heavily during the night; the trees were still weeping and the grass forlorn as the pillow of a girl who dare not sleep. If I swam, far out into the chill autumn sea, I might feel better.

I stood on the diving-rock; the rock on which the child Lucina had seen Clion as a gold statue against the blue sky of early spring. That child had also wept, for a lost island; but now there was no Clion to turn her tears to laughter. This sky was grey and sullen; it believed, as I did, that the clouds were too heavy to be driven away by a new wind. Below me the sea surged up to challenge the long endurance of the beach. It was dangerous to dive, even into deep water, when the waves were so high. Was Lucina afraid of the sea as well as afraid of love? Had she become a coward because she had lost everything. 'Everything,' the gulls screamed, 'You have lost everything...everything.' The gulls were mocking me, and humans can be more cruel than sea-birds.

I pressed the palms of my hands together for the dive; the spray was cold as grief. I felt some one grasp me round the waist and pull me back.

'It is too rough to swim.' Epicurus was out of breath as though he had been running. 'I came to join you...I saw you go out of the house. But the sea is too rough for us...yet.'

'Yes, the sea is rough,' I said. 'I am sorry I was too silly to recognize I couldn't swim against the current.'

He linked his arm through mine and led me back to the shelf rock where I had thrown my clothes. 'The sea is never too rough if the pilot is sure of his course,' he said. 'You need a pilot; I thought you would, so I have studied the charts of the future.'

I began to cry again; I had been prepared for mockery but not for this gentle understanding. His arm round my shoulder was strong and kind. He could feel that I was sobbing but I didn't mind; I had once seen Epicurus cry and he hadn't hated me for it...so it was safe to be grateful to him.

'You think everything is finished for you, but it is only beginning. In Elysium you would never have been able to use your talent, Lucina. This sanctuary is too small for real people: only wide enough for philosophers, and those who are content to be their echo.'

'Am I a real person? Am I anything?'

He laughed. 'Is a gull less real than a hen, because it needs a wide sky instead of being content to scratch for food in a midden?'

'The gulls mocked me; they said I was a coward who dared not accept the challenge of the sea.'

'Or did they only mock at Lucina's idea of herself: the girl who was going to let life be too strong for her because she had chosen to forget her strength?'

'Is there any other Lucina?'

'If you have forgotten her I shall try to make you remember...but I am not going to talk against this wind. You are coming back to the house; to put on dry clothes and then meet me in the storeroom, which can provide us with privacy and good wine.'

He sounded brisk and wonderfully ordinary. 'You won't tell the others I have been such a fool?' I said.

'If you dare to think so I shall tell you to stop behaving

142

like a naughty child...and then treat you as one, with a hard slap!'

'Dear Epicurus,' I said. 'Oh, *dear* Epicurus!'

'We are together in this,' he sounded vehement. 'I told you that I should never interfere unless I was sure my destiny was woven with your own. We shall never find our real strength until we have gone out to fight against life; we are not ready to accept, to contemplate, to be old. I came here because I was tired of fighting alone...but together we shall conquer.'

I looked at him as though I were seeing him for the first time; the heavy eyebrows, the black, resolute hair which grew in a straight line above the broad forehead; the grey, very direct, eyes; the square, solid body. He had none of the lithe beauty of Clion, but there was strength in every line of him: and now I needed strength above all things. And he was lonely, as I had always been lonely.

'We accept our nature,' I said. 'And we are both fighters, so we will fight together against the world.'

Epicurus had brought a brazier into the storeroom; we sat in its genial warmth, wine cups in our hands, a bale of wool to lean against.

'We will go to Rome,' he said. 'For a long time I have planned to leave Greece; I prefer not to profit by the stupidity of my countrymen. The Romans owe us everything of real value which their embryonic civilization has acquired, the debt can be paid, in part, to us; to Epicurus the merchant, and to Lucina the priest-philosopher, whom they will honour, and fear.'

'I don't want people to fear me, not even barbarians.'

'You must not be squeamish, Lucina. The world fears Rome; it may give Romans a modicum of humanity if they discover they are not invincible. Do you think any intelligent Greek enjoys being patronized by the robust young neighbour who allows us to believe this lull between wars will endure long enough for our culture to make another war impossible? We are playing the role of the docile wife who is permitted to continue in her female occupations so long as she admires the husband who gives her the security of his household.

'The Romans are excellent soldiers: they have a lust for discipline, they abnegate their personal lives for the life of the State. But they cannot fundamentally deny their right as individuals; and this makes them vulnerable to the desire for personal possessions, especially for any object which they believe to be unique. It will also make them abjectly eager for wisdom which can help them to endure their inner conflicts—which their method of living imposes on the senator as much as on the slave. We shall not need to employ extortion, as Romans do when they demand taxes from a subject people: they will be eager to barter with me for goods, which they think will endow them with a culture they do not merit; they will be even more willing to allow you to show them the source of their fears.'

'So you believe I am a tyrant?'

'No, Lucina. I believed you would be forced to dominate any environment which is not adequate to your capacity. But Rome is not an insignificant estate; already some speak of it as the centre of the world.'

'When do we go to Rome?'

'Soon. There are certain matters to which I must attend before we leave. I already have a small sum of money; Aesculapius has allowed me to take a just proportion of every transaction I have made in his name. I need more: and I have decided how this can be obtained.'

Something in the sudden hardening of the muscles of his jaw made me say, 'You are not going to steal it?'

'No; I am not going to steal. I have only learned that sentimentality is a luxury not permitted to the man who has decided to live by his own standards.'

144

PART TWO

CHAPTER ONE

East Wind

A tangle of masts made a restless pattern against the rising moon: behind me the lights of Athens starred the hills. Which mast belonged to the ship that would take us to Rome? Would I know to-night, or have to conceal my impatience until Epicurus considered he had made a favourable bargain with a shipmaster?

I saw him coming along the quay, threading his way between bales of merchandise, oil jars, disconsolate pack-donkeys.

'We sail at dawn,' he said. 'There is only one cabin: in any case one cabin is cheaper, though I could sleep on deck if you prefer it.'

'Of course not, why should you?'

He looked offended, which was odd as he was usually pleased if I showed a sense of the value of money.

The ship was larger than I had expected, and the sailors seemed friendly enough. Epicurus insisted on having our three chests in the cabin with us which left only enough room for the straw pallet. The blankets were grey with dirt and I saw several cockroaches.

'You had better get some sleep before we sail,' he said. 'It's going to be rough to-morrow, but the wind is in the east, which should be a good omen.'

He gave me three of the blankets and kept one for himself. He seemed to find it easy to ignore the rats which squealed above the creak of cordage, for he fell asleep very quickly. Cargo was still being loaded; people tramped across the deck above my head and heavy thuds told me when another bale was thrown into the hold which was separated from us only by a thin partition.

It was a relief when I knew we had cast off. I no longer had to wonder what I should do if Clion joined us and implored, or even commanded, me to go back to Elysium. Had Epicurus guessed why I had agreed to leave at night without saying good-bye to any one, or did he think me indifferent?

He was still asleep when I went on deck. The steersman stared at me, but did not return my greeting. Two sailors were trimming the sail and a third was coiling a rope. The hills were coming up from the mist, and I saw a small boat whose course would soon cross ours. I watched it idly, until I suddenly recognized the pattern of the sail. It belonged to Elysium, the boat Clion always preferred.

Now I should have a chance to use all the phrases I had so carefully rehearsed. I should be able to show him that it is not pleasant to learn that a woman can be as scornful of love as a man. Or should I weaken and allow myself to be persuaded to go back? Or worse, could I avoid showing how easy it would be to behave like a penitent child?

The steersman heard the hail and brought the ship into the wind. I saw a rope flung to the boat as it came alongside. The man who leapt to our deck was not Clion: it was only Narcissus.

If he realized I was disappointed he concealed it admirably. 'I hope you enjoy a rough sea better than I do,' he said amiably. 'If Poseidon is growing deaf he should appoint an efficient nereid to perform his duties. I asked for a suitable wind and he sent us a gale—*most* careless, though less embarrassing than if we had been becalmed.'

He turned to shout directions to the sailor who was hauling on board the chests he had brought with him. There were seven chests, and I recognized one as having belonged to my mother.

'Even when surprised, Lucina, you must learn to conceal it. The mouth half-open is disastrously unbecoming.'

I shut it so quickly that I nearly bit my tongue. 'How did you get here?'

'Never underrate the intelligence of your friends, or your enemies,' he said briskly. 'When I saw you coming back from the olive grove I took the trouble to search for a sign of disturbed earth. It was considerate of you to bury the white roses where we discovered Agamemnon's body. I thought it probable that your pride would not allow you to waste your time on sighs for Clion, who, to any one who has the wit to see him as he is, cannot be considered at all remarkable. Therefore you would decide to leave Elysium, for Aesculapius had already denied you an alternative outlet for your talents. Who would you go with? Epicurus: this would have been obvious to me even if you had not been so considerate as to make your detailed plans in the storeroom. The storeroom window is concealed by shrubs which provided me with an adequate though uncomfortable vantage-point. I am not ungrateful,' he added magnanimously, 'for if you had been more skilled in conspiracy I should have had to follow you to Athens instead of taking this easier method of interception.'

'But we are going to Rome! We shall probably starve....I don't think we have very much money. It won't be nearly so comfortable as staying in Elysium!'

'I have every confidence in the practical ability of Epicurus to provide us with tolerable comfort. He knows nothing whatever about women, but I can supply this deficiency in our plans. I have spent four years training you to use the weapons natural to the female; I shall now collaborate with Epicurus in taking tribute for Lucina from Rome.'

'Do any of the others know where I am?'

'Aesculapius knew you had decided to go. I think he expected you to give him the chance to tell you himself that he wishes you every success in your venture, and that you will always be welcome if you decide to return to Elysium. He sent a letter to Epicurus, containing a list of names, men of affairs who may be influential if we need help.'

So every one knew I was going! They were glad to get rid of me! They thought I should come crawling back to ask for shelter! How long would it take me to prove to them all that they knew nothing about Lucina?

It was difficult to see myself as the woman to whom Rome must pay tribute, for the voyage was increasingly squalid. Narcissus groaned in the cabin, imploring Poseidon to let him die. Epicurus played dice with the sailors and lost more than he would admit. For three days I found a temporary escape from a horrible sense of inadequacy by looking after a sailor who had crushed his hand. I set two of his fingers, and stitched up the torn flesh with a needle and thread which Narcissus had brought with him.

We entered the Tiber on a winter afternoon. Narcissus, cheerful though still pallid, stood with me in the prow. I watched a dead donkey float past on the yellow water, legs protruding from the carcase, a hideous parody of a wine-skin. Gulls were screaming above a mat of refuse, the tribute of a city's spew clutched in their claws. I shivered, but not only with the cold which drove down on us from the seven hills.

'You don't like the city you have come to conquer?' said Narcissus.

'Even snow would be dirty here: even a proud ship would rot if it stayed in this river.'

Epicurus joined us.

'Lucina has determined to despair,' said Narcissus. He put his arm through mine. 'My dear Lucina, you are seeing Rome at a disadvantage; how fortunate that we should have surprised her when she was unprepared. We need never fear a woman who cannot demand homage; we see Rome with her hair in curling-rags, wallowing in a dirty bath, a slut to her finger-tips! Even the weather has conspired against her; no suitor retains his ardour if the room in which he waits the presence is too cold for desire to flourish.'

I laughed, for the wind-driven sleet could no longer

threaten us. Narcissus was clever; he had stripped Rome of her power, he had made us see her through an unguarded window. Epicurus joined in the game, 'Even the hero cannot impress the slave who watches him wake blurred after a banquet, cursing Mars because his armour pinches a belly swollen with wind!'

Our small ship no longer seemed insignificant among the Quinqueremes, the trading barges, the pleasure boats of Roman nobles. We had come secretly, because our strength did not require the bombast of heralds. Greece was older than Rome, and much more subtle.

The shipmaster, to whom Epicurus had paid an extra stater, told us the name of a tavern where we could lodge until we found more suitable accommodation. It was in a narrow street which led from the quays; both Epicurus and Narcissus apologized for the squalor, so I could tell them that to me it was exciting. I had never been closer to a wine-shop than a glimpse through a lighted doorway, for Epicurus had hurried me past the taverns on our way through Athens, as once Elissa had hurried a child who made another journey by night.

Narcissus had all our belongings brought up to the larger of the two rooms, which he was sharing with Epicurus. My room opened out of it; there was a pallet bed, a stool, and a bucket of water in which floated wisps of dirty straw. A female, with one eye closed by a livid bruise, brought me a brazier, but seemed too stupid to understand my Latin. I combed my hair and put on a robe of dark-red wool. My hands were gritty with dust which I had tried to sweep from the floor before I took off my shoes, but the water was too unpleasant for me to wash. My opinion of the ability of Epicurus began to diminish rapidly: surely he would have made more effort to look after me?

Narcissus saw that I was disgruntled. 'Lucina is missing the cockroaches, the stench of bilge and dying sheep,' he said. 'Her ancestors must have been sailors; we must pur-

149

chase a pleasure barge for her so that she can take her ease on this salubrious river.'

'There are sufficient cockroaches here, and a stench which must be unrivalled even in the Augean stables. Perhaps one of you would like to play Hercules and clean my room before I try to sleep there!'

'We shall find a better place to-morrow,' said Epicurus defensively. 'I deliberately asked for an obscure tavern. Until we have found a suitable background it is wiser to avoid places where we might meet people of importance.'

'He is right, Lucina: we must not lose sight of the main plan in the temporary inconvenience of reconnoitering our objective. However, there is no reason why we should eat here, if you will deign to walk through the streets until we can provide a carrying-litter.'

By the time we had found a tavern, in a wide street that led out of a large, well-paved square, I had regained my temper. The main room was crowded with plebeians, whom I judged to be chiefly shopkeepers or mercenaries. There were not many women, so when the innkeeper showed us to a table set apart from the rest, most of the men turned to look at me. The food was good, or perhaps a sea voyage had made us appreciative of anything except millet porridge and salt fish. We had pasta, with a thick meat sauce strongly flavoured with garlic, followed by small fish stuffed with herbs and fried in oil.

Epicurus left us before the end of the meal, saying that he would meet us later and that Narcissus could take me home. 'Home' used to mean Elysium; now it was a dirty room in a foreign city.

'Have some more wine, Lucina. If you continue to look so miserable I shall begin to wish I had stayed in Greece. A gloomy woman finds few suitors in any country!'

I felt contrite: they had brought me here because I wanted to run away, and now I was being disgustingly selfish. I made a determined effort to be cheerful, and found it much easier than I expected. It was amusing to see so many strangers, to invent stories about them, to hear Narcissus laugh because I had thought of a remark to amuse him.

A soldier came through the doorway with a woman hanging on his arm. She wore brightly coloured clothes and a necklace of heavy silver links studded with turquoise. I thought she might be a patrician until I noticed that her nails were ingrained with dirt, her face taut and anxious under the paint.

'He is a decurion in one of the foreign legions,' said Narcissus. 'You can recognize them by the colour of the plume in the helmet. You will notice that the innkeeper treats him with respect. If he didn't, this place would be wrecked by soldiers, sent here by the decurion of course, though nothing could be proved if a claim for damages was made.'

'Is the woman his wife?'

'No Roman would bring his wife to a place like this. You had better take your fill of these surrounding, for we shan't be able to bring you here, or anywhere like it, again.'

The expression in the woman's eyes as she looked at the decurion gave me a warm sympathy for her. Why did I feel she was the only person here who had a claim on my affection? She was in love with him; blindly, agonisingly in love, and trying to conceal it so that she would be able to be gay and hard, as he expected. Perhaps she knew how little she meant to him; or was he going away, to a foreign country where he would soon forget she had ever sat with him among a crowd, which for her had no existence?

Her hair was a brilliant yellow, and the dark roots betrayed the dye. Only her eyes were really young; blue eyes with long lashes. The structure of her face would have pleased Praxiteles, who had often told me that no woman need fear age who has beauty deep in her bones.

She leant forward, speaking urgently, and put her hand on the man's arm. He shook her off, and she began to cry. The tears made streaks in the paint. He spoke to her in a low voice. I could not hear the words, only the tone which told me he was querulously angry. It pleased him to be desired; it embarrassed him to be seen in the company of a weeping woman.

Discretion suddenly seemed supremely unimportant. I got up from the table and walked across the crowded room. Every one stopped talking to stare at me. In the abrupt silence I heard my voice, a gay, trivial voice which Euripides had taught me to use for certain roles.

'How delightful and surprising to see you here! Last time we met was in Athens, at a banquet for the winners of the Games. I agree with you that one never really knows a foreign city until one has been to the taverns to watch the plebians. So quaint, so remarkable to learn that they are also hungry and require to be amused.'

The decurion, who had been leaning on the table, got quickly to his feet, his sword clattering against the bronze greaves.

'Perhaps your friend would like to join us?' he said; then added under his breath, which stank of wine, 'Why didn't you tell me you had been to Athens?'

The woman looked at me intently, and said, 'I thought that she might have forgotten *Helena*...it is three years since we met.'

'*Lucina* could never forget Helena,' I said. 'My dear, Narcissus will be delighted to see you again; he has talked of you so much that if I were not a docile wife I should have been abjectly jealous!'

The decurion stooped to pick up his helmet, and lurched against the table, nearly overturning it. Good; he was already in wine, which made him an opponent more than half disarmed.

The woman stared at me. Plainly as though she had spoken aloud her eyes said, 'Why are you doing this for me?'

I smiled to her: 'Because I am also a woman, and we must

join together against the men who make a mock of us.'

Narcissus had come quietly up behind me and overheard most of the exchange. He could not have played his role better if Euripides had rehearsed us. He not only accepted me as his wife, but endowed us with three children, the eldest a son of eight who seemed to be appallingly precocious. He invented a family, richly studded with illustrious names, aunts, cousins, even a grandfather who had been a general and an uncle whose oratory had been the pride of Athens. Helena became the third daughter of my youngest uncle, who had married a patrician of a small town in a southern provice of Rome; a marriage which the Family (by the time Narcissus had finished with the 'family' it deserved deep carving in marble rather than the small nobility of a mere capital letter) had considered a deplorable clot in the stream of noble blood.

We plied the decurion with the best wine the tavern could offer. If Epicurus complained that we had thoughtlessly squandered our resources he could blame his own lack of consideration in leaving us to pass what had promised to be an uneventful evening.

I learned that the man's name was Aulus, and that he expected to be transferred to one of the northern outposts in the immediate future. I thought it best to assume that he had been trying to persuade Helena to accompany him, and that marriage was the least he could offer to a woman who was so much better born than himself.

'Helena,' I said, as though reluctant to introduce a chill note of reality into a friendly conversation. 'I know how difficult it is to be worldly when one is young and in love. But have you considered how difficult it will be for you to live in the small circle which is all that can be permitted to the wife of a decurion?' I stared pointedly at his helmet, 'And only a decurion of a *foreign* legion? I don't want to stress the gulf which divides you socially...but...'

No fish had ever risen with such alacrity. He began to protest that as a soldier and a citizen of Rome he had no cause to fear any one. He even enumerated the tribute he had managed to exact by reason of his office. It was easy to see that to her this represented extraordinary wealth. To me it made little sense, for I had not yet learned the currency in which he boasted.

He lurched uncertainly to his feet and raised his winecup in a toast, 'I drink to Helena; and to her friends! I am only a decurion but I shall soon win promotion.' The 'only' affected him so profoundly that I thought he was going to indulge in maudlin tears. 'I am only a decurion, but I will not betray my wife...if Helena will consent to be the wife of such an obscure man as myself.'

He swayed, clutching at the table for support. 'Will you be my wife, Helena?'

'Yes,' she said, 'I will be your...wife.'

His voice was thick as felted wool, but he said, almost as though he were giving a battle order, 'You will have to marry me to-night...to-night, do you understand? If you are going to marry a common soldier you mustn't expect him to be sneered at by your rich, relations...you marry me to-night or I go away...I'm not going to be any one's fool!'

She took his hand and drew him down on the bench beside her, 'I will marry you to-night. Nobody shall have the chance to spoil things for us.'

He was so moved by this token of patrician generosity that he wept, a sign that we could leave them together to find their happiness, such as it was.

The woman came to the door with me. 'I shall never forget Lucina,' she said. 'I will make him a good wife. I love him, and I thought I was never going to see him again.'

I took the four gold staters which Epicurus had given Narcissus to look after and slipped them into her hand. 'Will you buy yourself a wedding gift from your cousins?'

'Thank you,' she said. 'I can only say—thank you!'

Epicurus was waiting for us outside our inn. 'You are late,' he said abruptly. 'I got back nearly an hour ago. I have found a suitable villa into which we can move to-morrow.' Then, as we did not appear suitably excited, he added, 'I am afraid you have had a very boring evening.'

'Not boring,' said Narcissus fervently, 'An evening with Lucina is never likely to be dull. No doubt in time we shall wish that it could be! Expensive, exhausting, a serious strain on the wits...but never, I assure you, drab or commonplace!'

'It can't have been expensive,' objected Epicurus. 'I asked the prices before I left, and they were exceedingly moderate.'

'Never be over-confident that Lucina will be restrained by the modesty of a tariff, and then perhaps you will spare your-self the need of recasting your tallies.'

Narcissus was laughing as he climbed the ladder which led to our rooms; so I laughed with him, instead of waiting to explain that I had enjoyed playing Apollo...even though I could not play the role for Lucina.

I was wakened next morning by the sound of excited con-versation coming up through the floor of worm-eaten boards. I leant out of the small window, and saw three litters, each with two bearers, in the street below. They obviously be-longed to a patrician, and my surprise at seeing them in such a poor part of the city was obviously shared by a crowd of urchins.

Epicurus came past the ragged curtain which divided their room from mine. 'You had better hurry, Lucina. The litters are waiting for us.'

'For *us*?'

'I told you last night that I had obtained a suitable villa. You and Narcissus were too occupied with your exploit to in-quire what I had been doing on your behalf.'

'I'm sorry,' I said contritely, 'it was horrid of me. I didn't mean to be unkind and I am very grateful for every-thing.'

His face softened, 'It was stupid of me to be offended. I

155

thought you were going to be excited, so when you seemed indifferent I sulked!'

'But of course I'm excited! How did you get the litters? How did you manage everything so quickly?'

'I went to see a merchant I used to know in Athens. He told me that a certain patrician had recently been banished to the provinces, a matter of unpaid gambling debts. I have purchased the right to live in his villa, with all the amenities including six slaves, for a year. Within a year we should be in a position to make permanent arrangement.'

'But you said we should have to live very quietly at first. You suggested we might find lodgings with a merchant. How can we afford to start with a house and slaves of our own?'

He hesitated, and then said abruptly, 'I decided that the plan required modification. It was agreed that the arrangements should be left to me, and you can question the details when I prove myself inadequate.'

He went out of the room, obviously to avoid further conversation. I heard him go down the ladder and speak to Narcissus. How had he managed to pay for a house and slaves, pay for a year?

I slipped into the other room. None of the chests were missing. I lifted the small leather sack in which our money was kept. It was apparently no lighter than it had been after he lost so much at dice. So he had not paid in coin. The chests were still corded, so he had not sold any of the things we had brought with us. Yet surely something was missing? Then I realized it was a small package, wrapped in cloth and heavily sealed, which Epicurus guarded with more care even than the money. I had asked him what it contained but he had always avoided the question. It had been very heavy: gold is heavy. But it was not coin, for I had felt it. What did Epicurus have which was made of gold and yet could not be shown even to me? It was puzzling, but I decided to be less inquisitive until a more propitious moment.

The inn-keeper bowed so low that I thought he was going to fall on his face. The slattern, who had refused to bring me clean washing-water the night before, was servile, her single eye rapacious as she counted the bronze coins which Epicurus had dropped in her dirty hand. I learned something important about Rome. People were not judged by their character, not even by their behaviour, but by their power to command money or slaves.

We travelled smoothly through the wide streets. I saw many litters with curtains more richly decorated than our own. A cohort of soldiers marched with a blare of sunlight on polished helmets. A chariot overtook us, and the people who thronged the square scattered to avoid the horse. A pack-donkey brayed in fear; tried to escape into a narrow alley, slipped on the cobbles and fell. One of the packs burst open; a shower of trinkets rolled into a gutter choked with refuse. The donkey-boy tried to gather them up, cursing the urchins who fought each other for this unexpected prey. The donkey screamed with the pain of its broken leg. No one paid any attention.

I learned something more of the Romans: they were indifferent to pain if it did not directly concern them. I would not forget the donkey. Rome should pay in its own coin for any agony they considered trivial, but which made me want to retch.

The buildings might have impressed a stranger who had not the wit to look at the faces of the people. Both were too gross, too concerned with the symbols of material power. Even the pediments were like heavy eyebrows which tried to conceal a defect of vision. The columns were strong, but with the strength of the gladiator rather than the suppleness of the athlete. Aesculapius had told me that a victory won through fear is only a defeat. But the Romans had declared the weapons of their challenge. If they wished to use Coin and Fear I might have to accept their terms; and win because I was strong enough not to be bound by their symbols.

Our villa was on one of the hills overlooking the main city. We entered through a courtyard flanked by the servants' quarters and the stables. A pair of massive doors led into the main hall, higher than the rest of the house and lit by clerestory windows. To the right were four bedrooms, comfortable but ornate; to the left a large living-room, with three arches opening on a terrace. Part of the terrace was covered by a pergola. In summer it would be pleasantly shaded by vines, which now were black, twisted shapes that still held a few withered grapes. Two opulent females in white marble stared bleakly at each other across a shallow flight of steps that led down to a small formal garden. The beds were freshly dug; the rose bushes still displayed a few wizened flowers, a clematis tried to retain the memory of purple in the white beards of ancients. In a pool slimy with rotting lily-leaves, a robust nereid supported a conch shell. There are few things more dead than a silent fountain.

CHAPTER TWO

temple of the tiber

A plume of water freshened the sultry afternoon. I lay on blue and violet cushions, considering the pattern made by vine-tendrils against beams of the pergola and the heat-heavy sky. I had to pretend an indolence I could not feel, to stop myself worrying about our insecurity. After six months in the villa we could still maintain an outward show of luxury, but even Tiro, our steward, must have begun to realize that our debts were unpaid because we had so little money left.

'Tribute for Lucina from Rome,' had been easy enough to say, easy enough for me to believe until I was defeated by its translation into actuality. Gradually I discovered, after I had watched their increasing anxiety and found myself powerless to effect a cure, what Narcissus and Epicurus had expected of me. I was to have been the main pillar of our security; the beautiful, mystical Greek, neither virgin-priestess nor hetaera but a subtle blend of both without the obligations, who was to become the envy of the circle to whom the letter of Aesculapius gave us entry. My insight into the Roman character was to have made my opinion, my taste, a criterion of culture. This is the scene as we imagined it: a banquet, Lucina the focus of attention, the envy of the women because she had proved herself more than the equal of the men. Lucina brilliant and remote; inviolate only because she was too subtle to be beguiled by Roman flattery. Then Narcissus, with feigned reluctance, would allow himself to be persuaded to design clothes and jewels for matrons who found themselves jealous of Lucina. Epicurus would be the link with the merchants, taking for us a substantial profit.

To this end we permitted ourselves a limited extravagance: I had certain essential jewels, Narcissus bought a chariot with two black stallions; Epicurus paid several merchants to keep selected antiques until we would require them.

But Lucina had failed in her role. The men we met gave me the attention due to any woman whose appearance is not entirely displeasing, yet when I tried to talk of serious matters they failed to conceal their boredom. The women, finding that I was at a disadvantage when they gossiped about people of whom I had never heard, pitied me for a foreigner who had failed to find a husband. I even had to pretend that Narcissus was my brother, to prevent myself being snubbed by women I despised—plump, indolent, *stupid* women!

It was not made easier when Narcissus frequently became impatient. 'Lucina, I have provided you with the right clothes, and nature gave you eyelashes—and a profile which would distinguish a coinage. But what do you do! How do you expect to please when you make no effort to conceal that the company in which you find yourself is, in your opinion, appallingly inferior? Why don't you treat them like children, flatter them, praise them a little...and then at least we shall never lack free meals!'

There was nothing practical I could do to help. I suggested going to market to get cheaper food, but Epicurus said that this would soon become slaves' gossip and destroy our credit. There was no point in doing the cooking, for old Porcia did it far better. I could have dug in the garden, but why should I, when the gardener could easily manage our small plot of ground? I wore my new bracelets, knowing they might have to be sold to pay a shipmaster to take us back to Greece, when we could no longer afford our pride.

I heard some one cross the terrace, looked up to see Tiro, and called to him to bring me a pitcher of fruit-juice. It was not sufficiently chilled, and I envied the women who had enough slaves to bring snow down from the mountains. Tiro had also brought me a letter, but for a while I was too lazy to read it. I broke the seal without interest, expecting it to be another invitation from some one who would give us an over-elaborate meal, and then take no further trouble when he found we could not return the hospitality.

It was from a man called Salonius; the name was unfamiliar. He said he had heard of me from a fellow-physician in Athens and invited us all to his house three days later. While I was reading it I heard a chariot drive into the stable yard.

When Narcissus joined me I said indifferently, 'We have got the chance of a free meal. We may as well accept, though probably the host expects us to pay for it with some of Aesculapius' formulae.'

'Let Epicurus do the bargaining and we may get a good price.'

'Fortunately I retain the elements of decency, even if you don't. I may have betrayed the hospitality of Elysium, but I can still keep a confidence.'

'No one is arguing with you,' said Narcissus briskly.
'And do, please, try not to be so depressing. This Salonius,
whoever he is, probably has better wine than we can afford,
and we still have litters to bring us home and beds to sleep in.
I could do with a cheerful evening even if I no longer have the
price of a Dionysian headache!'

So I agreed to go, though not without a certain display of
reluctance. We should be able to eat without adding to our
debts, and it would be satisfactory to show our host that
money could not buy everything, even in Rome.

Salonius was short, dark-haired, and decisive. He was
obviously prosperous, for his house had a large garden on the
south bank of the Tiber and the appointments were lavish.
The food was excellent and Epicurus was not disappointed in
the quality of the wine. During the meal our host spoke of
Athens and led me on to talk of subjects for which I felt
starved. No longer did I have to search for topics of conversation, no longer did I feel ignored. Respect and admiration
were stimulating, and for the first time I felt relaxed and
kindly in Roman company.

'You look really beautiful to-night,' whispered Narcissus.
'I must remember that you should wear violet more often...
most illuminating to your hair.'

'Give me intelligent conversation and you need not worry
so much about my clothes,' I retorted, smiling to show that I
did not resent his claiming my small success for himself.

Slaves brought bowls of rose-water for us to rinse our
hands, then left us alone with their master. I knew that now
we should learn the object of our invitation.

'I am aware that in Greece it is permitted to speak without
evasion,' said Salonius. 'In Rome it is more usual for Truth
to go disguised, so that if unwelcome she may be ignored.'

'Truth is always sure of hospitality in the house of a
friend,' said Epicurus smoothly.

'Then we are agreed. This meeting is, I hope, to prove
propitious to us all, especially to Lucina.'

I still thought he was going to make an offer for secrets which I had no intention of selling, so I continued to lie back on my couch.

'I have a full description of the events which took place in a certain cottage, close to an estate called Elysium.' I was so surprised that I sat bolt upright, but Salonius appeared not to notice the effect of his opening remark. 'I was permitted to read the correspondence between a valued colleague and a man who now prefers to call himself Aesculapius. It was only by chance that on my return from Athens I heard of a Greek girl who had arrived in Rome with two men who bore the names as two other pupils of Elysium. It was said that the girl was the sister of Narcissus. This did not coincide with my information, but the clue was too exciting not to be further investigated.'

'He is not my brother,' I said. 'We thought it sounded better. Platonic friendship seems beyond the comprehension of matrons.'

'Your action was fully justified: it is never politic to tell the audience more than they can digest. I hope you will forgive me if I ask a question which you may consider is none of my concern?'

'We have already agreed that truth need not go disguised among friends.' I could tell by the tone of his voice that Narcissus had also decided to trust Salonius.

'Did you leave Elysium because you could not agree with a way of life which claims to be realistic, but in fact avoids any issue which does not agree with certain preconceived ideas?'

'We decided that none of us could become philosophers in the school of Aesculapius...perhaps it was too difficult for us.'

'Again you must forgive me if I appear impertinent. Are you finding this new environment so fruitful as you expected?'

'We have not been here very long...' began Epicurus cautiously.

I interrupted him. We could no longer afford evasions... either we must trust Salonius or admit we had failed. 'We have spent nearly all our money: we have achieved nothing since we came here. Narcissus and Epicurus believed in me, they brought me away from Elysium because I was too unhappy to stay there any longer: and I have been a failure.'

'She hasn't...' said Narcissus.

'None of it has been her fault,' said Epicurus.

'Circumstances have in fact been extraordinarily benign!' said Salonius.

'Benign! You wouldn't think it benign to go to a few dull banquets, and not be asked again because nobody could understand our kind of conversation! You wouldn't think it benign to be sneered at by complacent matrons who couldn't produce a single intelligent idea if their silly lives depended on it!'

He laughed, but it was kindly laughter. 'I still call circumstances benign which refused to let you waste your talents, and yet brought you to the place, and if I may claim this without immodesty, to the man who can arrange for the field of their complete fulfilment. If you will agree to work with me I think that none of us will go...unrewarded.'

I liked him still more for the honesty which openly included himself in the prospects of reward; and so, I could see, did Epicurus.

'Can we hear your plan before we make a decision?' said Narcissus. 'Or is it too soon to ask for details?'

'It is not too soon. I was aware of the supreme importance of Lucina's faculties immediately I heard of their existence. At that time I did not hope for such good fortune as would let us work together. I have been searching for some other man or woman who could take the place, which I now realize, has been waiting for her.'

'So you really believe I can be of some use?' I said eagerly. 'That I can help people, who will pay me so that we needn't worry about money?'

163

'I have every confidence that you can help people. I am also sure that even if you had less effective powers they would still be of inestimable benefit, if properly presented. As to their value in terms of coinage: how much will a man, or a woman, pay for health? How much more will they pay for freedom of the soul? To answer that question you have only to count the temples in Rome, cults from every country which has come under our influence, and none of them can offer more than intercession with impatient and illogical gods! You will supply the power: I the method of its expression. I can provide the patients: you the insight into the hidden source of their disease. I will use my knowledge of the Roman's credulity, which is both the root of his extraordinary singleness of purpose and also of his passionate faith in anything he cannot understand.'

He poured snow-chilled wine into silver goblets and handed one to each of us. 'I give you Lucina,' he said. 'And to the four of us, prosperity...and power!'

Salonius had remarkable energy even for a Roman, and during the next few days I discovered in him a quality which I admired still more; faith in himself which allowed him to plan without the half-measures dictated by fear of failure. Immediately he had returned from Athens he had begun to build a small temple on an island which formed part of his estate, but he would not take me to see it until he had convinced himself, by tests similar to those imposed by Aesculapius, that my powers were not exaggerated. He told me the delay was caused because he wished me to see it after the portico was completed, but I accepted this evasion as an essential courtesy.

The island was oval in shape and had two landing-stages; one was being used by workmen and would later provide my private way; the other was on the far side of the island so that patients should have the illusion of a longer water journey.

'The approach to you must be sufficiently mysterious to

inspire a proper awe,' said Salonius. 'A special boat is being built, only large enough for a recumbent figure and a single oarsman. This water is the way to a new life, the crossing of a beneficent Styx. Therefore we have the white-robed youth instead of the sable ancient, the white boat instead of Charon's dark ferry.'

'Are all these trappings required? You seemed satisfied when I worked in your house.'

'You produced admirable results: they could have been attained with less effort in a more appropriate environment. Are the gods really so vain that they demand magnificent buildings in which to receive supplication? Rather it seems that men pray with greater fervour in a setting as remote as possible from their ordinary environment. No one paid due attention to you when you appeared no more than a cultured woman from Greece. You will find the situation entirely different when you are the priestess of a suitable temple.'

'I don't feel like a priestess! At least not like the ones I have seen in Rome.'

'Fortunately you don't look like them either! Those who are intent on preserving their virginity acquire an artificial holiness which I find most unpleasing. I was delighted when Narcissus mimicked them the other night; the mouth half-open, the flowers trailing from the loosely flexed fingers, was a triumph of intelligent observation.'

'And the other kind? The ones who are *not* intent on virginity?'

He had been talking lightly, but now he gave me a long, searching glance. 'Lucina, you would never find happiness in being only a female. I think you may have regretted this; never regret it again. In life there are certain exceptions to the rule that the lesser is always contained in the greater. You tried to be ordinary, didn't you?'

'Yes,' I said, and found a strange relief in this honesty. 'I tried; and failed completely.'

'We are both most fortunate that destiny was stronger

165

than immature ambition. My father wished me to become a consul; for a brief period I passionately desired to please him.'

'Yes,' I said softly, 'I am beginning to realize that we are both...most fortunate.'

Now I could see the temple through a green shade of young oak leaves...there were several old trees on the island and others had been planted as a grove. The portico had four pillars with elaborate capitals, and a pair of massive bronze doors stood open to show the room where I should preside.

'You will be enthroned on a dais, behind a curtain of thin gauze,' said Salonius. 'You will notice there are no windows, for a single lamp beside the patient will permit you to watch him while remaining only a dim shape, an oracular voice.'

Perhaps he thought I was not suitably impressed, for he said, almost brusquely, 'You and I love power, Lucina. We must always be willing to fight for it.'

'Power? How shall we use it?'

He put his hand on my arm and swung me round to face him. 'As a balm for wounds received in childhood; as a shield to protect us from an injury too deep to heal. Life has never been easy for either of us. For what it is worth I can affirm that I have no allegiance except to myself and my few friends.'

'Why have you been so hurt?'

'As a youth I believed implicitly in the ties of the family, in the importance of the State. I fell in love with the daughter of a Senator, and she with me. But, to my father's extreme displeasure, I had already decided to become a physician. Both families agreed that the alliance would be unsuitable. It was easier for my father to see through the eyes of another pupil of expediency than to remain loyal to his only son. I have never married: and, if you consider my advice worthy of consideration, you will also remain free.'

'I shall never marry,' I said, and to my surprise found the

166

words easy. 'I tried to drown myself because a very commonplace young man didn't want me. Now I am glad to be only Lucina. Glad!' I looked up at him, 'I think that at last this is really true. I am very grateful, Salonius...I shall not forget.'

He realized at once that I was shy at my spontaneous confession. 'You will notice that the ventilation has been contrived through concealed openings close to the ceiling...even in high summer the room will remain cool. The heating system is under the floor, far more effective than the old-fashioned braziers. Beyond the archway which frames the dais you will find another door; it leads into a smaller room where your robes will be kept and where you can rest. There is also a stateroom, for flower vases and anything else you may need...I consider suitable flower arrangements a useful adjunct to the general atmosphere.

'You are sure we need all this?'

'I am not a charlatan. My conception of a realist is some one who understands things as they *are*, not as he would find it convenient to believe. With free people, who can recognize the simplicities, it would not be necessary to destroy a set of false concepts by their appropriate opposite. But Romans are not free, otherwise they would not require to dominate the world...which, if my reading of the racial character is correct, they will inevitably try to do.'

'And they will fail?'

'Only when they have destroyed themselves. The tyrant can succeed until he becomes the victim of his own tyranny... or dies because the last conquest is too dangerous, the conquest of the self.'

One of the workmen, who was paving the floor with white marble, came forward and stood waiting for Salonius to give him permission to speak.

'There is flaw in one of the blocks,' he said. 'Shall I use a different stone, over in the corner where it won't show, or get another? I hear there is a boat in from Corinth which may have a good enough match.'

'See the match is exact,' said Salonius impatiently. 'I ordered material of the first quality.'

The man looked as though he was going to protest, then he turned and walked towards one of the boats used by the workmen.

'I used free labour because they are usually more skilled,' said Salonius, 'but slaves might have been more satisfactory. The flaw was probably due to careless cutting; a slave would have guarded against the skin of his back echoing the flaw, with a lash.'

'A temple which is to give freedom should not be built by slaves.'

'You still cherish some of the prejudices of Aesculapius?'

I knew he was annoyed though it pleased him to sound indulgent. 'I have been trained to dislike slavery, especially slavery to gods.'

'I thought you told me that gods were not accepted in Elysium? Surely Zeus was not so discourteous as to appear to you uninvited!' It was said with a smile, but he was looking at me as though he expected me to recognize an underlying seriousness.

'I see no preparation for a god in this building, or do you intend to place some suitable statue above the portico, further to encourage tribute from the faithful?'

'Men have made many images in the pattern of their ignorant morality: Aesculapius showed discernment in teaching you to ignore them.' He put his hand on my shoulder and I saw he was strangely moved. 'Lucina, don't let yourself be deceived because you have seen only the false images. Behind the dark facade I believe there are real gods, who command the springs of living water. I cannot reach this unpolluted source; yet I know, with a certainty more vital than reason, that these gods exist and cannot be denied.'

'So the physician is not without faith?' I tried to speak

168

lightly, for I knew he was embarrassed by this sudden display of feeling.

'No one who has seen many people die can sincerely believe that death is an end which is not also a beginning. Birth and death mark revolutions of the wheel whose circumference is eternity.'

'So you believe that we are not born as strangers to the planet? I have wanted to ask you that, many times, and until now I had not the courage. It was that question which made Aesculapius set a barrier against me...'

'There need be no barriers between us, Lucina. I am not concerned with the ultimates, only with the *here* and the *now*. If you prefer to believe, as do the Platonists, that you have had an actual physical existence before this century, it seems a matter for your personal convenience. I am concerned only with results.'

'But the results depend on whether I have real power or am only an unconscious charlatan! Was Agamemnon really the man whom Damocles tortured? Did the woman from Cos watch a child drown in mud? Don't you understand that to me it is of supreme importance to be *sure!*'

'Our work is to help people find freedom, and by that freedom to attain mental and physical health. We shall not follow the sterile path taken by too many philosophers, who neglected the immediate necessity and concerned themselves with fruitless speculation. I am content that the woman from Cos has been cured of her asthma. I recently had news of her; she is happy and expects the birth of a child in four months.'

'Agamemnon died. Was it because I failed him?'

'A surgeon has not failed if he cuts out a malignant growth and the patient dies because he was not properly cared for during the normal period of recuperation. The fault was with Aesculapius, not with you.'

I felt a pang of disloyalty because I was so grateful for this relief from a long anxiety.

'Don't try to take too much responsibility,' he said gently. 'Your role is to be the Ariadne who gives the scarlet thread to the labyrinth. When you have discovered the source of a disease the patient himself must slay his Minotaur.'

'How can I be an Ariadne if I don't know whether there is a real past in which to search for the thread?'

'The thread always leads from the centre. There is no inhabitant of a personal hell whose character does not contain the essential clue.'

'But I knew nothing about the character of the rich man who thought he was going to starve. I knew nothing about any of them. Don't you believe what I told you?'

'I believe it implicitly: the results are proof of the validity of the process. In my own work I have had ample evidence that the physical is not the only realm. Health or disease, sanity or madness, are no more than symptoms of the way an individual has reacted to various types of experience. If one can cause some one to mobilize all his resources he will emerge the victor in any battle, interior or exterior. Now you see the relevance of Ariadne? Bring the Minotaur into sight and you discover the hero to kill it.'

'Perhaps...if I have sufficient faith in myself. What is your faith, Salonius?'

'The belief in what I should be: which in time will become the certainty of what I am.'

The last of the workmen had left the island. Through the open doors I could see the calm river; the evening sun gilded the white walls of the room. 'You will work here, Lucina. Work for yourself, and for me...and for something much greater than either of us, which as yet we can only dimly comprehend.'

'The stage is set; but you have forgotten to teach the chief actor her lines. Even Euripides never expected me to write the play for him.'

'You will know the lines. A scribe will record them. She is a Greek slave I bought several years ago, her name is Iris and I think you will find her efficient. The patient will take a dream-drink, but less strong than the one used in your early experiments. Sometimes it may only be necessary for the patient to talk without restraint...that is why I have emphasized that you are more goddess than woman. One is not embarrassed by being truthful to divinity!'

'Why not make them drunk? In wine, men are not particular as to the audience of their confidences!'

'You underrate our Roman heads! Nobody attends many banquets without learning to guard his tongue, or else how to free the belly of such a dangerous guest!'

'My role as a priestess does not sound very exciting. Any skilled scribe would be better equipped to record the confessions of men in a stupor!'

'A scribe would not be able to ask the relevant questions. Your chief role, Lucina, is to enter, as a fully conscious personality, into the realm of your patient's phantasy. It will be as real to you as it is to him. I believe that by your special faculty you can destroy the destructive thought-sequence and substitute another which will provide the vital stimulus to freedom.'

'And if I encounter another cat of Bast?'

'You will destroy that too. You will never be in danger unless the patient's essential character is stronger than every resource available to you. I consider this so unlikely that the possibility need not be considered.'

This was small consolation. It was only too obvious that Salonius had never encountered Bast, or any other concretion of evil which might prove stronger than any single personality. He believed in real gods, but only those who were benign: yet he said that all things must have their opposites. It would be useless to try to explain to him that I knew the danger was real; for if he believed it he might try to stop me using my faculty, as Aesculapius had done. I had asked to be allowed to work towards further knowledge: it was much too late to regret that I had found the way.

the hetaera

Salonius decided that while the temple was being completed I should study his case-histories so as to learn his technique. These records were far more elaborate than any kept by Aesculapius, and at first I could not see the relevance of some of the details.

'One should try to see the patient as a *whole;* it is not enough to treat only the part which has succumbed to disease. Mind reacts on body, body on mind. We must cure the cause, instead of being content only to palliate the symptom.'

'That is understood,' I said. 'But why have you made notes of trivial conversations which seem to have no bearing on the case? Here is an account of a man who had nothing wrong with him except a simple fracture of the leg: you set it, the bone knitted without any complications. You have added a note describing a quarrel between the patient's third cousin, and the third cousin's wife. I could understand it if they lived in the same house, but they are not even close friends.'

'The cousin's name was familiar to me: he is a consul of some importance. The satisfied patient boasts of his physician: therefore I thought it probable that the consul might come to me for advice. It is always helpful to know in advance of any factor which may be relevant; it makes it easier to establish confidence.'

'Surely no one would find a leg, broken by slipping in a pool of spilt wine, a topic of interest!'

'My dear Lucina, that remark shows you have much to learn of the Roman mind. The Greeks, very properly, consider disease discreditable: the Romans appear to think it a sign that the gods have found them sufficiently important to suffer divine displeasure. Men and women boast of their afflictions with a fervour that would hardly be justified by laurels. I have heard two women argue about which of them had greater suffering in childbirth as might two Centurians protest their rival victories!'

He picked up the roll I had been reading and pointed to the note which recorded the quarrel. Beside it was a number, added later in ink of a different colour. 'We will refer to another roll,' he said, and walked across the room to fetch it from one of the many shelves which lined his library.

'You can read it later: I will give you a brief precis to illustrate my point. In due course the consul asked my advice for pains in the belly. Had I not known something of his family life I might have advised a change in diet, a prolonged rest; treatment which any other physician would have been able to give. Instead I told him to send his wife to me. I was able to make her understand that he ate not only the food which their slaves most admirably prepared, but the bitter words she forced him to swallow. I asked her whether she thought her position as a widow would be preferable to her status as a wife. She preferred silence salted with charity to the ashes of mourning. The consul made a most dramatic recovery.' He ran his finger down the page. 'A recovery worth three hundred aurei.'

'Three hundred gold pieces for telling a man that his wife was the cause of his indigestion! The Romans are certainly credulous!'

'You underrate me; I played a role of which Apollo need not be ashamed. I gave the woman some harmless powders, and told the husband that she alone could cure him, by putting one in his wine each evening. She had learned from me to curb her tongue: I gave him the confidence that his health would be restored by the beloved consort. They are both happy, and most grateful. The necklace she gave me as a token of gratitude fetched another hundred aurei. Not an inadequate return for the trouble of making a note which you considered so unimportant!'

'You and Epicurus will find much in common!'

'I have great admiration for Epicurus. I suggested that we divide the tribute you will bring to the temple in the proportion of a third to you; he insisted on a half. He argues well: I have accepted the portion.'

Epicurus had done even more: he had demanded a sufficient advance on my future earnings to pay most of our debts and to buy the villa and the six household slaves. So at last we enjoyed meals which were freely bought and slept in beds which really belonged to us.

When the day came for me to put on the priest robes which Narcissus had designed for me with such care, I felt unduly nervous. Why should I be more afraid than I had been with Aesculapius? I had a temple instead of an abandoned cottage: a sponsor who believed in me; a knowledge of human frailties which would have disgusted the younger Lucina. I was about to prove to Narcissus and Epicurus that they had not trusted me without cause.

Salonius saw through my surface of confidence. 'I have chosen your first patient with care, Lucina. You will find no cold, implacable intellect to challenge. But do not ignore the power of Cordelia; though she is not so secure as are the matrons, the Senator she has enslaved speaks with her voice in the affairs of Rome. She commands the service of all the famous soothsayers and on her word they increase their influence or find themselves diminished. I made sure she was one of the first to hear of you, knowing she would hasten to our new Delphi.'

Until now I had not been given the opportunity of getting to know Iris, the Greek who would act as my scribe. I had only seen her once, when Salonius made the formal declaration that henceforward she owed her obedience to me.

I found her waiting for me in the robing-room. 'Iris,' I said gently, 'we are to work together, to try to make people happier. We must both be worthy of Greece.'

'You are serving Rome. I am a slave bought by Roman money.'

'All individuals are free according to the capacity of their hearts...freedom does not depend on status or race.'

'Lucina, the boatman is a Greek too. Will you remember that...please will you remember?' She glanced towards the door as though afraid, then whispered, 'Salonius is strong.'

'Salonius is wise: but Salonius is a Roman.'

She bent and kissed my hand, 'Forgive me for trying to hate you because I thought you have forgotten the pride of Greece.'

The stage was set: a lamp burned on a silver tripod beside the couch where Cordelia would recline. The poppy-drink was ready in a gold goblet. A blaze of scarlet lilies filled the niche in the white wall. I had chosen the lilies because Salonius told me they were known to be her favourite flower. Suddenly I felt they were a disharmony. I told Iris to take them away, and went to the storeroom to see whether I could find something more suitable. Obeying a sudden impulse I took a handful of daisies, the precise petals edged with clear pink, and put them in a wine-cup.

Iris called to me that the boat was approaching the landing-stage. I took my place on the throne behind the gauze curtain: the silver ram's heads were smooth as linen under my hands.

Slowly the bronze doors opened: a woman who moved like wind on a field of corn closed them behind her. Except for a bracelet in the form of a serpent she wore no ornaments. In her right hand she carried a posy of daisies. I saw her smile, as though suddenly aware of an unusual happiness. She walked towards the niche and put her flowers with mine.

She was about to drink from the goblet when I again obeyed a sudden impulse. 'Unless you wish it, there is no need to pour poppy to this oracle.'

She put down the goblet and went to sit on the couch. I looked at her hands. They were relaxed so I knew she was not afraid. Surely this woman had no illness of body or mind, for her skin was lucent with health. I expected her to ask for an omen: probably to discover whether her protector would remain in favour. Unless she was insecure why did she consult soothsayers?

'I wait to hear your questions,' I said, in the impersonal voice which Euripides had taught me to use when acting an immortal.

'The greatest of these you have already answered.' She gestured towards the flowers. 'You have shown me that there is one oracle in Rome to whom I can at last entrust my secret.'

'You have found that soothsayers are charlatans, and yet you still consult them?'

'I hoped that one of them might cure me of my disease: and yet to none have I dared tell the source of my affliction.'

'You have made a votive offering to Aesculapius?'

'No, but many to Apollo.'

At least I had been right in thinking she enjoyed perfect health. Salonius had not been so well informed as he claimed, for he had told me that the Senator was lavish both with money and devotion. If this were true why did she seek aid from Apollo?

'I can trust you,' she said slowly, as though still trying to believe it true. 'I can trust you, for the flowers are a sign which no one could dare to doubt. Apollo brought me here; he has not been deaf to my supplication.'

'You wish me to ask Apollo that a lover shall not be forgetful?'

I saw her clench, then again she smiled, 'Forgive me. I betrayed the omen only because I have drunk deep of disillusion.'

'Ask of me in the name of Apollo, or in the name of your heart.'

'Am I to follow the daisies; or remain a husk?'

'What is the corn of which the husk was winnowed?'

'Power. The admiration of men, the jealousy of women.'

'And the husk itself?'

'The knowledge that the bread of my grinding is bitter; that my body will become the husk which leaves no seed for planting.'

'The price of the daisies must be paid in the gold which cannot be turned into coin. Scarlet lilies can be bought with copper. Which can you afford to pay?'

'I have so much copper; so little gold.'

'Can you afford to throw away the gold of which you have so little? Will the copper endure except as the hasps of a sarcophagus?'

'I accept the judgement of Apollo!' She went to the flowers and held the vase between her hands, then set it gently on the tripod beside the poppy-drink. 'I have read the omens. No longer shall I seek the little death of lethe which I have sought in Rome.'

The bronze doors opened and I watched her go into the quiet night.

I was tired and went straight home without telling Salonius what had taken place. To-morrow he would have the record taken down by Iris. He prided himself on his skill in interpreting dreams and symbols; he could discover whether he knew more of the facts than I did myself. I should not admit that though I had found myself speaking with confidence I was still ignorant of the probable effect, or even if there would be an effect at all.

Epicurus woke me next morning and I found it was nearly noon. 'I overslept,' I said, with a yawn. 'I meant to see Salonius this morning.'

'I have just come back from him. You must have done very well last night, Lucina. Cordelia sent a necklace of pearls as a thank-offering. I brought our share back with me; enough to pay the rest of our debts.'

'Salonius should be pleased; we shall soon be able to pay him back.'

'Yes, he should. For a moment I think he was, after I told him what the pearls are worth.'

'He is *not* pleased?'

'No; but he wouldn't tell me why. He wants you to go down early to-night so that he can talk to you before you work.'

'Some people are very difficult to please,' I said crossly. 'I'm still tired so I shall go to sleep again unless you have anything pleasant to tell me.'

'We are getting very grand,' he retorted. 'No longer to be pleased by a little matter such as pearls or freedom from debt.'

I found Salonius pacing up and down his room. He turned when he heard me and said sharply, 'Lucina, I thought I had made it clear that the protector of Cordelia was a man whom it is not wise to anger, and that because of her position she could be extremely useful to us. May I ask why you found it convenient to forget both these important items?'

'If she was dissatisfied why did she send such a rich gift?' I said defensively. 'She appeared most grateful, as though I had made her really happy.'

'I suppose you know what you have done? Though how you knew about the daisies is beyond my comprehension.' For a moment a note of grudging admiration warmed his voice. 'Another practical demonstration of your remarkable powers. But in future you must learn to temper intuition with common sense!'

'Why are you complaining? I had no preconceived plan: I said what came into my head. I had put scarlet lilies as you suggested, and then they seemed inappropriate so I used daisies instead. I have forgotten exactly what I said. It was mostly in symbols, husks and bitter bread. No, she said the bread was bitter. Anyway it cannot have been very important.'

'Perhaps I had better enlighten you. Cordelia, as she told me quite frankly after she left you, consulted soothsayers only because she wished to discover which policy they were adopting. Soothsayers have considerable bearing on the fortunes of influential people. She came here expecting to find another of the same kind; some one clever but not too scrupulous, whom she could bribe if necessary. On the way here the young man whose attentions she has succeeded in resisting threw a bunch of daisies into her litter; probably the first time a woman of her standing has ever been given such a tawdry present.' He snorted. 'Daisies...which can be picked by slaves from any field! I thought she was far too worldly to be influenced by so trivial an omen. I have over-rated the intelligence of women: she ran away with this man, with whom she believes herself to be divinely in love. And he is a plebeian! He owns a sausage shop!'

'Are they in danger? Will the Senator have them both murdered?'

'No; he will not have even that small balm for his anger. She told him that she had left a letter which described in detail some of his less dignified habits, and that this would be given into the hands of his most powerful rival should anything happen to either of them!'

I began to laugh, and though Salonius grew pale with suppressed annoyance, I could not stop. 'We must buy our sausages from them. I shall tell Epicurus to make a new dish worthy of their love.'

'Love! What will Cordelia feel for you when love has turned all her pearls to sausages?'

'She will have found out that it is better to live on sausages than to starve on pearls.'

CHAPTER FOUR

Son of Mars

To the contentment of Salonius, the next few months included no patients to whom my treatment brought inexpedient changes.

Women who had taken lovers, and then afflicted their
bodies which they thought had betrayed them into sin, left
me reassured. Sometimes I achieved a cure by reminding
them that Zeus was unlikely to be intolerant of amorous
adventures!

Men who could not digest their false pride found the pains
of their bellies decrease when I gave them a different standard
by which to live. Usually they accepted my judgement only
when I had found a way to make them realize that they must
choose between physical pain and ethical health.

I cured a Censor of a paralysed left hand, by telling him
that he must either cease wanting to strangle his wife or else
send her away. Her banishment caused a minor scandal, but
his spectacular recovery, which was attributed to my inter-
vention on his behalf with Artemis, considerably enhanced
our reputation. The Romans were too stupid to recognize
that I had chosen Artemis because of her aspect which was
said to bring sudden death, if provoked, to wives!

I discovered that it was much more effective to express
truth in the form of omens than to explain it in a manner
pleasing to the realist. However, Salonius never failed to
insist, we were concerned with results, not with theories.
Romans had faith in the remote priestess; yet they had not
even had the courtesy to listen to the opinions of Lucina. I
played the role they demanded; and was rewarded with the
tribute of increasing influence, and its counterpart, which
Epicurus recorded on tallies that now were slips of ivory instead of sheets of discarded papyrus.

Salonius never mentioned Cordelia, whom he still considered a regrettable incident for which my inexperience must demand forgiveness. I never told him that a Lucina who was an obscure Greek girl from a villa in an unfashionable quarter of the city, frequently went to a certain shop that was gaining a small, but substantial, fame for the excellence of its baked meats. From Cordelia herself I had heard the story of the daisies of fair omen, and wished that instead of listening in pretended awe I could have dared to tell her how grateful I was for this proof that I had not been entirely ineffective in creating happiness. Most of my patients were so determinedly Roman that I had little hope of helping them to become real people.

Tribute to the temple increased: Salonius was pleased to let me work with his approval but without his advice. Only a matter of unusual importance would have made him ask me to come to his house, on a certain evening of mild autumn, before I went to the temple.

'I wish I could have told you before,' he said, 'but I have only just discovered that the Centurian whom you will see to-night,' he paused, and then added with emphasis, 'is *more* than a Centurian.'

'Who is he?'

'If I were sure I would tell you his name: but it might be any one of three men of great importance in the affairs of Rome. Sufficient that he comes to you to discover whether the omens are propitious for us to acquire further territory; whether the time has come for the beneficent Rome rule to be extended.'

'Beneficent?' I said. 'You mean that Rome requires more slaves to increase her self-importance?'

'I find your Greek cynicism surprising,' said Salonius. 'If it were not for Rome your own country would have been over-run. We have a mission to extend our influence throughout the known world...'

'Just as I have a mission,' I said, in a smooth voice which I knew would conceal the thought behind the words. 'It is *good* for people to become obedient; their tribute is a natural expression of their gratitude.'

He smiled, oblivious of my real meaning. 'There is no disharmony between us, Lucina. I should have known it was unnecessary for me to warn you that in this case you must read the omens with meticulous care; the lives of legions may depend on your exact interpretation.'

Surely I was learning to understand human nature! I had thought that Salonius worshipped a realism too wide for Aesculapius; but now I realized that he, like nearly all my patients, believed only according to his concept of expediency.

'The victor of a campaign will bring tribute to Rome,' I said. 'He is unlikely to forget the source of the confidence which made his victories possible. Epicurus had better learn the barter value of the wealth which a people, as yet unconquered, shall lay as sacrifice on the altars of Rome.'

'We understand each other, Lucina,' said Salonius, secure in his confidence.

'Yes; we understand each other.'

As I was going out of the room I asked, as though the question was trivial, 'Do you know which country is to be honoured by our attentions?'

'No,' he said. 'Surely that is of no real importance? It is sufficient that it is worthy of five legions.'

I should have liked to decorate the temple with asphodel; the flower of graves, or, as Clion had once reminded me, a plant which can be used to decontaminate the odour of swine. But it was possible, though unlikely, that the knowledge of the Roman soldier might not be entirely limited by the concerns of strategy. So I made a not unsatisfying arrangement of elecampane; the flower said to have been favoured by Helen of Troy. She launched many ships; perhaps Lucina could restrain five legions!

On such occasions the poppy-drink was seldom used; the

man of affairs perferred to consult the oracle as would a minor state official go to his superior to receive further orders. When Iris told me that Lucius had put off from the bank, I took my place; to wait for a battle of wits against Roman arrogance.

The Centurion wore the uniform of a foreign legion; the helmet-plume faded and discoloured. I was intended to think that he was a veteran, perhaps to recognize that he had not received the advancement worthy of such arduous service. The sword he unbuckled before he lay down on the couch had a worn blade; the leather of his greaves was knotted where the greasy thongs had frayed. Had I not been warned by Salonius I might have believed these trivial, careful clues, taking him for a soldier who had fought hard but won no material advancement. Or should I have been deceived? I tried to remember where I had seen that face before: the heavy line of the brows, the hard jaw. Had I seen him at the Games, leaning, avid, over the balustrade of the arena; or in a triumph? The setting was irrelevant: it was sufficient that Lucina knew that somewhere a free people asked her to help them defend the right to live in their own way.

'Always try to understand the mind of the enemy; only then can you counter his strategy.' I had often heard Agamemnon say these words; now I heard their echo in the stillness of my mind. But was it only an echo?

I saw the soldier close his eyes, relax against the pillow of the couch. Iris sat forward on the low stool; the writing-tablet ready in her hand.

Gradually I became certain that Agamemnon was beside me. For the first time since I had seen his body crumble into ash on the white sands of Elysium I knew that between us there was a link too strong for any sword to sever.

It was not necessary to speak to him aloud, it was natural for him to hear me without sound carrying the words. 'Agamemnon; I shall not in this hour betray the sword which once was too heavy for us both.'

The answer was clear; I seemed to hear even the tones of his voice.

'He acts according to his beliefs, Lucina. He has the same fervour which drives priests to sacrifice on the altars of dark gods. He does not know that Mars grows ever more hungry on the blood-lust of the conqueror. He is loyal, brave, implacable. You will never turn him from his purpose unless you can make him believe that through him Rome will suffer.'

'I meant to read his omens in a way which would convince him that the leader of this army will die of a festering wound in the hour of victory...no, in the hour of defeat.'

'He is a tired man, Lucina. He is dedicated to death in battle. He is afraid only of being a soldier too old to fight for the glory of Rome. He has left himself no alternative spring of life from which to drink. He is not intersted in his family, not even in policy or fame. He will take others into death with him unless you can show him there is another way of living.'

It was becoming more difficult to hear Agamemnon, as though we were two boats which the current was drawing gently apart. 'Don't leave me, Agamemnon!'

'Do not hate him, Lucina. Nothing can be accomplished through hatred. He needs your pity. The children of Mars are pitiful, for the father they have chosen is very cruel. If you could make him see the white sword carried by the legions who war with Mars. If you could only make Rome remember the other sword....'

'What other sword? Agamemnon, answer me! What other sword?'

'Not Mars....' The words were so tenuous that I was not sure if they were only an echo of something heard very long ago: but I could not hear the source beyond the echo.

The Centurion spoke in a voice which might have been issuing orders for a battle plan, 'I asked the oracle to answer my question in the name of Mars!'

I knew something else about him; he was not used to consulting oracles, for they were well known to be exceedingly particular that all supplicants approached in a manner of correct humility, but he was confident that Mars viewed him with favour.

'Let the question be asked.'

'It requires the interpretation of a dream. I regret that my orders from Mars are in a code whose key is unknown to me.'

'Mars is displeased. His orders are not sent save to those who are willing to carry them into action. He wishes you to understand that he is occupied with many affairs: you will repeat your orders faithfully, so that he may discover whether he can entrust you not to distort his commands.'

In the calm, dispassionate voice of one delivering a message learned exactly, the man spoke, 'I find myself in a tent on the lower slope of a mountain range. I see a wide plain; fertile, for it is coloured by cultivated fields and well wooded. There are two large towns. One is partly surrounded by a wide river. With me are five legions. I know that the people whom I have come to enlighten with the wisdom of Rome are not your followers. They are unprepared: this I know for I have sent spies among them and discovered that their cohorts are untrained and their defences neglected. The scene changes. I see a triumph in the streets of Rome. On a bier is carried the sword and helmet of a man who died for this victory.'

'You dedicate your life to Mars, and yet fear death?'

I saw his face darken with a suffusion of angry blood; 'If Mars will ask his scribes to read my record they will find I have not failed in courage.'

'Mars is pleased that you have learned to keep anger as your slave.'

The taut line of his mouth relaxed; as may a wrestler who has countered a throw of his opponent.

'If the boon of death in victory is granted I need no further reward,' he said. 'I watched the triumph; I saw that the men

185

who wore the blazon of Rome marched proudly; but under the helmets were naked skulls. There were many slaves in our train: men and women and children who wore chains, gold chains. They were singing. Why should slaves sing before they have learned that it is better to be in bondage to Rome than to claim citizenship of any other country? Why did they sing *so soon?*'

'Do not your legions sing when they march towards victory? Do they wait until the city is conquered?'

'They sing to keep the rhythm of their march.'

'If their leaders cannot read my omens they chant only the melancholy beat of death. The false pride of a leader without wisdom is more deadly than ten thousand enemy spears.'

'I have no pride save that conferred upon me by the men I lead.'

'Then interpret my commands. Judge well, for the life of Rome depends upon your vision!'

'I cannot,' he said desperately. 'Would I be here, asking a woman to act as intermediary if I had not tried for sixty nights to dream again?'

'Remember the dead men who wore your helmets in an empty triumph; remember the gold chains of the singing people whom you thought Rome had enslaved. Do a people enter into bondage singing?'

'But the chains were gold: a sure sign that I was to bring new wealth to Rome!'

'Do slaves wear gold: or is it the seal of the victor?'

'I saw the gold: I saw so many slaves, more tribute to Rome.'

'You woke too soon. I am not pleased that you lacked the courtesy to wait until my orders were complete.'

'The heralds woke me, the trumpets that wake the men. We were in camp when you came to me.'

'Need you tell me that? Is it not more seemly for me to approach the soldier in his tent, rather than on some other occasion when he forgets the dignity of his calling? You had made a sacrifice to me. Would it not have been wiser to order silence for my voice than to allow Mars to be interrupted by the trivial pattern of the little men who make my wars?'

I knew this challenge was a risk; what if he had not made a sacrifice on the night before the dream? I knew that a vivid memory was far more probable after some definite act had made the mind receptive: but if I was wrong he might kill me to stop me betraying his plan. He would not be afraid to kill a charlatan. I felt a cold trickle of sweat between my breasts: a sword would be cold. . . .

'I made the sacrifice. Never again will I doubt that you answer; never again will I fail in the proper preparations to do you homage.'

'We will show you our clemency; but be not disobedient. I have many enemies to which men are blind. Disease and hunger are among the most implacable. If you had entered this campaign you would have brought my enemy into Rome. The conquered sang because they knew they brought with them invisible legions which would destroy our city. Slow death, disguised as fever; death to our women, death to the legions who will protect Rome in future years unless you slay them in infancy.'

'But the plans are made. The ships are ready, even the stores and horses have been sent to the ports! The Senate has approved: they were at first reluctant but I made them agree!'

'You will have an opportunity to learn that there are other weapons than the sword by which Rome may be saved from peril. Go to the Senate, and acquaint them with my orders! Or slay Romans in their thousands, and bring weary legions in your train to hear the condemnation of divine displeasure.'

Fear, doubt, passionate longing to cling to the standards by which he had lived, marked his face with a shadow of bitter age. I must dare another throw of the dice by which the lives of many unknown people would be gamed with destiny. I must give him a sign to weight the balance. . .

and if the sign failed?

'You still find it convenient to doubt. Do so at your peril; your peril and the lives of those who give to you blind loyalty.'

His voice was thick with emotion. 'Give me a sign. In clemency for the ignorance of a faithful soldier, give me a sign!'

'Have pity,' whispered Agamemnon. 'Remember his courage; remember that he lives according to his faith.'

'You will hear an owl hoot three times as you cross the river. You will not betray my orders when you hear my owl.'

He got to his feet; swaying a little, trying to compose himself. He took up the sword and his fingers fumbled with the unfamiliar buckle.

'That is not your true sword,' I said; 'but you will find the sword to fight my enemies.'

I watched him go slowly out of the temple. Iris looked up at me, her face pale with apprehension.

'You promised him a sign,' she said. 'What will he do when the owl does not fulfil your promise?'

I gestured to her to be silent. The silver ram's heads were cold against my palms. 'Agamemnon,' I said, 'please make him hear the owl. I heard the owl when you died. Please make him hear the owl!'

I ran down the path between the young oaks. The river was a dark flood between me and the lights of Rome. There was no wind; the night was very still as though it shared my listening.

I heard an owl hoot...and again. It hooted for the third time. 'Thank you, Agamemnon! Oh, thank you!'

And I felt tears running down my face.

I dared not forget that Salonius was a Roman, so I concealed that I had deliberately worked in defence of a people threatened by invasion. For the rest I gave him an accurate account: he found nothing disturbing in my awareness of

Agamemnon, and I was grateful that he did not try to pretend it had been an illusion. That the owl had hooted he took as irrefutable proof of the reality of the experience; neither of us could decide whether it had been a real owl, or only a subjective image, projected either by Agamemnon or myself into the field of hearing.

'I am convinced,' said Salonius, 'that nothing has a physical reality until it has first been created in a more subtle form. If you can effect cures by changing the pattern of a patient's thought, why should you not be able to make him see, or hear, the vital factor which you have decided is part of the essential chain? Is there any substance, however material, which cannot be modified, providing that one fully understands the forces required and how to dispose them? Is this, perhaps, the logic of creation?'

'I believe, as you do, that ideas are stronger than any one dare recognize...but I cannot explain the process. I am afraid that I have very little capacity for belief: I only know what I know, what I have experienced.'

'Never regret it, Lucina. For one actual fact there may be ten plausible theories...of which nine must be wrong. Keep your empiricism: leave others to provide the explanation. Keep faith with yourself.'

CHAPTER FIVE

the Soothsayer

I had worked with Salonius for nearly two years when the most famous of Roman soothsayers, a man who used the name Calchas, the Greek seer immortalized by Homer, said he wished to consult me.

'I suspect he has no more than ordinary powers,' said

Salonius. 'But I have heard too many stories of the effects he has produced, the influence he undoubtedly wields, not to warn you to be extremely guarded with him. He may be a fraud, and so become a dangerous enemy when he knows you could expose him.'

'And if he is genuine?'

'He will recognize you as a rival, and probably try to make sure you are no longer a challenge to his authority.'

'You meant I must not forget that I once fought with a cat of Bast?'

'Exactly. I may be unduly apprehensive, but I shall take such precautions as occur to me. Shall I act as your scribe instead of Iris? If my assistance is required I may not prove entirely ineffective.'

'If Calchas is only a man who grows fat on credulity Iris and I will be in no danger. It would make him suspicious if we altered our usual routine, and if he becomes physically agressive Lucius is always within call.'

'I accept your superior judgement. I am grateful for the tact which prevented your pointing out that I should be useless in a conflict which demanded more strength than the muscles of Lucius can provide.'

Calchas was younger than I expected, no more than forty-five though his hair was streaked with grey. His eyes were blue, pale as the sky in oppressive summer weather, his body lean, showing no sign of indulgence and yet not arid with asceticism.

'I come to consult the oracle of the Tiber,' he said smoothly. 'May I claim the privileges of a fellow...' he paused and then added deliberately, 'a fellow *artist?*'

As I did not immediately reply he made the second move. 'I use artist in its fullest sense. We interpret the essence of form, so that lesser men may see what before was hidden. We can interpret the realities of the world which is unknown to ignorant humanity. Craftsmen do not require to conceal their secrets from others who have proved the right to honour in the same fraternity.'

'You have come here to consult the oracle; or to talk with Lucina?'

'With Lucina; neither of us require an intermediary when we wish to consult the gods.'

The challenge was direct, yet I felt no hostility towards him. Perhaps he was doing the same work as myself; honest when his patients would permit him honesty.

I got up from the throne, drew back the thin curtain, walked forward and took my place beside him on the couch.

'If I had your beauty I should not hide myself,' he said courteously. 'You would find that Rome is not oblivious to the body through which the mind expresses wisdom.'

He smiled; the smile that any man accords to a woman not ill-favoured. This man had not come as an enemy; so what was his purpose? He was clever; already he had taken from me the advantage of the remote oracle. I was a hostess who had no wine to give her guest, nothing except her wit to offer.

I was further disconcerted when he said, 'Wine is only necessary when there is a lack of mutual interest to be concealed: so we do not require Falernian.'

'As we read each other's thought so well we need not concern ourselves with the exactitude of phrases.'

'Therefore I can admit without embarrassment that I came here with a certain apprehension. I feared an uncompromising rival; or to be disappointed.'

'And you are already convinced I am not...uncompromising?'

'Shall we say rather that I am not disappointed?'

This suave exchange would have seemed more suitable to a banquet than a temple; but I was not deceived as to its importance.

'When I first heard of you I thought that Rome had acquired only another cult. In this I did less than justice to the deserved reputation of Salonius, whose intelligence I have always rated highly. I erred only because I did not consider him capable of more than—intelligence.'

'Salonius does not lack subtle perception: if he did, could he be so successful?'

'In that recognition you forstalled me. I had become accustomed to regard the knife and the herb as useful, but very limited. You have the advantage of being born a Greek in this generation.'

Did he believe himself to have been Calchas, or only his follower in the same tradition? I had been foolish enough to underrate the integrity of my opponent; with this man I could not afford to be foolish.

'Have you no Greek blood?' I said.

'Not in my immediate ancestry; but the factors of hereditary genius do not depend on the paternal loins, nor on the attributes of the physical mother. Those who are born to rule do so irrespective of the race among which they find themselves.'

'Calchas could not accept an oracle wiser than himself,' I said. 'He died, as you will remember, because he could not accept Mopsus as a superior, or even as an equal.'

I wondered if he knew that Salonius had provided me with this useful information about the real Calchas, who had killed himself after being outwitted by a greater soothsayer on the island of Claros.

'Perhaps Calchas has acquired additional wisdom with the centuries. I have always been aware that there might be others who could claim the power of Mopsus; and now I am more than willing to work with them, instead of being destroyed by false pride.'

So Calchas was not immune to the superstition by which he flourished. Or had he real knowledge which I must recognize and honour? Salonius had given me every opportunity to work, but he had never been able to share the validity of my experience; he was only one of the many who either believed or disbelieved. Was Calchas perhaps the first friend I could accept as an equal?

Again he read my thoughts: 'The seer is always lonely; except in the company of those who share the same capacities.'

'Are not all rulers lonely?'

'Yes,' he said, and his voice rang out in the quiet room. 'We are always lonely; it is our strength, and we must insist that it is also our glory.'

Suddenly he got up, flung wide the bronze doors and stood looking up at the moon which flooded the marble floor and drowned the flickering lamp. There was power in the hands upstretched towards the sky, a radiant vitality. Then his arms fell to his sides: he closed the doors, came slowly back to stand in front of me.

'Lucina,' he said, 'I came here from curiosity: and then I recognized truth in you. I speak in the name of that truth, and ask your understanding. I said that neither of us required any intermediary between ourselves and—destiny; but we are both lonely. Is it the secret of our loneliness, that we never allow any one to share our responsibilities until they are so heavy that we are forced to put them down?'

His was no longer the sonorous voice of the prophet; he was pleading with me, as a friend who sees a danger he cannot fully explain, 'We both know that we use forces beyond the comprehension of our minds. We can interpret dreams and omens for those we try to help, but we have to discount omens in our own lives. We know we are masters of our destiny, but only providing we retain mastery of ourselves. We ride destiny as our Pegasus, from whose wings we discern horizons wider than mortality; but if we try to dismount from our perilous steed he is too strong for us to control.'

I knew exactly what he meant, 'We are neither animal nor man, man nor god. We are a kind of centaur: feared by the horses because we can talk, despised by humans because we have four legs instead of two.'

'We dare not listen to Pan: the music of his pipe might cause us to remember the goat. Lucina, I am not trying to frighten you. You have helped many people; will you accept help from a man whose real name is Porgius, whose father was a tanner and whose mother earned her living as a washerwoman?'

'I accept friendship from a man who knows that we are not bound by our heredity, unless this be counted in the long years.'

He smiled: for the first time I saw his face as the reflection of a spirit older than my own, and equally lonely. 'Lucina, we have a role to play which is not easy in our generation. Once we should have been priests to whom people came in love; now we have only a dim light by which to keep faith with our tradition. We wish to inspire love; but we are given homage born of fear. I have so often longed to flee from Rome, to live out the rest of this life as a farmer in clean fields. I have made a heaven for myself to which I escape in dreams: a small house among the hills; white oxen sleek in the sun, vines heavy with good grapes, children who laugh with me, a woman who is content that I am so ordinary a man. There I never have to pretend to be wiser than I am; I never have to be more than the stature to which Porgius was born.'

'I used to dream like that,' I said. 'But the gods were jealous of a girl who aspired to the freedom of Olympus; so they sent her away, to Rome.'

'I believe the gods are never unkind if we accept the necessities we have imposed on ourselves. We shall find our heaven, unless we demand it before the time of harvest.'

'The gods are not jealous gods?'

'What is jealousy?'

'The most cruel of all human emotions, the most destructive, the most evil.'

'Jealousy can be either the destroyer, or the star by which we seek a new horizon. We recognize some one, something,

194

greater than ourselves. If we see it by the black light of our own evil, it is a challenge to our lust for dominance; we try to destroy it, and set on our foreheads the seal of the black goat. If we see it as a beacon of a wider company we hasten towards it in love: and find the fire by which the phoenix in us is reborn.'

'You believe that we find our freedom in simplicity through which we earn our right to heaven? Porgius, you know something which makes you afraid that I shall be too impatient to wait for a rightful tenure of my dreams.'

'I saw nothing which I can express in words, not even an omen clearly delineated. I think you will soon be given a choice between fulfilling your destiny and trying to escape from it. I believe you will find fulfillment in this temple, and in the escape inevitable disillusion.'

'Can we ever escape from disillusion?'

'Only by holding fast to the courage which accepts reality.'

'No one has accused me of lack of courage: they have called me a fool, and a boaster, and an enemy, but never a coward. Do you want to take away this final defence of pride?'

'I want you to cherish your pride, you must learn to love the power you use for the freedom of other people.'

'Is my own freedom not important?'

'I know it to be vital to you, as mine is to me. At last I have discovered the real motive which brought me here: I wanted to find some one whose authority I could accept instead of always having to make my own decisions. But I implore you not to discard your personal authority; don't try to escape into blind obedience, to lose your vision in the small complacency of ignorant faith.'

'You think I am in danger of so doing?'

He took my hand between his, as Aesculapius might have done. 'There is an issue we cannot afford to avoid. You are young and lonely, and beautiful. You wanted power, and now you have got more than you need: and you have found that power is a cold companion. You desire to fulfil your heritage as a woman: if you meet a man whom you believe can let you do so you will long to escape from the role of the priestess. You will find every excuse for yourself: you will have to find your own excuses, for to you will be denied the exterior strength provided by soothsayers and prophets. '

'We are agreed that most people come to us only to be given the courage to fulfil their inclinations? '

'Of course: if not why would soothsayers who are only charlatans flourish as much as we, who once were priests? We are not alone in being weary of responsibility: that loneliness is shared by all who for some forgotten sin inhabit this planet of exiles from reality. A few, a very few, ask for their dreams to be interpreted because they want to learn more of their hearts which have grown cold with much forgetting; but for each one there are a hundred who beg us to remove from them the need to use their own authority, by which alone their freedom can be gained. '

'I have tried to make my patients think for themselves... but it is so very difficult, ' I said. 'I think I have always been honest with every one who really wanted to learn what honesty required. '

'How much I sympathize! How often I have cringed because I found myself paying tribute to expediency, giving false coin because they would not accept the gold which bore another profile than their own! They will pay tribute to any altar which does not make a sacrifice of their beloved complacency. Why do astrologers have so large a following? Theirs is the same power which is used by all tyrants: obey without question; do not try to fight against destiny. It is not easy to fight against temporal power; but the stars cannot be joined in battle. You will find the dominance of false stars wherever a race resents the dominance of the mother; and nowhere is the matron more deeply feared than Rome. Blame one's own weakness on the mother, at her greatest ascendancy which is the moment of birth, the moment of inertia between the dominance of the maternal host by the foetus and the gradual re-establishment of power by the growing child, and you can escape from personal responsibility. The adult finds it distasteful to admit he is still under the influence of his parents, but he is afraid to stand alone. He can no longer blame his mother for his faults, so instead he blames the stars. Men are very lazy in spirit; it is easier to believe in astrology than in themselves!'

'So you have also found it difficult to rescue people from astrologers?'

'I have broken their domination only when I have been able to convince my patients that the price of this tawdry comfort may be their own soul. It is not easy to live by the light of integrity. Until men learn that life can be loved even when it is not easy, there will always be astrologers— and all the other dark altars to the enemies, who laugh behind the masks that men have made for them, from their credulity.'

For the first time I knew from personal experience how a single conversation could break down a barrier carefully constructed against self-recognition. His sincerity demanded my own, 'Porgius, I am very grateful that there is one man in Rome from whom I need not hide how difficult it is to keep faith with myself.'

'You will never lose faith, unless you forget how desperately we are needed. People come to us because they have so little faith in themselves that even in the quietness of their minds they cannot accept brave truth who dares go naked. It is for us who ride Pegasus to show them both their weakness and their immortality; to make them weigh the one against the other; the return to the brute, and the soaring beyond the cold horizons. We can only *show* them the two courses: it is for them to choose.'

'I am not wise as you are wise, Porgius. I can only tell them to follow the heart, which I believe, I *must* believe, is clean; or else condemn them to continue in the service of desire.'

'Ride Pegasus, because we acknowledge kinship with the centaur?' He smiled ruefully. 'You see I am not yet free of concepts by which to overcome the circumstance in which I find myself: I even think in terms foreign to the land of my birth, in the symbols of Greece from which I took my name.'

'I was given the name Lucina: but shall I always have the courage to kindle a flame?'

'If it flickers will you remember Porgius?'

'Yes,' I said, 'I will ask him to remind me that we are pledged to our integrity.'

CHAPTER SIX

the Slaves

With decreasing success I tried to pretend that Porgius had not changed my valuation of myself. At last I had to admit that by uncovering a fear of the future he had awakened a deep unease. I knew that most of my patients could have effected their own cures if they had been honest with themselves: all I could do was to present certain character traits in a dramatic form which caused them to be modified by a deliberate act of will. I was too proud to ask Porgius to help me, and had too little confidence in Salonius. I must try to see Lucina as though she were only another patient: a dissatisfied woman who hoped I might re-establish her sense of importance. I had seen too many people suffer from futility not to be aware of its danger!

How well did I know Lucina? How much happiness did she give? How much would her death affect any one? I tried hard to be honest, to indulge neither in false humility nor complacency: and the result was not conducive to self-satis-faction.

Was I closer to Narcissus and Epicurus than I had been when we left Elysium? No; we were drifting steadily apart and had increasingly little to say to each other. How much was this my fault? Could I blame it on some one else, or on circumstances beyond my control? As I asked myself this question I realized with distaste that I had come to use 'circumstances' as a scapegoat; the role which other patients forced on the gods. So Lucina was trying to escape from responsibility, Lucina was trying to hide in a slough of self-pity!

Surely I was being unfair to her? Salonius had insisted that the influence of the priestess would be lessened, perhaps entirely destroyed, if it became known that she and the Lucina who lived in a small villa were the same person. He had tried to persuade me to live on his estate, so that there would be no chance of my being recognized on my way to and from the temple. I had refused because I was determined not to be parted from Narcissus and Epicurus, and knew they would find it difficult to live under the rule of Salonius.

But had it really been necessary to remain secluded while they lived the normal lives of their age and class? 'I did so only because I was afraid of losing our security: I have accepted these galling restrictions for their sake,' said Lucina, the patient.

'Are you sure?' countered Lucina the priest. 'Was it not an excuse to save you from having to go among people of whom you were afraid...afraid when you had to meet them as an ordinary human being instead of one endowed with an authority they could not wield?'

'Perhaps I was wrong; but I meant it for the best. I thought it was my duty to protect the people I loved. Our security depended on me: what would happen if I had no longer been able to earn money?'

'Have you nothing but money to give? Why have you

become so parsimonious with affection?'

'You cannot say I have been ungenerous,' protested the patient. 'I buy them whatever they want...chariots, slaves, everything. And they don't even pretend to be grateful!'

'Do you? Epicurus has greatly increased your earnings by clever barter. How often do you praise him? Narcissus has become a criterion of taste: his wit is a toast in Rome. How often do you let him feel he has amused you? How often do you laugh *with* him?'

'He never tries to amuse me, unless he wants to show off. He mocks me...when I am silly enough to give him the chance!'

'Can any one laugh with you when you have forgotten to laugh at yourself?'

'At least I am not *funny!*' said the patient desperately. 'If you stop believing in yourself you will destroy everything we have tried to build. You *must* believe in yourself...you dare not do anything else. No one believes in you as a person... no one loves only Lucina.'

Priest and Patient no longer sat in judgement on each other: in power and in pity they tried to conceal their loneliness.

That night I walked home, for I wanted a chance to think as one of the ordinary people with whom I shared the city. I had always been careful to say that it was by the small actions of daily behaviour, the trivial kindness, that the individual was assessed, but I had neglected my own advice. Now I had to learn how to be *nice*, to win back my place in the affection of the two men who meant far more to me than anything else.

First I must show that I was dependent on them for happiness. I must ask them to take me out and make a real effort to let them feel proud of me. Even if I was bored I should have to conceal it, even if the other people were unintelligent I should have to learn their idiom and pretend that children and the household were of absorbing interest.

While we had been poor we had made many plans of what we would do when we had money. We had decided to build a house on one of the Alban hills, and argued about every detail...deciding even the frescoes to be painted on the walls and the mosaic on the bottom of the bath. Now we had more than we could spend, in coin, in rare vases, in credit on the tallies of foreign merchants; but it was dead money which now we must bring alive.

At first it might be difficult to get me included in invitations again, for to explain why Epicurus and Narcissus could not return hospitality at home I had been made the invalid sister, too delicate to be disturbed even by noise from an adjoining room. I should have to produce a good reason for such a sudden return to health. It might be amusing to say that I had been cured by the Priestess of the Tiber. No, on second thought, this might be tactless: I would give the credit to Porgius, which in an oblique way was true.

As I set up the steep road to the villa I felt happy, an ordinary, human happiness. It would be enormously satisfying to be a real person again, even a chariot race would be more exciting than spending half my time secluded in the villa and the rest being an oracle whom I was beginning to dislike!

Narcissus was in the main room, pretending to read a roll he was holding upside down. Poor Narcissus! He must have been on his way to bed when he heard me cross the hall, and was afraid I should see he was a little drunk and make one of the sarcastic remarks at which I had become so adept. Perhaps I should have to learn to get a little drunk too...at least it would be more decent than the rigid sobriety which had been part of my rectitude. What a lovely surprise for him it was going to be, when he discovered we could enjoy each other again!

He looked up and said off-handedly, 'You are early to-night Lucina...how nice for the Olympians to go so soon to their celestial couches.... I suppose you told them you would not be requiring their services again this evening?'

It was interesting to notice that I could feel sympathy even to this remark, instead of being too intent on making an adequate rejoinder to feel either pity or embarrassement.

'Zeus was a trifle distrait, some trouble with the exact interpretation of a cuckoo's wooing, I believe. He strained a neck muscle last time he was a bull and is a little peevish. I thought it more seemly not to add to his distractions.'

'The company they keep in Olympus makes me resigned to my exclusion. Consider, my dear Lucina, how pompous you will have become in a millennium, if one may judge by the progress you have made in the last two years.'

I think I might have rescued the conversation even at this stage if he had not waved his hand towards a small jar on the table beside him, and said with real malice in his voice, 'I am assured that if you will use this ointment, it smells as though it is concocted of goose-grease and owls' droppings, your hideous rash will disappear. Pity I could not get anything better for you to-day, no flowers, no early fruit as offerings to my invalid sister...perhaps my friends are beginning to find you tedious.'

I tried to pretend I found this humorous, 'So I have now been endowed with a rash? On my face, I presume, so that I dare not go into the garden in case I frighten the swallows.'

'No, on your back, my dear Lucina. It comes from having to stay so long in bed. Your kind benefactor was most concerned to hear of your latest affliction. ''Poor creature,'' she said, ''how pitiful to live in bed...and alone.'' '

'How thoughtful of her! No doubt she also finds her bed exhausting...since she has to work in it so hard!'

He swung his legs over the side of the chair and stared at me with glazed solemnity. 'The invalid is fretful this evening? Never mind, I shall conceal this lapse from your usual divine patience. Sometimes I almost believe in my stories of you: the gentle smile with which you reward us for the smallest service, the frail body over-burdened by the radiant spirit. You would appreciate my sister—not that she would deign to stay in the same room with you! She is so delicate, so fond, so well beloved, that it is small wonder the gods are jealous of this pearl whose lack diminishes their treasure!'

There was an Attic vase on the table and I threw it, saw Narcissus duck, heard the crash as it shattered on the wall.

'Temper, Lucina? How vastly becoming...the flush almost resembles health...but your disease has robbed you of the skill with which you threw the discus.'

He lurched from the chair and walked carefully towards the door. Then he opened it again to say, 'You had better blame that on one of your slaves. No doubt you forgot that Epicurus gave it to you only last month...and I happen to know it cost him fifty aurei.'

'And who gave him the money?' I said bitterly. 'Your little sister to whom you cannot even return decent civility!'

'You flatter yourself,' he retorted. 'Romans gave it to us...a tribute to Greek culture with which we strive to leaven their stolidity.'

I heard him shout for his chariot. At least I had privacy in which to be miserable; privacy was the only thing which nobody grudged me, not even Salonius.

It was dawn before Epicurus came home. I had failed with Narcissus but he had always been more understanding. I found him in the hall with the broken vase in his hand.

'I broke it,' I said. 'I lost my temper and threw it at Narcissus.'

I meant to tell him that I was very sorry but he spoke too quickly, 'Four centuries of time are kinder than a moment of Lucina.' Suddenly strong emotion broke into his voice, as though he had seen some one thrashing an animal. 'Have you no feeling, Lucina? Does it mean nothing that you have destroyed something beautiful, something which has far more permanence than yourself, something which makes no demands and is content to be loved for itself? Are you jealous even of the beauty of a vase?'

'I will get you another.... I will go to every merchant until I find one even better.'

'If you bring the finest ever made I will break it in pieces, even though every shard drips blood! Will you never learn that there are some things you cannot buy? You can buy mosaics...they won't mind how much you tread on them. But even a priestess is not rich enough to buy hearts to walk on!'

I ran after him, but he banged the door in my face and I heard the bolt drive into the socket. Why should I plead with him when he preferred an old vase to me? How could I expect any other treatment from a man who boasted that the only real value was in *things*?

For the first time I was really afraid of unhappiness. Unless I could cure myself I should get ill, already I often found it difficult to sleep. I knew that happy people are seldom ill; nor are they destructive and cruel. It is natural for them to be kindly. Was that the answer? Was I so lonely because I had forgotten how to love? In Elysium I had tried to win love by commanding respect; in Rome I had thought I should gain love through power.

If Euripides was here he would be able to help me. He had so often warned me of the danger of being caught up in one of the roles. He might be able to rescue me from the priestess and so free Lucina. He had been right: the dramatist knew more than the philosopher or the physician—and much more than the priestess.

I must write at once and implore him to come to Rome. The matter was far too important to be entrusted to a ship-master. Which slave should I send with the letter? Menander, who looked after the horses...he was more intelligent than the others. He would find Euripides, even if he had left Elysium and gone to one of the islands or to Alexandria.

Suddenly I remembered hearing Aesculapius say, 'You can never ask a favour you are not prepared to grant.' I had recognized that Lucina had become a slave to her desire for power...but she longed to be free. It was no longer decent for me to be served by slaves.

Narcissus and Epicurus might find there was no one to cook their food or to wait on them. If we had to do our own work it might be easier to recapture the lost relationship...or if they insisted on buying new slaves they would at least have to realize that the power to do so had been given by me.

Instead of calling for Tiro I went to find him. He was in the kitchen, watching Porcia, the cook, prepare a dish of crayfish.

'Tiro,' I said, 'will you ask every one to come to the vine pergola...there is something important I want to tell you all.'

Porcia stared at me in astonishment, furtively wiping her hands on the towel she had tied round her waist to protect her tunic. The tunic belonged to me; she was afraid of getting it soiled because it was her duty to protect my property. She owned nothing...not even herself.

The slaves assembled. The old man who looked after the garden was rubbing his hands together as though trying to rid them of the ingrained earth. Porcia seemed close to tears, her lips pressed into a thin line to stop them trembling. Tiro stood apart from the others, betraying his anxiety only by a nervous twitching of the eyelid.

They were afraid that I was going to make them more unhappy. They thought I had decided I could afford better slaves and had summoned them to hear they could expect to be sold at a time convenient to myself. A tear crawled down my face: at least I had the decency not to try to conceal it.

'Please don't be frightened,' I said. 'I have been cruel to you all, but I ask you to believe it was only because I was ignorant. I have made you think that I value your kindness only if I cannot buy better service. You must have suffered many humiliations here. I ask you, most humbly, to forgive me.'

There was a long silence, broken at last by Tiro. 'No slaves in Rome have received better treatment. We have not had to fear the lash since you bought us from the last owner of this villa.' His face hardened, 'The last owner! May his soul rot in Hades.'

'You didn't blame me when the frost killed the vine on the new pergola,' said the gardener. 'You never make me suffer for the slugs or the blight: you don't count the bunches of grapes to see if I have stolen any.' His hands clenched, 'I stole six bunches last year, and bought forgetfulness in good wine, as though I had been born free.'

'You are all freed,' I said gently. 'I ask you to pardon a Greek woman, who forgot it is blasphemy to demand service which cannot be given in affection.'

'I don't understand,' said Porcia. 'I have cooked for you as well as I know how, and for the Lord Epicurus, difficult to please as he is. Far too little you eat, but it's not my fault. I would have made five dishes for each one you ordered...but you never gave me a chance!'

She began to weep, wailing to the gods to defend her from the unreasonable complaints of foreigners. I took her by the hand and drew her down on the bench beside me, 'Porcia, listen to me. I am not angry; I am only trying to explain that I am *sorry*.' I looked up at the gardener, 'My ingratitude could have been a real blight on the plants...thank you for defending them. I ask you all to forgive me for being such a fool as to think that one person can *own* another.'

'What do you mean?' said Tiro. 'In the names of the gods, tell us what you mean!'

'I give freedom to you all, and each of you shall have three hundred aurei.'

'I shall get drunk,' said the gardener, 'superbly drunk, twice every month. I shall buy a strip of land below here and get drunk on my own wine.' He looked at me, strong and belligerent, 'When I am no longer a slave shall you try to keep me out of this garden? You don't understand this ground, no one understands it except me.'

'It is your garden more than it has ever been mine. What

have I ever done for it except to pick the flowers which grew for you? I will bring the lower slope into your providence... it will be glad to have so kind a master as yourself.'

'A freeman,' said the gardener. 'It will be good to be free...so long as you don't try to send me away.'

'This will always be your home unless you choose to go.'

'I shall stay too,' said Porcia. 'I've got used to foreign cooking, and I don't like Romans, any more than my mother did when they brought her here. I was born a slave but she wasn't.' She stared at me, and then said slowly, 'I am free... I can't believe it yet...but I am free!'

She began to laugh, cried at the same time, covered her face with her hands and ran towards the kitchen. I started to follow her. Tiro put his hand on my shoulder, as a friend would do.

'I suggest that the Lady Lucina leaves Porcia alone to realize her incredible good fortune.'

'Thank you, Tiro. I shall think of you often, remember your many kindnesses.'

'I hope it will never be necessary only to remember. You will still require a steward...a steward who will always be proud to guard your interests.'

'You mean...you don't want to go away?'

'None of us want to go,' said Menander. 'We have been happy here, even as slaves. We shall be still happier now that we stay from choice.'

Surely the two boys who carried my litter could not feel the same inexplicable loyalty? They were standing beside each other; the one very dark, the other with red hair which showed he was also an alien in Rome.

'Don't *you* want to go?' I said. 'You will have three hundred aurei; enough to buy land, even to buy a slave if you want one.'

The dark boy threw away the whip of straw which he had been nervously twisting between his fingers. 'I want to stay with the horses. I love horses, and yours would never be properly looked after by any one else. I shall use my money: I want to drive a chariot in the Circus.' He held himself very straight, 'Whether I wear the Red or the White it will be your colours that win—Lady Lucina. And if I am hurt I shall not have stolen my health from my owner. Wait until I feel a quadriga in hand...you will never regret I am free.'

'The Lady Lucina is tired,' said Tiro. 'She must rest before going to the temple. I speak for us all when I say we are honoured to serve the Priestess of the Tiber.'

He dismissed them with a gesture: I might give them freedom, but to Tiro they were still the obedient servants of his stewardship. So Tiro had not been deceived by the excuse that I went to the house of Salonius because he was my physician and I was helping him to translate a manuscript into Greek?

'So you know I am also the priestess?'

He smiled, 'The Lady Lucina can now share the knowledge of other freemen. No patrician has discovered the identity of the oracle: the slaves know it, but they do not gossip except among their own kind. We know much about you that even the Lord Narcissus has never guessed. We rejoiced every time you diminished a tyrant, and we tried in our own way to show sympathy, to give you strength to fight in our cause. Did you never guess why Porcia made such good broth for you, why the best flowers were cut for your room? We tried to let you know we were not...unaware.'

'I took your kindness for granted. I was too ignorant, too blind, to be really grateful.'

'But we are grateful,' he said gently. 'We have never ceased to notice the charities which to you seem natural...to you who were not born in Rome.'

'And I was too arrogant to be comforted!'

'The slave is deprived of everything except insight. Although no patrician would accept it, I believe that when the gods judge a man's soul they are not deaf to the verdict of his slaves. To us you have never been only a foreigner or a priestess. We have seen, and loved, the *person*...and sometimes regretted that the person was not always ascendant!'

'I will try to remember the person,' I said, and for the first time knew the meaning of humility.

CHAPTER SEVEN

the SenatoR

That night everything seemed different, even me. I enjoyed the food which Porcia brought, and joked with the boys who carried my litter. We decided which of the fat patricians we saw would lose when they wagered against the future champion of the Circus.

Iris was waiting for me at the landing-steps. 'You are late,' she said. 'Salonius wanted to see you, but the patient is already with him, up at the house.'

'Who is it?' I asked indifferently. 'It can't be any one important or I should have been told sooner.'

'Nigellus: one of the few Senators who have real authority.'

I sighed. 'Another greedy old man who wants reassurance that he will find proper respect in heaven...and get there! Or does he require an omen, to clear his conscience before he orders the death of some unfortunate country which Rome envies?'

'I don't think Nigellus is one of those. I saw him. He is quite young, and too thin to be greedy. He looks more like an athlete, a Greek, of course, not one of the gladiators.'

It always warmed my heart to hear Iris' contempt of Romans. 'It pleases me to maintain the fiction that I am not bound by the ordinary standards of courtesy. Nigellus is

209

probably only too used to having people hurry to please him. He may find the cultivation of a little patience most salutory!'

In spite of Iris, I managed to take longer over my preparations than usual. I decided that the red poppies were unsuitable; so changed them for a few sprays of rosemary which she had placed ready in a jar in case I wanted them for a wreath. I let her dress me in white, and then changed it for a blue robe embroidered with small silver stars. Then, obeying a sudden impulse, I told her that she could go home when the patient arrived.

'I can't,' she said. 'You know Salonius never lets you be here alone.'

'I shan't be alone: I shall have Nigellus.'

'But you need me to write down anything you want to remember.'

'I shan't forget anything I want to remember; and I am tired of making notes to please Salonius.'

'I won't go,' she said. 'I dare not.'

'Then you can tell the Senator that the Priestess is not in the mood to listen to his troubles. You can also tell Salonius that I am too tired to work to-night...you needn't add ''and too bored'' unless you feel inclined to join in a quarrel!'

'I can't do that! Lucina, don't ask me to do such a terrible thing!'

'Well, the choice is your own. Leave me alone here, or take the alternative. Every one chooses the better of any two alternatives. I have proved that to the satisfaction even of philosophers!'

'Will it be enough if I wait in the oak grove?' she said desperately.

She looked so distressed that I was sorry to have teased her. 'Wait in the grove, and listen to Lucius. He will make much better hearing than a poppy-drunk Roman.' She blushed. 'You love Lucius, don't you? Never try to run away from love; unless you want to be so lonely that you haven't the spirit to run even from death.'

'I daren't love him,' she said. 'He is a slave. I can't afford to love a slave.'

I took her by the shoulders and shook her gently. 'Iris, stop trying to hide from your heart! You love Lucius: be thankful that you still have the strength to love some one more than yourself. He won't be a slave to-morrow, neither will you. I am going to buy your freedom.'

She looked at me, bewildered. 'Salonius would never sell us; we are too useful.'

'Salonius will also have to choose between two alternatives. He can *either* keep you and Lucius, *or* me.

She fell on her knees and kissed the hem of my dress. I tried to draw her to her feet but her hands were limp, so I knelt beside her. 'Don't cry, Iris. You mustn't cry.'

The gauze curtain held its usual placid folds: the lamp burned with a clear flame. I had waited here for more than seven hundred people: why did I feel this curious excitement, almost fear?

The gold cup, calm with poppy-sleep, waited beside the couch; the branches of rosemary cast their precise pattern on the walls. I heard some one walking up the path from the river. Some one who was unhurried, secure; for whom I waited.

A tall man stood between the bronze doors: the lines of his body were clean and strong, as though experience had scoured away all the unessential flesh.

I knew he would have been carefully instructed in the temple procedure. He would drink from the cup, and then lie on the couch beside the lamp. I would watch his eyelids grow heavy before he began to speak. He might take a scroll, on which he had written the questions he wished to ask the oracle, from a fold of his toga. He would try to inscribe them deeper in his mind before he let the drowsy peace assail him. I had seen this happen so often; why did I expect Nigellus to be different?

I watched him glance quickly round the room. He took the gold cup, and poured the pale draught on the floor, but in contempt, not as a libation. The curtain, tenuous as smoke, was no longer the protection of aloof omnipotence.

'I am not concerned with omens,' he said, 'nor do I wish to consult oracles. But I am aware that no one can be wise in every field. I have a problem which has not been resolved by the means I have been able to employ. As it does not directly concern myself I have to seek advice even by methods I have publicly rebuked.'

'So although you are not sympathetic to the soothsayers you have come to my temple? I am honoured by such discernment!'

'If your advice is to be sound, I must purchase it with honesty. I did not expect to consult you: I went to Salonius, whose skill I respect.'

'But you do not respect mine?'

'I hope that I can maintain an unbiased opinion of faculties beyond my understanding. Salonius tells me that you are possessed of greater wisdom than himself; until I have reason to doubt him I am prepared to accept his judgement.'

Certainly I had not been wrong in thinking this man would be different! I had become familiar with abject belief, and on occasion had fought with open hostility; never had I met this calm evaluation.

'That you have a small opinion of soothsayers need be no barrier between us: their methods are distasteful to me,' I said.

'You consider yourself to be an inspired intermediary between your patients and the gods?'

'Yes; when their gods are no more than a projection of unfulfilled desire or an embodiment of fear.'

I knew this statement was dangerous. If he claimed that I had admitted disbelief in the gods I should be in danger. The temple might be destroyed even if I managed to escape from Rome.

'I owe homage to your integrity,' he said. 'And I shall pay it in the coin of discretion. Is it agreed between us that we may speak with tongues inspired by honesty and unguarded by expediency?'

'It is agreed.'

'In this contract I do not include your scribe. I presume you have a scribe, for Salonius has the type of mind which would require an exact record of all that appertains to his province.'

So I had not been lacking in discernment when I sent Iris away! 'It is my usual practice to have a scribe in attendance: such records are of value in the treatment of future patients. For some reason, of which I am not fully aware, I said I wished us to be alone here to-night.'

I pulled aside the curtain. 'We are neither of us dependent on convention, nor on the trappings by which it is usual to maintain our authority. See for yourself; the Greek girl who acts as my scribe is not here.'

'Your word is enough,' he said courteously. 'I have sufficient honesty to recognize it in my equals.'

If even Salonius had called me his equal I should have taken it as a challenge: but from Nigellus I accepted a compliment.

'You are much younger than I expected,' he said slowly. 'I thought no woman could command the respect of Salonius unless she were old and ugly.'

'I thought that no Roman could be a Senator unless he were old and fat.'

He laughed. 'To-day has at least returned to us the capacity for surprise!'

'So you also have made of intellect a shield against disillusion?'

He looked at me, his eyes very blue, dark as the sea at the beaches of Elysium.

'I think we should drink a toast to a courage which can dare...illusion,' I said, and hoped my voice was steady as though I made only a trivial jest.

He laughed again, as a young man laughs whose head is not weary with bays. 'Is there wine here? We cannot drink in lethe for I threw it away.'

'We do not need lethe, and I regret that the wine is only a Falernian of the second growth...help me to fetch it.'

The wine was slightly acid, for the amphora had been opened several days and Iris had forgotten to replace it. There was a cold roast fowl and a bowl of salad, for I sometimes ate with Iris before going home.

We sat on the couch; eating chicken in our fingers. I told him about Elysium, as any ordinary woman would talk of her childhood to a man who found it exciting to hear of her life before their meeting.

'This is the first time for years, more years than I like to count, that I have been a real person,' he said. 'Always I am the Senator, or the husband, or the father...or the intellectual who has to make himself believe there is nothing else.'

So he was married? Of course he was married; he was a Roman, and a Senator. Why should I resent his wife, when I had had such ample proof that Roman matrons required only pity, or contempt?

'How old are your children?' I asked. I expected to hear they were small, perhaps still infants.

'My daughter is seventeen; my son two years older.'

Most Romans married young. He might have had older children...he must have lived with his wife nearly twenty years. Who was she?

'Was it about your children that you came to me?' I said.

'I am deeply concerned for my son.'

I tried to conceal how easy it was to share concern...for his son. 'What is wrong with him?'

'He takes no interest in women. I think this may be caused by the effect on his sister by their mother. He shows a disquieting affection for a foreigner.'

So Nigellus knew that his wife was not a wise mother to

her daughter; I was not surprised, but disproportionately pleased.

'Your wife is jealous of her daughter? If so, she shares this disease with many other matrons. Women will always be jealous of their daughters until they learn to welcome maturity instead of seeing it as an increasing weakening of their powers.'

'Roman women are seldom aware of the power of the spirit. They are concerned only with power which is bound up in physical dominance. There are few Roman faces which show the serenity of age.' He looked at me as though I were a statue he had carved. 'You will be beautiful when you are old, Lucina. You Greeks hold in your bones the secret of antiquity.'

'I will never be old,' I said impulsively; and then added, 'Age is only a habit of mind...it has nothing to do with the years since our bodies were born. Of course I shall live to be an old woman.... I am much too interested in living to die young; I am not so great a coward that I want to escape from life.'

'I no longer want to escape,' he said, and his voice was solemn as though he took an oath, 'I no longer want to escape from a living reality.'

CHAPTER EIGHT

attic Vase

I had left a message with Tiro to say I would try to be home early and that I hoped to see Narcissus and Epicurus before I went to bed. I had wanted to tell them that the slaves were free and to ask them to forgive me for having been so difficult. But it was the priestess who came back to the villa, deeply angry with Narcissus. Just before Nigellus left me I had discovered the name of the foreigner who dominated his son.

'Marcus is besotted about this Greek,' Nigellus had said. 'He is a man of culture, like most of your countrymen, and I must admit that I welcomed him to my house. At first I thought he came to see Flavia and was not displeased: most Romans would consider it unfortunate if their daughter married a foreigner, but I am only concerned that she shall find happiness...and happiness is a rare bedfellow in this city. I had heard that Salonius worked with a Greek woman, perhaps that is why I sought him instead of some other physician. The boy is enamoured of Greece, but I am not sure whether it is only because he echoes every opinion expressed by Narcissus.'

Narcissus! Surely there must be other Greeks of the same name?

'What manner of man is he?' I said, trying to sound casual.

'He lives with an invalid sister, and another man, in a modest property, but they appear to be people of wealth.'

'What is the sister like?'

'Narcissus told me she suffers from some illness which keeps her secluded. They brought her to Rome hoping to find a cure, but they have been disappointed. His concern for her made me think he would be a good husband for Flavia; which showed a lamentable lack of insight into the less attractive aspects of Greek culture. Lucina, what can I do to help Marcus?'

I had had to think very quickly; somehow I must make Narcissus promise not to see the boy again. I must never let him realize how deeply I was concerned. I had been proud of truth, and now I had to lie to the men who were most important to me.

I had been able to make Nigellus believe that it was not unusual for me to ask for seven days in which to consider his problem. I think he was not reluctant for this opportunity to arrange a second meeting.

I waited on the terrace until the sky was streaked with dawn, listening for the sound of a chariot. It was useless to wait any longer: Narcissus would not be in the mood to accept my appeal at this hour, for even a Greek cannot attend a Roman banquet and retain a clear mind.

There were no lights in the villa, but one of the boys drowsed in the forecourt, waiting to take the horses to their stable. He stood up as I passed, though I had tried not to wake him. We smiled at each other, and I was reassured because he was no longer afraid to have been found asleep.

I woke to hear Narcissus stumble towards his room. So he was very drunk; I should send for him during the morning, and find him at a disadvantage.

I deliberately chose to have the first meal served on the terrace, in the full sunlight, instead of under the vine pergola. I knew Narcissus was too proud of his capacity for wine to admit he did not feel inclined to follow it with goat's milk and fish fried with garlic. There was a greenish tinge to his skin, which gave me a certain malicious pleasure. He and Epicurus found it amusing that I accepted the role of the invalid for their convenience: it would be their own fault if they had forgotten that I could also be a woman of discernment.

'No appetite this morning, Narcissus? I hope you are not suffering from fever, I hear it is particularly severe this summer.'

'There is nothing wrong with me,' he said crossly. 'But I presume you asked me to join you for some better reason than to make futile inquiries about my health?'

'My insight must be infectious! No doubt with this new faculty you already know what I wish to say?'

'If you are going to talk in riddles at home as well as in your professional capacity, I shall go back to bed. An oracle would be intolerable under the same roof.'

'As the roof belongs to the oracle the choice for her guests should not be difficult: their welcome is absolute unless they find the laws of hospitality uncongenial.'

Narcissus leaned back in his chair. 'What's the matter with you this morning? You send for me almost before I've had time to go to sleep and then you try to be deliberately tiresome. Can't you vent your anger on one of the slaves and leave me in peace?'

'We have no slaves,' I said calmly. 'I freed them yesterday.'

'Don't be silly, Lucina. I heard Porcia singing in the kitchen, and Tiro brought me your message...no, ''summons'' would be a more accurate description.'

'Tiro and Porcia, and the others, will continue to work here, providing that you treat them with respect. If they leave us, because they find you intolerable, you will have to buy your own slaves, or learn to look after yourself.'

'Lucina, what *are* you talking about? Must you be clever so early in the morning? Have you lost all sense of decency?'

'We will not concern ourselves with the way the household is run; that, after all, is the concern of your little sister, who will continue to be docile so long as you do what she wants.'

'Well, what *do* you want? I would grant any request this morning if it could buy my release from this interminable conversation.' He passed his hand over his forehead and shuddered. '*Dear* sister, can I ask for your clemency in the matter of this revolting dish which offends my nostrils with the stench of garlic? May I tell Tiro to remove it, to bury it, to give it to the swine, to throw it in the river, anything rather than I should continue to suffer its assault?'

Tiro was looking out of the window of the main room and I called to him. 'The Lord Narcissus is not feeling in full health this morning. He finds the smell of fish disturbing, so will you take it away, but dispose of it so that Porcia will not think us unappreciative.'

With extreme gravity Tiro removed the offending dish: but I hoped that Narcissus noticed the smile in his eyes; a smile intended for me to share.

'How glad I am that you are not inclined for futile argument, Narcissus; it will save us both much needless conversation. You have agreed to grant any request I may choose to make; in gratitude I will escort you to your room where the pillow waits to comfort your aching head. You will not see Marcus, son of Nigellus, again. We are agreed?'

He stood up, leaning on the table. 'What do you know of Marcus? We don't interfere with you and I'll thank you to leave me to manage my own life. When I need advice from the oracle I'll come to the temple; and find you are a very old woman, for by then I shall be senile!'

'I wished the courtesies to be maintained so I made a request. But it is an order, Narcissus. Do you understand, an *order?*'

'And if I refuse?'

'You will cease to be my concern. Therefore you will not occupy my house, nor eat my food, nor ride in my chariots... we no longer have slaves, but no doubt you will find ways of buying some for yourself.'

'What possible interest have you in Marcus?' He sneered. 'Surely the famous priestess can use her talents to better effect than in trying to seduce a boy who is impervious to the deceits of women.'

'No doubt when I decide, or if I decide, to take a lover I shall not find the task unduly difficult.'

'Lucina with a lover! I will believe that when I see one of the statues expose the doubtful enticements which folds of marble so fortunately conceal! You will never take a lover, Lucina, you have not the courage. You only exist through your facility to dominate; you know that you would lose everything if you allowed yourself to believe any one superior. I think you would bite the coins that Zeus gave you if he became so besotted that he mistook you for a swan!

'Your mythology is at fault. However, that is hardly surprising, for you are in no condition to display intelligence or the most elementary recognition of your circumstances. I give few orders in this house, I play the role of the docile sister with commendable patience; but you will not see Marcus again, for reasons which are adequate and no doubt beyond your comprehension. Let it be sufficient that I consider it better if Rome remains free from certain Greek customs.'

'I find it amusing that you should consider the pose of outraged virtue at all convincing. If you suckle a child on Falernian is it surprising that it becomes a pupil of Dionysus? You are right in thinking that I fear women, for I see them in you, and in myself. You are ruthless as no man is ruthless; you are cold and clever, and have a hideous wisdom which taught me that even the revels of Olympus fall into embarrassed silence when Athene enters. You are worse than Julia, the mother of Marcus—who caused him to hate women.'

'There are many women in Rome; must I be blamed for their deficiencies?'

'You taught me to despise them, to expect the standard of conversation which was usual in Elysium. I see the peevish toilet behind the smooth, painted cheek, the endless preoccupation with trivialities which caused the exact folds of a dress, the greed which has inspired a banquet. You made me see all this, you broke the cup from which I might have drunk a sweet illusion.'

'You are unfair! I never bother to use face-paint except when I am in the temple...and you have never seen me there. You choose my clothes, have I ever complained about them; have I ever blamed Porcia if the food was badly cooked?'

'No, Lucina; but you made me see what other women value, and made me know I cannot accept their currency. You were clever, so very much too clever to be content with love! I liked women when I came to Rome, I enjoyed the few banquets we attended as obscure foreigners, when we were grateful for even a casual invitation because we could eat without worrying about the tallies that were mounting against us in the food shops. I laughed with you when you mimicked the matrons and showed us the silly little thoughts which lurked under the polished facade of eager virgins. I used to be in love with you; and when I found that you preferred Clion I tried to find a woman like you, a woman with a mind of a man housed in a body I was free to love. I was fortunate, I never found your equal. No man can be happy married to a goddess...for men are not ashamed of being human.'

'I don't try to be a goddess! Can't you understand that I have to pretend to be more than I am so that none of us will ever be afraid of poverty again? Do you want to go back to the time when we were always afraid, and had to be so terribly gay to hide it from each other?'

'It is better to be hungry for food than for power. You will never have enough power to satisfy you; it is a fearful appetite, gnawing away at your heart, always making increasing demands that have to be placated whatever the cost.'

'I don't want power,' I said desperately, clenching my hands so that he would not see they were shaking. 'Or only enough so as not to be afraid of people who would destroy us if they had the chance.'

'Didn't you want power over Clion? Aren't you glad that you can threaten me with poverty unless I am obedient? It must be amusing to be able to order people's lives, to take away the only happiness they have managed to find; and to do it with a sense of virtue, as a mother takes a toy from a child, unmoved by its screams because she believes it might suck off the paint and make itself sick!'

'If you prefer to think I am only a bully there is nothing more I can say. But, Narcissus, please Narcissus, try to remember that there has been much kindness between us. I didn't give you things because I wanted you to be dependent, I was so very glad that I hadn't betrayed your confidence which made you come with me to Rome. I wasn't jealous that I couldn't go out with you and Epicurus...or only very seldom when I thought you didn't understand how very dull it is being alone here all day, how very tired I get of trying to make people have the courage to see things as they really are instead of as they would like them to be. Won't you believe in me?'

His face softened. 'I would find it easy to believe in the Lucina I knew in Elysium if she would again have the charity to let her intimates live their own lives.'

'You mean you will either see me or Marcus...or neither. You will go on loving him even if it means going away and never seeing me again?'

'You overrate me, Lucina. I shall give up Marcus if you demand it; not because I love you more than him, but because I am too lazy to give up my comforts. He is dependent on his father who no longer welcomes me to his house.'

'I can't alter my decision, and I can't tell you why, for at least I have never betrayed the secrets told to me as a priest. But please don't hate me, Narcissus; I shall be even more lonely if you hate me.'

'I don't hate you,' he said sardonically. 'I love the man in you and seek it in other men: I only hate the woman whom I taught to copy the female I despise in myself.'

CHAPTER NINE

ΠιGellus

Salonius was so flattered at the first tribute sent to him by Nigellus that he agreed to allow me to buy Iris and Lucius; I made it clear that I would only work with slaves who owed personal allegiance to me, and for the moment he was more than content with my abilities. I concealed the fact that I had granted them freedom; it would be time enough when they left Rome. I should be sorry to lose the company of Iris, and a quarrel is an astringent balm not without a quality of healing.

Iris, however, showed a sense of the realities which I had not suspected in her: she wished to marry Lucius, but not until she became pregnant...a condition which, judging by the way they looked at each other, I thought unlikely to be long delayed. Part of me dreaded her going, the rest looked forward to the time when I should be spared the constant reminder that, though I had had a measure of devotion and more awe than I could digest, I had never been loved as a woman. It is easy to despise women, so long as one is clever enough to refrain from being envious...and perhaps I was not so clever as I thought.

Nigellus was coming to hear my verdict on the seventh day: I had often told people of the futility of trying to speed or to delay the natural passage of time, and now I learned that it is easier to give advice than to use it. I told myself that it was natural to look forward to telling a Senator how easily a woman had solved a problem which had been too difficult for him; but I was not really deceived.

I arranged the flowers slowly, discarding roses, and then salvias, in favour of flowering pomegranate in alabaster jars. I selected a Greek wine for which Epicurus had paid a ridiculous sum which now seemed reasonable, and Porcia made a poem of infant lobsters chilled with snow. Surely it was a coincidence that the Macedonian goldsmith had come to the villa with a necklace and wreath jewelled with emeralds which it would have been foolish to ignore? Ornaments had never been interesting, no more than part of a necessary facade which I accepted as due to a certain role, knowing always that it was no more than a role. But these emeralds were exciting, green as the moss in a secret grove where lovers are remembered.

Iris was unashamedly glad to be told that I should not need her. I even preferred to choose my dress alone: the white dress with silver ribbons, too young for a priestess, so I had never worn it. 'You look beautiful to-night,' I said aloud, secure that Iris had already left to wait for Lucius. 'You look beautiful, at least in this city where the women are often dark and over-plump.'

'I am sure Julia is fat,' I added, suddenly defensive. 'Fat because she is too lazy to think, too cowardly to find each day a new adventure. Such women deserve to be thrown back into the battle for security, to lose the things of which they have forgotten the value.'

I heard myself humming, a tune on four notes...the tune a goat-herd had played while a child listened. The sound was like cold water on the face of a sleeper. I was deliberately reverting to childhood, to the time when I could act without consideration, when I dared to feel, instead of guiding my emotions as a charioteer controls the quadriga on which his life depends. I felt suddenly cynical, and not a little foolish.

'Lucina,' I said, and sounded very like Salonius in a difficult mood, 'surely you have sufficient intelligence to be aware of your motives! Narcissus told you that no one would be such a fool as to wish to be your lover. You are lonely, and so have a pitiable vulnerability. The role of a mistress would be both unbecoming and ridiculous; the role of a matron, dull in the extreme and a deliberate discarding of your talents. Nigellus is only another man, of whom you have seen so many in their childish incompetence, wailing for something to add to their pathetic faith in their importance. They come to you when their mothers and their wives and their mistresses no longer provide them with sufficient material to shore up the tottering edifice of their self-worship. You have seen many women weep because the men they thought were gods have proved themselves only men. You have been sorry for them, and always a little scornful; are you such a fool that a taunt from Narcissus is enough to drive you to their shared disaster?'

The branches of pomegranate were no more than a device of interlaced shadows; the emeralds only green stones in an ornate setting. To-night was only another of the marks by which time is measured; to be endured with wit, with the evaluation of experience, with loneliness which pride has burnished from the tarnish of dependence.

The snow had melted in the bowl, the wine-jug was half empty. I had played the charming, aloof hostess, to whom the powers of the mystic were only a further accomplishment. Because I had made no claims, Nigellus was ready to believe that the change in Marcus, his sudden dislike of the Greek with whom he had been infatuated, was due to some supernatural influence. I was credited with being a foster-child of the blind Fates whose word would change the threads of destiny. I could be no more than a memory to Nigellus; I was secure that the living frieze I had designed was not within my capacity to improve. It only remained to think of suitable words with which to ease the moment of his dismissal.

'You have given my son back to me,' he said. 'The boy is hurt and angry...but the hurt will soon heal, the anger cool. I shall never cease to remember what I owe to beneficent powers I am too ignorant to understand.' He put his hand on my arm, the long fingers gentle against my skin. 'I shall never forget what I owe to Lucina,' he said.

'You are not my debtor,' I said passionately. 'If you let

yourself believe you owe me anything you will hate me...
you are not beholden for anything...for anything!'

'Is it no debt when a man who is old in disillusion has been
given back his dreams?'

'Is the Senator not content with reality?'

'Since I was eighteen, I have never known reality, if that
be the sanctuary which cannot be destroyed by the living
dead. Perhaps I always knew that circumstances would be
strong for my secret world.'

'Is Julia part of that world, or one of the living dead?'

He looked puzzled, 'I forgot that I had told you my wife's
name...or did you discover it through your finer intuition?'
Without waiting for me to reply, he went on, the words
urgent as a spring long sealed. 'When I was a young man, I
thought I should find a woman to whom I could be...every-
thing, as she would be to me. I had watched my mother and
father grow in hatred, that was limned on a background of
expediency with the brush of painful civility. The great
house in Rome was part of the background, the slaves a
chorus too well disciplined to chant the real theme of this
petty drama. A sum of money was left to me by an uncle.
With it I bought a small property in Umbria, concealing the
purchase even from my closest friends. There is a white
house hidden in an ilex grove. I thought there I should find
love in simplicity, free of the cold conventions of this city,
alight with a generous kindliness unknown to matrons. I
welcomed my betrothal to Julia; she was slender, beautiful in
the Roman fashion. I told her of my hill sanctuary and
thought to take her there. But her father gave us a villa by
the sea; she made me understand that it would be foolish to
offend paternal authority, squalid to bathe in a forest pool
instead of with the proper attendance, undignified to be content with the service of an old freeman and his wife when we
had twenty slaves, given by her mother as a marriage gift.

'We went to the villa; sometimes I wonder if Julia found
the same thorns among the yellow roses with which our

rooms were so carefully embellished. We have both followed the roles designed for us in ignorant affection by our parents: I am a Senator, as was my father; Julia is among the matrons whose verdict ruled her as a young girl. She has found it easy to barter dreams for authority, but I...I shall never forgive her, because she taught me that bays are more heavy than the lead with which a sarcophagus is sealed.'

'You wanted power, Nigellus; you could not cease to fear your father until you had more than his authority. You thought you wanted a girl who would let you forget your obligations; but the pattern you had chosen was stronger than yourself. The wife of the Senator is...Julia. Is it fair to hate her because she was not strong enough to make you change the aim of your ambition?'

'You think that even with another woman I should be only the Senator?'

'While you still lusted for power you would never have been satisfied with a bread which could not ease that special hunger. Have you ever been hungry, Nigellus? It is easy to despise greed when your belly is quiet; but I have known that the next meal can loom so important that nothing else matters. ''How shall we eat to-morrow?'' Once that was the question so much more vital than the most urgent concepts of philosophy: I shared it with more than half the inhabitants of Rome, or any other city, and found no solace in the sharing. The body hungers for food, the soul for power: now we find a new hunger because our old needs have reached satiety.'

'So the priestess is also lonely?'

'We both fulfil our roles without discredit: what more can we ask?'

'That question can never be spoken. You are the priestess to whom Rome gives homage, who has taught me that a house in the Umbrian hills must remain forever empty.'

I should not see him again. I was sending him away with a memory of the woman I had made him think might have been his dear companion. 'Be careful, Lucina,' I said to my heart. 'You dare not look forward to sorrow. Guard your courage to keep the present safe: in a few moments the drama you have written will be played out, and you at liberty to join the audience, and weep with them if you must.'

I intended to ask him to see if Lucius was at the landing-stage, but instead I heard myself speaking lines that were not in the polished dialogue I had rehearsed in my mind. 'We shall not see each other again, Nigellus; before you go to take the path you have chosen, the path which I cannot follow, I must take from you a memory I had thought would remain cherished among your dreams. I am not only the priestess, I am ordinary, as all women are ordinary. I pride myself that I do not find it necessary to lie; but to-night I have lied to you, or let you accept as a mysterious truth something which has a tawdry explanation.

'You believe that the change in Marcus is due to a power which is denied to other women. But is it unusual for a woman to exercise any powers she may command to gain an object which to her seems vital? Any woman would steal, and cheat, and lie if need be, to gain a desperate need when other methods have failed. I did not influence Marcus to give up Narcissus through any subtle strength; I told Narcissus that he could chose between your son and the comfort of an idle life at my expense. He chose comfort, and at least had the decency to tell the boy that his affection was not proof against the loss of easy security.

'I acted the tyrant, Nigellus, and found the role horribly familiar. Until now I have been able to afford to despise the tyrants of Rome, but now I have lost the right to feel superior to them. Perhaps Narcissus would not have fallen such an easy victim to expediency, or at least protested a little for the sake of his dignity and my own, if three days ago he had not ordered a new chariot with a harness of scarlet leather studded with silver...a child forgets its pride when its newest toy is threatened. The chariot has been paid for with my share of the tribute you gave to Salonius. I came to Rome with two men who were my friends; they stay with me because it is expedient.

'I became complacent, and I cling to it as my ultimate defence against the recognition that I have failed. I am a success in the role which a wise man warned me would lead only to a deeper knowledge of inadequacy. He called himself Aesculapius; and I thought that his claim to be a realist was only an old man's boast. If you had known me before I ran away from Greece I could have kept safe your dreams; but now I can only give you my honesty, to save you from allowing me to steal your house in the hills from some other woman who still has the right of entry in simplicity.'

All the time I had been talking he had been statue-still. He got slowly to his feet, and I thought he was going away without speaking to the woman who had betrayed his faith in her. He stood looking down at me.

'I knew before I came here that the name of the girl who lived in the house of Narcissus was...Lucina. It is not difficult for a Senator to make discreet inquiries; I knew the two Lucinas shared more than a name. I intended to threaten you with exposure unless you agreed to make Narcissus stop seeing my son. I played the comedy of our first conversation because I thought it amusing to be more subtle than the soothsayer. We both intended to deceive each other, but we have found that honesty is the only coin which dare pass between us.'

He went on one knee and took my hands between his. 'Life is too strong for us, Lucina. But love and dreams are stronger than life, and we shall gain eternity for our dreams.'

'Is life too strong for us? Dare we try to escape from our destiny?'

'We must not betray our strength; you cannot run away from the men and women who come to you for comfort, for health, for sanity. And I? I am only a Senator, but I have sworn my service to my countrymen. My voice cannot speak my heart to you, for it owes duty to the Forum where it may serve to keep in check the legions who would fight without just cause.'

'We may live to be very old, Nigellus. Will our dreams endure the tarnish of the years?'

'Can a sword-blade lose its power to reflect light if it is burnished every hour with sand? Time shall be the sand we use as burnish, the separate grains clean with honesty, sharp and defiant of destiny with our pride.'

'Pride, Nigellus? Are we not weary with pride?'

'I have never before known pride; until to-day when I found the woman who will wait with me for a fulfilment others cannot dare...a heaven we shall enter beyond the trappings of a Roman funeral.'

He kissed me; his body lean and hard under my hands. 'Good-bye, Lucina,' he said. 'I must go, to leave you guardian of our future.'

CHAPTER TEN

twilight

Because of Nigellus I found it difficult to remain unaffected by my patients: their emotions were now real to me, their troubles a menace, because I knew that I could so easily discover myself equally vulnerable. I, who had recognized that indigestion was usually a symptom of a more subtle failure, found myself disinclined to eat. I tried to hide my lack of appetite from Salonius to avoid the humiliation of receiving an explanation which I had already given myself with no useful effect. Epicurus seemed anxious that I was getting too thin; Narcissus remarked that my protest against resembling the Roman matrons appeared excessive. 'Perhaps,' he added, 'my taste is becoming blunted through this foreign environment; no doubt in Greece I should have agreed that the shadows under the cheek-bones were a sign of the proud spirit which proves the flesh is too well disciplined to make undue demands.'

Porcia implored me to drink goat's milk, and added cream to every dish. At least I had the decency to tell her I would eat when I got home and she never realized that the vines flourished on the rich diet which I often had to bury while the household slept. I think Tiro knew this small deceit, but kept his counsel and showed by an added kindliness that he was aware I was unhappy.

I knew he was excited when he came into the room where I was writing notes of several cases that would interest Salonius. I had heard a chariot drive up the hill and thought it was only Narcissus.

'There is a young lord from Greece; he says he is a friend.'

'His name, Tiro?'

'The lord Euripides.'

I ran into the courtyard and saw Euripides giving his cloak to one of the boys, smiling at him as no Roman would have done, as only one of us who came from Elysium would have found natural. In that moment I knew what was wrong with me: I had forgotten how to be natural, I had forgotten everything which Aesculapius had tried to teach me.

'How is Aesculapius?' I said. 'Oh, Euripides, I am so glad to see you! I want to hear everything about Elysium; I want to go back there with you.'

He kissed me on the cheek, but instead of sharing my excitement his eyes were grave.

'Is anything wrong?' I said, suddenly frightened.

'Come outside...it is easier to talk in a garden.'

I followed him to the terrace and watched him go to the balustrade and stand staring out across the crowded, alien hills.

'Aesculapius is...dead,' he said, and still he did not look

at me. 'He thought of you while he was dying, Lucina. He asked me to tell you that there is only love between you, that he understood why you had to go away.'

Loneliness was cold as a sword. Now I should never be able to tell Aesculapius that he had been right. Now I should never be able to return to Elysium in search of the courage to believe in love between equals. Now I should never learn how to be kind instead of only benign; to be brave enough to receive, instead of only giving what I dare not accept.

I heard a woman crying, sharp, desperate sobs that tore the throat like skeleton fingers. 'He can't be dead,' I heard her say. 'He can't be dead. If he is dead, Lucina killed him; and she isn't a murderess, she isn't! Lucina is only a fool who hurt herself so badly that she is cruel...but she isn't really cruel...she is only unhappy. He gave her everything and she threw it away...but people don't die because the things they have given are thrown away. They are sorry, but later they are happy because they learn they are right...the people come home and tell them they are right....'

I heard Tiro's voice, and Euripides asking him which was my room. Porcia was there...or was it Elissa? She was kind as only Elissa had been kind. I was a child afraid of the dark...yet there was a lamp burning among the shadows....

So I had gone to see Porgius...Porgius whom every one else called Calchas. He had given me the poppy-drink. Why didn't he recognize me? Soothsayers treat each other as equals...they don't have to pretend to each other...we can't always pretend...we can't go on being so much more than we really are.

'Porgius! Porgious, make them understand I am only Lucina. They think it is so easy...always being clever and knowing why people are unhappy and making them better again. But I can't always be clever, Porgius...sometimes I have to think about *me*. And I don't want to think about me...but I can't help it. I have to live with me, all the minutes and hours and days...and the nights too, Porgius. I am so afraid of the nights. That's why I walk along the quays and watch the pattern of masts against the sky. The ships could take me back to Elysium if only the pattern was right...but the pattern is never right. I made it; and I am not very clever. Won't they ever believe that I'm not very clever? Won't they ever believe I want to be ordinary?

'I know I wanted power...but you don't let a child play with a sharp sword. Aesculapius, didn't you know the sword was too sharp? It killed Agamemnon because I wasn't strong enough to take it away from him. Why didn't you believe in the sword and take it away from me? I would have given it to Clion, but he didn't want it. Couldn't Clion have taken it, just for a little while, until it was blunt and couldn't hurt any one...not even me? I don't like being hurt. Dying is no use...nothing is solved by dying unless you are ready.

'That's why you died, Aesculapius. You knew how to be ready for dying; you never tried to run away from anything. Did Socrates run away? You said that unless he had been ready he would not have been made to drink the hemlock. Have you asked him whether he wanted to go away to find the answer which no one alive was wise enough to give? But I want to run away...and I don't know where to go. I always thought I could go back to Elysium to find the answer, to ask the question. But now you are dead there is no more Elysium. It was only real because of you...now nothing is real...nothing...nothing...nothing.'

I must have had the summer-fever, for the next few days are not clear in my mind, a series of pictures which might have been painted on the walls of my room; Porcia talking to me as though I were a child or had been very ill...Dear Porcia, to please her I drank broth out of a spoon and said I was hungry for the smooth food she gave me. I remember Narcissus staring out of the window and biting his nails. He was proud of his hands; why did he suddenly bite his nails? Epicurus brought me toys; a string of amber with flies in their ageless honey, a Persian bird with jewelled wings, a vase on which the pipes of eager shepherds were never stilled.

Euripides was always there...I never had to pretend anything I did not feel while he was in the room. He knew when the pillow was hot even before Porcia did. He bathed my temples with rose-water, he talked of the play he was writing, so that I forgot I was feeling so weak that I dared not get out of bed. He did not feel embarrassed when he spoke of Aesculapius; he knew that it was necessary to remember that the past Elysium was safe in our hearts, that Aesculapius was somewhere...somewhere real, where the actors go when the little stage is empty.

'Did Porgius come to see me when I was ill?'

Euripides paused before he answered. 'Sometimes you called me Porgius; I would have sent for him but none of us knew who he was.'

'I'm glad he wasn't really here,' I said. 'I wouldn't have liked him to see me...see me like that. Will Salonius ever believe in me again? He thinks there are only two kinds of people; the mad and the sane...and I have not been very sane since I was ill.'

'Salonius?' his voice was hard as frozen ground. 'No we kept Salonius away; it was easy enough. Epicurus said it would be unwise if he came here. It was not difficult to keep Salonius away.'

'Why do you hate him? We should have starved if he hadn't given me a chance.'

'A chance to do what? To make him rich, to make yourself so unhappy that you wanted to die?'

'He is not an enemy. He didn't know why I got so tired of...everything. Don't be angry with him, Euripides. He didn't realize I was unhappy.'

'Do you want to go on working for him?'

'I must. I have got nothing else. I can't throw away everything. I thought I could go back and work with Aesculapius; but he isn't there any more. I must stay here; I don't belong anywhere else.'

'I have become successful, Lucina. Come back with me to Elysium. Clion is still there. Epicurus could come home too, I think he is weary of outwitting Romans.'

Should I go back? To a house which was empty because the man who had built it had gone away to the real Elysium. Clion would still be there, a little older, but nothing would change Clion. He could fall in love with the new Lucina, who had learned how to be clever with men, at second hand, from matrons and hetaerae. I could marry Clion, have children, occupy myself with kind trivial things. I should no longer have to weigh each word, each small decision, that to some one might make the vital difference between health and sickness, between freedom and a continued slavery to fear. I should be able to pretend that it was of great importance whether we ate pigeon or hare for the evening meal, to find security in a well-planned orchard, to share laughter with children, who, because I was their mother, grew strong in freedom. The days would be filled with small, beneficent triumphs.

But I had grown beyond Clion; he could never be more than my eldest child; beloved, indulged, and at last secretly despised. And his children would be healthy but too easily well-mannered; none of them would be really mine, for I knew I was not of the nature which can breed children after its own pattern. My children would always be like their father...and it was not Clion whom they might resemble if I were to love them without regret.

'I can't leave Rome,' I said, as though I made some decision which was unimportant because inevitable. 'I have made my life according to a pattern I decided a long time ago...and it is stronger than me, this pattern I have made.'

'Have you forgotten that the future is fluid? If I write a play I am free to change it from tragedy to laughter...and if the characters rebel I burn the manuscript and write on a clean page.' He came to sit on the edge of the bed and held both my hands. 'Lucina, you have written a play for yourself to act; and suddenly realized that the heroine is to be pitied. Don't follow the old lines; speak what is in your heart, tell the chorus that they must learn new words to describe the action.'

'You cannot stop a play once the actors hold the stage.'

'I have done it, Lucina. In the largest theatre of Athens, when I suddenly realized that the last act was wrong. I stopped the play and had the money given back to the audience. There was an uproar, and it was considered a proof that I was either a genius or a lunatic. When I put the play on again, which took some persuading and I only accomplished it by promising the theatre they could charge double for the seats, there were crowds waiting to go in from early morning. It was not the best of my plays, but after that I could write anything I liked and the audience remained faithful.'

'But I don't want to go back to Greece.'

'I know you don't, but you have got to be honest with yourself, Lucina. You intend to stay here because you want Nigellus.'

I sat up, 'What do you know of Nigellus? Has he been here?'

'Now don't get excited. You talked about Nigellus when you were too ill to be discreet. By Zeus, it is a hideous discretion you have imposed on yourself! Acting a part, too difficult for any one to sustain indefinitely, night after night; and shutting yourself up here until you nearly withered through boredom. Bored, that's what is wrong with you, Lucina! You behave as though you were a parched virgin of seventy, instead of a young, and very beautiful, woman...or you would be beautiful if you were not much too thin!'

I giggled, and realized with a shock that I had not done this for years. 'I *am* a virgin,' I said, and found it a joke instead of something of which either to be proud or ashamed.

'Yes, but that is an ailment not without a logical cure...
and as you are not also seventy, the remedy should not be
hard to find.'

'But I am a *priestess*, Euripides.'

'And is your body different from other women's? *Do* be a
realist, even if you happen to be living in Rome. What you
need is to be loved; not in some remote, nebulous way...
and if you don't know what to do about it I am sure that
some of the women you've helped would be glad to give you
useful advice! What you want is perfectly natural and right.
You happen to have chosen a Roman, but no doubt this city
has some remarkable inhabitants, though I personally think it
a pity you couldn't choose a Greek instead...especially a
certain Greek dramatist who understands you a great deal
better than any one else is likely to do. However, you have
made your choice, and nothing will content you until you
have found out for yourself whether he is real or not.'

'But it is impossible,' I said. 'He is a Senator, and
married, with two grown-up children. And he says we have
to wait until we are both dead.'

'When I see two corpses fulfilling the natural roles of
enthusiastic lovers I may be prepared to believe his story;
until then I prefer to appreciate the abilities which the gods
consider appropriate to mortals. And you had better accept
the fact that whatever you may want to do after you are dead
will probably be quite different to what you want to do now.
And *now* is the only thing that is ever really important.'

'But Nigellus doesn't want me *now*.'

'If he is really such a fool, the sooner you discover it the
better! My dear Lucina, I know you far too well to believe
that you will be deluded by a man who is too frightened to
take what the gods offer. Are you afraid of being dis-
illusioned? Surely you have not become a coward since you
left Elysium? We agreed, long ago, that if we wanted anything we would always have the courage to go after it. You
decided to be a priestess; so you ran away to Rome and found

exactly what you wanted. Now you want Nigellus; so go and get him, or find out that you don't really want him.'

'But how can I?'

'A famous Greek dramatist...I am not being boastful, I *am* famous...has come to Rome, bringing with him his sister. It is natural that she will be included in all the invitations which will be showered on him. Julia—oh yes, you talked about Julia too—will certainly not allow a celebrity to be absent from her parties. I shall choose your clothes, they shall be Greek, and we will make these Romans recognize that they are struggling to emerge from barbarism. They are pathetically vulnerable to anyone who has the courage to insult them!'

'Salonius would never let me do it.'

'I have seen Salonius, and the conversation we shared I found entirely satisfactory. I was quite firm with him; I said that unless he allowed you to do as you wished, which included going where you liked, you were returning to Athens with me next month.'

'Does he know about Nigellus?'

'Yes, he is not so stupid as to have been unaware of the change in you.' He paused, and looked at me intently. 'Salonius is willing for you to see Nigellus; he considers there is no likelihood of any complications. He says that a Senator would never consider a liaison with a soothsayer, and that when you find that men do not number intellect among the desirable accomplishments of women, you will be only too glad to come back to the temple. In fact, dear Lucina, it is his considered opinion that you are an admirable priest, but a complete failure as a potential lover.'

'Oh, is it!' I said. 'Perhaps it is time for Salonius to discover that he still has a lot to learn!'

CHAPTER ELEVEN

Roman Daughter

I lay on a couch watching my new, beautiful clothes being unpacked by Lydia, the slave whom Euripides had bought for me in Rome. I was supposed to be resting after my journey. 'You must be quite exhausted,' Julia had said. 'I have promised your brother that you shall both have a chance to relax. You will find we live very simply when we escape to Surrentium.'

Did I look tired, surely not? Or was it considered patrician to find a journey, in easy stages by litter, something of an ordeal? I had intended to be discovered by Nigellus in the garden, perhaps with a background of white roses, or where a solitary cypress could provide the vertical line to point my Greek draperies. Now I was condemned to stay in my room until the rest of the party collected on the terrace before the evening meal. I should have to meet Nigellus in public, with no chance to warn him of my presence in his house.

Julia had said, 'My husband hoped to be here to welcome you, but he has been detained—the Senate is greedy of his time. He will be back to-night, or to-morrow at the latest.' She had thrown an arch glance at Euripides. 'Nigellus is a great admirer of your brother's plays and we are so glad that you came here with him.'

I was far too excited to rest; could I explore the garden or would it be unwise? I told Lydia to return later and when the door closed behind her I opened the shutters.

My room was on the west of the house. The garden sloped steeply to the beach; marble statues were lavishly displayed among the flowering bushes with which the terraced ground was planted. There was a stone pergola covered with roses...so I had not been too optimistic in my setting!

'Do you like it now you're here?' I turned to see Euripides, who had come in through a door, concealed by a curtain, which I had not noticed before. 'I'm in the next room. Where is Lydia?'

'I sent her away. It is rather tiresome having a maid who doesn't know who I really am, but you were quite right not to bring any of our own.'

'Nervous?'

'No,' I said, and then added, 'Of course I am. One moment I am enormously happy and then I feel rather silly. Wouldn't it be awful if Nigellus isn't pleased to see me, if he thinks I shall be only a complication.'

'Wondering already if you will find him disappointing?'

'No...no, I don't *think* I am.'

'Julia is no fool; she could be a formidable opponent. I have been talking to her. I think she is already unsure whether it was clever to invite you. She asked me whether your marriage had been arranged yet and could not quite conceal that she regretted it hadn't! She said you might find Nigellus a little dull, as he was so much older. He *is* rather old for you, Lucina.' He looked at me without the usual laughter lurking behind his eyes. 'Are you sure you're not making a mistake? There are plenty of other lovers available if that's all you want.'

I sat down on the edge of the over-luxurious bed and tried to sound casual. 'I have come here because I was bored and needed a holiday. I may leave here and go back to Salonius, or I may decide to go to Athens...if your invitation still holds good. I may take a lover or I may not; it depends on whether I decide it is an experience I ought to have before I get too old.'

'But why choose a *Roman*?'

'Because any of the Greeks I've met would be too busy thinking about themselves to think enough about *me*. Women mean nothing in Greece, because the men are so sure of their masculine superiority that they don't even *try* to please their wives, except in a patronizing kind of way. And I won't be patronized!'

'We never patronized you, Lucina.'

'Only because I never gave you the chance! I had to show that I was as good as any of you and then you accepted me as an equal. With a Roman I can be a woman, and automatically the superior.'

'He will have my sympathy,' he said brusquely. 'You will soon get tired of an obedient lover, and I doubt if you will have the kindness to conceal your disappointment.'

He went out of the room, slamming the door behind him. So Euripides also thought I should be a failure as a woman? I picked up a mirror and studied my face carefully. Nobody believed a man could make me forget everything else! Why should I go on being lonely just because it was convenient to other people for me to be clever? I was young and I wanted to be happy: I wanted a husband and a child and a house, all the ordinary things. 'And I am quite clever, and quite beautiful, enough to get them!' I said this aloud, which made me feel foolish: surely I had not become so weak that I had to ask myself for reassurance?

When I reached the terrace—I knew Nigellus had not arrived for I could see the road from my window—I found Euripides talking to Flavia, the daughter, and a woman called Claudia who was a distant relation of Julia's. I liked Flavia, she was dark with a thin, intense face and she talked with surprising intelligence for one of her race and class.

Julia joined us, and immediately Claudia became the sycophant, anxious to make it clear she had only offered us wine because the hostess had not yet arrived. I felt sorry for Claudia: nearly thirty and unmarried, living in other people's houses and watching her vitality slowly eaten away by the acid of patronage. I knew her even before we had exchanged a few trivial remarks; I had seen too many of her type as patients not to recognize it, and known how impossible it was to cure them. What use would it have been to say,

'Break away from your environment, get a house of your own, even if it is a hovel; adopt a child if you are too old to bear one, find a man, almost any man, who will make you feel important to him.' They were too bound by convention to break free, too conscious of their background to risk changing it, too artificial to get a real friend, or even a lover.

I shivered: in Claudia I saw something that might become an echo of myself—if I became as bound to Salonius and the temple ritual as she was to Julia.

'You are cold,' said Julia. 'The sea air is treacherous until you are used to it.'

I had to let her send for my cloak. She watched me put it on, secure that she was the thoughtful hostess to whom no small discomfort of a guest could pass unremedied.

I found it difficult to make convincing conversation during the meal, which as usual stretched far beyond the time which eating should occupy. At any moment Nigellus might come into the room. The entrance courtyard was on the far side of the house and I would not hear his arrival. I had spent hours considering our meeting...what a tragedy if it took place when my mouth was full! We talked of interminable trivialities, while the moon rose and shone high through the arched windows. I began to feel sleepy, and to regret that I had not taken the opportunity to rest during the late afternoon. I felt a trickle of sweat run down my forehead: it was no comfort that Julia was also wilting in the heat. It would be better to go to bed, even if I could not sleep, than to continue in this cloud of ambiguity. I stiffled a small, deliberate yawn. Immediately Julia said it was time to go to bed, and for once it was easy to agree with her.

I left my door propped open with a sandal, in case I could hear Nigellus arrive. Later I wished that I had been less vulnerable to impatience: I had heard a man's voice and a woman answering. Against my better judgement I crept across the hall which divided our wing of the house from the owner's apartments. I saw shadows on the pink wall of the central room. Nigellus talking to his wife while she cut slices of cold meat and poured something out of a jug, an ordinary domestic scene which I watched and felt ashamed. She told him Euripides was here but did not even bother to mention me. Then she talked of household matters...a slave had broken one of the best dishes, the young vines on the south terrace were colouring well, Flavia had had a sore throat but was now cured, Claudia had been a little tiresome. 'Poor woman, it must be so difficult for her to be dependent on us for everything,' she added with contempt.

I saw Nigellus stretch, and heard him say he was tired. He put his arm round Julia and then kissed her on the forehead. Their shadows grew large on the wall before vanishing towards their own rooms. I went back to bed and took some of the poppy-drink, which was easier than staying awake, much easier than trying not to think of the future.

I woke early and went into the garden hoping the morning freshness would clear my headache. I thought Nigellus would be late getting up...he was probably sufficiently wary of Julia's guests not to see more of them than necessary. Three slaves were watering a bed of marigolds, they stared at me as I passed, no doubt surprised that any member of the household should be out so early. I walked towards the stables and watched one of the horses being groomed and two boys bringing in fresh bales of straw. A kitchen girl came out with a bucket of swill; she spilt some when she saw me and then ran back to the house, leaving a greasy trail across the cobbles.

I went back towards the terrace and then down through the small wood which shielded the side of the house from the sea winds. I found Nigellus writing at a stone table in a secluded pavilion. He stared at me without speaking, as though I would vanish if he broke the spell.

'Have you forgotten me?' I said.

He slowly got to his feet, the stylus rolling across the worn stone and falling with a brittle sound to the tiles.

'Lucina,' he said, 'Lucina!'

I felt suddenly maternal, as though he were a child I must reassure. 'It is not a dream, Nigellus. It was impossible for us never to see each other again. So I followed you here. Are you glad?'

He looked very young when he smiled. 'I have dreamed about this...but I always wake when I try to take you in my arms.'

'I am a very solid dream. Are you not brave enough to dare reality?'

It was so much easier to feel than to think...so easy to be only a woman. 'You are very beautiful, Lucina, so much more dear even than I remembered.'

I could feel his heart beating and for the first time knew why women find it wise to forget wisdom.

He looked down at me and I was glad he was tall. 'Lucina, I was a fool to think we could say good-bye to each other.'

I do not know how long it was before he suddenly said, 'Does Julia know you are here?'

It was like throwing a stone into a pool which had reflected a scene too bright for ordinary seeing...ripples spread out and the dark weeds showed beneath the surface. 'Yes,' I said. 'Julia asked me to come. As the sister of Euripides—she has no idea that I have any link with the ''sister'' of Narcissus.'

He did not bother to inquire further; he was satisfied that Julia approved, that he need not feel guilty. I had learned how to rescue people from petty tryants. Could I be sure that he wanted to be rescued from Julia?

It is difficult to give a clear picture of Julia, for my view of her underwent so many rapid changes. At first I felt sorry for her, the middle-aged woman whose husband preferred me: but that was before I talked with Flavia.

'You don't know mother,' Flavia said. 'It is no use your telling me to be more sympathetic when she tries to find out what I really feel. I used to want her. I used to be glad when she came to see me after I had gone to bed, and had cosy conversations. It was only her way of finding out if I was interested in any of the suitable young men she asks to the house, or the unsuitable ones that Marcus used to bring home. I was silly enough to tell her that I thought I might be falling in love with a Centurion...he was a patrician but his family weren't rich or important. He was sent abroad within a few days; she pretended to be very sorry for me when I heard he had died of fever. I almost believed her...and then I suddenly realized she had arranged it all. She probably chose the place where he was sent because she knew it was unhealthy.

We were alone on the beach and Flavia was sitting on a flat rock, her hands linked round her knees, her voice expressionless because she dared not allow emotion to flow. 'It is unpleasant to discover that your mother is almost a murderess, and that you have been blind enough to deliver into her power the man who would have been your husband.'

'She couldn't have known he was going to die,' I said. 'It is natural for a mother to interfere in her daughter's future... she cannot be expected to realize it is not really her business.'

'You underrate her. She is quite ruthless when any one tries to stop her plans.' Flavia laughed a hard, brittle, sound. 'At least I can embarrass her by refusing to marry; it is amusing to see how she dislikes the sympathy she gets for having an unmarried daughter. And it will be even more tiresome when she can't pretend it is only because no one sufficiently important has been selected! She tried to make me accept a *most* suitable person last summer; I only avoided it by saying I would kill myself if she went any further with the marriage contract. She had to stop then because she was afraid of the scandal...she couldn't afford to have both her children disgraced. Marcus isn't much of a credit to her; now that he never comes here, and is living with one of the charioteers, and drives in the Circus. I loved Marcus, and so did father; so she took him away from us.'

'I thought Marcus quarrelled with his father over a Greek.'

'You mean Narcissus? Oh, he wasn't the real cause. He was only something mother could produce to make father angry enough to join in the row. If Marcus hadn't seen through mother he wouldn't have disliked women. All the girls she produced for him were potential Julias, or else they were so spineless that we both despised them; you can be sorry for some one you despise but you can't love her.'

'Yet your father has lived with Julia for over twenty years; is he such a bad judge of character?'

Her face softened. 'Father? She has never let him forget that by marrying him they both lost the chance of falling in love. She makes it clear that she has always tried to make it up to him in other ways...the perfect hostess, the house so well run, constant devotion to his career...and of course she is so hideously clever when he gets interested in any one else.'

'So there have been other women?'

'Not many. She always asks them here until they feel so guilty at "deceiving" dear Julia that they go away, or else she arranges that they make fools of themselves. Father is not tolerant of fools.'

Was Flavia warning me? I nearly asked her if she knew about Nigellus and me and then thought it might be kinder to leave her in ignorance...if she were ignorant. There was a long pause as if she were waiting for me to speak, then she said, 'Claudia is a good example of what mother can do when she tries. I think father was a little in love with her. Anyway he wasn't at all pleased when he found she had been asked to stay here. She is a widow, you know, her husband fell on his sword because he lost a battle, and she was left very poor. Julia was so kind to her! She gave her a lot of clothes and kept on telling her she must eat more because she was so thin that her looks were going. Of course the clothes were all in the most unbecoming colours, and being told she was faded took away all her self-confidence. She thinks mother is *wonderful* and is always trying to justify her position here. If she ever loved father she doesn't now...she feels guilty every time she looks at him. He hates having her in the house, but whenever he suggests that she would be happier elsewhere, mother smiles and says, ''But, dear, you used to be so fond of her; we mustn't be unkind just because you have discovered she is a little *dull.''* She leaves them alone together, very obviously, because she knows they have nothing to say to each other. But it's a great asset to mother when she is telling other women how stupid it is to be jealous. It was just the same when I was small...she used to give me expensive toys I didn't want so that I could bring them down when I was summoned from the nursery and every one could see how generous and thoughtful she was! That was when she was in what Marcus and I called the ''devoted young mother'' period. We were taken in by it until we discovered she never bothered to be fond to us without a suitable audience.'

'Why do you stay here? If you could have a house of your own wouldn't you be much happier?' Already in my mind I had arranged for Nigellus to make his daughter independent. At least I could rescue *her.*

'I have money of my own...it was left to me by an aunt, the only person really kind to us when we were children. But I'm not going to let mother drive me away. I am the only thing father has got left. It is a pity I have decided not to marry...I should like to have had a child. It would be so easy to know what it wanted...just the exact opposite to everything I was given.'

'Why don't you persuade your father to take you to live with him in Rome? You know he doesn't love Julia but he loves you.'

'Julia would never let him go. You see, he is her career. She arranged for him to be elected to the Senate, half the things he says there are her ideas. She is much stronger than he is and inside himself he knows it. He *likes* being a Senator and he knows she would break him if he left her. She is much more clever than you realize, Lucina; every one thinks she is so dependable, so sane. If he was disobedient she would spread careful little stories that his mind was going, that for a long while she had been anxious about him, ''Overwork, overstrain tell on the strongest in the end...and dear Nigellus would never spare himself.'' Everything said in the strictest confidence, knowing that it would get to the right quarters before the end of the day.'

'But if he had the courage to make an open break with her?'

'Divide their friends into two camps, you mean? She would win, and father could not bear to be unpopular...it is the only thing which compensates him for not being allowed any real friends.'

'But if *he* won? Wouldn't it be worth the risk?'

'He wouldn't be happy long...unless the dead find the tomb amusing.'

'Why should he die?'

She looked at me in frank astonishment. 'I keep forgetting you are a foreigner. He would die because mother would arrange it. Poison I expect...it is not difficult to have some one poisoned if you really make up your mind it is worth doing. Dear Lucina, you look shocked! You are so understanding, and then so naive that I feel years older than you!'

She looked at me very straightly and then impulsively kissed me on the cheek. 'I love your being here, and so does father. But you must not underrate Julia. It might be healthier for you to go back to Athens...Rome is too close.'

For several days I tried to make myself believe that Flavia had been unjust to Julia. The child hated her mother, that was obvious enough, and surely she was exaggerating? Julia seemed so genuinely concerned for my welfare, so anxious that I should enjoy myself as her guest. She personally selected the fruit that was left beside my bed, chose the flowers for my rooms, gave me several small gifts.

She thanked me, almost effusively, for being so kind to Flavia. 'It is good for the child to have some one near her own age to play with.' She did it remarkably well, I might have been deceived if I had not realized that the remark was intended to be overheard by Flavia, who was supposed to think, "So Lucina is mother's confidante...I mustn't trust her anymore"; and by Nigellus, as a sharp reminder that I was more closely his daughter's contemporary than his own. She tried to find out more about me: I put her off by describing a house near Athens where I had lived with my brother since our parents died. It was only when I guessed she meant to make careful inquiries about me that I realized how greatly she could jeopardize my position and how powerless I should be to stop her.

When I first came to the villa I thought, if I thought intelligently about it at all, that I should either grow out of my need for Nigellus or else contrive to meet him in some suitably romantic setting.... I might even have insisted that Salonius give me his cottage where I could go when I felt inclined. But Julia always knew what Nigellus was doing; now she was sufficiently suspicious to have him watched even more closely. What would happen to me when Julia spread the story that her husband was having an affair with the priestess who worked with Salonius?

Salonius knew Rome; he had told me that a Senator could not afford to be associated with soothsayers...he did not need to tell me that no priestess in Rome could afford to have her virginity in doubt. What would Epicurus and Narcissus think if they discovered I had thrown away our career? Yes, *our* career, for if they had not helped me we would still have been poor. I should have to go back to Athens with Euripides...if he still wanted me. Had any woman ever been a greater failure at being a woman? Sixteen days in another woman's villa, a few kisses, a few delectable, dangerous embraces...and everything I had worked for was destroyed, by Julia whom I had been complacent enough to pity!

I had run away from Elysium and made a new life for myself. Now I should have to run away again. I made my decision without consulting Euripides, and announced it that evening, when we had assembled on the terrace.

'It has been lovely here,' I said to Julia. 'I shall have such pleasant memories to take back with me to Athens.'

'You are going to *Athens!*' Nigellus betrayed his dismay.

Euripides smoothly took the cue. 'At the end of the month I have a new play in rehearsal...we dramatists are the slaves of the theatre.'

'Athens,' said Julia and put her hand on my arm to lead me into the room where we ate our meals. 'How wise of you to go before the autumn gales.' Then in a lower voice so only I could hear, she added, 'I never thought the climate of that little island in the Tiber was really suitable for a girl brought up in...Elysium was the name, was it not?'

So she knew! Had she known all the time, or had her spies just earned a fresh reward?

I pleaded a headache and went early to my room. How could it still be early after such an interminable ordeal? Julia, very much the possessive wife, complacent, secure; Nigellus eating nothing, drinking too much, making only disjointed efforts to keep alive the flickering conversation; Flavia glancing at her mother, knowing she was the cause of the tension but not knowing why; Claudia discussing Greek drama with Euripides in a determined effort to avoid the silences.

I left the door open into Euripides' room for I wanted to talk to him, to escape being alone. The hours lengthened and at last I felt I should scream if I stayed indoors.

The marble steps linking the terrace were white under the moon. A young wind stirred the myrtle trees; vine leaves pattered against the stone pillars of the pergola like the stealthy feet of fugitives. The smooth, clear-cut path gave place to a rough track, steep among secret bushes whose presence in the shadows was betrayed only by their whispered response to the night air. Below me I could hear waves breaking on the rocks, solitary and changeless.

I threw off my clothes and ran into the sea. I swam far out until I grew tired and had to turn back, gaining the beach only with a final effort of aching muscles. My hair, heavy with sea water, clung to me and I had nothing to dry it with. I tried to comfort myself. It would be easier this way in the end; easier never to see Nigellus again than to know he left me to return to Julia; who would welcome him with that assured smile, the kiss on the cheek, the casual talk of the small intimate matters of their daily lives in which I played no part. He would never have been happy if we had become involved with the tawdry necessities of deceit. In time he might have returned to Julia to seek peace of mind, seeing in her formal living an escape from an illusory freedom too difficult to maintain.

I did not hear Euripides until he stood beside me, his cloak like the curve of a sail against the uneasy sky.

'Poor Lucina,' he said. 'So you must run away again... the idyll did not materialize?'

'At least I shall keep my illusions. I shall never have a chance to discover that I might have fallen out of love with Nigellus, and it will protect me from falling in love again.'

'I had not thought of that,' he said slowly. 'Won't you forget him... when you come back to Greece?'

'Why should I allow myself to forget? How can he forget me... if I am not there to show I am a failure? I could almost be sorry for Julia when I think how he will grow to hate her. He hates her already, but he doesn't know it yet.'

'Aesculapius said that Hate and Envy are the two great enemies... wouldn't it be stupid to deliver yourself to them?'

'How can I help hating Julia, how can I help being envious of every woman who is lucky enough to be ordinary?'

'If you had Nigellus would everything be different? Lucina, are you *sure* you want him, are you sure you wouldn't be disappointed?'

'If I had Nigellus I should be kind and wise and loving. But I can't have him, he doesn't want me enough. So instead I shall be clever and powerful...I am not sure how, but I am not entirely ineffective...and there are probably as many fools in Athens as there are in Rome.'

He picked up a strand of seaweed and tore it slowly in shreds before he spoke. 'You can have Nigellus if you want him.'

'How? What do you mean?'

'I misjudged the depths of his affection; he is willing, more than willing, to give up his career if he can have you instead.'

'And wait for Julia to poison us at her leisure?'

'He is perfectly aware of Julia's potential danger...I thought it more tactful to conceal that I had already been warned by Flavia. He says that you will never be safe unless Julia believes that you and he are beyond her jurisdiction. At first he was so distraught that he couldn't talk coherently; it is quite extraordinary how these Romans wallow in emotion once they lose the facade of imperturbability. But when I had calmed him we constructed a suitable plan of action. You and Nigellus will go out in his sailing boat the day after tomorrow...we must hope for a wind. You will land on the island and hide for a few days...he says there are several large caves which no one ever visits. The boat will be washed ashore further down the coast; you will be presumed drowned. Julia will be so engrossed in acting the broken-hearted widow that she may not have time for unjust suspicions.'

'And what happens to me? Do I live in a cave; eating raw shell-fish and dressed in seaweed?'

'You give me too little credit for attention to detail. I shall send suitable supplies to the cave and arrange for a boat to pick you up, after sunset and as soon as possible. It will land you further down the coast where you will have to make further arrangements for the journey to Umbria. Umbria, you may remember, is the place where the villa is situated to which Julia declined to go on their marriage journey. He has made the place over to me; I will in turn make a present of it to you, together with certain properties with which Nigellus has also entrusted me, sufficient to ensure you both an adequate income. Aren't you pleased with my efforts? It would make a delightful play...the comedy of the lovers in contrast to the sombre colours of the Roman funeral; the laughing girl and the wailing widow...not that I think Julia would wail, it would be too undignified.'

I had thought of myself returning, a failure, to Greece; now everything was changed. I was going to have my idyll, I was going to be loved and cherished. I was going to be the heroine of a great drama, two famous people who gave up the world for love.

'We shall be remembered long after ordinary priestesses and Senators are forgotten,' I said. 'I thought I was a failure and all the time Nigellus loved me more than he loved Rome.'

'You must remind me to write your story,' said Euripides. 'Fame rapidly decays unless embalmed in suitable prose!'

CHAPTER TWELVE

Idyll

When I left the house to join Nigellus, who had gone ahead to wait for me at the landing-stage, I saw Julia reclining on a couch under a purple awning. She was reading, but looked up when she heard me.

'The sea is a little rough,' she said. 'I hope you won't get chilled on your last day here...though you Greeks don't mind such minor discomforts.'

She smiled, the genial hostess concerned with the pleasure of a guest. I could almost hear her saying to herself, 'I can well afford to be tolerant, she won't dare to be any further trouble. If it amuses Nigellus to show off his new boat, what does it matter? She will get drenched and look bedraggled as a wet hen when she comes back. What a fool she is not to make a more becoming exit!'

She would have been an inefficient general, withdrawing her phalanx at the peak of battle! She returned to her scrutiny of the household tallies.... I might have guessed she would not have been reading anything more impersonal. Surely no antagonist had ever been more carelessly dismissed, or with such lack of insight!

As I ran down to the beach I was glad that Euripides had taken Flavia out for the day: I knew she would be happier when she no longer had reason to stay with her mother, but it would have been difficult to watch Nigellus saying farwell to his daughter and trying desperately to sound casual.

The wind filled the sail and we drew out from the shelter of the cove. We talked very little until we were in the open sea; I was concerned with showing that I knew how to handle a boat, and both of us had too much to say for the words to come easily. The wind freshened from the east and I began to wonder if I had prayed too fervently for rough weather. Nigellus knew what I was thinking, for he laughed, and shouted, 'You had better explain to Poseidon that we don't really want to be drowned!'

'He knows,' I said. 'I am careful to be exact in my prayers. I put my appeal tactfully so that he should not think we considered him an unwelcome host. I explained we were too concerned with each other to want even a God as a third to our company!'

'I love you, Lucina! I hope Poseidon can hear....I want

every one to hear!'

A wave broke over the side and sluiced us both in green water; I turned the boat into the wind.... I had neglected the course in watching Nigellus.

'You look even more beautiful wet,' he shouted. 'The nereids are sulking in their caves because they are jealous.'

'Julia would think I look bedraggled!'

'Julia! May all the Gods be praised...at last I can laugh at Julia!'

He laughed so much that the veins stood out on his forehead and he had to cling to the mast. 'Think of Julia with the ashes of mourning on her head...or will only the slaves wear ashes for me?'

Another wave broke over us. 'If we don't watch the boat we shall give her real bodies to bury,' I said, and hoped that I concealed that I really meant it.

It was dark before we reached the cave on the island; and if the boat had not been drawn into a favourable current I think we must certainly have been drowned. My teeth were chattering and blood was trickling down my face—I had been too slow to dodge the boom when it swung over in a sudden gust. My tunic was torn and my cloak a sodden heap. The boat was leaking and we doubted whether it would float long enough to be washed ashore after we set it adrift.

The grotto, for it was too large for a cave, had a wide ledge above high-water mark. Nigellus took the boat into the current and then swam back to me. The water was deep and calm in the grotto and I could just see him by the trail of phosphorescence. He swam well, but I had to help him up to the ledge. He was exhausted, and lay with his head on my lap sucking in gulps of air.

'Sorry...I shall be all right...in a moment. Silly...to get tired.'

'I'll start a fire. Where are the things?'

'They must be further along the ledge...there should be everything we need until Euripides picks us up. I meant to get here before dark.... I didn't allow for the storm.'

I felt my way along the ledge and came to a blank wall of rock. 'I can't go any further,' I said. 'Are you sure this is the right ledge?'

'This is the only ledge!'

A magnificent stream of oaths took up the echoes. If only they could have been translated into a different heat we should have had a blazing fire. I realized there had been a flaw in the plans; the supplies must have been left in the wrong cave.

How unlike Euripides to be so careless! He had helped me to select the few clothes I dared bring with me, chosen violet cushions and even insisted that we must have a mattress. 'Pebbles, or the ubiquitous thistle, can be to an idyll as a pin to the ephemeral radiance of a soap-bubble,' he had said. 'Lucina diving naked is a treasured image; Lucina shivering in the evening wind suggests goose-flesh rather than a dance of poplar leaves.'

So I had agreed to take two cloaks and a robe of fine wool, white with a scarlet girdle. There was to have been dry wood here and a jar of oil so that the fire would light at the first touch. It was too dark to collect driftwood...even if there had been any. I had seen Nigellus take a small leather bag out of the boat and by a sudden spurt of flame saw him looking at it disconsolately. He was trying to kindle a few stands of seaweed, but they were too damp to burn.

'I brought enough money to buy anything you might want: now I can't even give you a fire,' he said abjectly.

Inappropriately I began to laugh. 'Dear Nigellus, please don't look so miserable. We wanted an adventure nearly as much as we wanted each other. Now we have both, so why have regrets?'

'It is my fault,' he said, in the tone which is used to indicate that the speaker is entirely without blame. 'I should have seen to all the arrangements myself. Euripides seemed confident that he could be trusted with these minor details and that the slave fully understood his instructions. But one is a fool to rely on foreigners!' The words had slipped out and he tried to cover them: 'I was referring to the slave. I bought him in Syracuse. My dear, please be sure that I in no way meant my foolish remark as a reflection on Greece.'

'Perhaps this is not quite the time or the place to engage in discussions as to the rival merits of our countries.'

Suddenly he seized hold of me. 'Forgive me, Lucina! Please don't be angry. Please don't leave me! I will make it up to you. I will never fail to protect you. I love you so much! Lucina, I love you so much!'

He was crying! He thought I was going to blame him; to punish him by sending him back to Julia. He was not the lover, he was the child imploring comfort; desperately afraid that the companion he trusted was going to side with the grown-ups and send him back to loneliness.

Hatred for Julia was much stronger than disappointment: a temper for the will which had determined that I would try to give back to Nigellus his lost illusions, and in that giving find some of my own.

I am glad that Julia never knew how we passed our first night as lovers; with rock for a pillow and not even a thought of passion to bring us warmth.

Next day I found it a little tiresome to have to search each cave on the island, for until every possibility had proved ineffective, Nigellus remained convinced that somewhere we should find our carefully chosen supplies. At last he decided that a freak wave must have washed over the ledge and so disorganized his careful plans. Perhaps it was my finer Greek perception which suddenly told me that our situation was not due to any lack of efficiency on the part of Euripides, but to his view that an idyll in the primitive setting would have been flawed by the anachronism of Roman luxury. I should have preferred to share this insight with Nigellus, to cut short this frenzied search, this penetration into caves which gave no more than a redundance of seaweed or the spars of foundered ships. But how could I deliberately sever the link with the only friend whom I could take with me into this new life? How could I expect a Roman to appreciate such a very practical joke?

I recognized, a little ruefully, that the discomforts were easily offset by the recognition that they gave me an opportunity of showing I could be instructor as well as pupil. When Nigellus made love to me, which he did with surprising skill and variety, I was, for the first time in my life, entirely content to learn. How different can be reality from the most meticulous study of abstractions! As a colleague of Salonius I was not unversed in the emotional consequences of certain transmutations of vitality: as a priest I had listened to manifold complexities, and given judgement with profundity, and extraordinary ignorance: as Lucina I learned how much I had to learn, and how seldom academic knowledge can outweigh empiricism.

But would I have found it so smooth to be compliant unless I could have shown that when it came to such vital matters as having enough to eat that I was the superior? It was easy enough to collect dry grass and seaweed for a bed, but I thanked Poseidon with fervour for letting me discover an old fish-spear in a tangle of wrack among the rocks. I sharpened it on a stone, and in one afternoon caught enough for three meals. To my credit I did not laugh when Nigellus overbalanced and fell headlong into the sea, swallowing a lot of water before he came, blowing like a triton, to the surface. It would not have been unfair to laugh, for he had been convinced that using a trident must be easy because I could do it so well.

Euripides, in a fishing-boat, reached us on the fifth evening. Only when I saw it nearing shore did I realize how odd I looked. My tunic was torn and stained with sea water. I had forgotten to bring a comb with me, and a rock-pool is not a reassuring mirror. Nigellus, after an ineffective attempt to shave with his hunting knife, which I had blunted when opening mussels, was pitiably conscious of his stubble of beard. It is not easy to look noble in the remnants of a toga, but I think he would have managed to do so if only he had not developed a cold in the head. I felt very sympathetic, and yet a small part of me was ashamed because he sniffed, and found no comfort in telling myself that he would have remained healthy, and in full dignity, if only I had refrained from visiting my fish trap at midnight. We had caught a large lobster and two crabs: they had tasted good when roasted in hot ashes, but they were one of the luxuries which I could no longer afford.

The fishing-boat came alongside the natural quay of flat rock. Euripides was leaning over the side, smiling as though sure of his welcome.

'Do I look hideous?' I asked Nigellus, and received a most comforting reply, proving again that I need not have feared that Romans were inarticulate.

Euripides, with suitable expressions of sympathy which would have deceived any one who knew him less well than I did, listened to the story of our mishaps. He said how fortunate it was that we have suffered nothing worse than a cold in the head, and that in future we must make due allowance for a certain mischievous trend in the minions of Poseidon.

'For myself it was unimportant,' said Nigellus. 'But Lucina might have suffered grievously from exposure. She has been magnificent, and eaten the most unsuitable food as though she enjoyed it!'

'Lucina is very hardy,' said Euripides gravely. 'You must not be worried if she appears frail; wait until she challenges you with the discus, you will be surprised how strong she is. Personally I think she looks charming with tangled hair, and the green smudge on her nose brings out the colour of her eyes.'

'Lucina always looks charming!' said Nigellus hotly.

'But of *course*! I intended the remark as a compliment of the highest order. Any woman can look beautiful with

259

emeralds in her hair, or even roses. It takes Lucina to make do with seaweed. '

I smirked; as a smile it was not convincing even to me, and hoped Euripides was unaware how close I came to slapping him. So he thought that a few days on an island without benefit of unguents would cure me of an infatuation! Or worse, he thought it would cure Nigellus! It was a pity that Nigellus had a cold, but it only made me feel more protective towards him. How could I change my mind at this stage and send him back to Julia? There was a momentary vision of how ridiculous Julia would look, combing the ashes of mourning from her hair, ordering the slaves to cease their wailing, wondering whether she could get back the funerary gifts.

But of course I could not send him back to Julia. I had promised that to him in the grotto on the first night, and the promise was far more binding because it was not spoken in words. I was extremely angry with Euripides; but, hidden in the back of my mind, was small regret that I could not laugh about the idyll with him.

Dear Nigellus! Perhaps I should be able to teach him to laugh at himself: or would it be unfair?

CHAPTER THIRTEEN

Stone Apollo

To avoid passing along roads where Nigellus might be recognized, we sailed down the coast until we reached a small port where we could take passage on a trading-ship which would land us at Ancona. Again Euripides made a needless complication: or did he really consider it a wise precaution? Fortunately the accommodation was so limited that we had to share a cabin.

Euripides was travelling to Umbria by land, and would have left for Athens before we reached the villa. The night before he left, he again asked me whether I was sure I would not prefer to go back to Greece with him.

'It is never too late to change your mind,' he said. 'We have always been able to laugh together. Are you *sure* you won't come with me? We never have to pretend with each other; even when we play an unfair trick we can always see the joke.'

He sounded forlorn, as though for a moment he had lost is self-confidence. Did Euripides need me more than Nigellus?

I hesitated: Elysium seemed very close, compellingly urgent.

Then I saw Nigellus coming along the quay followed by a boy carrying an enormous bunch of flowers, another with a basket of fruit, a third staggering under a load of parcels. Presents for me, presents I did not want. But how could I betray him?

'I go to Umbria,' I said.

Euripides shrugged his shoulders. 'I will come to stay with the matron, if she is still interested in news of the world.'

'Please understand I am not just being stubborn...' And then I could say no more, for Nigellus had joined us and he must never know how difficult it was for me to say good-bye to Greece.

The winds were contrary, and it took us nearly a month to reach Ancona. Nigellus tried to keep me amused, but he thought it odd of me to enjoy talking to the sailors and was annoyed when I asked permission to steer. At the little ports we visited I insisted on eating in the small taverns and wandering through the markets. I had to make myself forget our early days in Rome; for even Narcissus had never found it difficult to talk as an equal with ordinary people. Nigellus had often described himself as 'the spokesman of the plebeians': reluctantly I learned that this only meant that when he made a speech they could provide the audience. I frequently reminded myself that it was impossible for him to find my way of living easy: it would take time to cure him of the infection of Julia.

Euripides had installed four servants in the villa; and there was the steward, Caius, and his wife Sempronia, who did the cooking. I was glad they were all free, for it saved me having to discuss the awkward question of slaves. The house was rather small and the heating system inadequate by Roman standards. Nigellus was soon engrossed in plans for improvements, eager as a child playing with bricks. He left the garden design to me. I soon had several masons building new retaining walls, for the ground sloped steeply down to a valley and was sheltered from the north by the ilex grove. I changed the course of a mountain stream so that it fell in a series of waterfalls into a narrow pool. Nigellus wanted this to be tiled with mosaics and used as a swimming bath, but I insisted on keeping it as a future retreat, when it would be concealed by flowering thickets and the harsh new marble covered with deep moss.

We agreed that there should be a vine pergola on the south terrace, but I refused to accept formal beds planted with marigolds for they reminded me of Julia. He was also a trifle difficult about statues, and bought me several which would have made Praxiteles laugh. The worst were a Juno who looked as though she would melt in the sun, and a Mars which might have been the portrait of an over-fed centurion.

In the barn of the farm which Nigellus added to the property I found an ancient statue of Apollo. It had obviously been brought from Greece, but I could discover nothing of its history except that it had been dug up in the ilex grove. Nigellus was disappointed that I wanted it, for I had dismissed his presents on the plea of an illogical dislike of statuary: so I told him I only liked it because I thought it suitable for us to make a daily votive offering to Apollo. He was always delighted to indulge me, providing I pretended it was a feminine whim instead of a conflict of taste or a logical deduction. How easy, and yet how difficult, I found it to be female!

I was happy when he made love to me, which he did whenever I gave him the opportunity. I enjoyed seeing my house grow, so long as I could make myself believe that each detail of fresco or mosaic was of real importance. Toilet became a ritual, clothes a horizon, perfume an incense: when I could remember that it was more necessary to be beautiful than to be wise. In a thousand ways, Nigellus showed that he was content with his return to youth. I had only to wear a new dress for him to start designing a jewel to be its complement: even the flowers I grew he saw as a wreath for me to wear or colour for my rooms.

He was always busy; first with the house, then with the farm, then with breeding cows and oxen which apparently must have pedigrees impeccable as his own. But what was I supposed to do? How did other matrons occupy the long hours of day? I tried to superintend the household, but Sempronia was more than competent. I searched for dust, but it had always been removed before I got up in the morning. Why should I scrutinize the tallies, when Nigellus enjoyed doing it and I knew Caius was honest?

What did other couples talk about, when one day was like another as links in a chain? I listened with convincing attention to stories of earlier triumphs of Nigellus. I acquired a mass of useless knowledge of Roman Law, Senatorial Procedure, Roman Victories. We did not discuss philosophy, for he found it too insubstantial, and I discovered that anything which reminded me too sharply of Elysium was best avoided.

When I knew I was going to have a child I lost the sense of futility, which, I suddenly realized, had been making me intolerant. I discovered that a pregnant woman acquires a kind of animal contentment, her thoughts flow in rhythm with the seasons, the world narrows and seems honest as bread. I no longer wished to acquire still more gardeners, I wanted to feel the earth under my hands, to plant small green shoots and watch them grow under my protection.

Nigellus became even more tender, and my every wish was satisfied almost before I had time to express it. Julia must have resented child-bearing, for I learned, though she was never mentioned directly, that she had produced every symptom of the rebellious womb: sickness, vertigo, and an extraordinary demand for unseasonable foods. Nigellus was at first proud that I remained healthy and then began to worry lest I was hiding discomfort because I was too proud to admit it. Or did he think that I ought to have produced a patrician protest against such a commonplace experience?

I thought I had driven Julia out of our lives, but she began to be such a barrier between us that at last I decided it would be better to discuss the problem openly.

'Nigellus,' I said, 'I know we have agreed never to mention the past, but we can't go on pretending this is the first child you have fathered. Julia may have found it an ordeal, but it will be quite different with me. It is a perfectly normal process; I shall probably do it more easily than one of your pedigree cows.'

'My very dear, your magnificent courage inspires me to yet further devotion.' But I *implore* you not to try to keep me in ignorance.' He shuddered. 'Julia, with all her faults, is a brave woman; but she told me things that made me appalled at masculine brutality. Do you realize that if you die I shall have *murdered* you?'

'It's a pity you didn't murder Julia!' I said crisply. 'Don't you realize she was trying to make you feel under such a heavy obligation that she could bully you without being afraid you might defend yourself? Why does she take so much trouble about her appearance if she doesn't want men to find her attractive...and why does she dare to resent the logical sequence? Oh dear, I have shocked you again!' A peacock screamed from the edge of the woods. 'What an excellent example,' I said. 'The male bird spreads his tail and does everything he can to beguile his mate: would you have sympathy with him if he later complained he had been seduced? It is just as true in reverse.... I wanted you as my lover, and I find it right and natural that the process follows the natural sequence. I *want* this baby, you dear, silly Senator.... Julia never wanted anything except herself!'

For three months he was happy and free from anxieties, but as the time of the birth grew closer, though it was not yet imminent, he became insistent that I should not be allowed to have it with only Sempronia to help me.

'I have made discreet but meticulous inquiries in Ancona,' he said fondly. 'There are two physicians who are most able men. One used to be famous in Rome until he came into property and retired from practice. I was afraid you might think me over-anxious, so I have engaged their services and they will be coming to see you to-morrow...just to make sure that everything is going well.'

I was about to protest, and then realized it would be a waste of energy. Both physicians were old, ignorant, and riddled with superstition. Salonius would have had them thrown out of his house if they had dared to enter it! I suffered myself to answer a multitude of impertinent and irrelevant questions; I listened to advice which I had no intention of obeying; I solemnly received several flasks of noisome concoctions which I would not have given to a sick goat. I found it difficult not to laugh while they were with me, and regretted that I dared not joke about them to Nigellus.

Although I knew their forebodings were spurious, and delivered only so that the patient would increase her fee out of a mistaken gratitude for escape from imaginary perils, I found it annoying to discover how receptive of ideas I had become. My mind knew the fears were nonsensical, my body discovered an excuse to become the centre of attention. I really *did* find it difficult to walk briskly up-hill, and so of course had to walk even further than I had intended. At least

I could refuse to be bullied by my body which had dared to become more gullible than my intellect!

If only Nigellus had had the wit to understand that I was a Greek, with a disciplined mind and natural instincts, I should not have been forced to suffer even these minor discomforts. Surely it was enough to have to tolerate being such a ridiculous shape! I gave him pompous talks, based on the knowledge I had used while with Salonius, about the vital need for pregnant women to remain uncontaminated by fear or ignorance. He listened, kissed me, told me in all seriousness not to dwell on dangers which he was sure would never materialize...and continued to treat me as though I suffered from some severe, and probably mortal, illness.

Eventually it became easier to play the role he designed for me with such passionate devotion, and with such curious stupidity. I developed desires for food which I knew would be difficult to procure, and then changed my mind when it arrived and demanded something else. Or else I ate it because I was feeling guilty and was usually sick. I shall never forget the effect of prawns that cost more than their weight in gold but had wilted on the journey.

Sempronia was the only person whose company I found congenial; she had had fourteen children, now all grown-up except two who had died in infancy, and she was delighted to describe in detail the circumstances of the various births. She had certain illogical beliefs as to herbs which should be strewn on the floor, and gods who must be placated. But providing she was allowed to carry out these harmless rituals I knew she would be no source of trouble, and I had confidence that she knew quite enough for my needs. Or did she? Should I bear a dead child, or slowly bleed to death after it was born? Was there really a fundamental difference in the structure of slaves and patricians...even Greek patricians? When I found these thoughts crawling into my mind I drove them out with well-rounded oaths which Euripides would have appreciated. It was easy to defeat them in the daylight, but sometimes they assumed a certain dominance when I found it difficult to sleep.

I longed for even an hour's conversation with Salonius. I had heard him say to other women, 'If you will only accept the fact that birth is natural, providing the child in your womb is welcomed and not resented, you need no more attention than an animal. And if you have your husband to share your pains you will find them trivial or even ecstatic.'

Why did I want to hear Salonius say this to *me*; why would the sound of his voice have made so great a difference when I knew the truth as well as he did? 'You may as well recognize that you *can't* have Salonius,' I said to myself firmly. 'He thinks you are dead, and physicians don't use their skill for ghosts!'

And then I heard myself answer, with the voice within the head which can be so much louder than sound, 'Do women who die in childbirth still cry for a physician to release them from their pain? If Lucina was still a priest could she help women who are beyond the skill of more ordinary leeches?'

There was a dream which followed such sequences. I was back in the temple and a crowd of people were gathered outside the door. Some of them were very old, some were women with children at the breast, and there were the lame and the blind, and through their rags I could see running sores. I could have healed them...they needed only a word to make them whole. But they waited for me to open the door; and I could not move. I could not even call out to them.

I used to wake hearing myself scream, drenched with sweat. Nigellus would hurry to me, bring hot stones wrapped in wool to warm my feet, heat broth and feed me with a spoon as though I were a small child. Then he would kneel beside me, holding my hand, soothing me with small comforting love-words until I fell asleep. The next day I would try to repay him, in so many small ways, for loving me so much more than I could return.

'When we have a child to play with everything will be different,' I said to reassure myself. 'When I have a child of my own I shall love it so much that I shall be able to give every one what I owe to them. I shall be proud with loving.'

Sometimes I nearly told Nigellus that I had lied to the physicians, telling them that the baby was due a month later than it really was. But I never quite had the courage. I knew I should be safe with Sempronia, but those unwise old men might bring fear with them, might drive me away from health when I was not strong enough to defend my body with my mind.

I counted the days carefully and intended to arrange for Nigellus to be away from home. But this plan failed, for nothing was sufficiently important to take him away for more than a few hours. Every morning we paced through the woods, I, who would have still found a fast walk reassuring, clinging to his arm. Every evening, though the spring was unusually mild, I let him wrap a cloak round my shoulders when we sat on the terrace to watch the sunset. If it made him feel happier, what did it matter that I was rather too warm?

It was easy to conceal that the first pains had begun. I told him I was going to spend the morning arranging flowers, an occupation he considered suitable even to my delicate condition. Fortunately it was the last day of the month, which he reserved for the tallies of the farm. As soon as he was out of sight and the dust thrown up by his chariot had begun to settle, I dropped the basket of hyacinths and went to find Sempronia. As soon as she saw me she knew what was happening; she ceased to be the cook and became the confidante.

'He's gone,' I said. 'We shall be clear until this evening.'

'Men are much better out of the way...fuss they do and more trouble than rats in the flour barrels!'

She opened a cupboard and took out the herbs which she

had so carefully hoarded against this occasion. 'Better go down and give something nice to Apollo,' she said. 'I'll take him a jar of the best wine later...when everything is satisfactory.'

I had reason to regret that I had put the statue so far from the house; it seemed a long walk and I was glad that several marble benches, chosen by Nigellus, had escaped my veto.

When I heard the chariot coming home I told Sempronia to bolt the door. Poor Nigellus! He sounded distraught, but I was by then too concerned with my own feelings to be sympathetic. I heard a chariot galloping down the road. 'I expect he has sent to Ancona,' I said. 'We are quite safe... they can't get here before to-morrow.'

'Sooner than that...so you had better hurry. A few more good pains and we shall be finished...if you put all you've got into it.'

Even curiosity was nearly subservient to the demands of the body, but I asked, 'How can they get here sooner?'

'He's not so stupid as most men; he has said to me several times that he thought you would have it sooner than you thought. The two old charlatans have been hidden in the village for the past seven days, and making a rare commotion about the bugs in their beds and demanding to be brought here.' She shook with laughter, her three remaining teeth yellow against the hard, pink gums. 'But the master wouldn't tell you, he won't let anything disturb my pretty... he thought they would get here in time. None of the men are as clever as old Sempronia...bear down hard and we shall make fools of the lot of them.'

I had underrated the fortitude of women: it was only by biting my lips until the blood was salt in my mouth that I managed not to scream. I should like to have been inspired by the heroic conduct of the Spartans, but they never entered my mind.

'It's a boy: as like to his father as two beans in a row!'
'Is he all right...there's nothing wrong with him?'

Even when I had *proved* I had been right I was still capable of being influenced by the threats of monsters! Those accursed old men!

'He sounds very healthy,' I said. 'Let me see him, just to be sure.'

He was a very ordinary baby, but to me entirely different to any other of the human species. Surely all babies were ugly? How magnificently clever of me to produce such a beautiful child! Instead of red he was the colour of a spring sunrise, and his skin...and his delicate nails, like almonds, and his hair...most babies were bald but he quite definitely *had* hair!

'He's so like my first that they might be twins,' said Sempronia. 'I could weep that my old dugs are too dry to give him suck.'

I suddenly took her hand and kissed it. Without her I might have had a dead son. What did it matter if she wanted to pretend she had had a magical baby too?

I had often rehearsed this scene in my mind...Nigellus coming into the room, and I looking calm and beautiful with our child in the curve of my arm. I had never decided what sex it was going to be, though Nigellus had been sure it must be a son. I was too tired for heroics, but I think I could have been adequate as the young mother if only I had not heard the chariot come up the road, in such haste that the horses were driven across the lawn. Then the raised voice of Nigellus, who had obviously been waiting their arrival in a torment of impatience. What a fool he was, to wait outside instead of offering to do something *useful*. That he had repeatedly implored me to open the door and that there were plenty of servants to carry out any orders given by Sempronia I found it convenient to ignore.

'You had better take the baby to show him,' I said. 'I feel too tired to think of the right thing to say.'

She nodded and wrapped my son in a blanket. 'I'll just give him a rub with oil and then come back to settle you down...a nice sleep is all you need.'

The door shut firmly behind her, and then I heard it open very quietly. Nigellus tiptoed to the bedside; I thought that, after all, his presence would be restful...but he was crying, the sobs shaking his body as though he had fever.

'My Lucina...my sweet, beautiful Lucina! Will you ever forgive me for letting you nearly die with only a cook to help you!'

'She isn't a cook...she's the nurse. If you want to see our son you had better ask her to show him to you.'

'I don't want to see him.... I don't want anything except you...are you sure you're safe...no, of course you're not, but you will be soon.... I've got the physicians here.'

So I had gone through all this and he didn't even want to *see* the result! He was still trying to pretend it was *his* foresight which had saved us both! I made an enormous effort to be tolerant and found it required too much energy.

'If you bring those horrible old men in here I shall be excessively rude to them. If you had a crumb of intelligence you would kill them for making everything so difficult for me! Can't you understand? I'm tired...I want to go to sleep...I want to be left *alone*.'

He put something under my pillow and crept out of the room, as though I had whipped him, as though he were suddenly old. I knew he would blame himself, not me: he would hate himself, not me...so I had no defence.

I put my hand under my pillow and felt a smooth circle. It was a bracelet...plain gold, and I remembered I had once said to him that gold was the symbol of all the great realities. It was inscribed, 'To Lucina in love.'

Could I ever learn to love my son enough for his father never to know I was so great a failure? I pulled the coverlet over my face, so that at least I need not add to his disappointment with the sound of the tears I was too weak to restrain.

SOUR WINE

'There has never been a drama, or even a comedy, which cannot be rewritten,' said Euripides gently.

We were in the ilex grove above the villa: I could see Nigellus sitting at the stone table in the shade of the pergola, working at his history of Rome, in which, because of me, he could not play a part.

'Once the stage is set only the old lines are fitting,' I said. 'It is a good stage: I have seen the vines fruit, I planted them, so I must be tolerant of the vintage.'

'Sour wine, Lucina?'

Suddenly it was no longer decent to pretend. 'Sour, bitter...the lees thick as clotted blood. I am only twenty-six years old...and I wish I were eighty, so that without loss of dignity I could withdraw from a role which I no longer have the wish, or the ability, to act.'

'You are out of love with Nigellus...and with Marius?'

'Out of love with myself. How can they love me when I have grown so small? It is terrible to grow small, Euripides, terrible to run away from life and watch yourself getting smaller and smaller in the distance. And I can't stop running. Even two years ago I might have broken the mosaic I made with such hideous care and built it into a new pattern...but now it is too strong.'

'Nothing is ever too strong if you don't try to escape.'

'How easy that must sound when you still have the courage to face everything.' I was shocked by the cynicism in my voice and hoped Euripides had not noticed it.

'Don't forget you are *all* the Lucinas...far more than those of which Praxiteles made statues. You can have the health you enjoyed in Elysium, the wisdom of the priestess, the faith in love of the young woman who made a certain journey to Umbria...if only you will accept them.'

'And accept their memories! No, Euripides, they can keep their strength so long as they allow me to forget.'

'You used to be proud of memory.'

'And where is the necessary pride? Can a wife be proud that she has stolen the fruits of a just ambition from her husband? Can a mother be proud that her son will come to know that she resents his likeness to his father? Can I be proud that I basely deserted all the people who helped me, and the others whom I might have helped? Can I be proud that I am no longer lovable?'

'Nigellus loves you, and so does Marius.'

'Nigellus is too kindly to recognize that the dream is over. He is nearly fifty; young for a Senator but too old to find his only justification as a lover. He knows, even though he will not admit it to any one, least of all himself, that I have robbed his age of dignity. It is terrible to watch him trying to stay young; the medicinal baths, the massage with curious ointments, the draughts taken in secret which are supposed to increase potency, the oils rubbed into his hair in a vain attempt to stop the bald patch spreading. To hide from his increasing desire to be free of desire he makes love to me: neither of us is deceived by the antics of two sorry puppets whom we watch dancing to strings that echo no magic.'

'Was it always a failure, Lucina? Has this house always been less than an illusion?'

'It is difficult to be honest about a dream that turned out to be only...a dream. Euripides, don't let me lie to you; *make* me tell you the truth, for I am starved of honesty.'

'Lucina was never afraid to be honest with herself...and she never bothered to lie to me. Don't forget you are still Lucina.'

'Am I, are you sure? Sometimes I think that the real me is in prison, in several prisons. I dream that I am back in the temple, waiting for people to come to me. The lamp is lit, the poppy-drink ready in the goblet. I wait for the sound of footsteps on the path from the landing-stage. I think that if only some one opens the door and sees me as I used to be I shall *be* that person again. But the door never opens: they think I have gone away. I can't find freedom in dreams any more, Euripides. I go back to Elysium to look for Aesculapius: the house is empty, the plaster cracked on the walls, the garden a wilderness. I run into the garden looking for some one who may remember me...and I suddenly remember Agamemnon's grove and am afraid.

'I never knew, until this last year, that ghosts could be part of people who are still alive. I don't mean people who died in other centuries and have been reborn, but part of their present self, split off from the centre, knowing a terrible loneliness of separation. Nigellus is growing old much faster than his years demand. Why? Because only half, or less than half, of his soul inhabits his body. Is that why people grow old? Because they leave behind so much of their souls that there is only a husk?'

Euripides by the tone of his voice tried to give me the detachment I used to find so easy. 'What a theme for a drama! We must write it, Lucina; you must come to Rome for the first performance...or shall we give it to Athens? The chief characters surrounded by ghosts of themselves...wailing or mocking...could ghosts laugh, do you think, or would that be a discordant note?'

'Is there nothing you don't see in terms of the stage?'

'I trust not, for then I should know I had relinquished my right to sit in the audience...and I think the experience might bring with it a certain discomfort!'

'*Think!* Keep on thinking, but never be fool enough to know it. I used to be a good actress, you did not waste your time when you trained me to speak your lines. How often have you said to me, ''You have got to *become* the character before you can make any one else believe in it.'' And I was a faithful pupil. I acted the boy when I came to Elysium; I was the priestess in the temple; the physician with Salonius; the hetaera, and then the wife—Nigellus married me after Julia died, last year. Now I have no role into which to escape.'

'You are still the wife, the mother, the benign despot of your little world. The plants grow as you demand, the servants conduct their affairs according to your wishes...is it not enough?'

His eyes were alert, bird-bright. 'Don't bother to answer. I did not come here merely to give you news of the world outside, I came to take you back with me. You had to go through this phase, but I knew it would fail: you cannot make a plant grow in a pot too small for its roots, and Lucina demands much more than a plant!'

'So you intend to write another drama for me? Shall I be your sister, or only a distant relation, a little faded but still passably good looking, whom you have befriended?'

'Sarcasm never became you, my dear.' I saw I had hurt him; and was glad that he found sombre reality disquieting. 'Poor, sweet Lucina,' he said. 'Forgive me for not seeing how sharply life has driven you. I am very selfish, and therefore very elated that I shall not have to be lonely for you much longer.'

'Have you been lonely for me? Have *you* been lonely?'

'Have any of us been anything else since we became exiles from Elysium?'

'You want to go back there too?'

'I want to take you back.'

'To find the ghosts? To see the house we loved fallen into decay? To find no Aesculapius, no Narcissus, no Epicurus....'

'Perhaps they will make the same journey.'

'Not Narcissus, he hated me because I was such a clever pupil, and in me he saw himself. Did I ever tell you what he said to me the night before I left for Rome? He didn't know I was never coming back or perhaps he would have been more kind...and less honest. He told me that if I had only had the courage to be a woman he would have been bold enough to be a man. He surrounded himself with painted boys because they were a mirror which he held up to himself, a mirror so merciless that he had to try to forget that there had been another alternative. He told me that I had taken from him the power to be a real person; now he was only a reflection of what other people thought of him. I could have given him the confidence that he needed: but I was too lazy, too selfish, too cold.'

I shivered. 'He was right, I am always too cold. Even when the weather is hot I never sweat; even in bed with a lover...(always I boast, for I say 'a lover' to conceal I have never had more than one), I am cold right down to the core of my bones.'

'Virginity has other qualities than a lack of warmth.'

'Virginity? Isn't that another word for integrity, and can integrity be worn except one is stripped naked of deceit?'

'Why are you so afraid of being a woman? It would be easy if you lived with a man who could see below the surface, who knew that you are so reasonable because you are terrified of your intense emotions, who honoured you for your intellect, but loved you in spite of it.'

'No man loves a woman in spite of her intellect...except when he forgets his masculinity, or before he is conceited enough to demand compliance from her.'

'Don't judge all men from your knowledge of an ambitious Roman, whom you loved only because you were tired and wanted to run away for a little while from responsibilities which seemed too heavy. That's where I was such a fool: I ought to have known you only needed a holiday, I ought to have told you to go away with Nigellus for a month. It could have been arranged discreetly, if I had been able to see an ordinary human situation without trying to make high drama out of it.'

For the first time for months I was almost able to laugh at myself. 'Dear Euripides, what should I have done to you if you had told the ecstatic young woman in Surrentium that all she needed was a gay, robust interlude of carnal love! How could I have possibly believed it, when I was so sure that mine was the flesh which could melt only in the fires of immortal romance! And anyway, a month would have been too short: I should have returned thinking that I had relinquished a paradise for the drab course of duty; I should have become embittered and vented my spleen on the unfortunate women who came to me for advice...at least I have not added to my burden by foisting my guilt on them!'

Small in the distance, I saw Marius run out of the house. He stopped when he saw his father and then went more slowly along the path to the waterfall. 'If I had gone away only for a month I could not have had Marius,' I said slowly, then made myself laugh again. 'At least I could have got him, but a pregnant priestess would not have been agreeable to Salonius.'

'You need never lack a father for your children...unless you are afraid to risk them having red hair.'

It was lightly spoken, but suddenly I realized that Euripides was offering me more than I had ever expected from him.

'Would people like us ever be satisfied with an ordinary human baby? To you and me it would always be a potential genius, a dramatist in little. You wouldn't be content to follow the pattern of slow fecundity: nor was I, until I told my mind to sleep, to sleep without long dreams. Marius was a Roman baby: fat and contented and greedy. He yelled when he was hungry, and never bothered to consider whether the milk, my milk, was a proper prelude to future Falernian. He slept when he was tired, brought up his wind before it gathered force to trouble him, beguiled me with his dimples and bullied his nurse. Fish lived in pools for him to catch, the cat had a tail for him to pull, the chariot rocked over an uneven road because it amused him. He breaks his toys because it makes him conscious of his strength, and ignores me when he feels inclined because it reminds him that in due course other women will weep at his frown. A typical

Roman, with the world to explore, and dominate. His father thinks him nearly perfect, and I have recognized that in a few years I shall have nothing to say to him, and he will always consider it a misfortune that he has foreign blood in his veins.'

'If you could dictate to one of the Fates, would you send Nigellus and Marius back to Rome?'

'They couldn't do without me,' I said quickly, aware of a sudden, almost physical pain in my heart. 'I am stronger than Nigellus; he has given up everything he valued for me, at least I can still try to guard him from disillusion.'

'But I thought you had admitted that neither of you believed in the idyll any more?'

'He doesn't know it. He must never know it, Euripides. He has made me into some one who never existed and it would kill him to discover the reality. He thinks I am entirely content to plan new flower-beds or to talk about the inefficiency of servants. He thinks my only anxiety for Marius is if he shows a sign of fever; he doesn't know I am far more anxious about the man he will be in twenty years. Only to you dare I admit I have most lamentably failed; but somehow I shall find the courage to keep this from the two who love me in their fashion.'

He took my hands between his, 'Lucina, think carefully before you answer. If it were possible for Nigellus to go back to Rome, taking Marius with him, would you be content to let them go? Would you have the courage to return to the path of your destiny, which is so much wider than this narrow field in which you have tried to hide.'

'Why talk about ''ifs''? Why torment me with a freedom of choice which is impossible for me to accept? How can I run away again, run away from the man who trusted me, who still trusts me, to guard his dreams. The second time he met me he told me that I could guard his dreams and make them come true...no one, not even I, could betray a trust of that nature. In some ways Nigellus is younger than

Marius, more vulnerable. Even if the hurt is only to his pride it could be mortal. If I left him he would think it because he is inadequate as a lover. I should drive him into the arms of other women whom he would have to pay to conceal from him that his manhood was growing old. I couldn't do that to him; I couldn't make him feel old and lonely, and ashamed. That is why I am afraid of dying: I don't know what would happen to Nigellus. I try to believe he would be happy putting flowers on my tomb and keeping lamps always burning in my rooms. They would be kept just as I left them, the flasks of perfume still on my toilet table, a ribbon on the floor...or would the servants have tidied away the ribbon before I died? He would take great pains to build me a suitable tomb, and the lettering would be a poem of spacing and good taste. But death would be no freedom for me: he would be so sure that I was waiting for him that I should never have the courage to disappoint him. I might die years before he did, and have to wait in some ante-room of Olympus, carefully setting my hair in ringlets and perhaps with a six-months' curve to my belly to give him a sense of proprietary security! And even that might be no use, for he would probably refuse to enter Olympus because it was inhabited by foreigners. And I should refuse a Roman heaven—plump ghosts and an excessive abundance of rich food would be a poor inducement to a tranquil acceptance of eternity.'

Euripides smiled and leant back against a tree with his hands clasped behind his head. 'I have found, in a somewhat varied life, that when all logical possibilities seem fruitless, the only sensible course is to believe in some solution which appears entirely impractical. If, with my exceedingly fertile imagination, I was able to think of a plan which would allow you to take your freedom without in any way giving disillusion to your husband, would you find this agreeable? You need not answer...your face has done that for you.'

He went on, 'You have died once, in the eyes of the world: you might die a second time. The river in which you sometimes bathe, not, I may say, without causing anxiety to your husband, is swollen by the spring rains. You are again presumed drowned: Nigellus enjoys the usual period of mourning, through which I sustain him with good counsel and plenty of excellent wine. He then finds a natural desire to return to his old life. I invent a plausible story of a Senator who was taken by pirates while floating on the wreck of his overturned boat. He has escaped after sundry adventures which he finds it too painful to describe, and with him he brings his adopted son who was given into his charge by some noble who assisted this providential rescue. Nigellus is restored to Rome. Marius takes up his natural position in society. I shall be careful to assign him suitable heredity.'

'It is a charming story...almost I wish it were true.'

'And why shouldn't it be? Why shouldn't you and I go back to release the ghosts which you say are causing you considerable discomfort. I should enjoy seeing you tackle a ghost, especially so charming a ghost as any of you would be.'

I saw the servants setting a table on the terrace and Sempronia coming to get Marius ready for the evening meal which Nigellus preferred him to take with us. 'We shall be late if we don't hurry,' I said. 'Nigellus doesn't like me to be late for meals, it upsets the routine of his day. He will have written exactly ten pages, no more no less, and after dinner he will read them aloud to us and we shall make appropriate comments. We must make at least two minor corrections or he will think we have not given it our proper attention. This especially applies to you, Euripides, for whom he has a great respect...as a user of words.'

The evening passed as had so many hundred evenings. A moth fluttered into the candle flame, a bat flickered among the vines, I watched the steady light glowing from the unshuttered window of the room where Marius slept. The drone of my husband's voice merged with the sound of the waterfall. By the glow of the single flame he looked young, younger than I had known him. Euripides sipped his wine and indolently peeled an apple. I watched my fingers threading coloured flax through a piece of linen, which, because I thought it suited the domestic scene, I had for months been embroidering as a curtain for my bedroom. It was already rather soiled, for I was apt to leave it in remote corners of the garden.

Euripides made the right comments, a mere suggestion as to the exact meaning of a Greek word used in the text, an allusion to some ancient philosopher whose view might be used to strengthen an argument. The men looked at each other with the unspoken agreement that on this point I could not be expected to contribute anything useful. Nigellus found it convenient to treat me with kindly patronage.

I went to my room and found Sempronia's niece waiting for me. She told me that the girl who usually attended me was ill. I tried to sleep, hoping that Nigellus would place his usual kiss on my forehead and then tiptoe with elaborate caution into the adjoining room. But I was so restless that it was futile to pretend I was not awake. Nigellus got into bed, and soon began to breath slowly and deeply. How often had he told me that if I paid proper attention to the rhythm of my breathing I should not need to tire my eyes by reading far into the night? Moonlight shone through the open window and made it easier to believe in the impossible.

Nigellus turned towards me, pathetically defenceless and trusting in sleep. I put my arm round him and his cheek found the familiar curve of my shoulder. He woke for a moment to murmur 'Lucina...I love you so much...I love you.' He smiled and drifted into a dream.

A cloud covered the moon: if I ran away from Nigellus I should leave an apologetic ghost watching over him, weeping because she had added one more betrayal to her score. I got out of bed and went to see if Marius had kicked off his covers. The stone of the passage was cold to my bare feet, but my forehead was hot. I kissed him; his skin smelt like warm fruit, his hair was yellow as barley. I trimmed the wick of the lamp...at least I could see that no child of mine awoke in a dark room....

Odd that I am hot on a chill night. And I am thirsty...my throat hurts. I must not be ill again: it would be absurd to be ill while Euripides is here. When I lived in Elysium I was never ill.

PART THREE

CHAPTER ONE

the Stream

Further up the stream, under a chestnut that grew close to the water's edge, the ground was covered with white cyclamen. I wondered why I had not noticed them before: there were so many, far more than I could remember planting. Euripides was to meet me here. I seemed to have been waiting for him a long time, though it could not really be long for it was not yet dark.

'Euripides, where are you?' I heard my voice echoing through the ilex grove, down towards the house. And the house was empty, for I had watched Nigellus and Marius go down the white road towards the village.

When they discovered I had left them they would go to Rome and be happy. Euripides was right; they would soon get used to being without me, there was no need to worry about them.

'Euripides...please hurry or I shall be alone when it gets dark.'

A fawn walked unafraid from the shadow of the grove. I held out my hand; it came closer and let me stroke its head between the soft pointed ears. I took off my sandals and splashed across the stream. The fawn followed me until I reached the far bank, then turned and trotted back into the grove of dark trees.

The water was pleasantly cool, and it washed the blood from a long scratch on my right knee. I must have got it coming up the valley where the brambles had grown over the path. Or had I climbed by the waterfall and fallen on one of the sharp rocks? I could not remember and was too idle

283

to bother about it.

It was colder on this side of the stream, so I followed the steep bank until I found another place to cross. I could not find my way back to the cyclamen, though I wanted to show them to Euripides.

'Euripides! Please hurry, Euripides...we ought to leave here before dark.'

But it didn't really matter if he were late; it was very pleasant alone in the woods, and if I wanted him I could go back to the house and shout to him from the garden.

Then I saw him standing on the far side of the stream. He looked ill; his forehead was beaded with sweat and he was pressing his right hand to his side as though in pain.

'I came as fast as I could,' he said. 'I have been revoltingly sick. How unromantic to be sick at the start of a journey!'

I was relieved to know there was nothing really wrong with him, nothing which would delay us.

'It's warmer on this side of the water,' I said. 'Come over and join me.'

'It's very deep,' he said anxiously. 'The current is so fast that I doubt if I could swim across.'

I laughed, for I knew he was trying to be funny. Euripides had been the best swimmer in Elysium, and the stream was so shallow that the water only reached to my knees. But it would be unkind not to share his game...he would get caught up in it and forget the shame of being sick.

'Shall I get you a boat,' I said solemnly. 'Or look for an easier crossing higher up?'

'Did you cross by boat? He sounded anxious: no one could enter into a game so well as Euripides.

'I had a boat, with scarlet oars and a violet sail. Then it turned into a cockle shell and I fell out and had to swim the rest of the way. I will make a boat for you.'

I picked up the husk of a chestnut and threw it across to him. 'Hold it and wish very hard and then it will carry you across the stream.' He clutched it in his hand and put a tentative foot into the water.

'That's right,' I said, as though encouraging a child. 'One foot in front of the other, and remember your boat.'

I saw him take a deep breath and shut his eyes. Then he walked slowly through the water. It was shallower than I thought; it only covered his ankles and I could see his feet clear against the white sand, as he picked his way carefully between the rocks.

He looked so funny that I heard myself laughing. I stretched out my arms to pull him up the bank and found he was shaking with cold. I picked up a cloak—I must have left it under a laurel bush—and wrapped it round him.

'Do you still feel sick?' I said anxiously. 'If you do you had better *be* sick and I'll hold your head...it's difficult to be comfortably sick standing up.'

'I shall be all right in a minute...but don't talk about being sick. Don't *ever* remind me of it.'

'I'm sorry...I meant to be helpful...and you seemed so dizzy. What was it you ate?'

'I drank it. It seemed the obvious thing to do. But don't talk about it,' he sounded unnecessarily vehement. 'Don't ever mention it again, do you understand?'

'Are you warmer now? How lucky I brought a cloak big enough for us both. We had better spend the night here: it's getting darker...only dusk yet but we shall find the road easier after dawn.'

He put his arms round me and the cloak wrapped us both, warm and secure even if the night should turn cold. It was a blue cloak, the colour we wore before I went into exile; the same weave as the cloak I had when I ran away from Elysium. It even had the same small tear in the hem that Narcissus had mended for me with thread that did not quite match, when we were poor, in Rome. But it was much larger than the old one; it covered both of us. We should not have to be afraid of the cold on this journey.

285

In the morning Euripides rolled up the cloak and carried it on his shoulder. I thought I knew all the paths leading from the grove, but we found a new one. In places it was so steep that we had to climb over rocks, and then it wound through small meadows, gay with buttercups and scarlet anemones: there were also hyacinths with a warm, sleepy scent.

'I should like some pomegranates,' said Euripides. 'I am not really hungry, but I think it must be time we had something to eat.'

'Pomegranates *and* figs,' I said firmly. 'Do we need milk too? If so we had better look for an accommodating goat.'

'Nothing to drink out of,' said Euripides, 'and I'm definitely *not* going to be suckled by a goat!'

At the end of the meadow we found what must have been an abandoned orchard. There was part of a wall still standing, supported by the serpent branches of an ancient fig tree...purple figs, the kind I liked best. There was also a pomegranate tree with ripe fruit, and Euripides made a wreath for me of the scarlet flowers.

We lay on the short, crisp turf in the genial warmth. I asked him whether he had a knife to cut the pomegranates.

'No,' he said. 'I was almost sure I brought one with me, but I must have dropped it when I crossed the stream.'

'It doesn't matter,' I said hastily. 'I hate knives...we should either blunt it or cut ourselves.' I thought he was looking pale, and said without pausing to think, 'You're not feeling sick again, are you?'

He turned on me with sudden intense anger. 'Will you never learn to keep a promise! I was quite all right...and now...'

He lurched to his feet and began to retch. His stomach must have been empty for he did not bring anything up, not even the figs though he had eaten a great many.

When the spasm passed he walked away and I followed him in penitent silence. After we had gone through two small woods, I said, 'I am very sorry, Euripides. I won't do it again...please forgive me.'

In answer he took my hand, and the feel of his strong square fingers was very reassuring. I knew he was not really ill, for we walked a long way without getting tired.

We avoided towns, for I thought strangers might be hostile, and try to make us turn back. Sometimes we called a greeting to people working in the fields, and once we found a child who had fallen and cut his head. He was running across a field and blood was pouring down his forehead. Euripides carried him to a stream and washed the blood away. The child told us where he lived...it was a small farm, beyond the stream. Euripides would not let me come with him when he took the child home.

When he came back he looked as though he had been sick again, but I remembered not to ask him. He said he had carried the little boy to his bedroom and left him in the care of his mother. I asked whether the mother had been grateful, but he said she had been too concerned to notice who had brought her son back. 'But the boy knew,' he said. 'And the boy was glad...he didn't think I had *driven* him back.'

He smiled as he said this, a gentle smile as though he were remembering something he would never wish to forget.

We did not ask any one for food or shelter until we came to Claudia's villa. When we were sleepy we wrapped ourselves in the cloak, and there was always fruit on the trees, even ripe almonds, though we saw the pink blossom in clouds on the hillsides.

Claudia's villa was crowded with people, though she seemed to have forgotten their names. I was glad she had a house of her own instead of having to flatter women like Julia. She smiled at us, the brittle smile of the conventional hostess, and told us to look after ourselves and to ask for anything we wanted. I was rather surprised she did not recognize us. Perhaps she only remembered the clothes I used to wear and the reputation of Euripides.

There was food in great variety, laid out on gold dishes, and boys in green tunics kept the goblets filled with wine. Most of the guests were richly dressed, but Euripides noticed that their clothes were ill matched, and several wore shoes of patched leather or had their feet wrapped in rags.

We explored the house, and found in the outer hall a chest filled with clothes. Beside it was a heap of discarded tunics, none of them of good quality. Then we went to the bath-house, which was elaborate enough to have served a town or a rich patrician. There were three men in the bath, but they took no notice of us. The water must have come from a medicinal spring, for I watched scabs float off a man's back and leave the skin clean.

Suddenly I understood. Long ago I had told Claudia she would never be a hostess until she learned to welcome any one who really needed her hospitality. She had stared at me, and complained to Julia that I had insulted her; but she had not forgotten. It was typical that in spite of her genuine kindliness she still had to pretend that the beggars she welcomed were patricians. Or did she give them new clothes so that they should be able for a while to forget poverty?

I thought it would be safe to remind her that this was not our first meeting, but she only smiled brightly and made a response which showed she had no idea who I was. She turned to welcome another guest. I judged him to be a farmer, for there was soil ingrained in his skin and under his nails. He wore the insignia of a Centurian, though he had added the plume of a different rank. She kissed him on both cheeks...so perhaps he was a poor relation.

She must have realized we had not eaten, for she insisted on taking us to yet another table, and heaping our plates with food. Roasted peacock followed by fish very richly cooked, and it made me feel heavy. When I tried to tell her I had had more than enough she looked as though she were going to cry, and said there was plenty more in the kitchens. 'Plenty here for every one,' she kept saying. 'Plenty to go round, more than enough.' She became so agitated that I had to accept a dish of almonds and cream over-sweetened with honey. She watched me with a fond, proprietary look, which made me suddenly ashamed that I had so often cajoled Marius to eat.

The arrival of another guest released us from her attentions. 'I had forgotten about Marius,' I said. 'We must go to Rome to make sure he is happy. I cannot go back to Elysium until I am sure he is not fretting for me.'

'Rome is in the wrong direction,' said Euripides. 'We have nearly reached the coast where the ship will be waiting for us. If we go to Rome we may lose our passage. Marius is all right: you wouldn't have left him unless you had been sure he would be happy. He is with Flavia: don't you remember how she always wanted a child?'

'I must go back to tell Flavia that he mustn't be made to eat unless he's hungry. It is wicked to force children to eat. I never knew it before...but if I don't explain to Flavia she will spoil his natural instincts and his body won't be able to look after itself when he's grown up.'

'It's too late to worry about that now. The boy has settled down and it would be cruel to disturb him.'

'But I must go back...I can speak to the nurse if you don't want me to see Flavia. Marius need not know I have been there.'

'*Please*, Lucina, don't go back to Rome.'

His voice was curiously urgent. How silly of Euripides to make a fuss about a small change in our plans! We argued for a long time before he gave way; I had to say I would go alone if he preferred not to come with me.

The road to Rome was much more hilly than I expected and the ruts were deep. I got a blister on my heel and had to limp along carrying one of my sandals. The thong rubbed the flesh raw, and there was another blister between the toes.

When I was too tired to walk any further we came to a

small farm. A woman was carrying water to a pair of white oxen. I knew I had seen her somewhere before. She smiled and said she had always hoped to meet me again. She took us into the house and gave us bread fresh from the baking and cups of warm milk. I did not remember her name until her husband came in from the fields where he had been sowing grain. She was Helena, who married her Decurion on the night we first came to Rome.

She seemed apologetic that they could only offer us clean straw in the byre, but we assured her it would serve us very well. Aulus was a typical soldier. He must have retired, but he talked of his experiences in a small garrison town as though they had happened yesterday. Helena never showed she was bored by these reminiscences; she shared them with him as though they were her immediate concern, as though she would have to go back there with him to-morrow.

Before they went to bed she said she might have to go out very early, before we woke, and that if we found the house empty we must eat the bread she would leave for us on the table. We asked if there was anything we could do to help her, as we did not usually sleep late, but she said, rather quickly, that if we would wait till she came back that was all she asked. Then they both said, rather abruptly I thought, that it was time for us to go to the byre. She went to make sure we had enough straw, then hurried away, back through the courtyard to the house. As the door closed behind her we saw the light go out in their window.

In the morning she said her husband had gone to look for a lost sheep, or it may have been a goat, I forget. She offered to lend us her oxcart, which was going to Rome with some sacks of grain she owed to her half-sister who lived close to the city. We protested, but she said it would be a kindness to make the journey for her. She gave us careful directions how to find the road. In any case, she added, the oxen knew the way so well that we could trust them to follow it.

The oxen plodded with emphatic deliberation. They took

no notice of our attempts to guide them, so after a while Euripides joined me among the sacks of grain. Helena had given us a flask of wine, which we drank because we liked the taste though neither of us was thirsty.

The oxen stopped in a narrow street. We climbed down from the cart. A woman ran out of the shop and kissed us both as though we were old friends. It was only when I saw the strings of sausages hanging from the roof-beams that I recognized her: Cordelia, the beautiful hetaera to whom I had given the daisies, the woman whom I had sent to follow her heart, to the intense disapproval of Salonius.

She opened a door at the back of the shop and I realized they must have moved to a new property. Instead of the small yard where I had once talked to her while she was washing her husband's clothes, there was a large garden which would have honoured a famous villa. How glad I was to find them so prosperous; had I known what their future held I should have had no anxiety for them.

I should have liked to gossip with her, but Euripides seemed determined not to leave us alone. Perhaps he thought I might be tempted to tell her I was running away again. What could it have mattered, for I knew I could trust her discretion. The gardeners must have had remarkable skill. Yellow roses, white lilies, tulips and hyacinths; carnations and mallows, lupins and salvia grew in ordered profusion. Almond and pomegranate trees were in bloom, their branches lively with birds.

'The birds sing for us,' she said. 'We never allowed lark's tongues to be sold in our shop.'

Before I could ask what she meant, Euripides interrupted to ask the name of a flower; he must have known it, for it was only a daisy. It was difficult to believe that Cordelia was older than I, but when her husband joined us I realized that the light in her heart demanded an echo in her body...she moved more beautifully than a dancer yet without any conscious effort.

Euripides sat up talking with them after I went to bed. I think they tried to persuade him to go straight to the harbour, but I did not resent their interference for I knew the intention was kindly. Seeing them together made me sorry for Nigellus. I was determined to make sure that he was not grieving for me unduly. A proper regret was only seemly, but I wanted reassurance that he had not grown suddenly old.

Euripides must have decided not to make any further difficulties, for he was cheerful in the morning and said that we could go to Rome in a double litter lent to us by Cordelia.

CHAPTER TWO

the RIVER

Marius was playing with Flavia in the garden. I called to him, but he was too intent on his game to hear me.

'Don't disturb him,' said Euripides. 'Can't you be content to leave him, now that you know he is happy?'

'Marius! Marius, can't you leave your game long enough to listen to your mother?'

He dropped the ball he had been going to throw and looked round as though he were frightened.

'Don't let him see you! said Euripides urgently. 'Can't you understand it would be disgustingly selfish?'

I let him pull me into the shelter of a statue of Hermes. 'Watch the child from here if you want to, but *don't* upset him. You promised not to disturb him if I let you see for yourself that he is happy. Lucina, you *must* learn to keep your promises.'

'I didn't know I had promised,' I said forlornly. 'It seems so little to ask...just to kiss my own child before I go away.'

'You should have thought of that sooner.' Euripides sounded severe yet not unkind.

I saw Marius begin to cry. I nearly ran towards him. Then I saw the expression on Flavia's face as she took him in her arms to comfort him.

'Take me away, Euripides. Take me away...there is nothing to keep me here any longer. Flavia knows much more about being a mother than I was ever able to learn. Take me away, before I cry or start to feel jealous instead of grateful, while I still have the decency to be *glad* Marius is happier without me.'

'Are you still determined to see Nigellus?'

'Yes, I might worry about him if I wasn't sure he is all right.'

'Would it do if you saw him making a speech in the Senate...or would you prefer the Forum?'

'How do I know where he is? Perhaps the litter-bearers will know...they knew where to find Marius.'

Euripides would not let me look out between the drawn curtains while we went through the streets of Rome. There was very little chance of our being recognized, but he was so insistent that I did not bother to argue.

Nigellus was making a speech in one of the public squares. There was a crowd listening to him, but Euripides hurried through the press of people so fast that I was not sure whether they were hostile or friendly.

Nigellus was standing on some stone steps which led up to a large building...probably a new temple as it had not been there in my time. He looked well in his yellow toga with a purple border. Either his hair had grown or else the laurel wreath concealed his increasing baldness, for he looked younger than I expected.

I was not close enough to hear what he was saying, or perhaps I was so used to the sound of his voice that habit made me forget to listen to the words...anyway it was probably on a subject which I should have considered irrelevant. I stayed until I heard the crowd cheering him. Dear Nigellus, he had been starved of cheers and now he could have his fill. Knowing that I could leave him without feeling guilty made me quite fond of him again.

'Satisfied?' said Euripides. 'Any regrets?'

'No regrets, and thank you for letting me see him.'

Euripides looked very pleased with himself as though he had done something very clever. I could not understand why, for it had been I who insisted on visiting Nigellus and he had done everything he could to prevent me. Perhaps he had always been a little jealous and was glad I felt so unmoved at this farewell to my husband...for in my mind it *was* a farewell.

I told the litter-bearers to take us to the harbour. I thought Euripides was going to protest, but after a moment's hesitation he got in beside me. For some reason best known to himself he did not draw the curtains and I could look on to scenes which once had been so familiar.

The Tiber was in flood; refuse was swirling down on the turbid water, the waves against the piers of the bridges might have been carved from yellow stone. The quays were not so busy as usual, but a cluster of masts against the sky showed that we should not have to wait long for a boat.

'Shall we visit your temple?' Euripides sounded casual, as though the matter were of small importance.

'No,' I said. 'I don't see any point in going back there. And Salonius might recognize me, which would be embarrassing.'

'Frightened?'

'Of course not! I only think it would be rather boring.'

'But you told me there might be a ghost there...we shouldn't leave any unnecessary ghosts in Rome.'

'I'm not sure I believe in ghosts. Anyway, I've outgrown the phase of being interested in the supernatural...I'm going to look after myself for a change...and you, of course. We must look after each other.'

'Then we will most certainly visit the temple. You said the ghost was one of the Lucinas. She must be feeling lonely, poor dear, and I think we had better take her with us, back to Elysium.'

'If I ever said anything so silly it was meant as a joke. How could I have left her there when I am *here*. Such a very *solid* "here".'

For a moment I felt peculiar and took hold of the side of the litter to reassure myself that it was made of ordinary painted wood and not part of an elaborate dream. One of the litter-bearers had a wart on the back of his neck. There can be something very reassuring in the sight of a wart!

'Well, I shall go there,' he said stubbornly. 'If you think it would be too difficult for you to use some of your old powers, though *why* you are deliberately pretending you never possessed any I simply can't understand, I shall go alone. You can stay on the bank by yourself, and I hope it rains!'

I think if I had not seen the heavy drops splashing on the cobbles I might have stayed behind...but I should look silly if I got soaked. It might be quite amusing to go to the temple, in any case it would probably make me feel better. If it were abandoned I should know for certain that Salonius had failed to find any one to take my place, and if there were another woman there she was probably quite inadequate and it would be amusing to make funny remarks about her so that Euripides could laugh with me. It was a slightly uncomfortable thought, how easy it would be to be funny about a priestess, even one who was quite sincere...all those robes and dim lights and the poppy-drink...and the awful solemnity of it all. Had any of my patients wanted to laugh?

'Not many of them.'

I was startled, not realizing I had expressed my thoughts aloud.

'Your sincerity was too obvious for any of them to have laughed when you were working properly,' said Euripides consolingly. 'Of course when you weren't really trying you might have seemed silly...but I think few of them were oblivious of the fact that you had got power, of a kind...and might have turned it against them if you grew angry. The risk of being cursed by an impugned priestess is a considerable strain on the most robust sense of humour!'

'If *they* had realized how funny they looked, lying on the couch and sipping that perfectly harmless draught as though it were hemlock!'

'I *told* you not to mention it again!' He raised his hand as though he were going to slap me. Then he laughed with an obvious effort and said, 'Sorry...forget it...not at all important.'

'What's the matter? Why shouldn't I say they looked funny? You said I did...which was unkind and probably quite untrue, at least I sincerely hope it was!'

'Forget it, Lucina. You *must* learn to take a hint instead of asking awkward questions...which won't get you any of the right answers.' Abruptly he changed the subject, 'I think that when we learn to laugh at ourselves we shall have gone a long way towards Olympus. Perhaps that's the greatest difference between immortals and the rest of us...the ability to laugh at ourselves without rancour.'

I was glad that he had found an abstract idea to cover what had seemed an awkward situation. Perhaps if he got sufficiently interested he would forget about the temple, for surely these sentimental journeys were in the worst taste! So I said, 'We have been assured that laughter resounds throughout Olympus, but I always thought it was because the Gods found the behaviour of mortals supremely ridiculous. I must admit that I agree with them, especially when humans are trying to think themselves sublime in the act of love!'

'Did you think yourself funny when you were in bed with Nigellus?'

I giggled. 'Not always, and not me really. But at times I

couldn't help imagining what we would look like to some one sitting on the ceiling...all those curves and antics. Sometimes I used to imagine he was wearing a toga, with his laurel wreath hanging over one ear, and that he would suddenly realize there was a crowd watching him, *us* I mean, who were patiently waiting for him to make a speech about the latest war or something equally pompous.'

'*How* amusing that must have been for your husband: no wonder he grew old so quickly, no wonder he is glad to be rid of you!'

'Surely we needn't be sarcastic in a friendly argument! Euripides, please don't be tiresome...it spoils everything when we have to quarrel.'

'You can pretend that I am a normal, difficult male... vastly your inferior, of course, who loses his temper without any just cause and is completely irrational. But if you go on talking with smug satisfaction about how you behaved *disgustingly* to a man who, with all his faults—and I will admit he was infuriatingly solemn on occasion—loved you sincerely and to the full measure of his capacity, I shall turn you over my knee and smack you. May it make you realize you are talking like a spoilt child, and not a very nice child either!'

It was a good row and I was thoroughly enjoying myself. 'Of course if you want to resort to your masculine advantage of physical strength there is nothing I can do. If you want a woman who will wrestle with you why didn't you choose a Roman girl...those fat arms and thighs are not nearly so pliable as they look!'

'It's not your fault really,' he said, and sighed. I knew him well enough to adjust myself for a more subtle attack. 'None of us had the sense to bully you when we saw you were going in the wrong direction. All we did was to bleat to each other like a lot of silly sheep and hang about waiting to help you when you got yourself into real trouble. We let you do just as you pleased with us, even Aesculapius never had the courage to tell you what he really thought of you. And Salonius! Poor Salonius, what a fool you made of him! In the end he was too scared to do anything except argue with you in a feeble sort of way. After you gave boils to the patrician who said rude things about you—which was exceedingly stupid, as I'm afraid you will discover before long—he never put up any adequate opposition to anything you did.'

'They were only very *small* boils,' I said soothingly. I had never felt entirely comfortable about this minor departure from the laws I had invented for my own behaviour and was startled that I had ever confessed it to any one. 'Two on the back of his fat neck and one between the eyebrows...to remind him that there is more to be seen through the forehead than he would ever recognize with his small, piggy eyes.'

'I'm glad to hear it, for I expect you will make a fuss when they catch up with you. I hope they remind you to look out of *your* third eye, it can't see less than the other two do!'

I put my hand furtively to the back of my neck to see if it felt sore, but luckily it did not. 'I think it very unkind of you to suggest boils on me! Salonius always said it was very unwise to imagine oneself in anything but perfect health...and I never realized how sensible of him it was. Salonius *was* sensible sometimes; it was really rather a pity I didn't take more notice of him.'

'Humility from Lucina! Real or false?'

'Aren't you being needlessly disagreeable? Do you think I'm incapable of humility? Is it my fault that I met so few people in Rome with whom it was *decent* to feel humble? You wouldn't have me grovel to my inferiors, would you? After all, we *are* Athenians!'

'And so, of course, immune from the laws which govern the conduct of less fortunate mortals.'

'Well you can't expect us to be bound by standards which were invented to control foreigners. They can't help being different, poor things, it's just that they have not evolved so far as we have.'

'Lucina, do try to use your imagination. When it was uncomfortable for us you were never at a loss for an unlikely idea; and now, when it might be useful, you are intolerably conventional, earthy in the worst sense.'

I knew he was going to start nagging me about the ghost, so I said, 'I'm ready to go to the temple...the river looks rather high so I hope we find a reliable boat.'

I expected a boat, but not a boat with Lucius at the steering oar. He greeted me without surprise, as though I were part of the ordinary routine. I thought it rather impertinent of him not to be glad to see me, so I did not ask him where he was living or inquire after Iris.

'You had better go alone,' said Euripides. 'I'll come if you want me, but unless you do I'd rather stay here...crossing a river makes me feel sick.'

I knew this was nonsense. He had been fond of sailing in rough weather...when a storm blew up he was always the last to suggest turning back. But if he thought I was going to implore him to come with me he was mistaken.

The waves broke over the low prow and yellow water swirled over my feet. The boat rocked dangerously and I nearly told Lucius to turn back. The storm must have been worse than any I remembered, for even in rough weather the passage to the island had been sheltered. It seemed much longer than before...and I knew it was only two hundred paces...less if you steered across the current.

At least Salonius had not allowed the island to fall into disrepair. The stone flags of the path were free from moss, and none of the oak trees had been attacked by ivy. So he *had* found some one to take my place...it would be amusing to see if she were genuine! I would go there as a patient and ask for her advice...I would even pretend to take the poppy-drink.

I pushed open the door and saw that the lamp was lit beside the couch. How well I knew the correct procedure! I took off my sandals and lay back against the violet cushions, pleased that the new priestess had not been allowed to alter the decorations.

I could see a female shape through the gauze curtains. She wore a robe similar to mine in colour...it was probably one of those Narcissus had designed. Salonius must have decided that new ones would be a needless extravagance. I could show her that I was familiar with the routine, which would make her try her hardest, for she would think I had been here before, to Lucina, her rival.

'I have come to plead for your advice and counsel before making a long journey.' (How easy it was to echo the phrases I had so often heard!) 'I lost my husband and my child and now I want to go back to the place where I was born. I want to know whether I shall make a safe journey, whether I shall find my home as I left it many years ago.'

'You will find the home you made. There is no other, however long the journey.'

She must have read my notes, for I had certainly used that phrase before! Surely Salonius could have found some one with more originality!

'In the multiplicity of Roman Gods I am undecided to whom I could make a votive offering before embarking,' I said.

'If you make it to any one save Apollo you do so at your peril; follow your heart...all other roads lead to disaster.'

This was too much! The exact words I had used to Cordelia who had so recently befriended me! But I would give her one more testing.

'Shall I agree to travel in the company of slaves...it may be that I can find no other boat which sails to-night.'

'Why should you be too proud to travel with slaves? There is no just pride except in integrity.'

The advice I had given to Iris when she could not decide to marry Lucius! It was disgraceful of Salonius to have taken

Iris's faithful recordings of my utterances and handed them to this creature to abuse!

I got up from the couch, my hands shaking with righteous indignation. I pulled back the curtains, so roughly that the silver rings clattered like the bones of skeleton fingers. The other woman must have been young to be so agile. Already she had escaped through the door into the robing-room. If she thought I was going to indulge in an undignified game of hide-and-seek round the island she was due for a sharp disappointment.

The silver ram's heads felt very familiar to my hands...almost as though I had never left this throne...this lonely throne. I must have been much more tired than I realized for my legs went to sleep...when I tried to get up I could not move. It was not cramp, for there was no pain: only a heaviness, a disobedience of the body which was rather alarming. It would pass off in a moment...how fortunate that there was no one to see me in this ridiculous situation! I tried to force myself upright by leaning my weight on my hands. The fingers remained flexed, as though I had deliberately relaxed. I could watch them, calm and unresponsive, long and pale against the silver of the rams.

I began to get delusions: I thought I was going to see the door open and Nigellus enter for the first time. It would be terrible if I saw him like that and had to love him again. Yes, *again*, for I had loved him until love became inconvenient to acknowledge. It was only when I began to regret the temple, to feel myself futile as a mistress, that I learned to hate him so that I could put the blame for my escape on his shoulders. It had been difficult to learn hate, but I had had a terrible persistence of scholarship.

'Don't come here, Nigellus,' I said, just as though he were really waiting outside the door. 'We shall only hurt each other again. You are too kind to break the cruelty in me, too young to challenge the age; too dishonest to make me see myself.'

301

The door slammed shut...it must have been the wind which had swayed it open. Then the wind played another trick on me: it made the noise of a crowd...many people sighing because they were lonely, or heart-sick, or bewildered. None of their sickness was too heavy for me to carry until they were strong again. If they would only open the door and come into the light of the lamp I should be able to talk to them. I should not ask them to lie on the couch or follow any of the ritual. I should just talk to them in small, ordinary words; for their problems would be things I had learned by ordinary living. I should not have to use the words Salonius had taught me, nor the phrases of philosophy. I should say, 'I know what you feel; I know how difficult it seems. But you are not alone if you will only remember your loving. It does not matter *what* you love; if you cannot think of any special person, an animal will do, or even a plant. Think back over your life and find some one, something, you loved more than yourself, even if it were only for an hour.'

Somehow I should find the words to make them understand how vitally important this was...just *loving*...Gods or people or things...it did not matter. It was not a truth which could break down disbelief like a sword, as logic can; it had not the colour of emotion which people follow like a scarlet banner without asking where they are going; it was so simple, so real, that no one bothered to look for it in the right place. They all knew it in their hearts if only I could remind them it was there.

Slowly the door opened. I waited for the press of people, who at last had come home to me. But a girl came through the door, as she had so often come before.

Iris smiled at me. 'I have brought you a cloak to wear on the ship,' she said. 'It is an old cloak...you gave it to me when I went to meet Lucius among the oak trees. You used to wear it when you first came here...but now you need it for your journey and Lucius will make me another. I shall never be cold with Lucius.'

She wrapped the cloak round me and then took my hand to lead me out of the temple, to the landing-stage where Lucius waited to take me back across the river...across the river where Euripides waited for the sailing of the ship by which exiles find their home.

CHAPTER THREE

the Sea

Euripides had gone to look for a shipmaster who would give us passage to Athens. The litter-bearers had gone back to Cordelia and I was alone on the quay, trying to shelter from the wind behind a stack of empty barrels. I saw him walking towards me across the wet cobbles and knew by the set of his shoulders that he had failed.

'I can't find any ship to take us,' he said. 'The ship-masters either say they are not calling at any Greek port or else they want more than we can pay.'

'How much money have we left?'

'It ought to be enough, if they will accept our currency. If only we had some one who would sponsor us it would be easier...they don't like taking passengers who have no responsible person to speak for them. Sailors are superstitious, they are afraid that a stranger might be an ill omen.'

'There must be *some* ship; it doesn't matter if it only carries cargo...I'm not afraid of being uncomfortable.'

'Don't you know *any one* in Rome who could use his influence? Think hard, Lucina: surely there is some one you could ask to help you.'

'I've never begged and I'm not going to start now!' I knew I sounded bad tempered, but I was cold and tired, and

303

the prospect of being stuck here indefinitely was most disagreeable.

He sighed. 'Then we shall have to stay until some one comes along to take compassion on us...and I hope it won't be too long. I think if I don't get to Elysium soon I shall decide to stay here and try to find something useful to do.'

'We can't stay here...it's a horrible place.'

'You didn't find it so bad before, even in the early days when you were poor.'

'We're poor now, so we can't afford to stay here. We shall starve, and we have nowhere to sleep. We don't *know* any one.'

'We might see if Narcissus is still living in the villa, or look for Epicurus. He will be angry with you for playing such a shabby deceit on him but he wouldn't refuse to help us. Narcissus won't be angry long, he's too lazy.'

'I'm not going to crawl back and apologize to them! I'd rather starve.'

'I doubt it, if you knew what starvation felt like! You've never been properly hungry, Lucina.'

'I'm hungry now...but I'm not making a fuss about it.'

I realized this was painfully true: it seemed days since I had anything to eat, and now I began to think about it the lack of food was like a cold hand twisting my empty belly.

'I've eaten less than you,' said Euripides. 'If we are determined to starve I shall go first...and then you really *will* be alone.'

'You're not feeling ill, are you? Oh, dear Euripides, please don't be ill!'

'You would find it inconvenient to lose me?'

To my intense mortification I began to cry. 'I know I'm horrid, but please don't leave me. You promised we should go back to Elysium.'

He shivered so I took off my cloak and wrapped it round him. I knew he must be feeling much worse than he admitted for he let me do it without protest, even though I only had on a thin tunic and it had begun to rain. I must get food for him...and wine, hot wine would be better than anything. After he has had something to eat I must look for a warm place to spend the night.

'Wait for me...I shan't be long.' I dragged three of the barrels to try to make a better shelter for him. He leaned back against them and closed his eyes as though exhausted.

The cobbles hurt my feet as I ran along the quay towards a cluster of dim lights, which belonged to a few squalid shops that sold cheap food to sailors. In each shop the shutters had been put up, and they would not open the door to me even when I banged with my clenched fists. I banged so hard that my knuckles were raw, but still they did not hear me.

I came to a wine shop, but the woman who owned it demanded to see my money before she would serve me. I gave her a handful of bronze and silver coins, but instead of becoming obsequious she looked at them disdainfully and told me they were false. I kept my temper and tried to make her realize she was wrong, but she told me to get out before her husband threw me into the street.

I became desperate. Somehow I must help Euripides...it did not matter now. He was too important to be allowed to starve; he could teach people to laugh at themselves, he said that was the key to real freedom. It was too difficult a lesson for me to learn, but at least I was discovering how to cry at myself, and the tears were not entirely self-pity. I would lie or steal or beg, but I would get food for him. I would not let him discover that loving Lucina always led to disaster. It would be easier to die than to beg, but not easier to let Euripides die.

I came to a crowded street and knelt in the gutter, holding out my hands for alms. I kept my head bent so that no one should recognize me, but the people hurried past, ignoring my supplication.

I saw a litter coming towards me: in it there was a woman who looked like Julia. For a moment I thought it was Julia's ghost who threw me the small coin which sank into the mud before I could find it. But this woman was younger than Julia; she may even have been a member of the same family...Julia was not an uncommon type. What would Marius think of his mother if he knew she was begging in the streets of Rome?

I should have to kill my pride and ask Narcissus to help me. I must go to the villa that once I had been proud to buy for them; go there to beg, to ask for charity. Would Epicurus be there too? It would not be easy to tell him that I had let them sorrow because I had found it more convenient to be dishonest.

The hill leading to the villa was steeper than I expected. There were no lights in the windows. Perhaps every one had gone to bed: if I knocked on the shutters they would hear and open to me. The shutters swung loose in the wind: the house was deserted. It was not so dark up here, above the city. I could see dirty straw, mouldy with age, in the empty stables, and dust was thick on the floor of the deserted rooms. In a corner I found a broken Attic vase. It was like the one Epicurus gave me. Was it the one I had broken long ago...and been sarcastic because he had been upset? I had told him that I could easily buy another, and he had said that I had taught him money could buy nothing worth having. Why had he said that, when he used to teach me that money was the only thing which was safe to love? Perhaps I could mend it if I collected all the pieces. I gathered them up and tied them in the hem of my tunic.

Only the garden was unchanged. There were grapes on the vines, unripe but eatable. They might help Euripides if I could find nothing better. I picked several bunches to carry with me and ate a handful: they were so sour that they made my tongue dry but they helped the hunger pain. I was glad the gardener had been allowed to look after the vines: at least I had not been unkind to *him*. I went a little further and saw that he had terraced the slope below the balustrade. The grapes were much riper there, so I threw away the green ones and picked others whose skins were flushed with purple.

But grapes would not be enough for Euripides and I must have money to bribe a shipmaster. Suddenly I thought of Porgius...Calchas he called himself; if I asked for Calchas some one would tell me where he lived.

'I saw you pass and followed you here.' Porgius was standing outside the deserted villa, looking down at me from the upper terrace. I ran towards him and he took my hands and kissed me on the cheek.

'I always hoped you would tell me when you wanted us to meet again,' he said. 'Salonius believed you were dead, and I thought it kinder not to tell him you had run away. It would have broken Salonius' faith if I had allowed him to lose his belief in you. You forgot that you were his only link with *our* reality: if you had remembered you could not have run away with Nigellus...and then Nigellus would have had courage too.'

'How do you know about Nigellus?'

'Salonius came to me after he believed you drowned. He hoped I should be able to assure him that you were happy; you had told him that to die suddenly can at times be dangerous. He was distraught to be without you; he believed that had he used a more tactful approach you would have returned to Rome before you went out on a too rough sea. He thought he had killed you by his lack of understanding. He kept on saying that he ought to have let you take Nigellus for a lover until you learned that your real role was not too difficult. Poor Salonius, he was in anguish; I also had misjudged him for I thought he was immune to such an intensity of grief.'

'What has happened to him?'

'He works as a physician, of the most ordinary kind, chiefly in the poorest quarters. He attends women in labour, washes sores he has no hope of curing, comforts the dying. He does this as a kind of penance for a sin he did not commit...the sin of driving you away.'

Tears were sliding down my face, but I did not bother to brush them away. So even Salonius had suffered because I had tried to escape. I had not realized that I had hurt so many people when I tried to run away from love. If I had had the courage to keep love in spite of its perils I could have protected them...I could have had clean pride instead of this slow shame.

'*Is* it love you feel, Lucina? Do you really want your pride to be clean? Do you really want to cure Salonius?'

'If you will look after Euripides I will go to Salonius.'

'Euripides is waiting for you on the ship which will sail tomorrow. He is well cared for; you need have no anxiety for him. It was he who told me where to find you.'

'But he didn't know I meant to come here. I told him nothing would make me look for Narcissus or Epicurus.'

'Perhaps he knew you better than you knew yourself: he sent a message to me, knowing I would not fail you.'

'Why are you so kind; why, when you know what I've done?'

He smiled. 'You gave me back my faith in myself when it was flickering. Is it surprising that I am glad to be able to remind you that Lucina has much of which to be proud?'

'How can I be proud?'

'Because there are many people who remember you with love. For each person who aroused in you only a lust for power there were many whom you really loved. It does not matter, Lucina, if you forget that you loved them; for love, however apparently fleeting, however trivial, is the only indestructible factor which exists. You have done what many would consider miracles: is it not miraculous to give happiness for sorrow, health for pain, truth for blindness? You seldom took a just credit for the real things you did, for usually they seemed so easy.'

'If I was kind, how could I be cruel? If I could love, how could I be so heartless?'

'The majority of mankind can afford to allow their souls to be grey, a darker or lighter grey according to the state of their essential nature. But you took the way of the priest: it was necessary for you to divide yourself into two arbitrary divisions; the black and the white…and all the other opposites. Is it surprising that at times you have swung between manifold extremes? It is not easy to remain still in the midst of conflict, to hold the balance true. You have many lessons still to learn: you must recognize your failures without guilt; you must see your triumphs without false pride; you must rejoice that you are chosen to carry out the wishes of your superiors. And now are you ready to go to Salonius?'

'Yes,' I said very humbly. Yet I felt happy for the first time…for such a long time.

Porgius told me that he would have to stay in the room while I was talking to Salonius…. I don't think it was because he wanted to be sure I had told everything…it made it easier for us to talk, though I am not sure how.

Salonius was sitting in a chair beside a brazier. I expected him to be startled at seeing me, but instead he said, 'So at last I can see you again, Lucina. I have prayed so hard that I should see you before I died…and now you have proved that you always told the truth. Do you remember telling me that it was worth having the courage to go on praying even when the Gods seemed deaf? Can I take your hand? Or would that spoil things?'

'Why shouldn't you take my hand…if you don't hate me too much? Please try not to hate me, for I have come to ask your forgiveness.'

'I didn't know,' he said. 'I can *see* you, but…'

So he thought I was a ghost! Dear Salonius, he ought to have known that if I had been a ghost I should have had more sense than to wear a torn tunic and sandals so old they were falling to pieces. But I knew I must be gentle with him in case he were startled.

'Your hands are warm,' he said. 'I expected them to be cold.'

Should I tell him I was not a ghost? I looked at Porgius, who shook his head, so I knew I must only tell him what had happened to me since our parting.

'Salonius,' I said. 'I have so much to tell you. Will you pretend that we are discussing some one else, as we so often used to do; some one who is in guilt and is begging for release? Let me sit at your feet and talk...talk until there is nothing I have to hide.'

'It will be like the old days, Lucina: sitting together in the firelight and talking. You used to tell me stories which were so much more real than my philosophies...you never knew a physician could have a philosophy, did you?'

He stroked my hair as I talked, and never ceased the gentle, protective caress even when I confessed my worst sins. These sins were little things; being indifferent when Nigellus made love to me, and laughing at Narcissus; the big things, like pretending to be dead, did not seem so important.

All Salonius said when I finished was, 'So there was never a real gulf between us...what a fool I was not to recognize your humanity. I put you on a pedestal to worship...and drove you away to look for ordinary, human warmth. We forgot that we never did anything except by the power of our loving, and we forgot to love enough.'

Happiness welled up in me, like water when you are thirsty, like fire on a bitter night. 'So you will forgive me? Salonius, can you really forgive all the terrible things I have done to you?'

'I love you, and is there any other forgiveness, when the eyes of love are open?'

Then he kissed me on the forehead and walked quickly out of the room...pausing to look back and smile as he went through the door: as though he were reluctant to go but had heard some one calling to him, some one he knew needed help.

'So it was not too difficult?' said Porgius.

'Is it ever too difficult to learn to be happy?' I said.

The house where Salonius lived must have been close to the quays. I walked with Porgius down a broad street lined with lighted windows and the people who lived there were happy for I could hear them singing. The rain had stopped and the river was coloured by the dawn sky.

It was a small ship of foreign build, there were two sails but no oars, to which he took me. It was half out of the water, though I did not notice this until I was walking up the plank which joined it to the bank. I looked at the river; surely they would never be able to launch the ship unless the river rose much higher?

Euripides was leaning over the side, with a wine-cup in his hand. He looked well, and was laughing as though he shared a joke with Porgius...I never knew they were friends. They took me to a cabin forward of the mast; it was small but very comfortably furnished. I was still anxious that we should not be able to sail because of the mud. I did not speak about it, but Euripides showed another flash of his insight.

'Come on deck to watch the launching,' he said.

The bank had been deserted, but now it was thronged with people; soldiers, foreigners and Romans, slaves, farmers, even women and children. They were hauling on two great ropes, tugging us down into the open water.

'How did they come here, how did such a great crowd know a ship needed help?'

'Why shouldn't they show their gratitude?' said Porgius as he leapt from the deck to the bank. He cupped his hands to his mouth and shouted, 'If it hadn't been for you they would have had to be killed in a futile war. The man who came to the temple disguised as a Centurion sent them to help you...it is sometimes useful to have befriended a son of Mars.'

CHAPTER FOUR

the fire

The voyage was calm, but the food must have been stale for I broke out in boils; the one between my eyebrows was much more painful than those on my neck. I did not ask for sympathy, because Euripides tried to pretend they were not due to eating hard bread which had gone mouldy. One of the sailors, a man with a scar on his hand, washed them for me, and they healed before we came in sight of the coast of Greece. The shipmaster said he would put us ashore at the landing-steps of Elysium instead of taking us to Athens.

I stood in the prow of the ship, straining my eyes in an effort to see the house. Gulls screamed over the ship and the vivid sea was flecked with spume. I felt Euripides put his hand, strong, reassuring, under my elbow.

'Frightened, Lucina?'

'No,' I said trying to keep my voice steady. 'Not frightened...only a little anxious. Until now I have never dared to think that Elysium may be deserted. Or worse, it may have been bought by a stranger who will send us away.'

'Elysium could never be bought: Aesculapius would have given it to some one who could never forbid entry to any of us who really belong.'

'But do we belong? You do, but I ran away.'

'And now you are coming home; we are *both* coming home.'

He said it so loudly that I realized he was also afraid. 'We must not be afraid,' I said. 'When I first came here I was frightened, I thought Elissa left me because she had never really loved me. But I found I was welcome...you were all so kind.'

'Remember how you felt then,' he said urgently. 'Come back to Elysium believing in goodness, see through the eyes of a child who has kept faith in kindliness.'

'I feel like a child, so it should be easy. Do you think there are still red sea-anemones in the rock-pools, and violets growing close to the water's edge? I will make a wreath for you, if there are still violets...'

Hand in hand we ran across the empty landing-stage, along the path under the pine trees, down the natural steps of dear, familiar boulders to the first cove. I suppose we must have said good-bye to the sailors, but I forgot the ship until I saw her, far out towards the horizon, sails curved to the west wind.

The rock-pool was deep and clear. I took off my patched tunic and slid into the warm, kindly water. I scrubbed my body with white sand; it was good to feel clean again, to lie naked in the sun, to feel my hair, clean and salt and alive, spread out behind my head on a smooth rock to dry in the vital air.

There were violets, night-blue and white, growing in the shelter of their scented leaves under the pines, far more of them than I remembered. Now my hands were so clean, I was aware of a greater subtlety of texture in their narrow stalks as I threaded them together...and my fingers must have become wiser, for I never broke a flower. Before, when I made wreaths I spoiled many of the flowers, but now I had not picked a single one too many.

Euripides had wandered off somewhere, but as I finished the second wreath I saw him coming back through the pines. He carried two white tunics in his hand. 'I found them in the pavilion,' he said. 'Either we were expected, or else their presence was a convenient coincidence. It would have been unsuitable to put on our old clothes.... I think they should be burned.'

I looked at the clothes we had discarded and realized how horrible they were; stained with mud and torn. They must have shrunk when I tried to wash them on the ship, for they were surely much too small?

'Why must we burn them?' I said. 'Wouldn't it be easier to throw them into the sea?'

'Aesculapius preferred discarded garments to be burned. Perhaps it was only a courtesy, to give them the freedom of fire...and perhaps it was not Aesculapius who instructed us in this matter. The pyre is an older tradition, not without significance.'

I smiled, even in so small a matter as the discarding of outworn tunics Euripides never lost his sense of the dramatic!

'We will build a funeral pyre,' I said. 'Drift-wood with streaming banners of flame against the blue backcloth of the sea. We will act as pall-bearers to these symbols of our dead selves—and you must compose a suitable oration! Surely, with all our faults, we have not been so inconspicuous during our sojourn among foreigners that we deserve to have our remains committed to ashes without due ceremony!'

'While I consider what lines would be appropriate,' he said, 'you can collect firewood...and be sure it is dry; it might be awkward if the fire went out.

Finding dry wood was more difficult than I expected. The trees were lively with sap and had no dead branches; even the cones and pine-needles must have been swept up by some over-careful gardener. Usually there was driftwood along the beach, but to-day there was only an unbroken line of quiet surf. Suddenly I thought of the cave where we had stored the wood which might have been needed for a different pyre...long ago, when we believed the cloaks of Tyrian purple had brought death into Elysium. Was it still there? Surely we must have used it, or had every one else forgotten it too?

As I ran along the beach, I saw that the house on the head-land was no longer deserted. The shutters had been re-painted, a pale, clear yellow and the garden was gay with flowers. A young woman was coming down the path from the stream carrying a water-jar on her shoulder; I waved to her but she did not see me. A man came out of the house and they stood laughing together in the sunlight. He looked a year or two older than she did, perhaps about twenty-five. He wore a short beard and his hair curling to the shoulder; it was the colour of pine bark, brown with a glint of copper. From the way they looked at each other it was easy to see they were happy just being alive together. I was glad the house was being lived in by the right kind of people; people who would never be afraid because a shutter banged forlornly in the wind, who would sit by the hearth, content to watch the fire of their own wood bring heat to the food they had grown, to the fish they caught.

I wondered who they were. Both of them seemed vaguely familiar, and so did the little boy who was playing with a puppy further along the beach. I intended to speak to him, but the puppy ran up the steps towards the pine tree and he ran after it. I could hear him laughing as I went past.

The cave was dark, and for a moment I was afraid to go in. I had not been here since the terrible day when I had brought my share of the wood here, and cried in secret because I was afraid the others would know I was afraid. But I had made myself go back, made myself collect my share of the fire we had built on the beach against the darkness...the night we drank too much and I had to be carried back to the house because my legs were disobedient! How funny I must have looked! Or were the others too drunk to notice? They could not have been so drunk as I was or they would not have been able to carry me!

The wood was surprisingly light; I suppose because it was tinder-dry. Driftwood...part of an oar, the leg of a stool...it had been inlaid with silver like the one Iris used when she acted as my scribe; a child's toy; a shutter that once had been painted blue...the wood was splintered close to the hinge as though it had been forced open, or weakened by swinging loose in the wind.

I built a pyre close to the sea; when the tide came up the sand would be washed clean of ashes. 'Give the ashes back to the sea; fire and water, in their marriage is freedom.' Who had said that? I could not remember, but it seemed important. It does not matter *who* said something that is true; truth is stronger than words, or the men who use them.

When the pyre was ready, I saw Euripides coming down the path, carrying a lighted torch. He looked solemn and yet he was smiling. I had put all our clothes on the pyre; the tunics, the sandals, the hair-ribbon I had worn on the boat. Hadn't I a cloak, the cloak Iris gave me? I remembered, I had given it to the shipmaster as a present...it was the only thing of value I could give him. I had forgotten I was wearing a gold bracelet; should I put that on the fire too?

'Yes,' said Euripides, 'the fire will clean it...gold loves being washed in fire.'

'But won't it melt? Nigellus gave it to me when Marius was born. I suppose I was so used to wearing it that I forgot it was still on my arm. I didn't bring any of the other jewels with me...only this bracelet he bought in the village. Oh, I hope he has found some one to make him happy, *dear* Nigellus!'

'Lucina, do something for me, and don't ask questions, before I light the fire.'

'Yes, of course. What shall I do?'

'Think hard, so hard that you feel as though you were there, of the statue you and Nigellus put in the garden when you first went to the villa, the statue of Apollo. Imagine yourself asking Apollo, the part of him which you called into the stone, to let Nigellus find a woman who will do much more than make him happy, who will give him the freedom to make himself happy. Stop! Don't try to do it unless you are sure you could let him find real happiness with another woman...are you sure you don't want to go back to him? Are you *sure*?'

I hesitated, but only for a moment. 'Yes,' I said slowly, 'I thought I should always be jealous of another woman meaning more to my husband than I did: but I don't feel that any more. I would be grateful to her...just as I am grateful to Flavia for making Marius happy. Have I stopped being jealous only because I have realized that he was never really my husband? No, it must be more than that for I was a very ordinary mother to Marius. Shall I start thinking of the statue now?'

'You have said your prayer,' his voice was gentle. 'Apollo heard.'

'But I haven't done anything yet.'

'Didn't Porgius tell you that you never noticed the real miracles because they seemed so easy? Don't think about it any more: put your hand on mine so that together we set light to the pyre.'

I watched the flames taking up the thin, worn clothes; they turned into colours as they burned, scarlet and green, blue and yellow. 'It is the salt in the wood,' I said.

'Yes, it is the salt.'

I expected him to make a long oration, but he only went close to the fire and said, 'We ask to endure by the power of the salt, from which the dead wood finds the colour of the morning.'

Such small ordinary words: but they made me want to cry without sorrow, to laugh without bitterness, to dance without the shyness of immaturity or the precision of age.

A wave broke over the cooling ashes. Euripides bent down to pick up the gold bracelet from the white sand: it was wet with sea water, salt water, as he put it on my right arm.

'The fire did not blur the writing on it. Before I gave it back to you I made sure you could always read, ''To Lucina in love''.'

317

the Gol∂

There must have been many more gardeners than in my time, although we did not see any at work as we wandered up towards the house. Even flowers so rare that Aesculapius had no more than a single clump, or a few cherished bulbs, now grew in wide swathes of colour among the thickets or flowed in scented rivers across the open turf.

The steps up to the terrace had been remade; white marble veined with malachite instead of worn grey stone; a procession of caryatids to support the elaborate balustrades.

'The taste of the new owner is a trifle ornate, but he must be very rich,' I said. 'I hope he is equally hospitable.'

'Hospitable enough to welcome you, anyway.' I looked up, startled, and saw Epicurus. 'I am sorry you dislike the marble; personally I consider it an improvement...but you were always hard to please, Lucina.'

'So *you* are the new owner! Oh, what a comfort! I was afraid we were going to find a stranger.'

'It isn't your fault we are not strangers...friends are unlikely to run away without a word of explanation! And I wasted an enormous amount of money on building you a memorial temple in Rome. I got Praxiteles to design it; he seemed pleased with the result though I thought it might have been rather more impressive considering the expense.'

'But you're not still cross with me? Please don't be cross, for it's so lovely to be back here...don't spoil everything.'

'I decided to forgive you some time before you arrived,' he said, a little stiffly. 'Clion interceded on your behalf and told me that you had been exceedingly foolish but were rapidly learning to repent...he insisted that you were made welcome and given your old room.'

'Is Clion here too?'

'He owns the place...I'm only the steward though with wider powers than before. Aesculapius handed it over to Clion before he died, on the condition that any of us could come here when we wished. But Clion doesn't stay here often, he just comes for a day or two to see things are all right.'

'Has he changed much?'

'Changed? No, I don't think so; there wasn't much in him which demanded change so far as I remember. He looks older sometimes, but that's only natural...now that he has a wife and four children.'

'Does he bring them here?'

'I don't think so...at least they haven't been since I became steward. She must be a nice woman or he wouldn't have married her.'

'No,' I said slowly, 'Clion would never have married a woman he didn't really love...and he only loved the right things.'

'You had better come and see the house...you will enjoy criticising my alterations.' But he laughed as he said it so I knew he was not trying to be disagreeable.

I slipped my hand through his arm. 'It is so lovely to be back.'

He smiled. 'I've missed you, much more than I like to admit. You can be infuriating when you try, but your absence leaves a highly uncomfortable gap...like a missing tooth!'

'I have heard more gallant compliments!'

'But probably none so deserved!'

The house did not give me any sense of unfamiliarity though it had been redecorated. The wall paintings were so vivid that they looked like real scenery, and the hangings were of a new material in deep, soft colours with a shimmer which echoed the wings of dragonflies. Vases, statues, carvings in ivory and bronze and lapis-lazuli; each single object of a quality which I had never seen equalled even among the

319

connoisseurs of Rome or Athens.

'Do you like it?'

'It's beautiful, Epicurus! The only trouble is I shall always be afraid of breaking something!'

'So you haven't forgotten the Attic vase?'

I blushed. 'I tried to bring back the broken pieces.... I must have lost them. But it doesn't matter now...you've got so many other things that the vase wouldn't mean anything.'

Euripides came into the room. 'I took these out of your old tunic before we discarded it,' he said. 'I don't know what they are but I thought you wouldn't have taken so much trouble to bring them here if they had no significance to you.'

The black and red shards lay on my open palm. I held them out to Epicurus. 'I thought you could tell me how to mend them,' I said. 'I have learned how to value beauty now, I won't throw it away again.'

He took the broken vase and began to fit the pieces together. 'I have some special glue,' he said. 'When I have finished with this you won't know it was ever broken.'

'Thank you,' I said. 'Thank you for so many things...for so much more than I shall ever be able to repay.'

He sighed. 'It is curious to be so rich and yet not to be able to find the only thing I really want to buy. After you left I went to Alexandria, to Heliopolis...to every likely and unlikely market, but I could never find it. I sold it for a hundred gold pieces.... I would give a hundred thousand more to buy it back. I always wanted to be rich, and when I was I couldn't find the only thing I wanted to buy. Funny, isn't it? You wanted power, and when you got it you were so lonely you threw it away for an illusion of marriage. I wanted a different kind of power, and got it only to find I was poorer than I thought possible! That's why I keep on ''improving'' this place...those steps cost more than a small war, and, as you rightly said, are an error of taste.'

'Perhaps it can't be bought...I tried to buy love, not with money for I knew I should never have enough. But with cleverness and authority, even with magic. And the only love I got was given to me as a free gift. I only saw the love I couldn't buy, that's why I thought I hadn't any.'

We had gone out on the terrace leaving Euripides looking at a collection of manuscripts...most of them lettered in gold on scrolls of vellum. 'What is it you can't buy? We never had secrets from each other...at least we didn't before I became so horrible. But I'm like I used to be, only kinder, I think.'

'You were never really horrid...except to yourself. You needed smacking sometimes but none of us had the courage!'

'Then tell me what you have lost. How can I help you to find it unless I know what it is?'

'Did you ever know what I took in that small, heavy parcel to Rome?'

I remembered the night in the inn beside the quays: going into the adjoining room and lifting the parcel and finding it was so heavy that I knew it must be gold.

'It was gold? The gold that paid for us until we could earn enough? Did you steal it? From Aesculapius?'

'It was gold and I stole it. I stole it from a dead man; I stole it though I had had enough charity to put it with him in his tomb. Until I give it back I shall grow more and more like him...not the real him but the thing he became. Already I am richer than he ever was. What will happen to me if my heart breaks, as his did after my mother killed herself? I have no son to look after me when I become an idiot, no gold toy to make me forget I am deserted....'

'You took the statue of Ptah; you took it to help *me*. And I never knew, oh, Epicurus, I never knew.'

'While you were in the temple I never felt I had committed a sin in stealing it. You were curing people, and Ptah is the god of healing...a brother to Aesculapius. He would have approved, at least I used to believe it. But we should never rob the dead to help the living...living brings its own strength, or it should if we don't try to escape into death.'

He tried to smile. 'Don't worry about it, Lucina. I shall find it one day. But I am so tired of going to merchants and asking them if by chance they have a small statue, no larger than I can span with my thumb and little finger, holding a rod of power between his hands from which life flows. I have made drawings of it and sent messengers to every country... but they never bring back what I want.'

'May I see the drawings?'

'They are in a chest beside my bed...look at them whenever you like.'

I pretended to change the subject. 'Does Praxiteles ever come here?'

'Not often, he is too busy now he is famous. But he has put several new statues in the garden: he works very quickly now and I must admit that his technique has improved enormously.' He grinned. 'Since meeting you again I think he did not overcharge me for your memorial! I must invite him to come here more often.'

'Does he announce his arrival?'

'No, usually the first intimation is the sound of hammering from the room where he used to work. He carves direct in the stone now, saying clay is a waste of time.'

As soon as I could slip away without being obvious I ran to the studio. 'Praxiteles,' I said, as though he were close and could hear me. 'Praxiteles, please come to Elysium...I want you for something very important.'

I thought that at best it would be several days before a messenger of Hermes brought him to me, so I was surprised when he walked in through the door. He must have been asleep in the adjoining room for he was yawning and rubbing his eyes.

'Oh, it's you,' he said. 'Did you call me? You woke me from an enjoyable dream. I was just receiving a string of compliments on my new aqueduct...not my usual line but I agreed to do it, for a very generous fee. However, the banquet was really very dull, one soon grows bored with compliments when they are deserved. In the old days, when my women looked as though they were modelled in lard, I wouldn't have missed the praise for anything...even if you had yelled your head off for me.'

'Always the flatterer! At least you haven't changed...a little fatter, I think, but the same Praxiteles.'

'I suppose you wanted me for something more important than to comment on my girth,' he said amiably. 'I'm always delighted to do anything for my friends...though if they ask me to debase my art I charge them double. Really, those steps! It cured any twinge of guilt I may have had about not doing your memorial for nothing. It is charming my dear; a poem in stone, a flight of imagination translated into temporal existence.'

'I must go have a look at it sometime,' I said a little sharply. He might have been glad to see me alive instead of being so interested in my memorial! 'No doubt one day I shall be most grateful for it...when I have established a more valid right than is given by a false verdict of ''death by drowning.'' '

'Didn't you drown?' he said. 'Sorry, how tactless of me, of course you didn't. What do you want me to do? Hurry up, for I may have to leave soon...I'm due at a banquet...or something. I'm almost sure it's a banquet but it may be a conference about the new public baths.'

'Would you make a small statue for me: I've got several very exact drawings of the original?'

'I never copy,' said Praxiteles loftily, then he grinned. 'If I borrow an idea I don't admit it! However, probably one of my pupils could do it. Let me see what you want.'

I handed him the drawings and he studied them carefully.

'My early training was not wasted on you, Lucina. Too difficult even for my pupils. Bother, I shall have to do it myself.'

'How soon can you bring it here?'

'Probably much quicker than you expect...commissions undertaken in Elysium proceed with remarkable alacrity. I shall need gold, your gold. Have you enough?'

'It is for Epicurus...and he has lots of gold.'

'You are giving this to him...so it would not be a proper gift unless you provide the material. Of course if it is not worth the trouble I shall be delighted...save my having to spare the time to do the job for you.'

'I haven't any gold.' It was difficult to admit even to Praxiteles that I had returned from Rome so poor.

'What's that on your arm?'

'Only a bracelet...it's not valuable except to me. It's more of a talisman than anything else.'

'Pity,' he said coldly. 'I thought you were fond of Epicurus...surely he's given you enough to be worth a small sacrifice? You used not to be mean when I knew you, but the Romans must have infected you with their acquisitiveness.'

I pulled off the braclet and handed it to him. 'I am sorry...it was disgusting of me to hesitate.'

He smiled and I watched him anxiously as he weighed it in his hand. 'Is it enough?' I asked.

'Almost exactly, so far as I can judge. I suppose you want to give it to him yourself? Don't like being indebted to any one, do you? At least you must have learned something if you don't still insist on keeping people under an obligation.'

'I don't think any one is really under an obligation to me...it's the other way round. They give me things and I break them...vases or faith or hearts, it's the same with everything.'

'You were a generous child...you gave us plenty of affection.'

'I hadn't anything else...you were all so much cleverer.'

'And therefore poorer in some ways...perhaps in all the ways which matter. Don't you know why Epicurus gave you so many presents? He did it because he thought affection wasn't enough. So you broke the things, because they reminded you that they were given instead of what you wanted. It wasn't just clumsiness or temper. If you give him this statue it will be much more than all the things he gave you; because he wants it with all his heart and he only bought you gifts with his head.'

I was ashamed of the picture I had made; of Lucina giving Epicurus the one thing which he could not get for himself, and feeling so smug because she need no longer feel guilty of taking so much and giving so little. How selfish it would have been to take from him the personal triumph of his search.

Praxiteles looked at me, one eyebrow higher than the other, kind yet quizzical. 'Well done, Lucina! It would have been very comforting to have done the giving...but Epicurus needs the comfort more than you do.'

'Forgive me for being so slow. First I nearly spoil everything by being mean, and then I should have spoiled it more, if you hadn't reminded me.'

'Well, I must be off,' he said briskly. 'Too busy to come here often, but I shall send this along soon. I'll get one of my pupils to dress up as one of the merchants and deliver it to the Steward of Elysium. Run along now...I want to have a nap before I go back to Athens...I am almost sure it is Athens, but one grows a little absent-minded about details.

He patted me on the shoulder and then went into the other room and closed the door. Dear Praxiteles, he had always been so determined not to become vague. He used to say that artists ought to be more efficient than ordinary people, that artistic temperament was more wasteful of energy than trying to carve with a blunt chisel. I was grateful for this small sign that he also sometimes had to act as his companions considered proper, even when he knew it was silly!

the Garden

The gardeners remained even more inconspicuous than when Aesculapius ruled Elysium, so I was surprised when a man whom I presumed to be one of them was so frequently in evidence. He looked like an ex-gladiator and seemed eager to increase his already over-developed muscles, for he was either carrying heavy stones or else brandishing iron bars which an ordinary person could scarcely have lifted. I intended to mention him to Epicurus, with a hint that he was neglecting his duties; fortunately I realized in time that he was not an employee but a fellow guest, having seen him lying on a mattress in the shade while a servant massaged him with oil.

I nodded to him, but instead of acknowledging the courtesy he reached for more wine, which the servant poured for him. Then he drank greedily, and wiped his mouth with the back of his hairy hand. Epicurus found me watching this curious barbarian.

'What do you think of our new inhabitant?'

'Hardly the type one would have expected you to welcome,' I said.

'You bring with you a vertible breath of Rome, my dear Lucina. No matron could have expressed herself with a more authentic blend of patronage and nausea! But wait till you meet the rest of the family.'

'A troup of circus performers? We shall not lack entertainment.'

'The wife would be most offended if she heard you. A lady not without charm, even if these are a trifle emphatic for my taste.' He pointed towards the house. 'It is her custom to relax in the garden after the arduous duties of the toilet. If I am not mistaken she is coming out now...from here we shall have a clear view of an excellent performance.'

A woman, plump though graceful, came slowly down the rose pergola. She was preceded by two girls wearing embroidered tunics: one carried a silver mirror, a flask of perfume and a bunch of hyacinths, the other a box of sweetmeats and a robe of red fox. They arranged purple cushions on a day-bed where their mistress languidly reclined. They then set their offerings beside her on a silver stool and taking up fans of white and amber ostrich feathers waited to supplement the gentle breeze should it prove insufficient.

'She must find her husband somewhat gross.' I said, 'and he must think her excessively distinguished. I presume they have no children?'

'They have a boy: you are fortunate not to have made his acquaintance. He is petulant and spoiled, pretty and intolerable...a living incentive to the foot, for his bottom was created to feel the impact!'

'Why don't you send them away?'

'The hospitality of Elysium cannot be refused, and they have as much right to it as any of us. Anyway, I thought you sent them here.'

'Of course I didn't! Am I likely to have befriended a broken-down gladiator with no manners!'

'Don't call him that, or you will have to watch him perform a dreary sequence of athletic impossibilities. You will grow either so pitiful, or so bored, that you will have to applaud, for until you do he will refuse to stop: he is very conscious of his dignity.'

'Are they fond of the child?'

'They dislike it intensely...I doubt if you will ever see either of them it its company.'

'Do they like each other?'

'So far as I know they have never exchanged a civil word. In fact, now I come to think of it, I have never seen them together.'

'Meals must be delightful,' I said sarcastically. 'I seem

to remember Aesculapius insisting that harmony was a requisite of digestion.'

'We eat in our rooms, when we are hungry. I tried to maintain the old routine but found it had certain disadvantages.'

'How fortunate, now that the company has deteriorated!'

'You needn't talk to them if you don't wish to; she seems perfectly content to think about herself between one toilet and the next. I must admit that she has the most startling range of garments. Persian one day, Roman the next, and a gamut of foreign conceits. Very becoming to her they are too, for she is a good-looking young woman, even you will have to grant that.'

'With all my faults,' I said coldly, 'I have never been jealous of other women's beauty.'

'So long as you could remain contemptuous of their minds, and undisturbed by their powers.'

'You talk with the cynicism of Narcissus...he had an extraordinary faculty of remaining undeceived by women.'

'Was Narcissus a cynic, or a passionate idealist? I think he expected so much that he lost everything...even himself. You might have saved him, Lucina, but you were too ignorant. Or was it easier to accept him as an instructor in certain female arts which your pride would never permit you to use?'

'I was not entirely ineffective as a woman.'

'You didn't make much of a success with Nigellus. Poor Nigellus, it meant so much to him when you bothered to put perfume between your breasts, or whispered delicious nonsense in his ear. You might have made a compact and ductile heaven of your bed, instead of turning it into a dusty anteroom of the Senate in which he discovered he wore wilting laurels. You consistently made a fool of your husband, and only the fool knows the bitterness of the fool's tears.'

'Nigellus was extremely intelligent!'

'Not in his choice of women; first Julia and then you.' He

grinned, 'You're much better at taking insults than you used to be: you didn't even wonder whether I deserved a few boils or whether it would be more amusing if I fell down the steps!'

'I think Euripides might have kept quiet about the boils... they were most uncomfortable when they came home to roost!' I said with feeling.

'By the way, Lucina, when you have settled down here you might see what you can do with the, er...family.'

I could see the ostrich feather fans waving slowly backwards and forwards in the distance. 'You mean, *her?*'

'Any of them: they are trying desperately hard to pretend they are happy, and we can't let people be miserable in Elysium. I have done what I can: given them things and provided servants but it hasn't done much good. Isn't it time you stopped pretending you have forgotten everything you learned from Salonius?'

'I don't want to get involved with other people's troubles; it sounds horribly selfish but it's true.'

He took me by the shoulders: 'Lucina, you haven't been really happy for years...far longer than you realize. You will never be happy until you recognize that centring on yourself instead of feeling outwards is certain to make you miserable. Why do you think you fell in love with Nigellus instead of loving him? Why didn't it last?'

'I don't know,' I said forlornly. 'It just happened, quite suddenly and for no particular reason. One day I was in love and the next the magic had gone.'

'You were happy when you first went to Rome; you were thinking about Narcissus and me, fighting for us, making plans for our future as well as your own. You were happy when you first worked for Salonius; you were grateful to him and determined that he shouldn't regret his faith in you. The people who came to the temple were important; their troubles were real, you wanted to help them...not merely for them to be cured so that *you* could feel more important.'

'Yes,' I said, 'I was happy for the first two years...and then...'

'And then you started to make a private world to rule, a narrowing circle with you as the centre. Before that happened, Narcissus and I were eager to hear what you had been doing; to us your work was vital, enormously exciting. And you wanted to share the things we had been doing while you were away.'

'But you never took me about with you...I was so tired of not being wanted.'

'Lucina, you *must* be honest with yourself. You know perfectly well that Salonius only told you to rest when you got home because you worked too hard. You know he would have preferred you to see fewer patients. It was you who insisted on having more and more people come to the temple. You know that the story of our little invalid sister was your own invention...it started as a joke and then became a reality because it suited your plans. We tried to take you to parties and chariot races, but you always said they gave you a headache. You were too tired to try with us, too lazy not to be bored. We did what we could to please you: I gave you more and more presents, and saw they meant less and less. You ignored Narcissus...and you knew that nothing could have hurt him more.'

'But I *was* tired...sometimes I could hardly crawl into bed when I got home.'

'Not too tired to be the priestess.'

'I don't know why, but I always felt well in the temple... energy seemed to come into me, though not enough to use for ordinary things.'

'So loving was too ordinary? Don't you see what you did to yourself? You threw away the power which was the real source of everything. You could only see through your own eyes, not through the eyes of the people you loved...and so you were gradually going blind. You were afraid when you knew you would soon be alone in the dark. When you heard

Aesculapius was dead you became ill; for you thought he was the only person who could have helped you. While you were ill you could accept help from ordinary people...me and Narcissus, even from the servants. Then you went back to the temple, more determined than ever to prove that you were self-sufficient. Of course you weren't enough for yourself, nobody is: so you had to make yourself believe that falling in love with Nigellus would be the cure. But you never really loved Nigellus, he was only the audience you selected to make you feel confident in the new role.'

'The stage is empty, so where is Lucina?' I stooped and picked up a handful of earth, crumbling it between my fingers. It felt like earth, it smelt strong and clean as spring furrows after rain. 'Where is Elysium?'

'Here, where we made it. How can we be anywhere, ever, except ''here''?'

'But the air is too clear, the flowers never fade, there are no dead leaves under the trees. Nothing is dead here...except...'

'Except us? Is that what you are trying to say?' He put his arm round me. 'Do you feel dead? Do I?'

I could feel the texture of his skin, smooth and warm over the shoulder muscle, see the fine hairs on his arm, his white, slightly irregular teeth. He hugged me and I began to laugh.

'I never knew that ghosts could be so solid,' I said. 'I never knew that dying could be so unimportant that one forgot to notice it!'

'Neither did I, until you gave me back the Ptah!' He was laughing so much that he could hardly speak. 'What a magnificent joke! You, who told every one that ordinary people were immortal, and yet never really believed it; and I, who was convinced that death was real. Both of us dead for years...and surprised because we are alive. We must tell Euripides...it's the funniest thing that ever happened to us.'

'Is Praxiteles dead too? Could we ask him, or would it be

rude.... I mean if he doesn't know he might find it embarrassing.'

'I asked him...when I thanked him for the Ptah. I wasn't quite sure about *me* then, and I was afraid he'd think me insane! He is asleep when he comes here. He says it is refreshing to be young in Elysium now and again; it prevents him being pompous and making scathing criticisms of the work of the younger generation.'

'He is still rather young to be patronizing...he can't be forty yet.'

'As a matter of fact the banquet you interrupted, the night when you called him here, was to celebrate his eightieth birthday. Don't worry,' he said airily. 'Time in Elysium is different to the kind we used to work by. I don't yet fully understand it myself but I don't think it's particularly important. We always made our own time without realizing it; it was only when we *believed* in hours and months and seasons that they had any real control over us.'

'It is a little confusing, until you get used to it,' I said. 'Are you *sure* I've been dead for more than forty years?'

'Only by their time, not by your own. You have been here for years, but it seemed like a few days because you are happy. Time only seems slow when you try to go against the current...I forgot who told me that but it seems to work.'

'But why did we all come back here?'

'Because we wanted to. Heaven is the place you want to go to and hell is where you think the Gods will send you if they are feeling in a bad temper!'

'So you've caught up with yourselves at last!' Euripides was laughing at us from a branch above our heads. He jumped down. I still found it reassuring that his heels made a little dent in the moss on which we were lying. 'How delighted I am to hear that I shall no longer have to make conversation adapted to your curious delusions. Lucina, how often did I tell you to use your imagination...and all you did was to make conditions needlessly limited. That rain on the quay, for instance...so cold it made me shiver! Of course at first I found certain difficulties myself...but then I had an unfavourable start.'

'*Please* fill in the gaps for me! I know we are all dead, or really alive, or whatever it's called, but I haven't lost my curiosity! Why did I die, and what happened to you and all the rest of us?'

'It is a long and not altogether creditable story; how fortunate that you will be able to listen without thinking it is time you were hungry...and so making yourself need food! Nor will flies tickle your nose, or your legs get cramp...in fact you will be able to listen with proper attention and without fidgeting. What an audience! Imagine a theatre packed with people and not a cough or a whisper, not a fruit-seller, or a bored child screaming to be taken out. No, don't,' he added urgently, 'or we shall bring a crowd here and then have to build a theatre for them, and I shall start rehearsing a play. I have suffered great embarrassment, deciding to write a play and then making the audience before I had written more than the first few lines. It is *so* easy to get caught up in your own creation.'

'I want to hear all about that, but not until you've told me about *us*. How much of our journey was true, and how much were you and I imagining it, and...so many questions.'

'All of it was true; nothing is true to any one except personal experience. A tree is a tree whether it was the idea of the God who first made it, or the man who planted the seed...or if it is a dream tree, or a tree you made, or a tree somebody else made. They are all quite *real*. Everything is some one's idea...it doesn't much matter *whose*...though some are more solid than others, and take longer to change.'

'He'll turn this admirable source of shade into something else if you don't bring him back to the point,' said Epicurus. 'He adores being a conjurer. He turned my favourite vase into a bowl of cheese and forgot how to turn it back again properly.'

'A little lop-sided perhaps,' admitted Euripides. 'I forgot what the original painting looked like. But you didn't make such a good job of it even when I explained the technique. You forgot to make the other side so it fell over, and broke, just as you *believed* it would!'

'Never mind the vase. *Dear* Euripides, please tell me what happened before we left the villa...it will be such an exciting story and I promise not to interrupt.'

'That will be a change! However, I suppose it would be unfair to ask you to control your curiosity...curiosity being one of your most charming attributes, though on occasion awkward for your friends. You wouldn't like the tree a little thicker before I start, or more moss? I could easily manage some silk mattresses to lie on, or a Nubian fan-bearer... though my Nubians are not entirely convincing to the critical eye?'

'No tricks,' said Epicurus firmly. 'And I want to hear the story too. Which reminds me, I must have been knocked on the head in a back street of Alexandria. I distinctly remember going into a most unsavoury quarter. I had heard that a certain merchant had got some rare manuscripts, the source was said to be dubious so the price would not have been too high. The next thing I can recollect was arriving here and being welcomed by Clion, who said I had better take on my old job of steward. However, more of that later. You tell your story first.'

CHAPTER SEVEN

the Road

Euripides leant back against the tree, made sure we were giving him our complete attention, and began, 'So far as I could discover, the last thing Lucina clearly remembers is returning to her room in the villa and being aware that her feet were too cold and her forehead too hot.' I nodded, and he went on, 'The next morning it was distressingly clear both to Nigellus and myself that she had something more serious than an ordinary fever. I will spare you the details, but it was obvious that no one could long survive so grievous a flux of the bowels, which caused the body to shrink with lack of moisture. Our sole comfort was that she appeared to be totally unaware of our efforts on her behalf, nor was she perturbed by the supplications of her husband.'

He paused to look at me, not without a certain severity, 'You misjudged the degree of Nigellus' affection; he was distraught and entirely forgot the frequent occasions on which you had proved yourself excessively tiresome. However, I run ahead of my narrative. On the evening of the second day you died, or rather you decided not to return to the body which was rapidly proving itself a most distasteful tenement. But did you hover round us with thoughts of reassurance? Did you attend the funeral rites, carried out with extreme care? Did you even bother to listen to the magnificent prose which I created for your adulation? No, my dear Lucina; you walked out of the house and amused yourself in the grove... more concerned with the cyclamen which you had imagined several years earlier than with the distress of your devoted admirers!

'It is not my intention to bring up an old grievance: indeed I should be grateful that my entirely unjustified presumption that you would attend your funeral inspired me to a degree of eloquence which I had never before attained. You were stupid to miss so well chosen a tribute, a certain lack of the dramatic sense which, on your behalf, I most sincerely regret.'

I thought I ought to feel strongly about this, but could only produce the vague regret which I might have felt on hearing that a party I had considered too boring to attend had proved amusing. 'Was it a lovely funeral?' I said.

'Lovely is hardly the correct description. Nigellus was *most* difficult. Under their mask of imperturbability the Romans are excessively excitable, utterly sentimental in their sentiments. He was anguished that he might perform some rite which would not be entirely in accordance with your wishes. Did you wish to be burned? Did you really mean it when you said you would like to be buried in the grove? Should your ashes be carried to Greece and there laid in a tomb where your history should be inscribed on tablet of finest marble? Fortunately the weather was unduly warm for the time of year, so in the absence of an embalmer, a decision had to be reached.'

'It was a good body,' I said. 'I don't blame you for taking trouble with it—after all, so did I!'

We might have been discussing the disposal of an old tunic; something I had worn with affection and which could not be thrown away without at least a trivial sigh.

'*Not* such a good body after Nigellus had failed to make up his mind for rather too long! I thought you would be annoyed by a Roman sarcophagus so I persuaded him to burn you. With the finest wood, of course, and perfumed oils which must have cost a fortune! He wanted to keep your ashes in a gold vase.... I must admit it was a charming shape, even Epicurus would have approved it; but I thought it more poetic that we scatter your remains in the grove. Even the weather was dramatic, a storm with really magnificent light effects on the western hills. My oration sounded exceedingly well with the thunder acting as chorus.'

He smiled and patted my knee. 'In actual fact I was quite absurdly miserable, Lucina. You have a capacity for inspiring affection which cannot be explained away by logic, and a quality of leaving an absence that is not to be gainsaid by intellect. I shed my secret tears, and returned to the house determined that Nigellus and I should get thoroughly and rationally drunk. I had even taken the precaution of telling one of the servants to bring from the cellar an abundance of an appropriate vintage.

'I, too, had misjudged Nigellus. Imagine my embarrassment when on entering his room, already I must admit more than a little unsteady, I found he had fallen on his sword! The only comfort was he had been competent to the last; attending such a wound would have tried my capacity beyond its limits.'

'Oh, poor Nigellus! If he died with us why didn't he come to Elysium?'

'Fortunately, though he could deceive himself while bounded by mortality, he showed a more stable vision afterwards. The Nigellus who killed himself intended to pursue you through the Shades; the wiser man was content to return to the heaven which circumstance, and your charming self, had denied him. I admit that when you insisted on visiting him in Rome I thought I should have to make an objective picture, to convince you that your anxiety could no longer prevent our return to Elysium. I experienced a degree of disquiet unequalled even at the first public performance of my worst play. Imagine my relief when I found that the scene we both witnessed owed nothing to my art: Nigellus had come into his own, haranguing Romans, both dead and sleeping, with the vigour and purpose which had always been his primary motivation.

'I anticipate: having made sure that Nigellus was dead, I returned to my room and continued to drink until I sank into a restful sleep. I was awakened by the wailing of the servants, who had discovered their master at the appallingly early hour that such creatures habitually commence their tasks. There is much to be said for the methodical habit of Romans: he had left papers giving me sole power over his property and making complete provision for Marius.'

'What happened to Marius? Wasn't he real when I saw him with Flavia? He looked so happy...surely you didn't invent that just to pacify me?'

'Do not distress yourself. He was perfectly content with Flavia, as I knew he would be before I sent him to her. Nigellus was more fond of his daughter than we realized, and had kept himself informed of all that had happened to her since he ceased to exercise his authority. He knew she was independent financially, for that he had arranged before he ran away with you. He knew she had established her own household; he knew she had decided not to marry but would make an excellent mother. He had left a document which assured that she would adopt Marius; it established that he was her half-brother and that in the event of the child's mother dying before he was adult he was to be put in her care. It was not necessary for him to add that he dare not send the child to Rome until after Julia's death; Flavia was not ignorant of her mother's nature.'

'Tell me more about Marius.'

'Immediately it was established that you were suffering from a disease which might be infectious, Nigellus sent the boy with Sempronia to the farm. You will be glad to know that I forbade his attendance at the ceremonies which disposed of your corpse. I, in spite of feeling far from well and importuning Dionysus for aid without avail, wrote a suitable ode for my host; divided his property, save that portion due to Marius, among his dependents; and then considered that I owed no duty to any one except myself.

'At that time I had little real confidence that we continued to exist beyond the span of our earthly existence: but I had written a quantity of excellent plays which ended with the withdrawal of the principal characters to some undefined place...Olympus, the Shades, the West...the names are manifold and equally vague. Lucina was the only person I had met who really believed that such a state existed; I thought that if death was in fact oblivion I should never become aware of my disappointment, but that if her vehemence was not unfounded I should journey in good company. Is there any dramatist who doesn't want to see the end of his play, what happens to his characters when the auditorium is empty? I decided that at least I could die in the great tradition: I remained ignorant that I lacked skill as an apothecary. Hemlock I could recognize: do you recall, Lucina, that you pointed out that ineffective plant to me when I first came to the villa? I gathered a quantity and stewed it in a silver vessel: Socrates, rather naturally, did not trouble to leave the recipe of a brew imposed on him by ignorant contemporaries.

'I drank the hemlock, and lay down on a couch with writing materials close at hand. It was probable that I should think of some suitable message to leave as a guide to less far-seeing mortals. I waited for the stealthy chill to approach, humble and subservient from my feet, leaving my brain as a final blazing torch to burn against the cold. For a while nothing happened, and I began to feel a little foolish: it would have been the supreme anti-climax to have risen from my state of purple cushions to gather more of this noisome herb. I waited in an agony of indecision: I continued in an agony to vomit! How sick I was, how angrily the body can rebel against the rape of the soul. The servants heard me retching. They put hot stones, for which I was grateful, on my belly; they tickled my throat with feathers; they forced me to drink vinegar and the whites of raw eggs. Their concern for my welfare made me eager to live. I produced prodigies of effort to stay in a body which I had derided and provoked. I fought to retain my hold on it. I suffered the leech—it would be unfair to Aesculapius to give that man the title of physician—to commit upon me the most humiliating indecencies.

'I even committed the ultimate obeisance to mortality: I admitted I had taken hemlock and implored them to provide an antidote! I think this was my final remark, the last words of Euripides who had thought to die with epic lines which history would enshrine! The cocks were crowing when in a final spew my soul was driven from the flesh. Then there was a period, of its duration in days or months I have no accurate knowledge, during which I apologized to a series of people for having acted towards my body as an assassin. Some of these looked like animals, others wore the clothes of remote historical periods and yet seemed more intimate than ancestors, the later ones resembled Euripides during various periods of my growth. It was all highly distressing, and always, like a drum rhythm behind a chanting, the retching tweaked my more than mortal bowels. I could, by a deliberate act of will, discount this resonance, but, needless to say, Lucina persistently reminded me of it!'

'I am sorry,' I said fervently, 'but if you had only told me why I mustn't mention being sick it would have been much easier to be tactful!'

'And encourage you to ask a spate of questions I felt inadequate to answer! I found the crossing of the Styx alarming; to you it appeared as a small stream in which it amused you to paddle. At least I had the kindness to leave you undisturbed so long as your creations were more comfortable than mine.'

'Did you know we were dead all the time?'

'To be honest, I was exceedingly bewildered. I thought it probable that I was delirious and that at any moment I might wake to find myself spewing again. I was further puzzled when I wished for pomegranates and instead of their appearing spontaneously, as I considered suitable to a dream environment, or our remaining unsatisfied, as we should have done on earth, we found them in what seemed to be an abandoned orchard. Was it too apt a coincidence, or just Lucina being lucky again?'

'If it were I, that proves it is sensible to be optimistic! Did I invent the people who let us sleep in their barn?'

'No, they were real...asleep, of course, that's why he talked of the garrison as though he were going to be there to-morrow...their to-morrow, not ours. At the time I found it very confusing. Claudia was dead; playing the hostess was her heaven. She didn't believe in herself enough to entertain patricians so she welcomed beggars and gave them new clothes. Rather pitiful to be a snob even when you're dead! The beggars were real enough; only too glad to have a meal and a rest, if only in a dream.

'Cordelia and her husband were dead too; they must have made the outside of the sausage shop when they heard we were coming, so that we shouldn't feel embarrassed at not knowing the new language properly. I asked her to help me in letting you see Marius, that's why she sent one of her friends with us as a litter-bearer.'

I found it difficult to realize that Marius was no longer a little boy. 'He must be grown-up,' I said.

'Over forty,' said Euripides briskly. 'A general with a considerable following among the more belligerent Centurions. He has a wife whom he bullies and five children.'

I looked down and was reassured that my breasts were still young and my belly flat. 'I have worn well for a grandmother!' I began to laugh, 'How surprised my grandchildren would be if they could see me now. It is odd to be asking whether people we know are dead or only sleeping, as though it were no more important than if they had been to the chariot races this summer. Was Porgius dead?'

'No, but he is a remarkable person. It doesn't seem to matter what his body is doing, or whether he happens to have one at the moment. He appears to find it perfectly easy to be in two places at once without getting them confused. Rather as though he could paint two superimposed pictures on the same wall and see them simultaneously...not a very adequate image but it conveys the rough idea. Salonius was asleep; he was delighted to see you for it gave him a proof of personal continuity. After that he could talk with real authority instead of having to rely on theory.'

'Even in my most ignorant phases I retained the sense to prefer empiricism to theories,' I said with feeling.

'Until you had put it into practice!' retorted Euripides. 'In future, when you experience a tendency to feel smug you had

341

better remember how long it took you to realize you were only a ghost!'

'Am I a ghost? How very curious!'

Suddenly Euripides was serious. 'Not nearly such a determined ghost as Narcissus. He has turned himself into three people instead of only one, like us. The strongest is the woman. We can't leave her here, so you had better try to do something about it. When we try to reason with her she only tells us that she can't be bothered to talk to madmen with no manners!'

CHAPTER EIGHT

the Ghosts

I tried very hard to persuade the woman to admit that she was a ghost of Narcissus, but she only stared at me as though I had suddenly spoken in a foreign language. Yet with certain careful reservations she enjoyed my company. Provided that I discussed clothes or unguents, the futility of men or the superiority of women, she was absorbed, even eager, and showed a child-like gaiety incongruous in some one who seemed so mature.

If I asked about her plans for the future, she became evasive, and would only say that she was waiting for a ship to take her back to Rome where her presence was urgently required. 'I shall have a villa which will be the envy of every one, and even the Emperor will obey me.'

When I led her to speak of the gladiator she did so lightly and with patronage, as though he were a chance acquaintance to whom she owed a trivial obligation. 'He was useful to me in his time,' she said. 'He fought certain battles when I had less subtle powers at my command. His gross strength gave me confidence: it was interesting to see how easily he punished people who annoyed me.' She laughed, 'Sometimes I almost envied him! I thought it might be amusing to have that obvious antagonism, to own a body so hard and insensitive.'

I was sorry for the gladiator. He was always civil to me, but seemed unable to sustain a lengthy conversation. He would drift off into a recital, dulled by repetition, of some test of endurance; a soldier who had marched until his feet ran with blood, or a galley-slave whose prowess of muscle had been the envy of his fellows. When I mentioned Narcissus he stared at me with blank eyes, and either said he had never heard the name, or else went to the hard couch on which he spent most of his time, and fell into a profound sleep.

I was no more successful with the boy until I found him hiding behind a rock, furtively watching the child who lived in the house on the headland. Perhaps it was because he felt specially lonely that he allowed me to approach. Was he talking to himself, or did he intend me to overhear?

I learned that as a baby he had been as other children: requiring ordinary, human affection, content with trivial joys, brave enough for his small enemies. Reluctantly he came to realize that his parents had wanted an heir instead of a son, a projection of their pride instead of a free companion. Then affection which could find no natural channel hardened into the barrier of a secret world where he hoped to be safe from disappointment. When this failed to give him the security he craved, he created a phantasy woman to be his protector; a woman more beautiful, more compelling even than his mother.

To hide from other boys his longing to be a woman he had to conceal this phantasy with another, modelled on his father, the dominant, aggressive male. This became the gladiator, who served his master, the child, leaving the woman in power over them both.

Slowly his dreams took independent form, assuming a vampire dominance over their creator. The boy was afraid to grow into either; so when Narcissus was aged nine, the boy also became a ghost. The gladiator took relatively little energy from Narcissus, for it is much easier to maintain a pattern than to cause it to change. But the woman grew in power, on his desire. He found it convenient to obey her, for she offered him a kind of security, drawing on his vitality in exchange for an insight into women, a patronage of men.

Could Lucina have rescued Narcissus from his ghosts if she had loved enough not to seek an escape from herself? Could I free them all, by taking the boy away from Elysium and creating for him a sanctuary where he might gain the strength of a happy childhood? I would be his mother or his sister: we could play together, as Lucina might have played with other children if she had not learned solitude too young.

Suddenly the boy became aware of me, turning quick as a fox, flinching as though I had thrown a stone at him. His face was unchanged; the yellow curls above the broad forehead, the pouting mouth. But the eyes were bitterly old.

He pointed towards the house where the woman luxuriated among her slaves. 'I made her,' he said. 'And now she is too strong for me. Until I no longer envy her I must be obedient. She is going away soon: and I with her.'

'Together we are stronger than she is.'

His eyes were bright as metal. 'But I love her!' he said passionately. 'What does it matter that I hate her too? I will kill you if you make me disobey.'

In a single movement he sprang to his feet and ran away from me. Past the sleeping gladiator, towards the woman who included him.

Across the silence I could hear the memory of Narcissus long ago. 'I love you, Lucina. I only hate the woman I despise in myself.'

I stood up. The sand was cold, the wind lonely among the

pines. 'I love you, Narcissus,' I said gently. 'When at last we have dismissed our ghosts we shall find our lost integrity.'

CHAPTER NINE

the tree

I met Epicurus coming out of the gallery he had made to house his treasures. He looked unusually light-hearted.

'Lucina,' he said, 'I shall be leaving here soon, any day now. I want to clear my things away before I go, unless you need them.'

I thought I knew the purpose of his journey and wondered why he tried to conceal it from me. 'You are taking the Ptah back to your father?'

He laughed. 'I did that when you sent it to me. I did not know I was dead then, so I started walking down the road to Athens. It was to have been a melancholy pilgrimage. You know the kind of thing, dirges in the distance and cypresses dripping in the rain. I intended to open the tomb and reverently place the statue among the lonely bones. But when I reached the boundary I saw two people sitting by the roadside. They seemed to be waiting for me, so I stopped to speak to them. The man was obviously a peasant, not a Greek but I forgot to ask his nationality, it seemed so unimportant. He was young, no more than twenty, and his wife was about the same age. They asked me whether I should like to live with them: an odd invitation from complete strangers but I knew they expected me to accept. They said their cottage had two rooms, and that the leak in the roof would be mended before the rains. The woman assured me there would be enough to eat, and plenty for two or three more besides ourselves.'

He paused, and then went on more slowly, 'I was bewildered by their generosity, but still intent on paying my debt that I did not recognize them. Suddenly the woman smiled and said she was hungry. Instinctively I handed the Ptah to her; perhaps because it was the only thing I had brought with me. The gold statue turned into a loaf of bread: it sounds unlikely, but it seemed quite natural. The woman broke the bread in three pieces, and we began to eat. Then I knew they were my father and mother; strong, and confident, and full of health.'

He smiled. 'You were right, Lucina, when you said she wanted to be loved as an ordinary woman; that they both died because possessions made a barrier against affection. I am happy as their son: because they both want me.'

'Are you sure you will be content in a cottage? Will you be happy there when you grow up?'

'Happy!' How can I be anything else when I shall have everything I really wanted instead of all the pitiful compensations? I am a very healthy baby; already I am six months old, and I assure you that milk can taste better than a vintage. When Euripides is born he will be more proud of his first tooth than ever he was of his first play!'

Before I had time to answer, he added, 'I shall miss you, my very dear Lucina: but we shall find each other again. We learned that affection is stronger than death: now I know it is stronger than birth.'

Laughing, he vanished: which I still found a little disconcerting.

So Epicurus had no further need of Elysium: how long would it be before Euripides also became weary of our little heaven? I wandered through the garden, along paths which were too smooth, among flowers whose changeless petals seemed a little pallid.

Several times I had seen the house which still existed on Earth, where Clion gave children a chance to grow in freedom. On those walls the plaster was cracked, the rooms untidy. But there was laughter, endurance, beneficent solidity. Clion was old, but his heart had a youth I could not echo, until I had the courage to be young again.

I found Euripides sitting on the quay, staring disconsolately towards the horizon. 'So Epicurus has gone,' he said. 'Don't pretend you are not depressed. I know how you feel: I heard the children again to-day; real children, who would pity us for still wanting to be only ghosts.'

'We are bored,' I said despondently. 'For Epicurus everything is beautifully solid. *He* doesn't have to trouble about everything changing into something else the moment he gets absent-minded.'

'He came to say good-bye to me, and I made him admit that teething had certain disadvantages.'

'What a silly thing to fuss about,' I said unsympathetically. 'His teeth will grow without his having to *think* about them. He will meet new people who are less boring than himself.'

'Bored with Lucina?'

'Aren't you bored with Euripides?'

'It seemed so unlikely that for a long time I considered it impossible,' he said frankly. 'But I am. I can't write any more plays for I need new characters. I am getting hideously tired of watching arrangements of the same old themes; there is something pathetically tenuous about the cheers of a self-created audience!' Then he sounded more like the familiar Euripides, severe yet tolerant. 'It might have been different if you had taken me to Olympus; the conversation there would have been sufficiently stimulating to enliven us for several millennia. Or would even Zeus have been repetitive?'

'I don't know. We couldn't get to Olympus because we never believed in it enough. I talked a great deal about Gods and Immortals, but never really believed in anything bigger than my silly little self.'

'We are ghosts,' said Euripides gloomily. 'We have got

everything we desired and find our heaven an error of taste, a distressing failure of perception.'

'I agree that my blue roses were a mistake,' I admitted. 'They might have been quite pleasant if I had used more restraint instead of making them larger than cabbages.'

'No worse than my theatre,' he said consolingly. 'That quantity of pink marble, that plethora of fountains! And the audience must have been composed of idiots, to have sat so still, to have endured so placidly, to have cheered with such determination!' He sighed, 'Oh, for one honest jeer, one bawling fruit-seller!'

Side by side we had been wandering along a familiar path towards the headland. 'Do you remember the Tyrian purple?' I said wistfully. 'We were real people then; even though the enemy could be explained away as insubstantial.'

'Nothing is insubstantial if it teaches you to love, or even makes you fight,' said Euripides. 'In future we had better be sure what we want: there is something very inevitable about heaven.'

'The real heaven is being with people because you love them enough. We are only ghosts, because our immortality cannot accept us into a company we have forgotten.'

'You think we are more than ghosts?'

For the first time since I reached Elysium I knew a confidence which Lucina had found in the temple. 'We are wide as the sea and enduring as the stars, if we will but believe it. You and I have held millennia as grains of dust in our hands; we are old as the rocks, patient as the trees, free as the birds of the air. We share the rhythm of Heaven and Earth, but only the seed of the harvest may endure beyond the small confines of Time. Above the limitation of our shade the tree of our growth is strong in the sun of our loving. We, the ghosts of our transient selves, are the seeds which require the earth to make their growth. We are lonely because we have forgotten our kinship with the tree; impatient because we have neglected the twig which links us to the branch.'

He smiled, 'Sometimes, though I was only an acorn, my plays brought a memory of the oak to remind my friends of the warmth of the long growth. Now for the first time as Euripides I realize that I tried so hard to write plays because through them there could be recognition of affection.'

'I know that as Lucina the priest I tried to bring to other acorns the knowledge of the tree.'

We found ourselves looking down at the house on the headland. I knew the name of the man who sat on the bench under the pine tree with his wife beside him: I knew the name of the child who played at their feet.

'Even Aesculapius had a ghost,' I said softly. 'He was so proud of being a realist, so wise that only a little of his soul stays here in the fulfilment of desire. But we must never mock the loving ghost, for it is by loving that the tree of immortality discovers its stature. Aesculapius and my mother refused to accept their humanity: they have come back to find the peace which they both denied because they were blinded by a light beyond their vision.'

'The child is Agamemnon,' said Euripides. 'He tried to force his way to the tree, and the sword was too sharp. To heal him he required gentleness and the kind inevitability of time. Aesculapius is giving to the little boy the peace he denied to the man.'

He took my hands in his. 'I am shy of making a speech, but I must speak with sincerity of subjects too wide for polished words. All roads lead to the tree, all ghosts find their immortality. But this I say to you with all the fervour of my heart: we, the artist and the priest, twin names of the same purpose, dedicate more than our souls in a service beyond our temporal understanding. We shall always think ourselves inadequate, for we try to express something beyond the limits of our wit. We shall be praised beyond our merit, and derided when we know we have earned honour. We shall never be able to find enduring refuge in our ghosts; that is why we shall find it hard not to envy the many who have chosen an easier way to the tree.'

'Often we shall fail,' I said. 'But may the Gods, whose names we have forgotten, remind us that we have only to choose between the desire to become yet another ghost, and the integrity which receives the freedom of Olympus.'

He kissed me on the forehead. 'I am going back to life, Lucina. We are all going back, but if we remember that the trees of the forest interlace their branches we shall never be lonely.'

CHAPTER TEN

phoenix

My dreams were becoming increasingly vivid. Already the house with the white pillars, where a woman waited the birth of a child, had brighter colours than Elysium. Or was Lucina no more than a fragment of the child's dream?

It would be exciting to enter a new span of living; I should find friends who could not enter Lucina's narrow heaven, and others who had shared it with her. I knew so little of the new country, only a few lines from a play not yet written. Narcissus would be my half-sister, but I should not meet her until I was grown-up. My mother would be Greek, my father a Roman. Later I should find some one who would tell me the simplicities which Lucina had never heard. Had I known him under a name forgotten, in a time wider than can be seen by a ghost's vision?

When I went away would Elysium cease to exist, or other ghosts seek it to regain their loving? There was nothing to keep me here: only a faint nostalgia for scenes I had known and loved, desired and slowly outgrown. Would birth be solemn, or smooth and natural as death?

I stood alone on the cliff above the sea as dawn spread phoenix wings across the sky. To-day Lucina would be given a new name.

THE FAR MEMORIES

Ariel Press is proud to announce that it has brought all seven of Joan Grant's "far memory" novels, plus three more of her books, back into print in a uniform collection. They may be purchased either individually or as a set. The books, and their prices, are:

The novels:

Winged Pharaoh. $15.99.

Life as Carola. $14.99.

Return to Elysium. $14.99.

Eyes of Horus. $18.99.

Lord of the Horizon. $14.95.

Scarlet Feather. $10.95.

So Moses Was Born. $14.99.

The others:

Far Memory, her autobiography. $10.95.

Many Lifetimes, a study of reincarnation with Denys Kelsey. $12.95.

A Lot to Remember, a memoir of her supernatural experiences traveling in France. $10.95.

These books can be purchased either at your favorite bookstore or directly from Ariel Press (include $6 for postage; $12 for Canada and overseas).

For those who prefer, the entire set of 10 books may be purchased as a set at a substantial discount for $120 plus $6 shipping ($12 out of the country)—a savings of $21.

All orders from the publisher must be accompanied by payment in full in U.S. funds—or charged to VISA, MasterCard, or American Express. Please do not send cash. Send orders to Ariel Press, P.O. Box 297, Marble Hill, GA 30148.

For faster service, call toll free 1-800-336-7769 and charge the order to VISA, MasterCard, Discover, or American Express. Or fax your charge order to (706) 579-1274.

In Georgia, please add 7% sales tax.

You can also order online at our website at lightariel.com.